"Tector's characters are a delight to follow, both through the streets of modern Paris and through the histories they uncover of three strong, unconventional women from the past. This novel, as beguiling as the jeweled necklace at the center of the story, celebrates the power of friendship and of following your heart with an irresistible mix of action, humor, and empathy. A fantastic debut!"

—Stacey Swann, author *Olympus, Texas*

"Amy Tector's gorgeous writing had me hooked from the first pages of *The Honeybee Emeralds*. This propulsive, atmospheric novel whisked me off to the bustling streets of Paris; I could feel the cool shadows on the walkways of Place Vendome and smell the old letters and books in dark European archives while following Alice's discovery of the honeybee necklace and her adventure as she, along with a stellar cast of supporting characters, delved into the necklace's storied past. Prepare to be mesmerized by this gem of a debut."

—Liv Stratman, author of *Cheat Day*

"In Tector's intriguing novel, a rich set of characters are brought together by Paris and its secrets. Women who have come to Paris in search of a new life, women who never left, women whose lives passed away many years ago. The book bubbles over with Tector's warm humour, but don't be fooled. A seriousness and a poignancy lies in each woman's longing for love, for belonging and for an achievement to call her own."

—Alette Willis, author of *Dancing with Trees*

THE
HONEYBEE
EMERALDS

THE
HONEYBEE
EMERALDS

Amy Tector

KEYLIGHT BOOKS
AN IMPRINT OF TURNER PUBLISHING COMPANY
Nashville, Tennessee

www.turnerpublishing.com

Cover design by Emily Mahon
Book design by Karen Sheets de Gracia

Library of Congress Cataloging-in-Publication Data
Title: The honeybee emeralds / by Amy Tector.
Description: Nashville, Tennessee : Turner Publishing Company, [2022] | Identifiers: LCCN 2021026163 (print) | LCCN 2021026164 (ebook) | ISBN 9781684427581 (hardcover) | ISBN 9781684427574 (paperback) | ISBN 9781684427598 (ebook)
Subjects: LCSH: France—Paris—Fiction. | Female friendship—Fiction. | Necklaces—Fiction. | Research—Fiction. | GSAFD: Mystery fiction. | Biographical fiction. | LCGFT: Detective and mystery fiction. | Biographical fiction. | Novels.
Classification: LCC PR9199.4.T393 H66 2022 (print) | LCC PR9199.4.T393 (ebook) | DDC 813/.6—dc23
LC record available at https://lccn.loc.gov/2021026163
LC ebook record available at https://lccn.loc.gov/2021026164

Printed in Canada

To Violet
and to Andrew

CHAPTER 1

Opening the Lockshields

ALICE AHMADI SLOWED HER HEADLONG RUN. THE DARK TANGLE of hallways was a different world to the shabby yet bright magazine office somewhere above her head. She stopped and blinked. The sharp, toothy panic that had driven her to flee into the pitch blackness was easing. She couldn't see a single thing. Bloody hell, why was this basement so mind-bendingly vast?

She remembered the stories she'd heard about the Parisian catacombs. How befuddled tourists would get lost in them for days before being retrieved by the exasperated gendarmerie. Did *Bonjour Paris*'s basement actually lead into the catacombs? Was she about to be confronted by the bones of a nice couple from Wichita or the ghosts of some Tokyo schoolgirls?

She took a deep breath, her first since the lights had unexpectedly turned off and plunged her into blackness. Well, her and Alexander.

Oh God. He must have thought she had gone stark raving mad. When the lights snapped off, she had bolted like Alexander was Dr. Jekyll. Or was Mr. Hyde the monster? Bugger. So much for her degree in literature.

Alice turned to make her way back to where she had abandoned him, keeping one hand on the slightly damp brick wall to her right. In her defense, it *was* unnerving to be down in this absurdly creepy basement with a man she had only met half an hour ago and who was, let's be honest, decidedly rude.

Alice remembered how last night, her boss, Lily, had told her to come into the magazine's offices early today. If *Bonjour Paris* still didn't have heat, Alice was to go next door and, in Lily's parlance, "shoot the breeze" with their neighbor. Like many large Parisian blocks of flats, theirs had several street-facing offices, including *Bonjour Paris*. Alice should get the "dealio" from their right-side neighbor on why the building's heating was, according to Lily, "kaput."

"Shooting the breeze" was not in Alice's repertoire. She didn't have Lily's easy American confidence or tendency toward aggressively slangy expressions. She couldn't even summon a smidge of British arrogance, despite having lived in the UK for so many years.

Still, Lily was the editor, and her word was law. Well, Madame Boucher, their terrifying office manager, actually ruled the roost. Either way, as the magazine's intern, Alice knew these types of tasks fell to her. So this morning, when it was clear the heat still didn't work, Alice had ventured outside to the neighboring office and knocked on its black door.

No answer.

There was a light rain, and a woman wearing a beret with a poodle on a leash sauntered past, needing only a baguette and a cigarette to complete the Parisian stereotype.

Alice had banged harder, smashing the heel of her palm against the door. There was something satisfying about pounding away at an immovable object.

The door was wrenched open. Alice had taken a step back. An enormous man, at least six foot five, stood before her—not just tall but heavyset and thick bodied. Even his hair seemed big—brown, curly, and wildly uncombed.

"Bonjour," she had said. She'd never actually talked to the neighbor before. He had simply been a shape she occasionally passed on her way into the office.

"What do you want?" he growled in English.

"I'm sorry, but I was wondering if you—" She stopped. The most amazing scent, like honeysuckle and tangerines, wafted out from behind him.

It reminded her of the hedgerows in summertime when the whole family, her mother, Dale, and her two half-sisters, would drive out to visit her grandmother in Skidby. Technically, Florence wasn't Alice's real grandmother, but she never made a fuss about that. Alice had always been grateful that she had one granny to lay claim to, given that all of her blood grandparents had been wiped out by ill health, stress, revolution, and state violence. "What is that smell?" she blurted.

"You like it?" he asked, his scowl softening. His English was inflected with a slight accent that wasn't French.

"It's brilliant," she said.

"Good," he said. Then he had stepped outside and shut the door. He towered over her on the sidewalk. His belly overhung his jeans a little, and she could see the tip of it peeking over his waistband, like a hairy animal trying to climb out of his shirt.

"Why are you here?" he demanded.

"I just—well . . . Lily sent me over."

He stared at her blankly.

"You know, from next door—the editor of *Bonjour Paris*."

"That magazine," he said dismissively.

Alice's irritation got the better of her shyness, and she surprised herself by speaking firmly. "Yes. I'm Alice." She stuck out her hand. "You are?"

He hesitated, as if debating whether to tell her. Common courtesy won out. "Alexander," he said. They shook hands, and it felt like his massive paw might engulf her entire arm.

Alice continued, "Our heat has been out for ages. My boss, Lily, wanted to know if you'd had any luck getting in touch with the landlord."

"The landlord is a wanker," Alexander said.

"Yes," Alice agreed with a surprised laugh, her annoyance easing. "Did your heat go out too?"

"Yes."

"Well, maybe we could work together to get that sorted, then?"

"No," said Alexander.

"Oh." She'd lived in Paris for six months, so was used to racism and condescension. Flat refusal to help was a new thing.

He seemed to realize that his last reply might have been a bit blunt. "I fixed mine myself."

"You did?" she asked. "How?"

"I made sure the lockshields on the radiators were open—"

"Great, then maybe you could—"

"Then I had to bleed the air out," Alexander continued.

She waited a moment, not daring to interrupt again.

"In the end, I needed to change the TRV."

"So, do you think you could do that for us?"

Alexander stared at her.

"Could you come over and do that thing, with the TRV or whatever?"

"It depends. You might need to open the lockshields."

"Right," Alice said tentatively. "Could you open those?"

Alexander shrugged, a rolling movement like a chunk of ice calving off a glacier. "I'd have to turn the boiler off."

"Okay," Alice said.

"It's in the basement," he said.

And so they descended to this network of interconnected arched brick hallways lit (unreliably, as it turned out) by flickering light bulbs. Once in the basement, she and Alexander had spent ages snaking their way through twisty hallways past the occasional half-open storage room containing random items. One room she glimpsed was stacked with aquariums; another held the contents of what appeared to be a 1950s living room.

Alice had grown increasingly nervous as they walked on, seeming never to come to the utility room. What did she know about this man? Where was he leading her? When the lights had flickered and then gone out, she had panicked and run away.

Now, alone in the dark and lost, she deeply regretted her mad dash. She stumbled down the hallway, relying on her sense of touch to guide her back to Alexander.

Oh dear, a fork in the hallway. Had she come from the left or the right? She had been running so fast she couldn't remember. Alexander had called to her as she bolted, his tone bewildered. That call had come from the right, she was sure of it. "Alexander!" she shouted. Her voice was too small, unable to carry through the network of brick hallways. There was a skittering sound to her left. "Alexander?" Her voice echoed back to her. The noise resumed. A mouse, or probably a rat. Alice shuddered and called out Alexander's name again, but there was no response. Her eyes did not acclimate to the light, because there was no light to acclimate to.

Unexpectedly, a warm breeze tickled her from the left, and she shivered, remembering her mother's tales of djinni, or mischievous spirits, riding the sandstorms, bestowing either prosperity or misfortune on the humans they encountered.

Her outstretched hand brushed against something soft. She screamed and fell back, hitting her head into the brick wall. She rubbed the spot.

What had she touched? She grabbed for her phone. Why hadn't she thought of it before?

She turned on the torch app, sending a small circle of light to the ground in front of her. Immediately she felt calmer.

What was that soft thing? She flicked the light toward it. A coat rack, laden with garments, stood against the wall. She stared at it, trying to process what she was seeing. The clothes were beautiful—three jewel-colored gowns, sparkling in the dim light. She touched the fabric on a sapphire-blue dress, and the satin slipped through her fingers like water.

There was a door behind the rack.

Without thinking, she pushed it open. She entered the room, and the small beam of light picked up sequins. As she moved deeper into the space, the light fell on feathers, silks, and shimmering patterns of embroidery. She flashed the light higher. Racks of clothing crammed with bright, colorful dresses—polka-dotted, striped, and patterned with flowers. Her heart beat with excitement.

She followed the wall across to the far side of the room, where she found a little stool on wheels and a table covered in sewing supplies. Needles, thread, safety pins, and an enormous pair of silver scissors. As her heart rate slowed, she realized that somehow, despite the dank cold, she was covered in a thin film of sweat that chilled her body. She shivered.

A sudden hum raised the hair on the back of her neck, then the room filled with brightness. She laughed in relief. The lights were back on, and she could finally see.

Now the glory of the racks of clothes was revealed: three rows of lavish and sequined finery. Some were party dresses with fluffy chiffon underskirts, giving them a full-bodied look, as if awaiting a dance partner. There were gorgeous heavy velvet gowns in deep, rich colors that looked like something Eleanor of Aquitaine would wear, a few leather jackets, a section devoted to bejeweled brassieres, golden sheaths, floor-length ball gowns.

It was an Aladdin's cave of vintage clothes. The jumble and brightness and verve of the room made her smile. Along one wall, she found stacks and stacks of hats—feathered, sparkling, embroidered, wide-brimmed—and a pile of fezzes of different sizes. Drawn irresistibly to the clothes, she forgot her need to find Alexander.

A thick layer of dust covered everything, and spiders and moths had been busy. She was no fashion expert, but despite the damage, these clothes seemed expensive and well made. At the back of the room was another surprise, a dozen wigs, each one sitting on a beautiful wooden stand. She rubbed her hands together, partly in delight, partly to warm them up.

She walked up the far aisle, occasionally pulling something out from the racks that caught her eye. Her hand brushed against a soft sleeve. She tugged the garment out. It was different from most of the items. Rather than a satin gown or feathered headdress, it was more of an everyday jacket, but a beautiful, opulent green velvet. Hand-embroidered flowers and fruit were stitched over the pockets, and there were intricate brass buttons on the sleeves, with tiny matching ones adorning the front. It was like something Mr. Toad would wear to afternoon tea.

Couldn't she borrow it to warm up? She shrugged her shoulders into the coat. It was long in the arms but cinched in perfectly at her waist. It was heavy and cozy. She wiped the dust from the shoulders and wished for a mirror to see what she looked like.

A moment later she heard a faint voice calling her name. Alexander. She went to the door and shouted for him.

"Alice." His voice was distant.

She was oddly flattered he remembered her name. "Here!" she shouted back.

"Stay there," he yelled. There was silence for about twenty seconds, and then he called her name again.

He was closer this time, and she poked her head out in the hall. "Alexander, I'm here!" she shouted.

He rounded the corner and she felt only relief at the sight of him coming toward her.

"The lights came back," she said inanely.

"Yes, I fixed them," he said, looking through the doorway at the gowns, the wigs, the feathers. She had the impression that his brain was filing every detail away.

"How?" she exclaimed.

"Found the fuse box and replaced the burned out one. The lights are on an old system. Temperamental." His tone was disinterested as he continued to absorb the costumes.

"How did you find the fuse box in the dark?" she asked.

"It was there next to the boiler when the lights went out," he said.

"The boiler was right there?" She recalled seeing a large shape in the corner of the room before it went dark. "I freaked out."

"Yes," he agreed. There was no sympathy in his tone. "What is this place?" he asked. His voice held a hint of wonder, and she felt a quick jolt of connection with him.

"I don't know. It's a wardrobe room or something." She looked around again, feeling that same wave of excitement. It was like the inside of the Wonka Chocolate Factory, filled with overwhelming bounty, dazzling treasures, unique abundance. It felt magical and, oddly, like it all belonged to her.

"Wardrobe?"

"You know, a place where a theater company would keep its clothes?" As she said the words, she realized that was exactly what this was. The clothes, apart from the jacket, were far too extravagant to be anything but stage costumes.

Alexander nodded. "There was once a theater in the building. It closed down many years ago."

"You mean all this is abandoned?" Alice hugged the jacket closer. Maybe she could keep it.

Alexander shrugged. "I guess so." He sniffed. "It smells forgotten."

He was right. There was an odor, damp, mildew, age, neglect. "How mad! Do you think it's been sitting here for years? No one claimed it? No one found it? How is that possible?"

"You got very lost. We are quite far from the main hallway. Perhaps they forgot about it."

"We should find the owners. It would make a great story for the magazine."

"Maybe so," he said, turning to go. "Now we must fix the furnace."

With a last lingering look at the treasures, they exited.

They walked a couple of steps and Alexander surprised her by stopping. "'Wardrobe.' That is an uncommon word. Like the book with the lion and the children."

"*The Lion, the Witch and the Wardrobe!*" Alice said. "They go through a cupboard and fall into Narnia. I loved that story."

Alexander nodded. "Yes, it was a good one."

They walked a few steps, turning a quick right into a much wider corridor.

"Wait," she said. She raced back to the room and searched through the sewing supplies. She grabbed a spool of thick red thread, tied one line to the coat rack, and unrolled it back to where Alexander waited. "We can unspool this to the main hallway, so we can find our way back to the wardrobe room."

"Clever," he said, and Alice stood a little straighter.

As they walked down the larger corridor, Alice made sure that the thread lay unobtrusively on the floor, a guide back to that room of wonders.

The lights stretched down the hall as far as the eye could see. About ten feet farther along, a hallway split off to the left.

Alice was again disoriented. "How do you know where we're going?"

"I remember from when I fixed my heat," he said. His deep voice was reassuring in this dank place—a reminder that if they came across malevolent basement creatures, it might be useful to have a large man by her side.

Alice wondered how big Alexander's breakfast must be. It had to involve a lot of eggs. Maybe a whole dozen. The thought brought to mind her beloved Mr. Men series, some of the first books she had read upon arriving in England. A caseworker had handed her and her mother an Asylum Seeker Welcome Packet: toothbrushes, change of clothes, bars of soap, and there at the bottom, five little square books. She'd studied enough English in school to read their simple words.

She remembered marveling at how many eggs Mr. Strong consumed. The illustration was of a whole plate of them, heaped in a great bounty. Mr. Strong's red arms stretched wide with joy, and his little yellow tongue stuck out at the side. "Eggs, eggs, eggs!" he exclaimed. There was something calming about seeing all of that abundance safely before him. Young Alice understood that feeling of relief. She and her mother were safe. They had left Iran behind. They could stop moving. The pinched look would leave her mother's face. They belonged now. Eggs, eggs, eggs!

She stroked the sleeve of her green velvet jacket and thought again of the jumble of clothes and sequins they had left behind in the wardrobe room. Lily was always exhorting her to get out and find stories—she wanted the kooky, the fabulous, the intriguing. The wardrobe room had a story behind it—Alice could taste it.

Alexander had slowed down, pondering a left-hand turn down a narrower hallway. Alice nearly banged into him. His clothes retained that faint smell of honeysuckle she had caught when she had knocked on his door.

If the lights went out again, she could still find him in the dark—trace him by that scent. In *A Midsummer Night's Dream*, Shakespeare had called honeysuckle "luscious woodbine." There was something rich about the smell, wanton. She blushed.

Their feet echoed down the hall in the silence. "How can the boiler be so far away from our office?" she asked.

"Very inefficient," Alexander grunted disapprovingly, and Alice stifled the urge to apologize, as if the poorly designed heating system was her fault.

They walked on, passing an arched door made of wooden planks with huge black hinges. It was closed, but Alice could imagine Bilbo Baggins behind it, fussily brewing up a pot of tea and second breakfast. "What do you do?" she asked, surprising herself with her boldness.

Another silence. "I'm a perfumer."

She was shocked. Bricklayer, sure. Welder, absolutely. In fact, it was easy to imagine him as that blacksmith god, Vulcan. "You make perfume?" she said doubtfully.

"Yes." He stopped and turned to face her, arms crossed. "I am a certified perfumer."

She could tell that the doubt in her voice had offended him. "I'm sorry," she said. It made sense and explained that wonderful scent wafting from his workspace.

"I don't look as you would expect?" he asked belligerently.

What was a perfumer supposed to look like? Maybe someone with a pencil-thin moustache and slicked-back hair. Someone skinny who wore bow ties and had enlarged nostrils. Essentially the human version of Pepé Le Pew. At any rate, slovenly and enormous were not words that sprung to mind. "No, it's not that," she stammered. "I was surprised. I've never met a perfumer before."

He nodded, although still ruffled. They walked on, and the silence was unbearable.

"Where are you from?" she asked.

No answer. For a moment she wondered if he had decided to ignore her. At last he spoke. "Iceland."

"Really!" she exclaimed.

"Yes," he said. "Does that surprise you as well?"

"It's just, I haven't met anyone from Iceland before." That definitely explained his Viking aura.

"Well, today is full of discoveries for you," he said.

She couldn't understand why she was pleased about his snarky rejoinder until she realized he hadn't returned her question and asked where she was from. As a Persian woman growing up in the UK, that had been a standard question and had only intensified since she'd arrived in Paris.

Alice checked her phone. Hopefully, Lily and Mme Boucher weren't at the office yet, annoyed she wasn't at her desk.

They turned into a spacious room. It looked familiar. Alice realized it was where the lights had gone out last time. She could see a huge metal machine, like something from the Industrial Revolution, hulking in the corner. This must be the boiler.

"Thank you so much for helping us out," she said. "How long will this take?"

"Perhaps a half hour." Alexander's head was already buried deep within the furnace's mechanisms, giving her an unobstructed view of his tree-trunk legs and the faintest hint of a bum crack.

Still chilly, she thrust her hands deep into the jacket pockets. Her fingers brushed against something cool and hard. Gently she pulled it out and gasped. Alexander turned toward her.

She held the thing up to the light—it was a diamond necklace with a large golden bee pendant in its center and an enormous emerald shining from each wing.

Alexander's eyes widened. "Fallegur!" he breathed. "Beautiful."

She dangled it by the diamond chain, letting the gorgeous pendant glint and sparkle in the basement's dim light. In a flash, she understood why she had wound up in the basement this morning, why she had stumbled upon the wardrobe room and pulled on the jacket. She was meant to find this necklace. This treasure. It was her destiny.

Villeneuve-sous-Dammartin

France, 1864

The necklace was cold in her hand, but the gems were weighty and satisfying. She held the jewels up to the light from the candelabra: a double strand of diamonds flanking an intricate golden honeybee, its wings outstretched, an enormous emerald on each wing.

She did a quick count—forty perfect diamonds, two exquisitely cut emeralds. Judging from their clarity, they must come from the Americas. She bit the pendant lightly. The gold was undoubtedly twenty-four karats. The bee design was charming. He must have commissioned it especially for her; he knew she found the creatures amusing.

The faint crunch of gravel on the drive caught her attention. His carriage was pulling away. Leaving her forever. She stroked the cool diamonds. This was what remained of their passion. Their affair had once been the talk of Europe, and now she was left with a handful of stones.

She was being dramatic, of course. The very nice château she stood in, overlooking a fairly sizable park, was another reminder of that love, as was the generous annuity that would be delivered to her bankers in quarterly installments for the rest of her life.

She sunk into the chaise longue by the window, clasping the necklace more tightly in her hand, and closed her eyes. Her talent for dramatics was what had earned her this house, this view, this necklace, and, of course, the brand-new baby sleeping on the other side of the château. Well, her talent for drama and a few other skills . . .

CHAPTER 2

La Vie en Rose

LILY WILKINS SIPPED HER CAPPUCCINO, ITS WARM, SLIGHTLY nutty aroma chasing away the final vestiges of sleep. She sat up straighter, smoothing her navy blazer and fiddling with the silk scarf at her neck.

She didn't usually get so dressed up for work, but Luc's invitation to a "power breakfast" at one of Paris's most elegant restaurants called for a little effort. She shifted uneasily. Le Chou Élegant—with its linen tablecloths, crystal glasses, and waiters trying to trick her into eating snails by calling them escargots—wasn't her usual kind of place.

She wanted to stand up and pace, but she contented herself with drumming her fingers against the tablecloth. What could Luc want? Nine in the morning was obscenely early for any kind of Parisian business meeting. She had to assume the news was going to be grim.

True, Luc hadn't explicitly said that he was planning to kill the magazine, but she had been in publishing long enough to read the signs. *Bonjour Paris* was the city's longest-running expat magazine, but it was struggling. If she couldn't work some magic, Luc was within his rights to shut it down. Then she, Alice, and Mme Boucher would be sent packing, and *Bonjour Paris* would be donezo.

The waiter stopped by her table, and as always, Lily insisted on using her French. She was determined to improve, which meant speaking it every chance she got. Ignoring his pained expression, she explained that she was waiting for someone. Despite over six years in Paris, her French still sounded more like Mansfield Union High, Jericho, Vermont, than the Sorbonne, Paris.

She glanced up to see Luc weaving his way through the tables, and she smiled in greeting. Dark-haired, dark-eyed, and broad-shouldered, Luc wasn't handsome exactly. His nose was too big, his stature too short, but he had an air of confident authority that had undoubtedly helped him make his millions.

"Forgive my suggestion that we meet here," he said, his flawless English evidence that it was his mother tongue. "I have another meeting nearby and thought I could kill two birds."

"Chirp, chirp," Lily said, immediately wishing she hadn't.

He raised a perfect eyebrow—did he get them professionally plucked? Half American, Luc nevertheless oozed a French superiority that always made Lily nervous.

She gestured for him to sit in the chair opposite. He raised a finger and the supercilious waiter was upon them, now minus the attitude. Luc ordered a complicated coffee, but waved the waiter away when he suggested something to eat. Lily's stomach rumbled. She'd been looking forward to trying out the menu, but apparently power breakfasts didn't involve actual food.

She was still trying to figure her boss out. Since starting as editor a year ago, she hadn't met him very often. Luc was a hands-off owner, spending most of his time doing something complicated with hedge funds in La Défense, the Parisian financial district.

Luc smiled. "Truthfully, I prefer meeting here because the magazine's office reminds me of Maman." Olivia Seguin, Luc's mother, was *Bonjour Paris*'s founder and only other editor. She had died a year ago, and Luc was obviously still grieving.

While Lily had never met her, Olivia's presence hovered over all aspects of the magazine. Everyone from advertisers to the mailman got misty-eyed when talking about her—she was a firecracker, a force of nature, une femme formidable.

While the French were often suspicious of Americans, Olivia got a pass from the usual distrust.

"What made you call this meeting?" Lily asked. Might as well cut to the chase.

He cleared his throat. "Next month is May," he said.

"Yes, and I think the month after that will be June," she said brightly.

"Before Maman's death, I promised her I would keep this magazine going for one year. The year is now up, and, unfortunately, I don't think we're going to survive."

Lily's stomach knotted. She leaned forward to speak, but Luc forestalled her.

"Do not blame yourself. I wanted to honor my promise to Maman and give the magazine a fair shot, which is why I hired you away from the *International Tribune*. But this is a dying business. The magazine is a drain on my revenues. I can't operate something out of pure nostalgia—that's bad business."

Lily frowned. While for the fifty years of Olivia Seguin's editorship *Bonjour Paris* had reigned unchallenged as Paris's only expat magazine, six months ago a rival had appeared.

The new magazine's owner, a big wine distributor who wanted to tap into the market, was pouring in money and talent to target the wealthy expat experience. *La Vie en Rose* covered the same turf as *Bonjour Paris*, but threw in aspirational extras—reviews of exquisite five-star châteaux in the Loire Valley and service journalism pieces on the best place to get one's Ferrari repaired in the 16th arrondissement.

Lily told herself that *Bonjour Paris* offered real stories and not glammed-up puff pieces, but the truth was that *La Vie en Rose*, and its editor, Yvette Dufeu, was always one step ahead of her, consistently scooping Lily on stories and juicy advertising dollars.

Luc's voice held regret. "It is time to throw in the towel. *La Vie en Rose* is hastening our death. Yvette Dufeu is a formidable opponent." His voice held a tinge of admiration.

"You know Yvette?" Lily asked in surprise.

Luc shrugged. "Years ago she worked for *Bonjour Paris*. She would never have dared challenge Maman, but she must see us as weak. Alas, I think she might be correct."

Lily flinched, but Luc's defeatist attitude fired her up. "We shouldn't go down without a fight," she exclaimed. "I can turn this magazine around."

Luc cocked an eyebrow. "That is quite a can-do attitude—very American."

Lily nodded. "It's what beat Hitler and made Kim Kardashian a thing."

Luc let out a bark of surprised laughter.

"Your mother did something amazing, creating and running this magazine, and we shouldn't let her legacy die. What if you reinvest in *Bonjour Paris*? We could become the byword for strong, exciting, relevant stories about Paris."

Luc frowned at her. "You are passionate." It almost sounded like an accusation. "I am a businessman. Convince me with hard numbers."

Lily's heart raced. This is what she had been preparing for since Luc had suggested they meet. "*La Vie en Rose* is hurting our bottom line. They are stealing advertisers, authors, and subscribers. It's not enough to remain flat—we should be building our readership. I propose that we think bigger."

Luc leaned forward. As she suspected, he had an appetite for risk.

"Why are we limiting ourselves only to the expat market?" Lily asked rhetorically. Her voice was stronger, confident. "We write amazing stories about Paris, and in the age of the internet and fake news, we have a fifty-year pedigree. We should expand our editorial scope to find stories that anyone who loves this city, whether they speak English, French, or Swahili, can relate to."

Luc nodded cautiously. "How do we do that?" he asked.

"Well, it will require some investment," she said. She glanced down at the notes she had made. This was going to be the tricky part. "We need to ensure that we're taken seriously. I want to increase our photography and freelance budgets so we can scope out edgier, more offbeat stories. We'll put out a weekly e-newsletter and a monthly podcast and charge customers extra for that premium content. We could host live events—readings, debates, book signings—put *Bonjour Paris* on the city's map."

"That doesn't sound cheap," Luc frowned. "Have you costed it out?"

Lily passed Luc a sheet of paper with the budget and proposal outlined. She had spent all evening looking at what other magazines did, researching the costs, estimating the outlay. He studied her figures, and she held her breath.

He looked up, his eyes thoughtful, and her heart fluttered with hope. "Your figures are solid," he said, indicating the sheet in front of him. "Produce a June issue that shows me what you can do with the budget you have, and I'll consider investing longer term in the magazine."

A June issue? Usually they worked with months more lead time, but if this was the lifeline Luc was throwing to her, she'd grab it. "We can do it," she said, smiling resolutely at him.

He surprised her by smiling back. "It is a nice break to think about such a small enterprise." He gestured to the paper with her calculations again.

She tried not to be insulted by the dismissive way he was treating her career.

He finished his coffee with a quick swig and stood. Lily rose to join him. "Please," he said. "Stay and finish your coffee. Have some breakfast. The crêpes are magnificent." He gestured to the waiter, who appeared at once. "An order of crêpes for mademoiselle. Charge it to my card," he said.

"Thank you, Luc," she said.

"The least I can do, after you promise to save my mother's legacy."

"I'll do it," Lily said. "You'll see."

Luc nodded, looking thoughtful. "My mother devoted her entire life to that magazine. It was her passion. She spent every spare moment there. Our dinners were interrupted by work phone calls. She missed family vacations because of deadlines." His voice was steady. "I don't think Maman could have named one of my childhood friends or told you what position I played on the rugby team, all because she was consumed with making this business a success."

"Did you resent it?" Lily was shocked to be asking her boss such a personal question, but he seemed to have opened the door.

"Probably," he admitted, "but I admired her as well. She was a good businesswoman. I think perhaps I was also jealous that she immersed herself in this creative life. I never had much imagination, but Maman, well, she could bring a room alive with her stories."

Lily's father had died when she was twenty-five. She recognized the complicated love, admiration, and discontent you could feel toward a dead parent, one you'd never get another chance to talk to. "I'm sorry," she said, and impulsively put her hand on his arm.

"Bah," he said. "I am being sentimental. Talking of the magazine brings it out in me." He gave her a brisk nod and departed.

The waiter arrived with Lily's order. Luc had been right: The lacy, featherlight crêpe combined with the buttery, cinnamon-dusted apples melted together in a way that needed to be savored slowly to be appreciated. Unfortunately Lily, the third of four children, knew that if you didn't act quickly at mealtimes there would be no seconds. She looked up from her two minutes of concentrated eating to see the waiter's startled expression. She grinned at him and shrugged.

She pushed her plate away and started to think. Luc was giving her the chance to save the magazine, and she wasn't going to blow it. She would ditch their planned cover on the state of Parisian parks. She needed a honking big June story and a superstar writer . . . a familiar face came to mind. Chiseled features, deep-blue eyes, dark-blond hair—like they'd blended all those Hollywood Chrises together and chucked in a dash of some old-timey Gene Kelly hot guy.

Jacob Meyers was one of her oldest friends. They'd met drinking cheap whiskey by the pond at Bennington and had bonded over their mutual love of writing. After college, Jacob's parents had subsidized his assault on the New York literary establishment.

While Lily had lived with four roommates and taken temp jobs in writing-adjacent professions like marketing, Jacob suddenly got serious. He didn't need to worry about paying rent and could devote his time to ill-paying gigs that got him name recognition. Now Jacob had hit the big time. The real big time. The New York big time. His byline was everywhere, from BuzzFeed to *The Atlantic*.

She couldn't be happier or prouder of him. Yes, that was the correct emotion: pride.

It just so happened that Jacob had arrived in Paris last week, here for a monthlong dream job working on a series of stories about Paris for the *Hudson Magazine*.

Despite his previous success, this gig resonated the most with Lily, maybe because getting a short story published in the *Hudson* had been her fantasy. Once upon a time, she had thought she was going to be the next great American novelist, but between fending off a mountain of student debt and the writing world's lousy pay, she never had the money, time, or space.

Lily jotted down Jacob's name in her notebook. Given his increasing luster, it would be a huge coup if she could get him to write their June cover. She doodled his name, making it bigger and shading it in.

It was weird that she hadn't seen Jacob yet. In the past, when he'd traveled to Paris he'd texted her from the airport. Their first meeting after a long absence was always the best. They were like two puppies, both yapping excitedly, grinning like fools, blurting out their stories, thrilled to be in one another's company again.

A movement at the restaurant's door caught her eye and she glanced up. Oh God. Just what she needed. Yvette Dufeu stalked in. It was unsurprising, really. This ritzy place was exactly Yvette's cup of tea, or café allongé, as the case may be.

Lily and Yvette often ended up at the same events, and she had come to dread these encounters. The other woman's astounding self-confidence and needle-sharp malice were grating to say the least.

"Leelee, darling!" Yvette drawled, approaching her table. Yvette's petite frame was clad in a long silk kimono-style coat in beautiful emerald greens, which parted to reveal a sleek black dress, undoubtedly from Les Suites or some other chic atelier.

Lily immediately felt enormous, unkempt, and oily. She stood, and the two women did the traditional double cheek kiss in greeting. A cloud of Chanel Grand Extrait enveloped Lily. It wasn't overpowering, of course; Yvette would never do anything so gauche as wear too much perfume.

"Yvette, how are you?" Lily asked. She didn't dare try out her French. She couldn't imagine how the other woman would react to her pronunciation.

"Marvelous. Now, the last time we saw each other was that exhibition opening, was it not?" Yvette asked. "You were wearing the most darling Dior dress."

"That wasn't Dior," Lily said.

"Are you sure?

"I don't own any Dior."

"Oh no," trilled Yvette. "My mistake."

Lily's mouth attempted a smile.

"I must say, Leelee," Yvette said, changing tack, "I am surprised to see you here. Le Chou Élegant is not your usual haunt."

Lily smiled tightly.

"But I am being so rude!" Yvette exclaimed, gesturing to the empty seat. "You are awaiting a companion."

"No, no," Lily said, but before she could explain that Luc had already left, Yvette spoke up.

"Ah, dining alone," she murmured compassionately. Yvette's keen eyes caught her notebook, where to Lily's horror she realized she had been doodling Jacob Meyers's name all over the page, along with a list of potential story ideas.

Yvette's mouth dropped open. "Jacob Meyers—the American writer? Is M. Meyers writing for your magazine now?" Yvette's tone was aggressive.

Lily hastily turned the notebook over, but the damage was done.

Yvette continued, "I had heard he was in Paris, but I am frankly quite surprised you managed to secure someone of his caliber."

"What do you mean by that?" Lily bristled. She knew exactly what Yvette meant by that.

"Voyons donc, Leelee. *Bonjour Paris* is not at the same level as M. Meyers's usual publications—it is not the *New York Times* or the *Hudson*.

Let's be truthful." Her voice hardened. "It is more of a glorified series of advertisements for lousy flats in bad neighborhoods and mid-tier restaurants filled with tourists."

Lily gasped. Yvette had never been so naked in her disdain for the magazine. "Actually, Jacob is writing our June cover." Oh Lord, now she was in it.

Yvette had regained her poise. "It's true your little magazine covers some amusing topics now and then. If M. Meyers wants to learn about the real France, however, he should do a piece for us. We are running a very compelling article on yachting in the Mediterranean. I might get in touch with him, to see if he'd like the assignment. Of course, it would involve spending two weeks in the South of France aboard a number of fine vessels. All expenses paid."

Yvette turned on her heel and sauntered off to join a table of men in expensive suits. Lily felt sick. In the arms race of niche Parisian expat magazines, she had handed Yvette a Jacob-shaped nuclear warhead. She picked up her phone. She needed to convince Jacob to write her June cover, pronto.

CHAPTER 3

The Honeybee Emeralds

LILY PACED TO THE FRONT OF BONJOUR PARIS'S OPEN OFFICE plan, ignoring Mme Boucher's annoyed look.

There was something daunting about their office manager, Mme Boucher. She sat at her desk at the front by the door, swathed in black, like an aggressive crow guarding a nest. Mme Boucher (never Élise, never Mrs. B.) had been around almost as long as the magazine itself. Indeed, there was a framed photograph from the early '70s on the wall: Mme Boucher, or maybe she was still Mlle Nadeau, with a foot-high blond beehive and a miniskirt showing off surprisingly good legs.

Lily turned and paced to the back of the room, taking in the office with fresh eyes. She saw the faded yellow paint, the walls plastered in old *Bonjour Paris* covers, posters from Parisian concerts long past, and large framed photographs of the staff, interns, and writers who had helped fill the magazine over the decades. The magazine had a history worth fighting for; certainly, she wouldn't let Yvette, that mean-spirited harpy, destroy it.

Jacob was her ticket. When she'd called him from the restaurant, he had agreed to drop by later this afternoon. She was going to have to convince him to write for a publication with much less cachet than he was used to and at a rate far below his usual price. She bit her lip. The trouble was that Jacob was a loyal friend but not necessarily a generous one. He liked the idea of doing good more than the actual doing of the good.

In college, he had always been the first to sign up for a Habitat for Humanity shift or a car wash fundraiser, but when it came time to roll out of bed at 6 a.m., he'd suddenly have a midterm he had to study for. There was also the funny fact that he had been in the city for a whole week and hadn't bothered to get in touch until she reached out.

She rapped her old pine desk with her knuckles. She was being ridiculous. Jacob was one of her oldest friends. He'd help her out. He had to. He was by far the biggest writer she knew. Alice, the intern, wanted to be a writer. When the younger woman had confessed this, Lily had smiled hugely and encouraged her, but her heart had squeezed a little. A part of her wanted to tell the truth—writing was a brutal game that required commitment and passion and offered no guarantees. Successful writers, people like Jacob, were the aberration rather than the norm.

She swung her arms, heading up to the front of the room again. The movement helped warm her up. The office was still cold. Yesterday she had told Alice to ask the neighbor for help with the furnace, but it obviously wasn't fixed. Where was Alice, anyway? She'd sent the girl a text half an hour ago. Lily looked at her phone and noticed that the message hadn't been delivered. She frowned. It wasn't like Alice to be gone for so long without checking in. She called the intern's number, but it went straight to voicemail. It was almost 10 a.m.

"You haven't seen Alice, have you?" she asked the office manager.

"She's not here." Mme Boucher stated the obvious, managing to make Lily feel stupid for asking the question.

"Yes, but I wondered if you'd heard from her."

Mme Boucher shrugged. "She was not here when I arrived." A pause. "While you were breakfasting."

"It was a power breakfast," Lily said weakly. Mme Boucher didn't roll her eyes, but Lily could tell she wanted to.

"I am going to do the banking," the office manager announced, picking up her black handbag and rising from her perch. "You should review the advertising for May."

Mme Boucher had a habit of issuing stark orders, which Lily tried to take with good grace. Élise Boucher kept *Bonjour Paris* running. From her encyclopedic knowledge of English-language writers in Paris to her deft ability to manage the bureaucratic labyrinth of small-business ownership in France, the magazine would be lost without her.

Still, Lily breathed a sigh when the older woman walked out. The bank was on the other side of the city, and Mme Boucher would be gone for a while. The air in the magazine was always a bit lighter when the office manager was absent.

Lily had decided to go look for Alice when the girl herself walked in, followed, weirdly, by Alexander, their office neighbor. To her surprise, the normally quiet Alice was babbling.

"Oh, Lily, have you been to the basement? It's amazing. We went down to fix the furnace, but it's a whole other world. There are piles of junk, but buried in all that are some real treasures. We came across a room filled with absolutely stunning clothing and wigs. All of it sitting there."

"Really?" said Lily. "How bizarre." Alice actually initiating conversation felt even weirder.

"Alexander says there used to be a theater in the building, and maybe it's their old costumes. Apparently, they've been closed down forever, so their stuff is basically up for grabs," Alice said.

"Well, I wouldn't know about that," Lily answered. She was impatient to get back to her brainstorming. She needed to come up with a few great cover story ideas for Jacob.

"I found something down there," Alice said.

Lily looked at her more closely; the younger woman was vibrating with excitement. Even Alexander, usually so stone-faced, seemed animated. For the first time, she noticed that Alice was wearing a gorgeous, deep-green velvet frock coat with brass buttons down the front. "Was it that jacket?" she asked.

Alice bit her lip and blushed. This was nothing new. She'd blushed once telling Lily she'd seen a dog peeing in the street.

"No . . . well, yes," she said in confusion. "I found the jacket down there. I'm going to keep it. No one has been in that wardrobe room for ages, and it would get moth-eaten and ruined if I left it there."

Lily put her hands up. "It's none of my business, Alice," she spoke mildly. "If you want to keep it, go nuts."

"Good," Alice said with a trace of defiance. "I will."

Lily smiled. She hadn't realized that Alice was looking for her approval, and it was a reminder of how young the other woman was. Lily would bet her bottom dollar that this was Alice's first time living away from home.

Alice continued, "The thing is, I didn't only find the jacket down there. I found this, in the pocket."

She held an object in her hand.

"It's a necklace," the young woman said.

"Are those emeralds?" Lily gasped. She stifled the urge to rub her eyes in disbelief like a cartoon character. She had never seen such a beautiful piece of jewelry.

Alice laid it out on the desk in front of her, and Alexander and Lily gathered to gawk.

It was gorgeous. It had two thick strands of diamonds, but they were the supporting characters to the main event: a golden honeybee pendant with filigreed wings that held two perfectly matched green gems, each about as big and thick as a thumb.

"This can't be real," Lily said, tracing her finger along the bee's outstretched wings.

Alexander picked up the necklace, running his index finger over the stones. "I don't think it is fraudulent," he said.

"How can you tell?" Lily asked.

Alexander shrugged. "I am not an expert in jewelry, but it is very well made. You see the stones? They are set nicely. This is very good work, I think. Perhaps also quite old."

Lily had no knowledge on which to base her opinion, but she agreed instinctively with Alexander. This was not a fake. The necklace exuded an aura of sturdy authenticity.

"It's missing some diamonds," Alice remarked.

They looked to where she pointed. Sure enough, there were settings for four more diamonds, but they had fallen out—or been pried off. Lily did a quick count. There were thirty-six diamonds, each as big as a shelled peanut. The deep greens of the emeralds shifted in the fluorescent office lighting, hinting at hidden depths.

"This came from the jacket?" Lily asked. Her heart fluttered with excitement.

"Yes," Alice confirmed. "I found it after I had put the jacket on while we were sorting out the furnace." The intern reached out and stroked the diamonds, her hand lingering over the hard stones.

"We should call the police," Alexander said. "Someone must have reported this stolen or missing."

"We don't even know if it's real," Lily said. "It came from a wardrobe room? It might be a prop."

Again, they all gazed at the necklace. Even though she voiced the doubt, Lily didn't really believe it.

"It must be reported," Alexander repeated.

If the necklace was real, then there was a story to how it had ended up forgotten in a dusty basement. A story Lily wanted *Bonjour Paris* to tell. "We need to authenticate this," she said.

"We could find a jeweler," Alice said.

Lily shook her head, her brain whirring through possibilities. "They'll ask us all kinds of questions—things we can't answer yet—and it might look suspicious." She had a plan. "My friend Daphne runs the International Art Registry," she said.

"What's that?" Alexander asked.

"It's a tiny United Nations organization. They keep a database of lost and stolen art to assist police forces around the world in returning items to their rightful owners. She could help."

Alexander grunted, although it was impossible to tell if it was in agreement or dissent. Lily chose to believe the former.

"Don't they work with art, not jewelry?" Alice asked. "I thought your friend was an expert in painting."

Lily bit her lip impatiently. "She's in that milieu. Plus, she knows all about diamonds." She saw the doubt in their faces. "Trust me, she would not shut up about clarity and cut when she and Philip got engaged. She did in-depth research and can size up a diamond at fifty paces. She's a red-blooded American woman."

"But Lily," Alice said. "You're American. Can't you tell us if they're real?"

"I'm from Vermont," she replied, waving a distracted hand. "We're different."

"Ah," Alice nodded wisely. "Bernie Sanders."

"Ben & Jerry's," Alexander murmured in agreement.

Lily opened her mouth to inquire exactly what they meant by that, but then thought better of it. "So, we get my friend Daphne to examine this necklace?" she confirmed.

Alexander put up a hand. "Halt," he said. "Alice was the one to discover the necklace. She should be the one to make the final decision."

Alice blushed and touched the necklace. "Let's find out if it's real," she said. Lily grinned in gratitude at her intern.

"Yes," Alexander nodded. "When it's authenticated, we can inform the police."

Lily had other ideas. A lost treasure found in a forgotten Parisian basement. If this necklace was real, they had the front cover of their June issue.

CHAPTER 4

Hearts as Big as Fiats

"I AM THE HEAD OF THIS HOUSEHOLD, AND MY WORD IS FINAL. We are moving. Give your notice." Henri Boucher stood in front of their open door, blocking his wife's entrance and, most distressingly, speaking loudly enough for their neighbors to hear.

Élise slipped past him into their tiny front room. "I'm not ready to move," she hissed, conscious of Mme Savoie next door, sweeping her stoop.

"You're an old woman," Henri said. "It's time to quit that ridiculous job."

Élise had worked at *Bonjour Paris* for almost fifty years. Henri had resented her job for every single one of them.

"They need me," she said, putting her purse down.

Henri laughed, an unpleasant sound. "You could be replaced by a computer. I'm retired, and I want to leave Paris—to return home."

Élise opened her mouth to argue further, but he stomped out the door. Off to the café for a Friday afternoon apéro with his buddies.

Mme Savoie's sweeping resumed next door, the scratchy sound somehow imbued with a smug satisfaction. Well, her neighbor had nothing to be smug about. Élise remembered Mme Savoie's husband drinking too much at the Feast of the Annunciation supper and pinching Sister Marie-Marguerite's bottom.

Élise removed her wet raincoat. She had gotten drenched on her walk from the métro. Spring in Paris was always rotten. So much rain, so many tourists. Tulips being sold everywhere. They weren't real flowers—big, waxy, overbright, too confident, too tall, too Dutch. She recalled the flowers of her childhood: blazing golden asters, sweet fairy's thimble.

Henri was right: The idea of returning home, going back to La Rosière, held some enticements. Coming across a field of small, white edelweiss bending in the clear mountain air was magical. It was fitting that a song had been devoted to those blossoms, but vexing that it was sung by an Englishwoman. Her hair was too short, like a boy's, and her nose too long. Not even a jolie laide, just laide. What's more, she was a terrible nun. Was that actress even Catholic?

Élise walked into the kitchen, turning on the gas for the cooker. Summertime at La Rosière was magical. They used to return for summers when the boys were young. They would run up and down the hills, searching for wild strawberries. They'd fill baskets with them, even stuff their pockets, and for once she wouldn't fret about the stains. The berries were tiny, but carried such powerful flavor. Her mother always said it was the sweetness of the sunshine itself.

Mountain strawberries were nothing like the enormous monstrosities you bought in the épicerie nowadays. She could almost pity her fellow shoppers, buying those overblown bits of cardboard. They did not know the taste of a tiny, sun-warmed strawberry picked from the side of a mountain.

She was so tired of fighting Henri. Was it perhaps time to retire? To give in? For a moment she allowed herself to entertain the idea. It might be nice to stop. To rest.

Yet the idea of returning to La Rosière, as beautiful as it was, made her shoulders hunch.

As a girl, Élise had felt stifled rather than inspired by those enormous peaks staring down on her house. In those days everything was difficult and everything felt dark—there was not much employment, not much money. Despite this pinched existence, or perhaps because of it, neighbors did more than know one another's business—they surveilled each other.

After Olivia's death, Élise had presumed *Bonjour Paris* would close. The magazine couldn't continue without her as editor. Nothing would be the same. Yet, Olivia had surprised them all (again, always) by leaving the magazine to her youngest son. Élise had been skeptical last year when Luc had hired Lily.

Unlike Olivia, who was American but seemed more French than the French themselves, Lily was 100 percent Yankee—full of loud enthusiasm and overbearing sincerity. Could this Lily safeguard Olivia's legacy? Non. Lily's French was atrocious. How could she be trusted? Élise's father always said that proper French was a gift, the most elegant piece of jewelry a woman could wear.

The latest intern, Alice, spoke good French, but she was British. *Bonjour Paris* had often hired British writers. The Brits had changed their tune over the years—going from arrogant, globe-bestriding conquerors when she had started in the early 1970s to chastened Brexiters anxious and apologetic in equal measures.

Élise nodded in contentment. While she disagreed with most modern societal shifts, the humbling of Les Anglais was satisfying.

Yes, Alice was une anglaise, but not a white. What was this Alice? She was not so dark as to be African. More brownish. Her real name was Aliyeh; Élise had processed her paperwork. "Aliyeh Ahmadi" sounded suspiciously Middle Eastern, perhaps Arab.

Still, the younger woman didn't wear the headscarf, and Élise had seen Alice eat a croque monsieur, so not a Muslim or not a practicing one. Élise had never worked with a Middle Easterner before, and she didn't like it. She could never be sure of what the girl was thinking behind her dark eyes.

The office had been surprisingly busy when she returned from meeting with the bank. The atmosphere was charged—a barely suppressed excitement. Furtive conversations. Oddly, the dirty Viking from next door was on the premises, whispering with Lily and Alice. Monday she would figure out what they were up to, make sure it was nothing idiotic. Today she simply hadn't had the energy.

Élise opened the refrigerator, looking for the sausages for dinner. Her eyes lingered on the whale magnet stuck to the door. It had been there for more than thirty years, a gift from her youngest son, Thierry.

Blue whales are the largest living animals on Earth. Not only are they the biggest currently alive, Thierry had told her one day when he was about eight years old, but they are the largest animal to have ever existed on the planet. Thierry had been like that as a child—from whales to *Star Wars* to race cars, he would become immensely passionate about a topic, absorbing everything and then immediately needing to share it.

She recalled the day when Thierry had come home from school, full of his lesson on whales. She had barely listened to his monologue, focused on the meal she was cooking. She was out of pepper—Henri was sure to comment. "These whales are bigger than elephants?" she had asked distractedly.

"Yes," Thierry nodded, his smile lighting up his little triangular face. His sharp chin always reminded her of Henri.

Thierry was still wearing his school clothes. If she had told the boys once, she had told them a thousand times to change from their uniforms as soon as they got home. In those days Élise was constantly sewing and patching, trying to save last year's jumper for the next boy, but it was futile, and inevitably, in September at la rentrée she would have to ask Henri for extra money to buy new trousers, clean T-shirts, new shoes. He would sigh and open his well-worn leather wallet.

She earned money from the magazine, of course, but Henri barely tolerated her job and forbade her from ever seeking out promotion or extra responsibility. He was suspicious of her work for an expat magazine— obnoxious foreigners—and he was especially suspicious of Olivia.

The few times they had met—her husband stolid, hardworking, and taciturn, and Olivia so charming, vibrant, and erudite—had been disasters. Instead of falling under Olivia's spell as most men did, Henri stood with his arms crossed, snapping out answers to Olivia's thoughtful questions about his job, his garden, and his sons. So every two weeks Élise handed over her paycheck to Henri, a sacrifice on the altar of marital stability.

Thierry had spoken in an excited rush. "Blue whales can be as much as thirty meters long. That's two coaches placed end to end. They live up to ninety years, and they were almost hunted to extinction." He hopped from foot to foot, the laces of his school shoes undone. "Their hearts are as big as Fiats. Their largest artery is so big a child could swim through it."

That caught Élise's attention. She could imagine one of her three boys— at that time still so small—swimming alone through a whale's bloodstream, and the image caused her a moment's panic. Thierry continued to talk. "Scientists use the whale's earwax to tell how old they are. Blue whales' tongues weigh three tonnes. A baby blue whale at birth weighs as much as a fully grown hippopotamus."

When had Thierry stopped being so passionate? She returned to the present with a frown. When had her youngest son's imagination dried up? Now the only thing he cared about was his video game console and his big-breasted girlfriend. Forty years old and bagging groceries for a living. Shameful.

Where had she and Henri gone wrong? Two of their three boys were layabouts. One unemployed, one barely employed. After Mass the other women clucked around in sympathy, asking in concerned voices if the boys had "had any luck" on the job market.

The only one who had flown the nest was David, and truthfully, he was the only one she wished were still home. You were supposed to favor your youngest, but David was her first and her favorite, no point in pretending otherwise. He had beautiful green eyes and a mischievous smile, and even though he was given all the responsibilities of the oldest son, he shouldered them with grace and competence.

His younger brothers adored him. His father even smiled when he walked into a room. Perhaps David had set the bar too high for the other Boucher boys. The younger two saw what their oldest, golden brother had done and, lacking any strength of character, thought it easiest to give up. They were unsatisfactory copies from the original mold.

Of course, David was no use to her now. He had moved to Canada fifteen years ago for a good-paying job, where he promptly married a lovely girl and produced their only grandchildren—little Justine and Camille. Élise loved those two girls with a fierceness that still caught her by surprise. She had always longed for a daughter, and she delighted in their weekly

Skype calls when she was able to chat with them about their little hardships and dreams.

She and Henri had finally gone to visit them just over a year ago—a two-week holiday, the trip of a lifetime. Henri, fearing air travel, had resisted for a long time, but the lure of those granddaughters was finally too strong even for him. Once actually aboard the plane, Henri was perfectly fine, and she could have strangled him for having made them wait so long. David and his family toured them around Québec City, an old town that felt surprisingly French. They visited la Citadelle, admired the museums, and delighted in the little girls.

The highlight for Élise was to be their whale watching tour up the Saint Lawrence River. Ever since Thierry had sparked her imagination so long ago, Élise had longed to see a whale in the flesh. Something about their immense, quiet lives in the cool of the ocean called to her. David had promised them a magical experience—a guaranteed sighting in the windy Saint Lawrence River.

The day before the cruise, they got word from Paris that Olivia had died. Élise insisted on returning home. Henri thought she was being ridiculous; she was only the office manager, for God's sake. She didn't need to go back.

Élise let her hand fall from the magnet and bent over the refrigerator to find the sausages. She thought of *Bonjour Paris* back in 1970 when Élise, an ignorant country girl fresh off the train from La Rosière, showed up desperate for a job. Olivia had offered her a cup of coffee and listened to her story. She had a way of making whomever she was talking to feel welcome, important, and heard. For Élise, coming from a world where a woman's opinion mattered very little, Olivia's interest, more even than her kindness, had been intoxicating.

Yes, the day Olivia had died Élise had flown back alone, leaving Henri to see the whales without her. He lived her dream. She helped organize a funeral.

She had no regrets.

CHAPTER 5

Minecraft

DAPHNE SMYTHE-BAIRD HELD HER SON'S STICKY HAND, PUSHING open the door to *Bonjour Paris* with her hip. Glancing around, she felt the usual pang of dismay. Romantic comedies had taught her that a magazine's head office should be glassy, glossy, and staffed by sassy gay men.

These jaundiced yellow walls, dated posters, scuffed desks, and rows of filing cabinets felt like a personal affront. Lily never picked up on her hints about spiffing the place up. Instead, she waxed poetic about the magazine's storied past and authentic vibe.

In Daphne's opinion, a fresh coat of paint and some strategically placed succulents were infinitely preferable to "authenticity."

The office manager, an older French woman who always seemed angry, must have been gone for the day. Lily and her latest intern, the pretty one with the dark eyes, were sitting at their desks. A great big man bent over a radiator, looking up with a sweaty, round face as she tugged her son through the entryway.

Theo was being quite the little turd today—wriggling out of her grasp in front of the judgmental eyes of his Montessori teacher when she'd tried to strap him into his car seat, banging on the Audi's window as they inched through the Parisian rush hour. Normally she could tolerate these five-year-old antics, but with Philip once again traveling for work, the child was getting on her last nerve.

Before Daphne could say a word of greeting, the door pushed open again and Jacob Meyers walked in. Lily had mentioned he was in Paris, and of course, he would also be invited to Lily's urgent meeting about some mysterious project. Daphne's heart sank. He was Lily's oldest friend. A real golden boy with the entitled attitude to go with it.

Obnoxious.

"Lily Pad!" Jacob boomed, and Lily glanced up from her desk and ran across the office to throw herself into Jacob's arms, completely ignoring Daphne and Theo.

Daphne had to literally step aside as the tall man swept her friend up in a hug. Jacob took up too much space—he was too tall, too handsome, and too smart. Daphne bit back the urge to tell the two of them to get a room, instead standing aside with a polite smile on her face.

"Lily," Theo shouted, happily interrupting their hellos. Despite, or maybe because of, her own lack of children, Lily was a favorite with Theo. He ran to her for his own hug.

"Hey, kiddo," Lily said, turning from Jacob with a smile that made her look, briefly, like a teenager. After the quick hug, they did some sort of complicated high five—when had they practiced that? "I'm so glad you could make it, Daphne." Finally, an acknowledgment that she was even here. Lily swept her arm wide to encompass both herself and Jacob. "Come over and meet everyone."

"Can I play a game on your computer, Lily?" Theo asked.

Lily replied before Daphne could intervene. "Sure, kiddo." She brought him to her desk and scooped him into her lap, hitting a few keys on the computer in front of her.

Screen time was limited in the Smythe-Baird household. "Is it age-appropriate?" Daphne asked, approaching the desks.

"I bet it's a first-person shooter called *Welcome to Pimp World*," Jacob said sardonically. He always had to be so cool.

Daphne smiled tightly. "Well, I'm sorry for being a concerned parent." She hated the way her voice sounded. Self-righteous and pompous—a double whammy of asshole. She could imagine Lily and Jacob mentally rolling their eyes at her.

"It's *Minecraft*," Lily said in a soothing tone.

Daphne turned to the big blond, who was wiping his hands on a rag and approaching. "Hello," she said. "I'm Daphne, Lily's best friend." She emphasized the "best" to make sure Jacob knew his place.

He extended a hand, engulfing hers in his gigantic paw. "Alexander," he said with a scowl.

Had she done something to offend this man? As always when she was discomfited, she resorted to officiousness. "Theo, darling. Where are your manners?"

Damn it, now she sounded like an uptight Mary Poppins. Theo tore his eyes from the screen. "This is Lily's friend, Jacob," she said, and the other man waved at him. "This is, er, Alexander," she indicated the large man. "This is Lily's colleague . . ." Her voice trailed away. She had forgotten the younger woman's name.

"I'm Alice," she said.

"Like from Wonderland?" Theo asked, shaking her hand with interest.

Alice broke into a wide smile. "Yes," she said firmly. "Exactly like Alice."

Theo's attention was caught. "Doesn't Alice have yellow hair?" he asked.

Alice shook her head. "You've been misinformed," she said gravely. "I've been to Wonderland. I had tea with the Queen of Hearts and had to run away from the Jabberwocky."

Theo gazed at her for a moment. "You're teasing me," he finally decided.

"You're right," she conceded.

"I knew it wasn't true," he said. "Alice has white skin, not brown."

Daphne stiffened. Theo had only started noticing that people had different skin color, and she was always terrified of what observation might come out of his mouth. The other day at Les Galeries Lafayette, he had marched up to a sales girl hanging dresses and informed her that she was Black. Daphne had been mortified, although thankfully the woman hadn't appeared to speak English.

She flashed an apologetic look at Alice. "Theo, why don't you play your game while the grown-ups talk." Her son turned back to the computer.

"I am sorry about that," Daphne said to Alice. "He has lots of Arab friends at school. His best buds are Mohammed and Mufasa." Oh, God, she was making it worse, playing the old "I'm not racist, my son's best friends are Middle Eastern" card.

Alice looked down, and Alexander's scowl deepened. Daphne suddenly wished she had ignored Lily's text asking her to come to *Bonjour Paris* after work.

She didn't need this right now. Not when Philip had abandoned her yet again. This time for three weeks. He was the VP of sales with that goddamn multinational; didn't he have any say in his travel schedule?

He had left her, as usual, to keep their lives together: work full-time, parent full-time, don't forget to make the bake sale cookies, sign the permission form, remember it's Pajama Day, separate your recycling, take the car to the garage, organize playdates, eat clean, watch your carbs, update your goddamn gratitude journal.

Meanwhile, this morning Philip had boarded a first-class flight to Singapore to stay at a hotel with a rooftop infinity pool and a swim-up bar featuring twelve different varieties of Singapore Sling.

Daphne knew. She had checked the hotel website.

"It's fine," the younger woman said, still refusing to meet her eyes. "It is true—Alice Liddell was a little white girl."

The younger woman sounded defeated, and Daphne frowned in self-reproach. "Theo," she said sternly. He looked up. "You know that people in stories can be any color, and there is no right or wrong in our imagination."

He nodded, looking mystified as to why she was speaking so forcefully to him.

Lily seemed oblivious to the undercurrents in the conversation and turned to finish the introductions, calling Jacob her "oldest friend" and Daphne her "dearest pal." Which was better, to be an old friend or a dear pal? "Dear" was more affectionate, but the "pal" lessened its power.

Daphne was only in Paris thanks to Lily. Her friend had already moved to France when she sent Daphne a hot tip about an opening with the United Nations' International Art Registry. Before she even knew what was happening, Daphne was navigating a brand-new job in a brand-new country. Six months into her move, Philip, who she met over too many beers and a fully loaded baked potato at an expat pub quiz, was on the scene. Marriage and Theo followed in rapid succession. She owed career, husband, and baby to Lily.

Lily addressed her and Jacob. "Thanks so much for coming. I need your help."

Lily didn't often reach out—she was insanely self-reliant, undoubtedly a result of that hardscrabble upbringing. It was strange, even though Daphne had grown up in much more comfortable circumstances, she wasn't nearly as generous as Lily.

Daphne always knew just how much she should contribute to cover her meal, or exactly how many times she'd hosted the playdate. It was something she disliked about herself—this small, ugly, calculating, enumerating side.

Lily was looking at her. "We need your expertise," she said.

"Yes," she said. "What can I do?" Lily must be working on a story with an art angle. Maybe she'd be featured in the magazine. Daphne had a master's in art history, and though she used her knowledge every day in her current job, it was gratifying to know that Lily appreciated her know-how.

Daphne hadn't been in great shape, career-wise, when she had first met Lily at a 7 a.m. boot camp in Battery Park. They had bonded over their shared awe at their instructor, Sergeant Todd, and his impressive thighs.

Back then she had been working for peanuts at a middling gallery in SoHo. The artists were pretentious jerks, while the gallery owner was making so many bad business decisions she wondered if the whole thing was a money-laundering front.

Lily gestured to an uncomfortable, straight-backed plastic chair, and Daphne sat. She saw a flash of relief on Lily's face. Had she really worried Daphne wouldn't help?

Lily glanced at Jacob. "This concerns you, too," she said to him. She launched into a convoluted story, Alice occasionally offering a timid interjection in an attempt to clarify the rambling tale. By the time Lily wound down, Daphne was still not sure how the furnace or wigs fit into the whole thing, but she had the gist. It was some nonsense about a lost necklace.

Jacob was equally dubious, and she saw him sneak a glance at his smart watch.

She pasted a big, fake smile on her face, annoyed that she had driven across town on a Friday night when her backyard, such a luxury in Paris, and that glass of chardonnay awaited her. "That's quite a story," she said. "So, let's see this amazing discovery."

Alice pulled a necklace from a drawer. Jacob barely glanced at it, and she felt the three others staring at her face, awaiting her reaction. Her annoyance with them was softened by their sweet credulity. These dummies really thought they'd found a genuine jewel-encrusted treasure in the basement.

She leaned forward and picked it up. The necklace felt weighty and important, and her skepticism dissipated. She wasn't a jewelry expert, but she worked with old and sometimes even ancient artwork all day long. She had developed an "eye" for age and for the patina of value.

The double strand of diamonds alternated between cushion and circular, creating a pleasing pattern. She cleared her throat, straightening her shoulders. Her voice took on a slightly deeper timber, the one she used at work. "The cuts of the diamonds, especially on the cushion, are each a bit different—some more oblong, others more square. This could be mine cut, which would mean older than modern cutting techniques."

"Does that mean it's real?" Jacob asked. He was finally paying attention, but his voice was incredulous.

"The setting for each diamond looks individually molded," she said, not quite answering his question.

Daphne appraised it. Thirty-six stones, with four missing from the settings closest to the clasp. She pointed to the empty settings. "It's unlikely that you'd go to the trouble of individually setting stones unless it was authentic, or you were deliberately constructing a forgery."

She looked up and saw she had everyone's attention. While she was used to a certain amount of respect at work, it felt good to have Jacob and Lily admiring her knowledge. Theo was still engrossed in *Minecraft*.

Daphne turned back to the necklace. At the center of the whole thing was the exquisite honeybee. It was a rich, warm gold. "I suspect it's twenty-four karats," she said. The finish of the setting was mellow, something difficult to fake. She examined the back. "The gold has tiny dents, which might indicate that it was hammered rather than cast, another sign that it was handcrafted." Jacob nodded sagely, as if she was confirming his own suspicion, making her want to slap him.

At last, she turned to the two fluted emeralds. Each a good inch long. "I'm not an expert, but their cut and clarity are breathtaking." Daphne now held the whole necklace up, letting the honeybee swing in the air. It was about eighteen inches long, princess length. Designed to sit at the collarbones to more perfectly display the pendant.

"What's that, Mommy?" Theo asked, looking up from the computer and reaching out to grab the necklace.

"Be careful," Jacob said, swatting his hand away. Daphne flared with anger, even as she understood Jacob's reaction—the necklace was exquisite and must be protected.

"I think this is real," she said, placing it back on the desk.

The others visibly relaxed.

"I also think it's old—at least a hundred years. You should get it properly assessed," Daphne said briskly. "Then, of course, inform the police."

"We will," Lily said. Here she hesitated for a moment, as if debating whether to say any more. "But first, I wondered if we could do some research."

"What?" Daphne asked. "Why?"

Alexander also reacted to this news, leaning forward. "We had agreed to inform the police," he rumbled.

"Yes, we will," Lily said, twisting her hands together. "Only, I had an idea. You see, *Bonjour Paris* is struggling. I've got a plan to turn things around, but Luc Seguin, the owner, needs to see a real blockbuster June issue. If he doesn't see a future for *Bonjour Paris*, he's going to shut it down."

The intern, Alice, gasped. This was obviously news to her. Daphne looked around at the shabby walls. She couldn't say she was surprised.

Lily told them how *La Vie en Rose* had eaten into their market share, and their urgent need to pull away from their competitor. Daphne's mouth twisted guiltily. Every month she bought herself a copy of *La Vie en Rose*. Filled with gallery openings, fashion shows, celebrity profiles, and ads for Amélie Pichard shoes, the magazine catered to precisely the kind of expat life she aspired to. *Bonjour Paris* was more earnest, more arty, and if she was honest, a bit boring.

Her lack of affinity with *Bonjour Paris* didn't stop her from always buying two copies of that magazine when she bought her illicit issue of *La Vie en Rose*. It was like carbon offsetting, but for magazines.

"So you see," Lily finished, "Luc wants to secure his mother's legacy, but he'll keep the magazine going only if he can be assured that it still has an impact. Otherwise, he wants to cut his losses. If I can wow him with a June issue—say, something about the amazing Honeybee Emeralds," she gestured to the necklace, "he'll invest further in the magazine and we'll really be able to compete."

No one spoke. This was Lily's brilliant plan? Hanging all of her hopes on a necklace? It was ludicrous. It was unconscionable. "I'm sorry, Lily, but the necklace must be handed over to the police," she said. It went against all of her professional instincts to hide the origins of a work of art, and this necklace was just that.

"Please," Lily turned to her. "We need this. The paper is struggling. If I lose this job, I'll have to move back to the States."

Life without Lily in Paris would be grim. Sure, she had some mommy friends, and work colleagues, but no one who knew her the way Lily did. She looked at the "Honeybee Emeralds" again. How had it ended up abandoned in a basement? There was a story there, and she'd like to know the answer. For the first time in weeks, months, she felt the stirrings of real excitement. This was something different from the usual routine of work, laundry, and meal prep.

Alexander spoke up before she could. "It must go to the police."

"Oh, please," Lily said, now turning to him. "We'd only need a couple of weeks to do some background research, and then we could turn the necklace in. It's a win-win—we'd give the police information that would actually help them, and Jacob will write us an amazing cover story that blows everyone's minds."

"Me?" Jacob said, startled.

Lily bit her lip, "Yeah, I was hoping you could write an article for us. We can help with research. With your name attached, we'd be guaranteed attention. We could save the magazine. What do you think?"

There was a long pause. Daphne watched as Lily's hands twisted together.

"I don't know, Lily Pad. This isn't my usual beat. I like meatier stories, deep dives."

"You could do a deep dive on this one," Lily pleaded. "I'm sure we're going to find some compelling angles. Maybe these are blood diamonds?"

Was Jacob really going to make Lily beg, right in front of all of them? Daphne couldn't stand to watch. "Lily," she said crisply. "I'm okay with delaying the police contact while you guys look for answers. As for who writes the article, why don't you do it? You're a terrific writer. You could do something amazing. Very meaty." She placed particular emphasis on that last word.

Jacob flushed red and shot Daphne a peeved look. "I'll do it, Lily Pad," he said. He sounded like a king granting dispensation to a subject. Lily smiled in relief.

"Thank you," she said to Jacob. "Thank you too," Lily said, turning to Daphne, enveloping her in a hug. Daphne smiled as she returned it. Yes, the necklace needed to be reported. But as Lily said, if they could provide more details, it would only help the police.

"We cannot keep this." Alexander interrupted their celebration. He didn't raise his voice, but he seemed to somehow get even taller. "This is not ours," he said firmly.

"Could you give us two weeks, until the beginning of May?" Lily asked. "If we haven't found the owner by then, we'll turn it over to the cops."

Alexander frowned.

Daphne watched as Lily tried charm. "I feel we're on the cusp of an amazing story." She grinned at him, inviting him to join in the fun.

He simply stared at her, and Lily's smile faltered. Daphne had to admire this guy's commitment to his stoic Viking brand.

"Alexander," Alice spoke up. "The magazine is in trouble. We might all lose our jobs." Her voice cracked, and Daphne feared she might cry. "You could help save *Bonjour Paris*."

The large man stared at her.

Alice persisted. "If we go under, who knows who your new neighbors might be. Maybe noisy people, or some smelly restaurant . . ."

This last had an effect. "Fine," he said. "Until the beginning of May. Then we call the police department."

Lily smiled hugely, and they all relaxed. Theo, as if sensing a change in the room's vibe, slipped from Lily's lap and climbed into Daphne's. She bent her head and gave his soft hair a sniff.

Just then, the door to the office opened. Jacob moved to block the necklace from view. Daphne recognized the short, well-dressed man as Luc Seguin. Lily's boss was deliciously attractive.

"Luc," Lily said, her face breaking into a nervous smile. "Thank you so much for stopping in."

Luc shrugged. "It was on my way home."

Lily introduced him to Alexander and Jacob. "And you know Daphne," she said.

Luc held her hand, and for a moment Daphne thought he was going to kiss it, but instead he made eye contact and said, "But of course I remember your lovely friend." He grinned at Theo. "And this must be your charming husband." The boy giggled, and then buried his head in Daphne's shoulder. He was getting tired.

"I asked you to come by," Lily said, clearing her throat, "because we've made a bit of a discovery." Lily was nervous, and Daphne felt for her friend. She was usually hyper-competent professionally, but the presence of Luc obviously discomfited her.

Without the song and dance she had gone into earlier, Lily relayed the story of the lost necklace. She pointed to the desk where it lay.

Luc's eyes widened as he bent over it. "This is magnificent," he said, touching it gently.

"I work for the International Art Registry," Daphne said, inserting herself into the conversation. "I am pretty sure it's authentic."

Luc turned to her and nodded, and Daphne nearly flushed at the respect she saw in his eyes. Here was someone who knew the value of expensive things and understood the importance of caring for them. She spoke authoritatively, pleased that she could impress a man like Luc Seguin. "If the necklace is indeed authentic, it will be worth a great deal of money."

"How much?" Jacob asked eagerly.

"Well, there are thirty-six diamonds, plus the emeralds. Leaving aside historical value, these diamonds are all about two carats. If they are color-less and flawless as they seem, it would be about 160,000 euros for the diamonds, plus the emeralds, which are honkers . . . that's the technical term . . . I don't know, the whole thing might easily be worth a quarter of a million euros, but I wouldn't be surprised if it was actually much more."

Alice gasped, and Daphne smiled at her. Sophisticated people like her and Luc were used to hearing about such large sums of money, but obviously that would seem enormous to the intern. The girl reached out and touched one of the bright-green emeralds, her hand moving softly over the gem.

"This is the June cover," Lily explained. "Jacob will write it. Alice and I are going to research its history, flesh the story out."

Alexander cleared his throat. "I also will assist," he stated. He wasn't asking for permission. "I wish to ensure we find the rightful owners."

Daphne panicked. Were they all going to do this without her? She thought of Philip, swanning off to Singapore. Why couldn't she have an adventure for once? "You'll need my help too," she said.

"I don't know," Jacob broke in. "There are already a lot of us."

Five minutes ago, he hadn't even wanted to write the story. Now he was getting territorial? "I'm the only one of us with any art experience. I have access to information, contacts, and databases that you might need."

Jacob frowned.

"Of course you can help," Lily said.

Luc gazed at the necklace again. "This might be quite the story," he said. "Unusual, mysterious. It could grab the city's attention."

Lily grinned happily. "You should join us in the research," she said. "Solve the mystery with us."

Luc looked startled by her invitation. "I'm neither a writer nor a researcher."

Lily took a step toward him. "Think of your mother, how interested she'd be in this story." She pointed to a framed black-and-white photograph on the wall of a middle-aged woman looking up with a warm smile from her typewriter.

"Maman would love this," Luc admitted, his stern features softening.

Daphne almost applauded Lily's deftness. Involving the boss in the story was a brilliant move. Once he was invested in the outcome, it would be much harder for him to kill the story, or even close down the magazine.

Luc gazed around the room, its walls covered in the photographic history of *Bonjour Paris*. "I will help out," he said decisively.

Lily turned to Jacob. "Okay," she said to him. "What do you need for a killer story?"

He paused for a moment, then began rattling off a list of research areas they'd need to cover. Lily assigned people tasks: Daphne would research the necklace itself, see if she could narrow down its origins by identifying its era and style.

Work was to begin tomorrow, Saturday morning, and they were going to reconvene Sunday afternoon in the wardrobe room itself to discuss what they had discovered about the Honeybee Emeralds.

The meeting was winding down. "Time to go, Theo darling," Daphne said.

They said their goodbyes and headed to the door. Daphne was preoccupied. Her mind cycling through all the angles she could take to uncover the necklace's origins.

"Mommy?" Theo asked, pulling her back from contemplation.

"Yes, sweetheart?" she responded as they reached the door and she turned to wave to the group.

"What's a pimp?" he asked in his high, clear voice.

She shot Jacob a dirty look and opened the door to the street. "It's a kind of bird," she replied crisply, yanking him outside.

Villeneuve-sous-Dammartin

France, 1864

The sound of Louis's carriage wheels had long faded, but still she sat by her chair at the window. He had abandoned her. Thrown her over for another, or, knowing him, several others. The abandonment, though well-compensated, still stung. It had been many years since she was jilted. Normally, she was the one breaking with one gentleman to trade up for one with a heavier pocketbook.

She recalled the moment she had met Louis. Naively, she had not immediately known who he was. That part had not been artifice. She and her companion, Mme Champêtre, had been taking a turn through Saint Cloud Park when the heavens had opened. The rain poured down, and her parasol, much like the ineffectual twittering of Mme Champêtre, had been useless. They sheltered as best they could under the scant protection of the yew trees.

Over the small hill, his carriage had sailed into view, like one of those new 90-gun ships the navy was so proud of. He leapt from the apparatus and approached her with a firm stride. His aura of command, if nothing else, should have told her who he was. His voice was clear, his accent impeccable. "Are you in distress, mademoiselle?" He addressed her directly, correctly assessing Mme Champêtre as unimportant. She glanced behind him and saw the imperial coat of arms on the carriage. Her heart beat faster.

Her eyes met his, and in that moment, she had known what he wanted. It was that instinct for love, for reading men's desire, sometimes before they sensed it themselves, that had served her well since she had reached the first bloom of womanhood.

She cast her eyes down, and then fluttered her lashes up. He saw what she was thinking. She gave him her hand and demurely accepted any aid that he would be so kind as to extend. She left the parasol and Mme Champêtre behind in the park.

He was a serious man, an unbelievably powerful man, yet together they spent their time laughing. He was an indefatigable and highly efficient lover. Sometimes she didn't even have time to rearrange her facial expression before he had sated his desires yet again. Once she had looked up, midthrust, to realize that the vigor of his exertions had caused the wax of his moustaches to melt, making them droop down comically. It was all she could do to stifle a giggle. Despite these calisthenics, he was not the worst lover she had ever had, and they were able to find much mutual pleasure from one another. Their affair had lasted only two years. Long enough to scandalize Europe and produce darling little Charles, so chubby, so perfect.

She stood from her chair and walked over to the dressing table, her silks rustling in the stillness of the room, before sinking elegantly to the seat in front of the mirror. She placed the necklace at her throat, the clasp closing easily behind her slim neck, evidence of its exquisite craftsmanship. She looked at herself. The diamonds in their gold setting were cool against her skin, though the emeralds seemed to burn hot. He'd once compared her eyes to emeralds. She'd smiled and thanked him. The comparison was inept; her eyes were hazel, not this deep, rich green. But it was sweet of him to try—poetry from a deeply unpoetic man.

Ablutions

Daphne: I have started my nightly ablutions.

Lily: What the what what now?

Daphne: Cleanser, an oil cleanser, a toner, a serum, and a moisturizer, plus under-eye stuff.

Lily: Holy cow, where did you even get all that?

Daphne: I hit up Printemps Haussmann and let a twenty-year-old with flawless skin boss me around.

Lily: You're going to have the perfect pores of a hot, buttered baby.

Daphne: ??? Now I've oiled my décolleté.

Lily: Your what?

Daphne: You know, your chest area. Where that gorgeous necklace would sit.

Lily: It's pretty incredible, right?

Daphne: I've honestly never seen anything like it. Stunning.

Lily: If we can spin this into a big story—get some international coverage—it will give the magazine so much more security.

Daphne: It's kind of fun that we get to work together.

Lily: I know! It's going to be amazing. It will be like the old days!

Daphne: ???

Lily: You know, when you first moved to Paris—we hung out together a lot.

Daphne: I was sleeping on your couch . . .

Lily: Yeah, but we did everything together.

Daphne: It's true, we were totally inseparable—what happened?

Lily: You met Philip.

Daphne: ?

Lily: You did that thing that people do—you got the new boyfriend and kind of fell off the face of the earth.

Daphne: Yeah, we got serious pretty quickly, but I didn't completely ditch you!

Lily: Oh don't worry about it—it's the thing that happens with new relationships—you were cocooning.

Daphne: LOL—right . . . and now I'm a butterfly. Okay, next up, I'm dabbing snail essence to my under-eye area.

Lily: Is that really from a snail?

Daphne: Yup. Ingredients list snail secretion filtrate.

Lily: I have a hard enough time eating them, now you're saying I need to rub them in my eyes?

Daphne: Not IN your eyes, you dingus, UNDER.

Lily: I think I'm going to stick with soap and water.

Daphne: Tsk. Tsk. Every woman needs a skin care regime.

Lily: Regimen.

Daphne: What?

Lily: It's regimen—regime means like a dictatorship, or a military regime.

Daphne: Are you sure?

Lily: Yes. Look it up.

Daphne: Huh. You were right.

Lily: SRSLY—what's going on here?

Daphne: I'm thirty-five, it's time I started paying attention to my skin. Plus, it's self-care—there was an article about it in the New Yorker.

Lily: Okay. I want a full report on this.

Daphne: I already think my pores are shrinking.

CHAPTER 6

Wild Geese

ALICE WAS DISCONCERTED TO FIND RUE DE BEAUNE DESERTED. She had only ever come to the office on weekdays, when well-dressed commuters bustled past. On Saturday morning the wide street was empty, the shopfronts closed, the sidewalks holding only a few chained bicycles. She stuck her hands into the pockets of the green velvet jacket, reassured that for once she was looking chic enough to be on the streets of Paris. Upon closer inspection, she had realized that the embroidery on the jacket didn't represent fruit, but was a sprig from an olive tree, with its distinctive long leaves and oblong olives. Perhaps this hinted at a Greek or Italian connection to the jacket, and therefore the Honeybee Emeralds.

She had slept badly last night, thanks to a mixture of zinging excitement at the discovery of the necklace and sinking dread at the thought of *Bonjour Paris* closing. What would she do if she lost the internship? Return to Hull? Sometimes she missed home, her mother, Dale, and her half-sisters with a sharp, sudden ache. Other times she thought about that cramped house on Victoria Road and felt only a bubbly lightness, almost as if she might faint with relief. Return to Hull? It would mean failure.

The necklace, though. That was thrilling. She recalled her jolt of adrenaline as she pulled it from her pocket in the basement. For a brief time, while she and Alexander finished up with the boiler and walked back to the *Bonjour Paris* offices, it had belonged entirely to her. Now the group had wisely decided to lock it up in a safety-deposit box registered to *Bonjour*

Paris. Alice knew that was the right thing to do, but she mourned the necklace's absence. It would have been nice to run her fingers over those diamonds again. She contented herself with taking out her phone; she'd made her wallpaper a nice shot of the necklace, the pendant prominently displayed, and it soothed her to look at it.

Ignoring *Bonjour Paris*'s entrance, she knocked on Alexander's unmarked door. They had been assigned the task of following up on the Honeybee Emeralds' connection to the theater. He slid it open, his large face looking out in the street in inquiry. "Yes?" he said.

Had he forgotten they'd made plans to meet today, or was he being deliberately obtuse?

Her concern fled, however, when she detected the scent wafting from the space behind him. It was completely different from her last visit, much more exotic, almost musky. She took a big sniff. Wait, the honeysuckle odor was still there, small and harder to sense but persistent, like a child tugging at your sleeve. "That scent—it's the same, but different," she remarked. What a stupid thing to say.

Alexander didn't appear to notice, instead nodding. "I am experimenting. Layering some odors. Trying to capture a scent." His face softened as he spoke about his work. "You can come in." He made the offer as if he were bestowing the rarest of prizes.

It was only as she stepped inside that she realized he was.

The space was as big as the *Bonjour Paris* offices, but there the similarities ended. Instead of clutter and computers and fifty years' worth of print issues covering every surface, the walls were crisp white, and it was as pristine as a surgery.

Three enormous copper vats of different sizes and shapes lined one wall. One fluted bronzed pot was connected to another via an arched pipe. Complex valves monitored the pots' contents. She was dimly aware of Alexander watching her closely, gauging her reaction, it seemed, for any sign of disrespect. He didn't have to worry; she felt only awe. The warm glow of the vessels, presumably filled with bubbling liquids, made her think of alchemy and magic.

One long table, spanning nearly the entire room, was covered in sacks of dried flowers. A second table, under small, high windows, flanked the other wall. Here glass test tubes and flasks reminded Alice of her A-Level Chemistry class. Mr. Daniels had looked like Walter White from *Breaking Bad*, and the whole class had thought he was the coolest. It was a commentary on the dullness of life in her suburb, that cooking meth in New Mexico was seen as glamorous.

She wandered over to the table strewn with dried flowers. "Where do you get all of these?" she asked.

"Around the world," he said. "I only buy the highest quality, so it takes some time to find them." It seemed like perfume was one subject that made Alexander chatty, or at least less taciturn. He indicated a bag filled with petals. "This is damask rose from Turkey." The desiccated petals spilled out of the bag, deep pink at their outer edges, becoming lighter and almost yellowy brown in the interior. Alice itched to pick one up and sniff, but feared Alexander's reaction.

She walked over to the science class part of the room and peered in at the beakers containing what looked like oil. "Why does this look like a chemistry lab?"

"Glass is the best medium for perfume. It is neutral, so doesn't disturb the acid balances."

"What's the name of your perfume—like, what's your brand?" she asked.

He sniffed. "Brand! I don't sell my perfume at Monoprix, you know."

Goodness, he really was touchy. "Right," she said. "How do you sell your perfume if you don't brand it?"

He shrugged. "Women with taste and money find me. I often customize a scent for a specific client."

"That sounds pretty posh," she said.

"Yes," he replied.

She wandered around some more, peering into bags, sniffing at beakers, until he began to shift restlessly. "Shall we return to the matter at hand?"

"Yes," she agreed, pulling herself away from the magic. "We have to figure out where the Honeybee Emeralds came from."

Mentioning the necklace aloud gave Alice a happy, warm feeling, like thinking about a dear friend. She suddenly remembered that she had dreamed of the jewelry the night before, imagining it around her neck, its solid weight a confirmation of her place in the world.

"I have located the name of the theater company that had rented space in the building."

"How did you get that?" Alice asked, impressed.

"Last night I went back to the basement and retraced our steps. I found the wardrobe room. Then I looked for some information about the theater."

"That was good thinking," she remarked.

"It was a simple matter," he said. "Leaving that string was smart," he added.

She didn't know what to say and could feel a blush surge to her cheeks.

He didn't appear to notice. "There was no documentation in the room," he said.

She was grateful for his lack of comment on her blush. "Nothing? That's odd, isn't it?"

"Perhaps," Alexander said. "One would expect there to be some trace—a scrap of paper, an old program."

"How did you figure out who owned the theater, then?" she asked.

"I checked out the Registre du commerce et des sociétés de Paris. It's a registry of businesses in the city. It dates back to the First World War."

"Impressive," Alice said. "Do you have an owner's name?"

"It seems that Théâtre Rigolo closed its doors thirty years ago."

Her heart sank, but then she rallied. "Let me do some digging," Alice said. "I'm kind of a whiz with Google." Oh God, what a dumb thing to brag about. Thankfully, Alexander made no comment. After about five minutes of searching, she had something. "There is a Théâtre des Muses, which might be the descendant of Théâtre Rigolo. They have the same artistic director, anyway."

"What's his name?"

"Alphonse Marchal."

Alex furrowed his brow. "I think, perhaps that was the name I saw in the registre."

"That's great. He might know something about the necklace." She turned back to her phone and continued Googling. "I can't find a number for Alphonse Marchal, but I have the address for Théâtre des Muses—we could go over and check it out."

Alexander frowned. "The theater won't be open at ten a.m. on a Saturday. It is a wild geese chase."

"Goose," she said.

"What?"

"The expression is 'wild goose chase.'"

"But you are chasing many goose—geese."

She twisted her lips, considering his point. "It's not explicit in the expression that you're chasing a lot of geese. Maybe you're only after one goose."

"Nonsense. Why would you only chase one goose? You would want the whole flock."

"You would?"

"Of course. Why are you hunting them if not for eating? More geese, more goose meat."

There was something disgusting about the expression "goose meat," and the image that Alexander had evoked was chilling in its brutal matter-of-factness. "I think we've got offtrack," she said. "We should check out the theater."

"That is what I am saying—wild geese chase. Who will be at a theater at ten o'clock on a Saturday morning?"

"Listen," she said impatiently. "This Alphonse Marchal might be able to tell us all about the Honeybee Emeralds. What if he's the owner and we return a long-lost family heirloom? That kind of sentimental tearjerker is just the thing we need for *Bonjour Paris*. I'm going. Are you coming or not?" She was surprised at how assertive she sounded.

"Where is it?"

She checked her phone. "142 Rue Saint-Denis," she said.

"Saint-Denis?" Alexander frowned. "I will go with you," he decided.

She opened her mouth to argue further, then realized he had acquiesced. "Great," she said.

Alice and Alexander made their journey via bus, a mode of transport not often associated with Paris but one that was effective, not only for getting around the city but also for seeing the sights. They drove past the Louvre's forecourt and saw the tourists massing, like soldiers preparing to storm the castle walls. They were armed with selfie sticks and a hunger to see the rarest prize these days—an actual authentic object, rather than a bunch of backlit pixels.

Alice saw a security guard standing straight-backed in a building's doorway. When Alice was seven years old, she had made friends with a soldier. Intrigued by his upright bearing and crisp uniform, she had watched him carefully over several days. She had seen how straight he stood at his post and how seriously he took his role. She had admired his sense of purpose and his adherence to duty. These were things that Alice herself believed in. She was a serious girl, sure of her purpose in life, which was to listen to her mother and do as she was told. When she got up the nerve to wave at him one day she was surprised, and even a bit disappointed, that he waved back. Surely that wasn't allowed?

The wave was enough to initiate a change in the man's demeanor; he became relaxed and friendly. He would make a daft face or do a silly walk when he saw her coming down the pavement. She realized she had completely misjudged this man's character, and in later years she sometimes thought her whole life was premised on the lack of discernment that had led her to make one small, shy wave.

Of course, there were many things she realized in later years. She had thought the silly, overeager man was a soldier because that's what she was used to seeing on the streets at home in Tehran, but she learned that Dale was a security guard at the housing estate where the Home Office had briefly housed her and her mother after they claimed asylum. She also learned that Dale was as soft and easily amused as his wave had indicated. He was a man of big emotions—always ready to laugh lustily or cry with gusto.

At the wedding, when her mother had married Dale, he had broken down completely, crying with happiness. Alice hadn't realized you could do such a thing. He sobbed in front of the surprised officiant, while her poor mother, tiny next to this well-fed Englishman, tried to support him, digging through the pockets of her simple sundress for a tissue.

A cynical person would look at their marriage and think that her mother had married Dale for the security—an escape from the status of asylum-seeker and all of the tentative uncertainty it implied. Alice had lived inside that marriage, however. She saw the truth: Against all odds, Maheen and Dale loved each other. He delighted her mother; he was silly and kind in ways that spoke of his happiness in his own skin. Maheen, beautiful and fiercely intelligent, was his North Star. It was the thing that Alice loved the most about Dale—how deeply he adored her mother.

So far, she and Alexander had traveled in silence. Alice realized that if she didn't initiate conversation, they wouldn't speak the entire journey. There was something relaxing about this idea, but her curiosity got the better of her. "Why did you become a perfumer, anyway?" she asked as they rumbled up Rue Molière.

He shrugged. "Fell into it."

"It wasn't your family business?" she pursued.

"Definitely not," he said.

"It's very rare for someone to just become a perfumer," she said. "Usually there is a familial connection."

He looked at her sharply. "How do you know that?" he asked.

The heat suffused her face, but her voice didn't falter. "I've been Googling perfuming," she said.

He stared at her.

"I'm a curious person," she explained quickly. "When I'm confronted with something new, I want to know all about it. I did the same thing when I discovered that Mme Boucher is obsessed with whales."

"Whales?" Alexander asked, confused.

"Yeah, she's got a thing for them. I noticed a blue whale is her screen wallpaper, plus she's always reading these nature magazines. It's basically her one humanizing trait."

"What does that have to do with perfume?" Alexander asked.

"Nothing," said Alice. "It's just that I am a curious person. So, why did you get into the perfume business? It seems like a random thing for a kid from Iceland."

Alexander shrugged.

Alice persisted, "Come on," she said. "This is a long bus ride, and what else are we going to do?"

He sighed. "I grew up near Grindavík in a fishing village. The people are small-minded. It is a shithole."

Alice nodded. While Hull might be bigger than his village, she knew what small-minded people were like, and how their narrow outlook could force you into a version of yourself that simply wasn't true.

He continued, "One of the things we are famous for is making hákarl—the fermented shark meat."

"Wait, what?"

"Google it," Alexander said. "The meat has a very strong smell. I was surrounded by it. It was too much. My mother always said I had a sensitive nose, but my father thought I was ridiculous."

This might have been the longest she had heard him talk. He looked at her dolefully, his eyes asking if he needed to continue.

She nodded firmly.

"You know when you have something, something that makes you different, and instead of rejecting it, you really commit to it? That was me with my sensitive nose. We have a saying—Sá vinnur sitt mál, sem þráastur er—it means, 'He who is most stubborn will win.'"

"You became a perfumer to spite your father?"

"Perhaps," Alexander nodded. "Think of the life opposite to dwelling in a tiny fishing village surrounded by rotten shark carcasses." He gestured out the window to the beautiful city bustling about its Saturday morning.

"My father is certain I am gay," Alexander said as an afterthought.

"Are you?" Alice asked.

"No," he replied, and for a brief moment their eyes met. Then the bus rumbled to their stop.

As it turned out, Rue Saint-Denis was in quite a seedy area. Every second store seemed to be a sex shop. They passed Club 69 and a place called Top Sexy, the window filled with blow-up sex dolls, a tattoo parlor, and a used-car lot. It was 11 a.m. by this time, but there still weren't a lot of people around. They crossed Rue Réaumur, and Alice was sure the very young-looking women standing on the corners were prostitutes. Men lingered in doorways staring at them as they walked past. Alice shivered and was deeply glad that Alexander had chosen to accompany her.

"This is one of the oldest streets in Paris," he remarked.

It was rare for him to speak unprompted, and Alice wondered if he had noticed her nervousness and was trying to distract her. That thought bucked her up.

At last, they came to number 172. It was the middle shopfront in another long Haussmann building, although unlike the *Bonjour Paris* offices, it looked fed-up and tired, the stones chipped, and the sign announcing "Théâtre des Muses" was crooked and in need of paint.

They tried the door, happy to find that the building was open. The interior reflected the same sense of exhaustion and failure that marked the outside. They stood in a dumpy lobby, the walls water-stained, the carpet frayed. They walked up a set of low steps, leading deeper into the building, and a strong stench met their noses.

Alexander's whole face scrunched up as the scent hit him. "Helviti," he muttered. "Mildew, cigarettes, and body odor."

Alice gave a tentative sniff. That sounded about right. She was impressed. "Hello," she called.

A thin man with a thick mustache and balding head appeared from a door at the side. "Can I help you?" he rasped in French, his voice betraying years of smoking.

"I'm sorry to trouble you," Alice responded in French. "Are you Alphonse Marchal? We're hoping to talk about Théâtre Rigolo."

The man frowned, his moustache drooping as well, pathetic fallacy but for facial hair. "I am he, but the Théâtre Rigolo closed many years ago. It is officially wound up. Bankrupted. There are no funds for outstanding debts." He crossed his arms.

"No, no," Alice said, stepping forward. "We are looking for information about the theater."

The man's posture relaxed somewhat. "Really, why?"

On the way over Alice had formulated a plan of attack. "I'm Alice Ahmadi, and this is my coworker, Alexander," she said. "We're reporters for *Bonjour Paris*, maybe you've heard of it?"

"It rings a bell," M. Marchal said.

"We're writing an article on the history of theater in Paris." Alice was always grateful that her natural shyness melted away in a professional setting. Her desire to excel overrode her instinct to self-efface. "We wanted to include the Rigolo. We might even put in a plug for your current theater." She waved her hand.

M. Marchal's arms remained crossed, "What kind of article?"

"Oh, you know," Alice said vaguely. She hadn't given that aspect of her lie much thought. "It would be free publicity for this place," she said.

Whether it was the mention of the word *free* or the idea of publicity, Alice seemed to have convinced him. "I have some time now," he said. "I am waiting for a delivery, which is why I am here this morning."

"We were lucky to have caught you," Alexander said, speaking for the first time and giving Alice a meaningful look.

She could tell he wanted to say "wild geese chase," but she ignored him. His French was as good as his English, with only the faintest hint of an accent. Alice supposed that you had to be good with languages if you grew up speaking Icelandic. There couldn't be that many native speakers. She made a mental note to look that up. "Do you have somewhere we could talk, M. Marchal?"

"Of course. We will go to my office."

It was cramped; an old, beaten-up desk occupied most of the space, and the rest was filled, almost Tetris-like, with open boxes of old programs and stacks of posters from former shows. M. Marchal pulled in two chairs from an adjoining space, which must have once been another office but was now a storage closet. "Just stack those boxes on top there, and make room for the chairs," he said.

M. Marchal appeared to have lost much of his suspicion and was now delighted to talk to them. They all sat, and she turned on her phone's recording app, putting it on the desk.

"So lovely to have the press interested in our little enterprise," M. Marchal said, directing his speech to the phone. He reached into his bottom drawer and pulled out a bottle. "Would anyone care for a drink?"

"What is that?" Alice asked, surprised.

"Calvados—apple brandy," he said, pouring three healthy portions into some questionably clean glasses. A cat appeared in the doorway. She was a sleek black animal, her coat glossy, her whiskers magnificent. She stalked into the room with grace, ignoring the visitors and assuming a place under M. Marchal's hand, where he began petting her. He passed the glasses around, and Alice took a tiny sip. It was surprisingly delicious. Crisp, sweet, but with a real kick.

"It is only made in my region—Normandy, in the town of Calvados. Legend says we took our name from the Spanish armada. In 1588, the *El Salvador* wrecked off our coast on their way to invade England. The ship carried barrels of brandy, which washed ashore along with the dead. We found our calling and our name in one fell swoop. 'Calvados' is a bastardization of 'El Salvador.'"

"That's a good story," Alice said, guiltily realizing she had already sipped a quarter of the large glass away.

"Tell me about Théâtre Rigolo," she said. In the past six months Lily had assigned her a ton of interviews, an opportunity not always afforded interns. It was one more reason Alice loved her job and wanted to hang on to it at all costs. She liked to open interviews with a broad question, allowing the subject to relax and choose the path they wished to take.

"We were a group of dreamers, we were," he said fondly. "We opened in 1969, when all of France was rebelling. We started at a shitty little bôite in La Pigalle. Our vision was to reinvent theater in the tradition of Le Grand Guignol."

Seeing their blank expressions, M. Marchal sighed. "The young people know nothing of history," he said. "Le Grand Guignol was a naturalistic theater that ran for nearly sixty years. The plays were dark, bleak, and bloody. We wanted to do the same."

Alice had now consumed the entirety of her delicious boozy apple juice. She normally didn't drink much, and she was already feeling a thickening in her head and a murkiness to her thought process. M. Marchal noticed her glass was empty and went to fill it again, but Alice put a hand up to stop him. Alexander showed no such hesitation, and he and M. Marchal enjoyed another drink.

"Théâtre Rigolo put on horror plays," M. Marchal said proudly.

"Wait, like ghosts and monsters?" Alice asked.

M. Marchal shook his head impatiently. "Nothing so obvious as the grotesque. No, we delved into the psychological pain of insanity, panic, anxiety—uncontrolled intellectual horror." He leaned forward. His eyes were alight with memories of his work, and he actually licked his lips in pleasure. The cat suddenly jumped onto the bookshelf behind his head. It started purring. Alice shivered. Things were getting a bit *Phantom of the Opera*-y.

"Of course, the audience was not always so interested in the fascinating depths the human mind could descend to, so we had to coat everything in lots of gore. We used so much fake blood that our prop master came up with a recipe to make it ourselves—saved us many francs."

"Not very naturalistic," Alexander murmured.

M. Marchal didn't hear, or ignored him. Alice shot him a dirty look. The theater owner was opening up to them; she didn't want Alexander blowing it.

M. Marchal continued, "We put on shows about lobotomies, electric chairs, insane asylums, disfigurements. Our most controversial play featured a botched abortion, where the fetus returned to psychologically hound the beautiful young would-be mother. It would limp along on stage, trailing blood and placenta. Very technically challenging to execute. Eventually the mother stabs out her own eyes with some rusty scissors."

He rattled this list of horrors off in a calm tone, and Alice wished she had more Calvados to gulp. Still, she was glad she was recording everything, as this would be excellent color for Jacob's article. "So, what happened to the theater?" she asked.

"We were young and idealistic. We thought that we could show these complacent Parisians the true horrors that lurked beneath and it would snap them out of their bourgeois smugness. It didn't work like that, of course."

"When did the theater go out of business?" she asked.

"We hung on for a few years—by 1985 I knew we were done. Our creditors were everywhere."

"Is that why you abandoned the wardrobe room at Rue de Beaune?" she asked.

M. Marchal blinked in surprise. "Rue de Beaune?" he inquired. "Oh yes, we did briefly have our headquarters there. It was when we were in between performance spaces. I had forgotten about that place." His eyes suddenly lit up. "That's where I heard of *Bonjour Paris*—their offices were there."

Alice nodded. "Yes, we're still there."

M. Marchal gave a low whistle. "Still in business, that's impressive." He closed his eyes, apparently in an effort to remember. "It was for expatriates, was it not? English-language?"

"Yes," Alice agreed.

"They were our neighbors. That office manager was quite a bitch, but Olivia, she was a wonderful woman. She had style. She had smarts. She was the whole package." His eyes darted to the side and he licked his lips, a quick flick out of his tongue, the pointed pink tip visible and then gone. Alice was repulsed.

"She came to a few of our shows, brought her husband. He was a very handsome man, very successful. I remember they came to the twin incest one. She told me afterward she found it 'repugnant and alarming.'" He smiled happily at the memory.

"Olivia died last year," Alice said gently.

M. Marchal shook his head. "That a woman so vivacious and witty should be no more . . . we are all getting old," he remarked dolefully. "It is amazing that your magazine lives on, in this age of computers. It is the same for my theater. We are the last of the dinosaurs." M. Marchal poured himself another glass of Calvados, forgetting to offer any more to Alexander. He shot the liquid back and poured another.

"Coming back to your time at Rue de Beaune," Alice said.

"Yes, yes," M. Marchal said distractedly.

"Why did you leave there?" Alice asked.

"The landlord, that espèce de putain, claimed we were in arrears on our rent. I tried to barter with him, give him a lifetime pass to the théâtre, but he rejected it."

"I can't imagine," Alice murmured consolingly.

Alice could see the alcohol had started to affect him, and she figured they didn't have much more time before he was legless. "Did you ever store anything at the old address?" she asked.

"What?" he asked. His eyes were red, and it looked like he was about to cry.

"Did you store anything there, at that address? Stage props or costumes?"

"We didn't believe in costumes," he said. "We demanded our audiences furnish the details with their imaginations. After Théâtre Rigolo closed we decided to go much more experimental. We did away with scenery, the props . . . now, often our productions don't even have actors. We simply incorporate the audience into our experiments."

Alice considered his words. If Théâtre Rigolo never used costumes, then the wardrobe room couldn't belong to it. The Honeybee Emeralds had no connection here. This whole trip had been a waste of time. There was a long pause as she tried to absorb her disappointment.

The cat leapt from the shelf now, back onto the desk. "Allo, my little Josephine," M. Marchal crooned, scooping her up in his arms.

The movement roused Alice, and she recalled the pretext of their visit. She grabbed her phone from the desk. "Thank you so much for your time, M. Marchal. I think we have everything we need."

She met Alexander's eyes and could see her own disappointment reflected there.

M. Marchal stood, somewhat unsteadily, to usher them out.

Back on the sidewalk, Alice and Alexander blinked for a few moments in the sunshine. It felt like they had escaped from a Poe story—broken through the vault where they'd been bricked up. Alice didn't feel relief, however. Instead she was anxious their morning's work hadn't amounted to much. Sure, they might be able to do a story on this bizarre underbelly of the Parisian theater scene, but they were no closer to finding the truth about the necklace, and her job was still in jeopardy. She was grateful for Alexander's quiet stoicism; it meant she didn't have to verbalize her worries. They trudged on for a few moments in silence and then, when she felt like she had got her discouragement in check, she turned to Alexander. "I guess you were right," she sighed. "It was a wild goose chase."

"Geese," he insisted stubbornly.

It was only when Alice glanced up at him and saw the twinkle deep in those blue eyes that she realized he was teasing her.

CHAPTER 7

The Long Haul

DAPHNE LAY IN BED, LUXURIOUSLY ALLOWING SLEEP TO SLOWLY seep away. When Philip was around on a weekend morning, he inevitably bounced awake, noisily making breakfast and then undertaking some ostentatiously efficient chore, like sorting out the recycling. Would she have started dating him if she had known he was a morning person? That hadn't been apparent when they'd met at that pub quiz. Dragged by Lily, Daphne had gone to the Monday night events grudgingly—she was competitive by nature, and it infuriated her that all the sports questions were about soccer (or "football") and all of the pop culture ones seemed to relate to Eurovision. Still, her third time, while the Les Quizerables were down by fifteen points, she had met Philip, captain of the John Trivia-oltas.

She stretched and climbed out of bed, noting that she had begun sleeping diagonally across the whole space. She padded into the bathroom and saw her array of beauty products, but she couldn't face her essences, serums, and cleansers without coffee. She shrugged into her housecoat and examined her purchases. They looked nice in their tubes and glass jars by the window. She snapped a quick pic. Yes, one corner of her flowered Yves Delorme towel was visible, creating a bright contrast to the bottles and jars glinting in the sunshine. She typed a quick caption: I regret taking such good care of my skin—said no one ever! #Skincare.

Nailed it.

Feeling more awake, she checked on Theo, still asleep and curled up with his stuffed brontosaurus.

As she headed downstairs to the coffee maker, Daphne wondered about the necklace. Was there an actual story, or was the result of their research going to be quite dull? Rather than a spectacular theft or a Russian tsarina, they might uncover a mundane tale of absentmindedness or insurance fraud. It was always insurance fraud.

For Lily's sake, Daphne hoped they'd find something juicy. What would she do if Lily moved back to America? The thought literally made her shiver, and she hurried to the Keurig.

Jacob was writing the article, and as much as she hated to admit it, he had name recognition. She thought back to the way he had delineated what needed to be done, assuming leadership over the crafting of the story. He seemed to have good instincts for the angles to adopt. Right now they were looking into origins and where the necklace ended up. Once they had the start and finish, he said, they could fill in the middle. Daphne inserted the pod, waiting impatiently for the machine to deliver her cup of caffeine and alertness.

Jacob was very handsome, and Daphne wondered, not for the first time, if Lily had a crush on him. Lily's European romances had gone nowhere. Her French boyfriends had all worn scarves (hard to get away from that, really) and some of them had seemed like pretty good bets—one had been a talent agent, managing some big-name French actors (although not so famous that Daphne had ever actually heard of them). Another had done something with wind power, and a third, weirdly, had been a cop. Still, none had stuck. Was that because in the back of Lily's mind she was measuring them against that perfect guy? The one who looked and talked an awful lot like Jacob.

Once she had a good, strong cup to fortify herself, Daphne turned to her reference books. She could start her skin care regimen tomorrow. Her job today was to narrow down the necklace's time period. At work she concentrated on paintings and sculpture, but she needed a good understanding of major trends and styles in all the decorative arts, including jewelry. Over the years she had amassed a very useful reference library.

The Honeybee Emeralds was a unique design. That should focus the search. Her heart beat faster. She loved a juicy research project. Much as she tried to hide it, at heart she was a nerd. This was why she'd studied art history in the first place—delving into the past and seeing how ideas, design, and beauty incited passion across the centuries.

While she had loved some aspects of her time in grad school, one element she had not enjoyed were the men who studied art history. The few straight guys she came into contact with were arty types with dubious hygiene who claimed *Eraserhead* was their favorite movie but had really seen *Braveheart* one hundred times, or grown men who lived with their mothers because of their "artistic" jobs. That kind of lazy attitude to the creative process drove Daphne crazy. What was the point of making something if no one ever experienced your art and you could only afford off-brand toothpaste? There was nothing inherently noble about being an artist. It wasn't a more important job than plumber or road surveyor, and yet these self-indulged babies thought because they created images or poems or "sound sculptures" they got a free pass from basic adult behaviors. She infinitely preferred Rembrandt's sensible business practices (for the most part) to Edvard Munch's depressed Norwegian alcoholism.

She was therefore ripe for the plucking when she met Philip. He was nothing like those artsy types. He was stocky and muscular and wore a baseball cap like a bro-ish jock, but he was actually quiet and introspective. From Massachusetts, he had been living in Paris for years as a senior sales rep for a big farm machinery firm. While the work wasn't glamorous, it was well-paid, and Daphne had reached the age where being nobly impoverished had lost its allure. Philip showed her a different Paris from the scruffy expat one Lily had introduced her to. With Philip, they took cabs rather than the métro and ate "inventive" dinners in restaurants populated by other ambitious, serious people. It felt like Philip was an adult, and Daphne was ready to grow up.

She frowned, thinking of her text exchange with Lily. Had she really ghosted her friend when she had met Philip? She could hardly remember that time of her life; she and Philip had met, married, and had Theo in such rapid succession that it was all a blur. At the time it had felt romantic and exciting, but now part of her worried it was just desperate. There had been something wonderfully familiar about Philip amidst the swirl of foreignness of her new job, new language, new city, and new life. He got her pop culture references, pronounced words the same way as she did, and had paid for the most expensive satellite package so he could watch college football. Had she built her whole world on panicked home-sickness? Only now, with Theo in school full time, did it feel like she had the space and time to think about her life. The question was, did she like what she saw?

Moving to the computer, a good hour of online research confirmed that nineteenth-century France, thanks to massive amounts of colonial French archaeology work, was in love with classical motifs, and the bee in partic-ular. The ancient Greeks and Romans saw the insects as a sacred connection between the living and the underworld, and they plastered much of their jewelry with bees. While there was no way their necklace was ancient— diamonds only became common in jewelry in the eighteenth century— the creator of the Honeybee Emeralds was undoubtedly influenced by the nineteenth century's mania for ancient artifacts. She texted the gang her research finds, putting the date of creation between 1840 and 1890. She was pleased to learn that Alice and Alexander were en route to a theater following a lead. Daphne quite loved this feeling. They were all in this together. Working on a common problem.

Theo came down; she fed him cornflakes and then, after a particularly intense bout of whining, let him have his Saturday-morning screen time.

She returned to her laptop, wondering if she could identify the jeweler who had made the necklace. It was unfortunate there was no maker's mark, but given its unique style and expense, there couldn't have been many jewelry houses in the nineteenth century capable of making such a piece. Deep into her research, she was startled by the familiar Skype ring-tone. Shit. It was 11 a.m., and she and Philip were scheduled to talk. She hesitated, tempted to ignore the call, but then remembered Thérèse, their couples' therapist, admonishing them both to make an effort. Philip would win serious points in the ongoing blame game if she missed the daily check-in.

"I can't see you, the camera isn't working," Philip said. His voice held that querulous, almost petulant tone that reminded Daphne of Theo. There was something deeply maddening about hearing that inflection from a grown man's mouth. It made Philip seem so weak, so childlike. Very unattractive.

"Let's forget about my camera," she said. Was there a thin note of contempt in her tone? She knew. She *knew* that contempt was the marriage ender, the emotion you could not express to your spouse, because otherwise the whole thing was going to sink like the Titanic. Years ago, she'd listened to a podcast about the dangers of contempt. Its sour derision and sense of superiority signaled the time to call the divorce attorney.

Philip began talking about his most recent series of meetings, and Daphne listened with half an ear while scrolling through websites from various high-end jewelers. She was looking for companies that had been in business in the nineteenth century.

"We've got nothing scheduled this weekend, so Xiu Ying is going to show me the Botanic Gardens."

"Xiu Ying?" she asked, keeping her voice light. Philip had mentioned this colleague before. This female colleague.

Daphne's parents' relationship had been as rotten as a four-day-old fish wrapped in an infidelity newspaper. She was fourteen and her sister, Lara, was ten when her parents announced their divorce.

"Xiu Ying is a colleague," Philip said in amused exasperation.

Daphne remembered the day her parents had broken the divorce news. Lara had held her hand, crying. Daphne had been tempted to shake her little sister. Hadn't they been trying for the past year to do everything right in order to make Daddy stay? They'd obeyed their parents, did their chores, tried not to squabble. She remembered how lost she had felt as the realization sunk in. It was too late, Daddy was giving up on them, and stupid Lara was making sure he'd never come back by crying like a big baby.

"You're spending a lot of time with Xiu Ying," Daphne said, unable to keep the sharp edge from her voice.

Daphne had turned on her little sister that day, bending down to whisper in her face. "This is your fault," she hissed. "They had you to save their marriage, and it didn't work." This was true; she had heard them fighting about it once when she stayed up late to enjoy the sick thrill of eavesdropping.

She remembered how Lara's face had crumpled, appearing to lose all structural integrity, becoming loose and inhuman in the depth of the pain she, Daphne, inflicted. That moment was a touchstone for Daphne, a reminder, whenever she needed one, about just how evil one person could be toward another. Hurt people hurt people, and she had transferred her own torment to her baby sister. She closed her eyes. She hated remembering that moment.

"Daphne, Xiu Ying is a rotund, sixty-year-old grandmother," Philip said calmly.

Philip knew where her suspicions came from, of course. Her father, Merv's, infidelities had been a rich topic of discussion with Thérèse in her fern-filled office with the burbling aquarium. It was all well and good, in that soothing environment, to clearly analyze her own insecurities and rationally trace their origins. It was quite another when her husband was thousands of miles away, traipsing off to botanical gardens.

Thérèse had once suggested that perhaps Daphne's dissatisfaction with her marriage might be connected, in some part, to her own fears of abandonment. She was distancing herself from Philip before he had the chance to leave her. "No duh," Daphne had responded. It had not been a productive session.

"How's Theo?" Philip asked. He'd forgotten that his camera was still working and that she could see him. He looked at something on the wall, his eyes betraying boredom. His chin was beginning to soften, starting the slow melt into his neck.

"Fine, fine," she said, her answer equally disinterested. The thing, of course, was that Philip was a good man. He was a kind person who wanted to do right by his family. He was fiercely loyal to anyone in his small circle. If Theo returned from school with a story about a mean kid on the playground, Philip was alert, asking for all the details, fretting about whether they should call a meeting with the teacher, the principal, the board of trustees. Similarly, if Philip's mother complained about a member of her bridge club cheating, he would struggle to be polite to the old lady the next time they were home in the States. And Daphne? Once upon a time, they would share a glass of wine after dinner and she would recount her day to him. It gave her a thrill to hear his protective instincts come to life when she told a story about the métro doors closing on her too soon or a colleague's unfair remark. That was the essence of Philip's loyalty—he always sided with you, he was always in your corner and was always there.

When they got married, after the vows and their sweet, soft kiss, he leaned down and whispered something in her ear. When the ceremony ended, her friends clustered around her, asking what he had said. She smiled mysteriously and refused to tell them, letting them guess at the meaningful bon mots he had uttered. In actual fact, he had said, "I'm in this for the long haul." It was a stupid, unromantic thing to say—maybe even insulting? Would their marriage be something as prosaic as a "long haul"? Was she something to be hauled? And yet, over the years, whenever things got rough, she had repeated his promise to herself and it had comforted her. He would be there.

Lately, however, Daphne wondered if he was still in it for the long haul. Working much more than usual, his travel was excessive, and, according to him, the pace would continue for many more months. His constant absences weren't helping her sense of disconnection. It seemed like she was slipping out of Philip's inner circle of loyalty. Given his apparent lack of interest in her life, she had no motivation to tell him about the Honeybee Emeralds. That realization made her sad, because a year ago it would have been the first thing she raised.

Skype was cutting out, and sometimes she missed a few words Philip said, but she didn't bother asking him to repeat anything. As their desultory talk meandered on and she watched his finger absently climb into his nostril and do an exploratory sweep, she wondered if she even wanted him around for the long haul.

Her eyes strayed back to her computer and she clicked on a web page.

Philip stopped. "Daphne, are you even listening to me?"

This time she hardly noticed his sulky tone. She looked up, her eyes more animated than they had been for their entire conversation.

She had uncovered the designer of the Honeybee Emeralds.

A Moleskine

IN ANTICIPATION OF JACOB'S MORNING ARRIVAL, LILY HAD nipped out to her local boulangerie and picked up a bag of fresh, flakey croissants. The coffee she brewed filled the apartment with a warm, breakfast smell. Her place was modest—a series of small attic rooms that would have been the domestiques' chambers back when the building was constructed. Still, the tiny windows were numerous and looked out over the rooftops of Paris, recompense for the long hike up five flights of stairs. Lily had considered moving to a more convenient location, but given her worries about the magazine's future, that was off the table.

Now they sat in her tiny living room, their laptops out, researching the necklace. Jacob was in her secondhand armchair, the one she had bought at a seedy brocante and thoroughly inspected for bed bugs (you can take the gal out of NYC . . .). She'd had it reupholstered in a deep, satiny blue, which she just realized was the exact color of Jacob's eyes.

"These croissants are delicious," Jacob said. "Did you get them from La Maison Pichard? Marie-Pierre says they're the best."

Lily looked up. The way he said that name, as if reading a line of poetry, she knew he was referring to a lover. "Marie-Pierre?" she asked lightly.

His face broke into a broad grin. "Girlfriend," Jacob said.

Lily struggled to disguise her surprise. Jacob had never called any of the women he dated his "girlfriend." A true commitment-phobe, Jacob's singleton status was a given. And yet, for the next twenty minutes Jacob regaled her with story after story about the wondrous Marie-Pierre whom he'd met in Manhattan but who lived in Paris. Marie-Pierre had an incredible artistic eye, she volunteered at the French version of Girl Scouts, she found running hard on her joints! He revealed each item as if sharing a precious pearl.

"She sounds wonderful," Lily said, when Jacob finally paused for breath. Her tone had a slight note of sarcasm, but Jacob seemed oblivious. This girl-friend was probably why Jacob hadn't called her as soon as he had arrived in Paris. She pushed her croissant away half-eaten, before changing her mind and inhaling it. Marie-Pierre—undoubtedly small, dark-haired, dark-eyed, and gorgeous in that indefinable French way—was now the most important woman in Jacob's life. Her half-formed plans for Jacob's sojourn in Paris—their bike rides, trips to the Loire Valley to spot châteaux, the lazy Sunday afternoon brunches, the fun of a midweek meal and a wander through Left Bank bookstores—all gone. Jacob would now do those things with Marie-Pierre. Lily was second banana.

That hadn't always been the case. Her memory of her one night of romance with Jacob was a bit blurry, thanks to several very cheap and extremely sweet bottles of Canadian wine. It was senior year. In fact, it was the night before graduation. They'd started with a gang of friends at Madison Brewing Company. Five of them ended up back at Lily's room. They'd sat around talking about their futures and swilling that wine. There had been a lot of "I love you, mans"; a bunch of ironic high fives; many, many hours of urgent conversation; and an unfortunate series of dry heaves. The friends dwindled away until it was only Lily and Jacob.

The rest seemed inevitable. She remembered the night as a series of little moments. One of those flashbulb instances was Jacob tucking a tendril of her hair behind her ear and then cupping her chin in his hand. That moment, right before he bent down and pressed his lips against hers, was a perfect distillation of all the memories, laughter, and dumb shit they had done together. It was all the flirtation and accidental hand strokes, the many hours of conversation, the months of studying and encouragement. It included the spikes of jealousy when a new lover entered the scene and the hours spent dissecting their families. It was their entire relationship compressed into a split second. When Lily thought about that night, and the awkward, fumbling, funny half-drunken sex, that moment was most precious to her.

Fifteen years had passed, and while there was always a small, simmering frisson between them, neither had been interested in pursuing it. They had both locked that attraction away. Except, what was she feeling now? Was she jealous of Marie-Pierre? Maybe her attraction wasn't as locked up as she thought. She pushed the worry aside. She didn't need this now. Not when *Bonjour Paris* and her job were on the line.

Luc hadn't texted for an update today, probably because he had some big financial report to finish, but she wanted to get results for their meeting tomorrow. She needed to show him that she could deliver.

She returned to their task. They were trying to reverse-image search the necklace through Google. Lily had uploaded a photo she had taken into the search engine. Google's algorithm got to work, crawling the billions of images in its database, producing a listing of all possible matches. Unfortunately, they got thousands of results, and she and Jacob were now clicking through each one, looking at murky images of necklaces taken from photographs, paintings, movie stills, and a variety of other sources.

She stretched, shaking croissant crumbs from her lap. "I don't know how successful we're going to be. If that necklace was in the basement for more than thirty years, which certainly seems possible, then it was lost before the internet even really existed."

"Yes," Jacob replied. "But there might have been a photograph or a drawing made of it before that's now online."

Lily's phone chimed. Another text from Daphne. She smiled. They'd seen each other only yesterday, but Lily had received more texts from her friend in the last twenty-four hours than she had in weeks. For the past six months or so, Daphne had been a bit depressed, but this project seemed to have reinvigorated her.

Daphne had texted them a date range to focus on, but there were still thousands of results from 1840 to 1890 to sift through. They tried narrowing down the returns with keywords, but "honeybee necklace," "insect necklace," "diamond and emerald necklace" hadn't yielded better results.

A song came up on Spotify, and both she and Jacob hummed along.

"I recognize this," he said.

"It's Tegan and Sara—'City Girl.'"

"God, you played that album constantly," he recalled.

She grinned as the poppy, angsty sounds of the duo singing about a failed relationship filled her apartment with big emotions. All that betrayal and pain had spoken to her twenty-year-old self, but fifteen years and many relationships later, she didn't empathize as profoundly with the girl getting "crazy" over her ex and screaming so loud that the police were called. Now she felt bad for the officers wading into this drama, the neighbors enduring the girl's histrionics, and the woman's friends, who would have had to listen to City Girl's undoubtedly obsessive and self-pitying analysis of the broken relationship. Was this middle age? When you started to sympathize with the neighbors listening to the heartbreak, rather than the heartbroken?

The song made Jacob nostalgic. "You were always writing back then," he remarked. "It didn't matter what time I showed up, you had one of those Moleskine notebooks and you'd be scribbling thoughts down. You took it everywhere—the dining hall, the library, all your classes. I thought you were so cool."

Lily laughed. "I was pretentious writing in that thing so ostentatiously. I thought that's what made a real writer. A Moleskine."

"Yeah, but you were a real writer," Jacob said softly. "You wrote some amazing stuff. That essay about your dad? The story about the fresh-baked bread? Those were astonishing. I really admired you."

She noted his use of the past tense and tried not to be hurt. She had been on fire at college. So exhilarated at getting enough of a scholarship to escape her overcrowded house and her tiny hometown. So thrilled to talk about big ideas with like-minded people, so happy that the act of writing was not only respected, but somewhat worshipped. She had been on a four-year high at Bennington, and through it all, by her side, was her gawky, goofy, long-legged, handsome friend Jacob. They'd had such dreams for themselves and for each other. Their future paths were clear. Now, everything seemed harder and more complicated.

"How's the writing going these days?" He always asked this, and over the years, it had become increasingly difficult to answer.

"What writing," she said flippantly, hoping to quash the conversation before it got going. Her whole life she had been certain she would write novels, create stories to inspire and delight, but with every passing year that dream seemed sillier and more romantic.

He smiled kindly at her, his teeth flashing. "No, really. Are you working on anything? You have to put the time in with fiction—inspiration doesn't just strike. It's work." Jacob's own novel had been published last year. It was brilliant, but some small, unlikable part of Lily had been pleased that reviews hadn't been warm and sales weren't strong. Jacob was still speaking. "The thing you have to do is get your butt into a chair and sit there until something comes . . . I find early mornings—"

"Yes," she interrupted. "Thanks." Why was she being so bitchy? This was not how she had anticipated her reunion with Jacob.

"Wait, I've got something." Jacob interrupted her self-recrimination. He leaned forward. "I think this is it." His voice was excited. He stared at his screen. "I found the necklace."

Lily leapt up, hunching over Jacob's shoulder to see. There in front of them was the Honeybee Emeralds—maybe. Jacob's confident identification might not have been entirely warranted. It was a black-and-white illustration, so it was difficult to be sure.

A rotund, happy-faced-looking woman stared out from the pages of an old newspaper. Her hair was in an old-fashioned chignon, and she wore a dress that showed her décolleté. Around her throat was a double strand of diamonds that seemed to have an alternating cushion and round cut pattern. Most important, hanging pendulously from the strands of diamonds was a large golden honeybee, with an emerald on each wing.

"Where's this picture from?" Lily asked urgently. This was their first real lead.

Jacob clicked around, getting to the originating site. It was a small British archive that had digitized its newspaper collections from England's Penwith region. The image dated from the April 21, 1881, issue of the *St Ives Weekly Bugle*. It was a series of sketches taken from a fundraising ball held the week earlier in support of the St. Ives Church Benevolent Society. There were drawings of men in morning suits with ascots at their necks. The women's gowns were beautiful, intricate bodices with narrow waists and voluminous skirts. Every woman wore a dress that revealed décolleté and showed off shoulders. One woman sported a small tiara, and another had large sparkling earrings; and more than a few wore boas bursting with sumptuous ostrich feathers. None of the women displayed a piece of jewelry to match that of the twinkly-eyed matron. Frustratingly, none of the people sketched were named.

She and Jacob read the article that accompanied the images. Willoughby Somers's recitation of events the evening of April 21, 1881, was brief:

> All of St. Ives' grandees were to be spotted at last evening's fundraising "do" for the St. Ives Church Benevolent Society. Various amusements abounded, though the highlight was the dancing. Sir William honored the company with a brief address, followed by a lengthier disquisition from Reverend Bainbridge. Refreshments included lemonade, negus, and a variety of fowl. In a nod to the traditions of our esteemed benefactress, a hot soup was also served and a tremendous success it proved to be.

Lily read it through twice, willing there to be something useful in the description.

"There's nothing," Jacob said, his voice echoing her frustration.

Lily blew up the image of the woman, zeroing in on her neck, and printed the photo out in the highest definition possible. She jabbed at the image. "This looks like our necklace," she said. She was pleased; it was imperative to make good progress on the story.

They pored back over the images—about a dozen of them—from the party and then started Googling for other mentions of the event, or the people named. Two hours later, they didn't have much to show for their work beyond empty coffee cups, sore eyes, and croissant crumbs, which Lily picked absently off her chest.

Willoughby Somers seemed to have written extensively about St. Ives society, but there were no further links to the necklace. They figured out Reverend Everett Bainbridge's full name and that he lived in St. Ives from 1870 to at least 1896. As for Sir William, they simply didn't have enough information to track down anything about him.

"Okay," Jacob said, stretching. "I'm calling it. We're not going to find more images or further information online."

Lily's shoulders slumped. What if this whole quest was a silly pipe dream? What would she do if *Bonjour Paris* closed? She'd always told herself she'd do some serious writing if she had more free time. Would this be her opportunity? Who was she kidding? That ship had sailed. She closed her laptop with more force than necessary.

"Hey, hey," Jacob said. "This is far from over." His voice was tender. "We've made good progress," he said. "This is the first step. Now we'll hit up the library or go to the archives to dig deeper. This is going to be amazing, you'll see."

She nodded, still not convinced. Jacob must have realized it, because he took on a teasing note. "Look at the crack researchers we've got—an intern, a perfumer, a financier, and a Daphne." Here he rolled his eyes. "That's what I call the dream team."

"Hey." She whacked his arm in protest.

"Nah, I'm only kidding. This is going to be great. There is a story here, Lily Pad. We're going to find it."

Lily straightened her shoulders. Jacob was right. This wasn't over, and she shouldn't be getting down on herself. "At least we've got what's probably a positive identification of the necklace from 1881," she said.

"Exactly," Jacob agreed. "It bolsters the likelihood of its authenticity. It was much harder to forge diamonds in the nineteenth century, before the discovery of cubic zirconia."

Lily raised an eyebrow.

Jacob shrugged, "I did some diamond-research Wikipedia deep dives last night," he said.

"I'll text everyone and let them know what we've uncovered," Lily said.

It was early afternoon. Lily needed to put in a few hours at the magazine, and Jacob had to run to the arms of Marie-Pierre. They were headed in the same direction, and they walked along the high embankment, overlooking the Seine. "This is amazing, isn't it?" Jacob asked.

Lily looked around. It was one of those perfect Parisian days. "Yes, it is gorgeous," she agreed. The late April sun was finally shining, cyclists on the ubiquitous bike-sharing Vélib's whizzing past; a lady in a beret carrying a baguette; ahead of them a flower seller hawking tulips and hyacinths in a rainbow of colors; a nearby cherry tree in violent bloom, its profusion of pink flowers an exclamation point on an already perfect afternoon. On the street corner an old man in a flat cap played a mournful song on the accordion. She smiled. Sometimes she forgot how lucky she was.

They walked on in comfortable silence. Lily was relieved that the tension she'd been feeling earlier had dissipated. It was like the Honeybee Emeralds quest had smoothed over the jagged edges of their friendship that had been briefly exposed. Good. They had been friends for too long to let her unexpected jealousy ruin it now.

"This is me," Lily said, indicating her turnoff. She gave a little wave and made to leave.

"Wait," he said. He grabbed her arm, startling her.

She turned back toward him and nearly ran smack into his chest.

He lowered his head.

"What are you doing?" she asked, taking a step back.

He scowled. "Isn't this what I'm supposed to do? Two kisses to say hello and goodbye? I'm trying to be Parisian."

"Oh," she said, her heart beating in her ears. "You caught me by surprise."

Jacob stared at her expectantly. "So, how is it done?"

"Well, your instincts are right." She continued hurriedly. "When two friends, or even acquaintances, are leaving one another, they'll often do a kiss on each cheek."

He eyed her doubtfully, as if assessing a melon for rot. "How do you know which way to go first?"

"You kind of read each other's body language, see, like this." She took a step closer to him, but was thrown off balance by how tall he was. After all these years in Paris, she had forgotten how lovely and large American men could be. She put a hand out to steady herself and brushed against his chest. That was too intimate. She placed her hand on his shoulder instead.

She leaned forward and spoke, embarrassed to hear a husky note in her voice. "You sort of tilt your head forward and the other person reads what you're doing and moves their head the opposite way." They were so close she could feel the heat radiating from his body. She made the mistake of looking up, and her eyes met his.

"Like this?" he asked. He leaned down, and for a crazy moment their lips almost touched. She turned her head decorously to the side. His cheek, warm and faintly bristled, slid next to hers. She felt his breath whisper in her hair.

She took a stumbling step back. "Yup," she said, her voice sounding loud to her ears.

He looked confused. "Aren't we supposed to do a double kiss?"

"Nope, that's enough practice. You got it!" she blurted. "Okay, I had better be getting back to work now. Catch you later!" She practically yelled the last word as she turned and strode away from him.

Out to Dinner

Daphne: Get THIS

Lily: . . .

Daphne: I'm going out to dinner with Gisèle and Isaac Monday night. Remember them?

Lily: They're that super artsy couple—she sculpts and he does art direction or something?

Daphne: Yep

Lily: Maybe she's got an enormous mole on her face that should be gross, but instead she's so French and chic that it's just like a really stylish facial accessory?

Daphne: That's her. That mole is so cool.

Lily: Wait, isn't Philip out of town?

Daphne: Yeah, but we made the plans two months ago and I didn't want to reschedule.

Lily: Where are you going?

Daphne: Le Moulin.

Lily: What? That place is too loud. You're in trouble.

Daphne: ?

Lily: Gisèle and Isaac are low talkers. You are going to hear NOTHING. Last time I saw them I literally had to put my hand to my ear and lean toward Gisèle like an old lady to hear her mumbles.

Daphne: OOo. You're right. You know what's worse? Isaac is a slow talker.

Lily: OMG, that's true. So sloooooooow. It tricks you into thinking that what he is saying is super interesting, but

IT.

IS.

NOT.

Daphne: Yeah, like if you speak ponderously you're revealing some super important fact that's going to blow all of our minds. Spoiler alert, Isaac, no one cares about your commute route to work and how if you deke through that parking lot, you avoid a tricky roundabout.

Daphne: The worst thing about Isaac is that he's cool, which means that even when he's saying something so slowly, and so low, you have to pay attention in case it's really cool and you don't want to look uncooked.

*uncool.

Lily: He does have great hair though.

Daphne: Great hair.

CHAPTER 9

The Fellowship

IT WAS SUNDAY AFTERNOON AND THE FELLOWSHIP OF THE Necklace, as Alice had begun calling it to herself, had gathered in the lobby leading to the fancy flats above the street-facing businesses. The white marble foyer exuded expense. Shiny brass mailboxes were set in one wall, an art deco light fixture dangled from the high ceiling, and a tall, narrow set of locked glass doors opened to a richly carpeted hallway leading up to the flats.

Lily, Alexander, M. Seguin, Daphne, and Jacob stood in a clump in the center of the foyer, but Alice hung back. She wished she were wearing the green velvet jacket. It felt wrong to be returning to the wardrobe room without it, almost like she was missing its magical protection. The weather had warmed up, however, and it was too hot today to wear the heavier coat.

She took a deep breath, trying to manage her nerdy excitement about being part of this Fellowship. Working with Jacob Meyers alone was a massive boon. He was an internationally renowned author who had written incisively about climate change, homelessness, and American politics. He had also interviewed Beyoncé. BEYONCÉ. She had already learned so much from him. Back on Friday—was that only two days ago?—he had encouraged them to seek out the quirky, the unusual, or anything with a human-interest angle. Even at this early stage, he was looking for through lines: "Pay attention to the finances, follow the money; get me background on the historical influences; connect the players."

The rest of the Fellowship was equally impressive—an executive, an editor, an art historian, and a perfumer. They were mature, sophisticated professionals with their lives together. None of them had bad roommates, money worries, or persistent self-doubts. They had cars, families, connections, and nice clothes. Even Alexander, whose style was "Big and Tall indifference," owned his look and made it work. Now she belonged to this inspiring group, and they were on a quest to discover the truth about the Honeybee Emeralds.

Every time she thought about the necklace, a jolt of adrenaline zipped through her. The moment she had pulled it from the pocket of the jacket, she knew her life would never be the same. She kept dreaming about it: sometimes recalling the moment of its discovery, other times having terrifying, half-remembered premonitions of its loss. She woke this morning from one of those dreams, her heart beating furiously. Alice bit her lip. She knew the necklace was secure in the safety-deposit box. Yet she could not help worrying. Precious things could be lost or snatched away. There were no guarantees in life. You had to protect the things you valued.

Alexander turned to a small door set into the wall beside the double doors and painted an unobtrusive white.

"This door was here the whole time? I've never noticed," Lily marveled.

"Me neither," M. Seguin said. He was wearing jeans and a T-shirt, but Alice wasn't fooled by his casual look. She wouldn't be surprised if his outfit cost the same as her monthly rent.

Daphne and Jacob brought up the rear. Alice wondered where Daphne's little boy was this afternoon. She missed her sisters, especially Suri, the youngest. She was only nine. Little kids were so easy to be around; you always knew where you stood with them. No need to be wary.

Alexander produced a key so large it looked like a clown's prop and slid it into the lock. Alice had been expecting it, because she'd seen it when they last visited the basement, but it obviously struck Lily.

"We don't have one of those. How did you get it?" she asked.

"Took it," Alexander grunted, disappearing down the steep stairs leading to the basement.

What would it be like to be so intensely confident? To stride through life knowing how to vent radiators, take keys, and dismiss questions? It would be glorious, of course, but wouldn't it also make you kind of an arsehole? Alice recalled her old classmates at Colchester Primary. They had the blond hair, weak chins, and dropped *h*'s of the true Hully Gully, and they were terrifying in their unwarranted confidence and everyday aggression. Mind you, Alexander wasn't an arse, so there was obviously a way to be self-assured without being a twat.

She descended the stairs behind Jacob. He smelled nice. Not lemony like Alexander, more fancy than that. She didn't think he was wearing cologne, more probably it was a posh shampoo.

The stairwell was narrow and water-stained. There was a sharp turn halfway down the flight. As they rounded the corner, a cool breeze hit Alice's face and she smiled; she was sinking into Wonderland.

"We must be descending more than a single floor," Lily remarked from in front of her. "We're really going down."

"Paris has many layers," Alexander said, somewhat obscurely.

The walls narrowed, and the stairs steepened. There was a faint sound of dripping water. The stairwell ended at last, and she bumped into Jacob's back. She blushed in the darkness.

Alexander flipped on the light switch, and they spread out down the hall a bit.

Daphne, taking in the old brick walls and vaulted ceilings, said, "It's like we've gone back in time."

"Marvelous," M. Seguin agreed.

Lily shivered. "God, you can almost feel the weight of the building above us. The floors of the apartments, the furnishings, the people, the lead-lined windows, the mansard roof. It's all bearing down."

Alice, whose latent claustrophobia was never too far away, tried to ignore her boss's words.

"This is great," Jacob said. He took out a small notebook and tapped Lily on the arm. Alice was surprised when Lily jumped, as if he'd burned her. She really must be nervous about being down here. "This will be great color for the article," he said.

Alice peeked at what he was jotting: "Brick walls, anemic light, chill in the air, sense of otherworldliness."

Alexander hadn't stopped to marvel. Instead, he headed down the hallway with his long stride, staring at the floor as he went. They followed him like a flock of ducklings. Wait, *flock* wasn't right. It was a *paddling* of ducks.

They passed a couple of turnoffs, but Alexander ignored those. Alice sensed Daphne's anxiety rising, but she was confident in Alexander's sense of direction.

"Here," he said abruptly, turning down a narrower hall.

"How do you know?" Daphne asked, a hint of aggression in her voice.

Alexander pointed to the floor. There, unobtrusively, was the red thread Alice had laid down.

"Good thinking," Jacob said, clapping him on the back.

"It was Alice's idea," Alexander said, nodding to her.

The entire Fellowship turned to her with admiration in their eyes. She, of course, blushed.

After many twists and turns, they found the wardrobe room at last.

Alice felt proprietary pride as the Fellowship gasped in wonder at the rich colors and vibrant fabrics that greeted them. Daphne nearly shoved Alexander aside to get to the clothes racks. She pulled a gown out at random. It was a metallic-gray, long-sleeved, form-fitting dress with a tailored bodice. "These rhinestones are hand-sewn. Look at this attention to detail," she shouted.

Alice took in the room. There had to be at least two hundred gowns, furs, capes, headdresses, and wigs. It really was a treasure trove. Daphne was moving from dress to dress, making exclamations under her breath; Jacob wrote furiously in his notebook; Lily wandered around with a stunned look on her face; and Luc kept murmuring, "To think this was here the whole time."

Alice wanted to dance a little jig of pure happiness. Alexander caught her eye and actually grinned at her. He was enjoying the others' surprise as much as she was. She smiled back.

"So, Alice, Alexander," Lily said. "What did you guys find out about this room?"

They all turned to look at her. Alice cleared her throat, ignoring the heat suffusing her cheeks. She wanted to impress these people with her observations and be a key member of the Fellowship. Maybe not a Frodo, exactly, but at least a Legolas. Honestly, though, she'd settle for not being Samwise Gamgee. That servile little hobbit was pants. "We followed up on the Théâtre Rigolo angle," she said. "It doesn't seem to have any connection to the necklace."

"It was found right here in their wardrobe room," Daphne spoke quickly. "How can we be sure there's no connection?"

Daphne's tone wasn't aggressive, but it still flustered Alice. How to convey the creepiness of Alphonse Marchal and his dusty, depressing theater? Maddeningly, her blush deepened, and she found herself at a loss for words.

To her surprise, Alexander spoke up. "The theater did not keep a wardrobe room here. This does not belong to them. I was mistaken."

"Okay," Jacob said. "So that was a dead end." His deflating statement sucked the air from the room.

Alice flinched. Her membership in the Fellowship was not off to a good start.

"Still," said Lily, looking around her. "The necklace was found here, and it's obviously a pretty incredible place; there must be a connection. Let's see if we can find some clues."

"It is of no use," Alexander said. "I already examined this room thoroughly."

No one paid any attention to him, and for the next half hour, they all carefully searched the clothing, wigs, hats, fascinators, sewing supplies, and shoes for any insight. Unfortunately, no one found a thing.

"Not even a scrap of paper or an old receipt. It's almost as if they were deliberately obscuring where these came from," Lily said in frustration.

"Well, we've still got some lines of inquiry we can pursue," M. Seguin said.

"Lines of inquiry," Jacob said with a laugh. "Are we in a Sherlock Holmes mystery?"

"You're quite right, Luc," Daphne said, shooting Jacob a reproving look. "We've got a lot of possibilities to pursue."

After milling around for another ten minutes or so, Alexander led them back upstairs, and they reconvened in the *Bonjour Paris* offices.

They pulled up chairs in the filing area at the back of the room. There were no desks here and it felt cozy, the walls covered in old framed articles, magazine covers, and black-and-white photographs.

"Alrighty," Lily said. "Let's get back to it. Just to remind everyone, we've less than two weeks to figure out the Honeybee Emeralds's provenance and write a story about it. If we're not successful by that point, we turn it over to the police. Our field trip to the wardrobe room has convinced me we're onto something huge."

Jacob spoke. "I want to emphasize again how important it is to keep our discovery under wraps. No one else must know what we're doing, and that includes your office manager, Lily."

M. Seguin cleared his throat. Alice got the impression that he didn't like Jacob. "Mme Boucher is completely trustworthy."

Jacob nodded impatiently. "Of course, but let's keep this close to the vest. Stories have a way of leaking, and that would risk the impact and power of my article."

M. Seguin appeared about to argue, but Lily intervened. "I think you're right, Jacob." She smiled apologetically at M. Seguin. "We should limit the circle."

M. Seguin nodded, and Alice saw everyone else relax. What Jacob said made sense, but also Mme Boucher was quite dour, and her presence might have quashed some of the undertaking's sense of adventure.

"Okey dokey," Lily said. "Moving on, let's have our progress reports."

There was a pause reminiscent of that moment in class when the teacher asks a question no one wants to answer. Luckily, M. Seguin spoke up. "I made some quiet inquiries with a friend who is au courant with the wealthier and more exclusive Parisian scene, but alas, she has heard nothing about a lost or stolen necklace." He crossed his legs and took a small sip of the coffee that Lily had made.

Every word in M. Seguin's statement conveyed poshness and sophistication. Alice was positive that M. Seguin's "friend" was a current or former lover. What must it be like to be the kind of person who had lovers, rather than plain old boyfriends or girlfriends?

Jacob leaned forward. "Wait a minute. Are you saying you told someone else about the necklace?"

M. Seguin looked affronted. "Certainly not," he replied. "I simply asked her if she had ever heard any gossip in certain circles about missing jewelry. I didn't even specify I was asking after a necklace."

"Well, that kind of question seems a bit vague," Jacob said. His tone implied that by "vague" he meant "useless."

M. Seguin merely raised an eyebrow and took another sip of coffee.

Lily seemed oblivious to the tension, because she piped up, explaining what they had discovered. She passed around the printout of a lady from 1881 wearing the necklace, and they took turns studying it. Even in black and white, you could almost feel the Honeybee Emeralds pulsing with light and life. The necklace was a work of art. Reluctantly, Alice passed the image back to Lily. They all agreed that it was their necklace. Lily seemed relieved at their consensus.

"This is good," Daphne said. "It gives us some dates to hang on to. The Honeybee Emeralds was in England in 1881. This jibes with what I've uncovered. I am confident that the necklace is Second Empire."

"How can you narrow it down like that?" Jacob asked.

Daphne wasn't discomfited by a question the way Alice had been in the basement, explaining that the design was influenced by French archaeological finds of the 1830s.

"So this was a French necklace?" M. Seguin asked.

"It does seem most likely." The entire group was paying attention to Daphne's words, nodding thoughtfully as she expounded on the topic. "Whoever made this was attuned to the trends of the day. The exquisiteness of the setting and the quality and number of gems indicate to me that only a master craftsman could have created it. At the time, those jewelers were concentrated in Paris."

"Really? All the jewelers were here?" Jacob asked.

"Oh yes, France was the global center for style and craftsmanship. French jewelers were renowned for their elaborate creations."

M. Seguin's chest puffed out slightly, and Alice thought that his obvious pride in French skill made Jacob cross, since he glanced at him sharply.

"One more thing," Daphne said. "No jeweler, no matter how skilled, would make this on a whim. Given the expense involved for the materials—the quality of the gold, the size of the gems—this was made on commission."

"If we figure out who the jeweler was, it might give us a clue about who commissioned it," Lily said.

"Yeah," Jacob replied. "There can't have been that many major jewelers back in those days. We could do some research and see if we come up with a list of likely contenders."

"Well, I might have a lead on that," Daphne said. "I've done a lot of digging, and I think that I know who created the piece."

This caused a stir of excitement, and even Alexander, who had been staring intently at his water bottle, looked up. Daphne continued, "I wouldn't be surprised if it's a Medici dit Beauregard—they were a jeweler patronized by all the royals—they made tiaras for Marie Antoinette."

Alice shivered. She still couldn't believe she had uncovered something as amazing as that necklace. She had touched something ageless. What a thrill.

"Medici dit Beauregard made painstaking, elaborate pieces like our necklace," Daphne said. "Look at this peacock feather brooch from 1849. It features diamonds, sapphires, and rubies surrounding a large emerald . . . sound familiar?"

Daphne passed around her phone, which showed an image of the bright brooch—a cluster of small diamonds encircling gleaming blue and red stones, with a large, winking emerald in the center.

Alice held on to the phone, staring. She was less enthralled with the image, which was beautiful, and more with a question: How had she,

Aliyeh Ahmadi, who had been an asylum seeker as a child, ended up here, in Paris, sitting around a table with urbane sophisticates debating the provenance of a piece of expensive jewelry? "I love being part of this Fellowship," she exclaimed.

There was a pause, and she realized what she had blurted. The heat of her blush was painful.

"Fellowship?" M. Seguin asked, his bewilderment increasing her embarrassment.

"It's just a stupid thing I've been calling this group in my head," Alice mumbled, looking down.

"Like a research fellowship?" Daphne asked dubiously.

"No," Lily surprised her by speaking up. "Like *Lord of the Rings*—The Fellowship of the Ring—a group of disparate adventurers trying to complete a mission. I love it."

Alice shot her a grateful look, and Lily smiled back. Alexander was still gazing down at his water. At first, she thought he wasn't looking up because he was embarrassed for her, but then she detected the faintest smile tugging at his lips, and she relaxed.

Jacob spoke. "Getting back to what Daphne was saying, if we confirm the designer, then we can figure out who commissioned the work."

"Given the value and craftsmanship," Daphne said, "I think it might have been made for someone very wealthy, perhaps a minor nobleman or even a member of the royal family."

"Wait, you said the necklace was made in the nineteenth century," Lily interjected. "There was no royalty in France anymore—remember the whole 'off with their heads' thing?" Lily made a guillotine motion with her hands. "Chop chop."

"Oh, Lily, you really need to brush up on your history," Daphne said impatiently. "There were tons of attempts at restoration in France throughout the nineteenth century—Napoleon fell in 1814, then there was the Bourbon Restoration."

"Sounds intoxicating," Lily said with a laugh.

Everyone studiously ignored the terrible pun and Daphne carried on. "That's when Louis XVI's brother took the throne. Various pretenders battled for the crown over the next few decades. The dream of restoration only ended when Napoleon arrived on the scene."

"He was still around?" Lily interrupted.

Alice was glad that Lily asked these questions. Although she'd taken some French history courses at university, she had concentrated on the Middle Ages; Eleanor of Aquitaine was an inspiration. Nineteenth-century France, with its muddlesome number of revolutions and counterrevolutions, had not held a lot of interest. Now she was anxious. She was going to have to study it, make sure she understood every nuance. Knowledge made her feel secure and gave her a useful role in the Fellowship.

"Not Napoleon, Napoleon," Daphne said impatiently. "By 1850 we're talking about his nephew—Louis Napoleon III."

"What happened to Napoleon II?" Lily asked, obviously trying to keep up.

"Doesn't matter," Daphne said. Even she was impatient with her own history lesson. "Louis Napoleon established a new Napoleonic empire, hence—Second Empire. It lasted until 1871, then France got a president."

"Confusing," Lily remarked. It was a testament to how secure Lily was that she was willing to admit her own bewilderment. Alice would never cop to ignorance. Any sign of weakness was an announcement that she didn't belong in this conversation, in the Fellowship. She wouldn't make that mistake.

"Quite confusing," Daphne agreed. "The important thing to remember is that during this time the French nobility quietly reclaimed their place and France prospered, meaning there were lots of wealthy noblemen and aristocrats in Paris. Lots of potential people to commission our necklace."

"This is great," Jacob enthused. "Now we just have to get confirmation from the jeweler that they made it."

M. Seguin spoke, his voice sardonic. "Good luck with that," he said.

"What do you mean?" Jacob asked with a hint of belligerence.

Alice could see that M. Seguin's slow smile bothered Jacob, because the American's neck flushed red. She felt a kinship toward the other man. She wasn't the only one afflicted by the curse of the blush.

M. Seguin responded calmly. "I once had a small connection to Medici dit Beauregard—a friend of a friend worked there. I can tell you that it is one of the most exclusive jewelers in Paris. As Daphne said, they have been in business—a family-owned business—for centuries. They are notoriously discreet, and they guard their clients' privacy zealously. You don't waltz up to them and ask to have a look at their books." M. Seguin seemed to be taking a lot of pleasure in delivering this news, as if knowing something that Jacob didn't was satisfying. "There is no way they'd share confidential business information with just anyone."

Daphne coughed. Alice realized that although she had read the sentence "triumphant smile" before, she had actually never witnessed it until now, when she saw one spreading across Daphne's face.

"Luckily," the other woman said, "I'm not just anyone."

Villeneuve-sous-Dammartin

France, 1864

She continued to gaze into the mirror, stroking the beautiful necklace. Her lover's parting gift. Her story had really begun well before this villa on the outskirts of the city. Long before Louis and long before his rupture with her.

Even as a green girl, far from Paris, she had known that she could attract men, seduce them. That power fizzed through her with the budding of her breasts and the rounding of her hips. Not even the hours spent scrubbing the shit and piss from the sheets of the good citizens of Saumur, back bent, hands raw, steam robbing the air from her lungs, could quench that buzzing knowledge.

She'd sensed this power at sixteen, many years before she'd met Louis, when her first lover, a roguish lieutenant, had been stationed in Saumur. He was handsome and brash and utterly without morals. Despite her virginity, she had known what he was after and happily gave it to him, born aloft by the seething certainty that she was destined for something bigger than Saumur.

Months ago, lying in bed in this very house he had purchased for her, Louis had held her small hand in his perfectly manicured one, tracing the rough callouses on her palm, the place where the skin was still as hard as pebbles. Despite her delicate wrists and carefully trimmed nails, those calluses lingered, a brand on her flesh, earned in the hard toil of the wash-houses of Saumur. They were a reminder that she was not one of the aristocratic women Louis generally consorted with. Certainly, his genteel wife did not sport such evidence of labor.

He asked her how she came by such callouses. She'd closed her fist then, for once denying him something he desired. Instead, she had explained, to his amusement and delight, how before she had become an actress in Paris, she had been an acrobat and trick rider in the provinces. She had swung from the trapeze, high above her audience's heads, and then ridden bareback—straddling the horse, with only her strong thighs holding her steady.

Louis had been charmed at the idea, laughing and begging her to show him what she could do. She had demurred, saying that her body was starting to thicken with pregnancy and she was not nearly as flexible as she once had been. He would not be denied, and at last she acquiesced.

She slipped out of the covers, as naked as a jaybird, and executed a perfect back bridge. He'd laughed delightedly and then called her back to him.

The story of the trick riding had been true—a year in a provincial circus after the lieutenant had discarded her. At sixteen, he had taught her some hard lessons, the most important being that she could survive anything. Her ambition and pride kept her from returning to Saumur, and so, eventually, inevitably, she came to Paris.

Now another stage of her life was over. She was no longer a kept woman. Another reinvention was called for. She lingered in front of the mirror, staring at her reflection. The necklace Louis had given her was a comforting weight around her neck. It was an assurance that her child would never have to give a thought to how their household's soiled sheets and dirty linens stayed so clean. His connection to the washhouses of Saumur would be as faded and irrelevant as the slowly disappearing calluses on his mother's hands.

CHAPTER 10

52 Hertz

IT WAS MONDAY EVENING, AND THOUGHTS OF THE OFFICE intruded on Élise's mind as she made dinner. Something was going on at *Bonjour Paris*—there was barely suppressed excitement in the air. The young people talked in murmurs, but their voices were urgent. There were many comings and goings. The arrogant American, Jake or Jack, was underfoot. What's more, the Viking next door, so disheveled and surly, was always nearby, though he at least was helpful. She'd asked him to shift the back filing cabinets into alignment and been pleased at his quiet compliance and effective strength. Even Luc, Olivia's boy, had popped by today for a whispered conversation with Lily.

She caught fragments of their discussions. They were all working on a story. In the old days, Élise would have ferreted out the secret almost immediately, but the old days were dead, as was her curiosity.

Élise flipped the sausages and closed the oven door, her mind turning, as it so often did, to the ocean. Whale song is a deep, rumbling thunder that most humans can't even hear. It travels great distances, connecting one whale with his brethren dozens, or even hundreds, of miles away. Scientists only discovered whales' song in the 1950s. Hydrophones planted by the American military to spy on Russian submarines instead picked up unearthly melodies of such a depth and musicality it was as if the very ocean was singing to them. Those songs, especially those of the humpback, saved the animals. Someone released a cassette of their singing in the 1970s, and it sparked rallies to fight the decline of their habitats. "Save the whales" was born from the animals' own voices rumbling up from the ocean deep.

One of the things that Élise loved about whales was their families. They have deep connections, traveling in pods, taking care of one another, communicating through those songs. That's why Élise was so fascinated with 52 Hertz. Known as the loneliest whale in the world, for some reason he couldn't communicate at the same frequency as the other blue and fin whales. Scientists tracked him for years across the north Pacific feeding grounds as he sang his lonely song, unable to be understood by any of his fellows.

Researchers didn't know what to make of his vocalizations, a haunting series of bellows and echoes that Élise had listened to over and over again online. Scientists recorded the song for years—its strange music echoing over the ocean, but 52 Hertz never found a friend who could hear or answer the call. If Élise thought about 52 Hertz too much, her throat tightened and her eyes filled with tears.

She was making Henri's favorite—diot sausages cooked in wine and onion, the flavors filling the small kitchen with a rich, succulent odor reminding Élise of her own mother's cooking. She grew up in the 1950s and early '60s, right around the time when those Americans were busily spying on the Russian submarines. Despite this, her youth had not been marked by the endless Cold War, playing out on black-and-white television screens around the world, but by the Second World War. Her father lost an arm in the conflict, and gained a life of unrelenting agony. Phantom pain, that terrible joke the brain plays on the body—the ache of the lost limb blown away by a German bomb—plagued him. This unending pain soured his personality, making him angry and short-tempered. While her father suffered physically, her mother was simply sad. All four of her brothers had been killed in the war. Élise thought of her own sons, and her grip tightened on the spatula. Her mother wore her grief like a heavy coat, never shedding it, even in the brightest sunshine. Her parents' marriage was a union of sorrow. The attraction, such as it was, lay in their shared pain.

The sausages were cooked. She buttered the cabbage and drained the polenta from the stovetop. Henri preferred the traditional square crozet pasta, but it had been months since they had been back to the mountains, and her supplies were gone. Soon, when she finally agreed, they would return forever to La Rosière. Henri had brought up the move again last night. "There is nothing left for us in this city. Let's go home."

The problem was that La Rosière wasn't home to Élise anymore. Beautiful as it was, it represented the past. Returning there felt like an ending, rather than the next chapter. Henri couldn't understand her attitude.

"Souper—à table!" she called out.

Henri, Thierry, and Yanick came to the dining table, sitting in their usual places. She brought the meal out and began serving. All four could see the television playing the dinner-hour news in the background.

"Disgraceful," Henri grunted as footage of a Syrian refugee camp played before them.

"Dirty Arabs," Yanick agreed.

Élise craned her neck to look. They did look dirty—and tired and terrified. She thought of Alice, the only Middle Easterner she knew, and wondered for the first time when that young woman had arrived in England, and under what circumstances. Had she or her family suffered from conflict the way Élise's parents had? It was funny, but she had never connected the refugees she saw on her television screen to her own parents' war experiences. They hadn't had to leave their homes, but many in France had been displaced.

Élise could tell, from having watched Alice for months, that the girl was wary of others and nervous about letting down her guard. Insecure about her place in the world. Just like 52 Hertz, the intern was searching for a place she belonged. Alice never spoke of any tragic circumstances, but then again, had Élise ever asked? She pushed her sausage away, suddenly unable to eat.

CHAPTER 11

An Apple Turnover

LILY SNAGGED A WINDOW SEAT AT COUTUME CAFÉ. DAPHNE HAD been quite strict about rendezvousing at seven in the morning. They were meeting Daphne's contact at Medici dit Beauregard at eight, which explained Daphne's unaccustomed early hour.

A quiet Tuesday, the tourists who would soon flock to the nearby Eiffel Tower hadn't yet risen, and it was too early for ordinary Parisians. The café, near Daphne's house in Wealthy Expat Central, was very cool—subtle, flattering lighting, minimalist design, metal-and-wood furniture, and very fancy coffee machinery on display. Highly Instagrammable.

Knowing Daphne might be late, Lily ordered a café au lait and a basket of viennoiseries. She thought again of the meeting on Sunday. She loved the idea that they were now the Fellowship of the Necklace. Lily had discovered the *Lord of the Rings* series as a twelve-year-old and had immersed herself in Tolkien's fantasy world for a whole summer. Those books made her believe that she, too, could be a writer.

The one computer in her household when she was growing up was old, slow, and heavily used. Instead, her dad dug out his typewriter exclusively for her writing. There wasn't much in that house that was hers alone, and she prized the old Smith Corona. She was always looking for paper, using the backs of her siblings' homework, old bills, anything. She'd bang out stories of elves, dragons, and sword-wielding heroines, enjoying the process of writing almost as much as the tales she created. She loved the tap-tapping sound, the fact that there was no room for mistakes, ripping a sheet out and rolling in another, and the thick stack of finished pages after a successful burst of writing. She recalled how lost she would get in her tales of vanquished heroes and magical lands. She'd only abandoned the stories of dragons and swords and mythical realms when she'd shown up at Bennington, quickly learning that neither her professors nor her fellow students considered her beloved fantasies to be legitimate art. She wanted to be a real writer, someone to be taken seriously, and that meant stabling the dragons.

Her basket of viennoiseries arrived, containing a flakey croissant, sweet brioche, a bun, and a warm apple turnover. Lily felt a rush of affection for this city that provided such a cornucopia of delights as a standard breakfast. As a rule, France had no patience for gluten intolerance or carb counting.

Daphne showed up only a few seconds after the pastries. Her hair was in some sort of messy chignon that seemed effortless and probably was. She wore a soft cashmere sweater dress that managed to look demure and sexy at the same time. It was only as she approached the table that Lily saw how wan she was.

"You're actually green," Lily observed.

Her friend sank into the chair opposite, squinting at the warm sunlight filtering through the white curtains. "I'm hungover," she groaned.

"Oh no, how did you manage that?" Lily asked sympathetically. She bit into the brioche. The warm, dense flavor filled her mouth, and for a moment, she thought she might pass out from pleasure.

A young waitress, her hair pulled back in a thick braid, appeared at their elbow. "Du café?" she inquired of Daphne. "Un oeuf? Des viennoiseries?"

"No, no." Daphne shook her head, looking appalled at the thought of food. "Still water," she said in French.

The waitress frowned and disappeared.

"What I wouldn't give for a large Diet Coke and a Pop-Tart," Daphne moaned, rubbing her temples.

Lily snorted. "Can you imagine if you tried to order that? They'd deport you."

Daphne's water arrived, and Lily broke off a piece of her plain white bun—fluffy and as light as air—and passed it over. "Try this," she said. "You should be eating a little bit. See how it goes."

Lily took another bite of the brioche, but in deference to her friend's ill health, quashed her moan of pleasure.

"It's been a brutal morning," Daphne said. "Since Philip is away, a neighborhood mom takes Theo to school, which means getting him up and moving even earlier than normal. He's miserable about it."

Lily had a hard time picturing Theo—that cherubic kid with blond curls and enormous cheeks—being grumpy about anything. Whenever she saw him, he was swathed in smiles.

"Why are you hungover?" Lily asked.

"Remember my dinner with Isaac and Gisèle? That was last night."

"Oh no, was the restaurant really loud?" Lily asked.

"The restaurant was fine, but it turns out Gisèle wasn't even there. She and Isaac have broken up! He hadn't realized that Philip was out of town, so it was like this super awkward date."

"God," Lily said sympathetically, "that's so weird."

"Yeah, and the kicker was that I dropped fifty-five euros on a sitter for the privilege of spending three hours listening to Isaac talk about what a bitch Gisèle was. That is one lousy thing about being a parent—any evening away from your kid is super high stakes, because you've invested a small fortune on the babysitter."

"That does suck," Lily agreed. The older she got, the more of her friends paired off and started reproducing, and the more she heard babysitter complaints, car seat bitching, and a surprising amount of nipple talk. Lily had always known she didn't want children; seeing how much her parents had struggled to put food on the table for herself and her siblings had made the prospect of being entirely responsible for someone else profoundly unappealing. Whenever a friend complained, she felt vindicated in her decision.

"It's so weird that Gisèle and Isaac broke up. Destabilizing," Daphne said.

"What do you mean?"

Daphne surprised Lily by looking confused, not an expression she was used to seeing on her friend's face. "Gisèle and Isaac have been together for a decade and now they're done. I mean, if they can't make it work, can any of us?"

"Hey, you and Philip are rock solid," Lily said.

"Are we? What if he dumps me the way Gisèle ditched Isaac?"

"You're being paranoid. That guy loves you like crazy."

"Hmm," Daphne said. "Anyway, maybe you should get on this. See if Isaac is interested."

"What?" Lily demanded, genuinely startled. "You just finished saying he's hung up on his ex. Also, he's a low talker, a slow talker, and boring. Why would I want to go out with him?"

Daphne shrugged. "I don't know. He's got a good head of hair and a decent job. . . ."

Lily frowned. She loved Daphne dearly, but her friend wasn't immune to the kind of lazy assumption that married people often made about the unattached. "Just because I'm single doesn't mean I'm desperate," she said.

Daphne looked surprised by her sharp tone. "Right," she said mildly. She took a sip of water and muttered, "I forgot Jacob was in town."

"Jacob?" Lily spluttered. "What does he have to do with anything?"

"Dude," was all Daphne said, but her tone spoke volumes.

Lily's cheeks flushed. "I don't have feelings for Jacob," she said. For the thousandth time, Lily recalled Saturday's awkward almost-kiss. She was desperate to talk it through with someone, but Daphne was a bit self-absorbed at the best of times. Hungover, she simply wouldn't have the mental space for empathy. Plus, Lily recalled Daphne once saying that Jacob was a smug douche nozzle, so she might not be exactly unbiased.

Daphne stared at her and didn't say anything.

"Come on," Lily said. "Jacob is a friend. He proofread my term papers, counseled me through breakups, he even helped me move into my first New York apartment—a third-floor walk-up."

Daphne remained quiet.

"I've only involved him with the necklace story because he's a legit genius and I need his help."

Daphne took a sip of water.

"He's got a girlfriend." She wished her voice didn't hold that telltale note of defeat, but who was she kidding? Jacob getting serious with someone had shifted their whole dynamic. Talk about destabilizing.

"You know who you should be concentrating on?" Daphne asked, picking at the piece of bread roll in front of her.

Lily forced a laugh, relieved they were leaving the topic of Jacob. "Keep your horny married-lady thoughts to yourself."

Daphne continued, undeterred. "That Luc Seguin. He's sort of deliciously commanding. Very attractive."

"Luc?" She had honestly never considered him. It was unsurprising that Daphne was crushing on the dapper Frenchman. Her friend loved the glossy, the sleek, the well turned out, and Luc with his expensive watches, gym-honed body, and elegant suits was right up her alley. "He's my boss. Plus, he's short and sort of intense."

"Mmm, and decisive and smart. He'd keep you on your toes."

Lily snorted. "I don't want to be kept on my toes, thanks. Anyway, I am happy being single. I don't need whisper-talking Isaac or intimidating Luc or even Jacob." Happy, handsome, successful Jacob.

Daphne made a little disbelieving click of her tongue, and Lily was fed up. Why did everyone assume that if you were single you were on the hunt for a partner? What was with society's insane need to pair everyone up?

"Sometimes it's better to be single than to be with a jerk," Lily said, with more heat in her voice than she intended. "One isn't the loneliest number when the alternative is some ass who sneers at you for watching Netflix Christmas specials, or suggests you wear more A-line dresses because they 'skim those problem areas.' Not all men are sweet like Philip, Daphne."

Her friend flinched. Lily knew Daphne was going through a bit of a rough patch in her marriage, and she hoped she hadn't inadvertently touched a nerve. Daphne was a good friend. Indeed, Daphne's pure, undiluted delight for Lily when she had announced that she landed a job in Paris had helped erase Lily's own doubts about the big move and pushed her to take a chance. Daphne had been so happy for her, and it was nice to have someone so polished and smart rooting for her.

She didn't express any of this to Daphne, who had taken the hint and changed the topic to the necklace. "Medici dit Beauregard are definitely our best bet for the creators of this piece. They've been around for over three hundred years, and their style resembles our necklace."

"Why do we have to be there so early?"

"We're trying to keep this visit on the down-low. Strictly speaking, Catherine Medici dit Beauregard is not meant to share the company records with anyone. They are obsessive about client privacy. Even if their clients have been dead for a hundred years."

"Why is she helping us, then?" Lily asked.

Daphne leaned in, the gossip obviously taking her mind off her hangover. "Catherine's the youngest of the family, and she was always a bit wayward. A couple of years ago she started to get her act together, but her boyfriend didn't get the memo. I was involved when he stole one of the family's Chagall sketches."

Lily's mouth formed an *o*. Sometimes she forgot what exalted circles her friend now moved in. Her position as the director of the UN's International Art Registry meant she was involved in some high-profile cases related to extremely expensive art.

"The sketch was recovered, and Catherine begged me to smooth things over with the police. Because the artwork was undamaged and returned within twenty-four hours, I agreed. Luckily, I have a good relationship with a senior officer on the Police Nationale's cultural heritage unit. I explained that the whole thing was a 'misunderstanding.' We left it at that."

Lily pulled at one of the turnover's crispy edges, its flavor caramelized and slightly crunchy. She was saving the gooey apple bit for last. "So we're blackmailing this woman into helping us?"

Daphne made a "tsk-ing" sound and reached over to Lily's pastry, breaking off a sizable piece. "I like to think of it as calling in a favor," she said, before popping it into her mouth.

CHAPTER 12

Père Lachaise

THE SAFETY-DEPOSIT BOX KEY BEAT LIKE POE'S TELL-TALE *Heart* in Alice's jeans' pocket, and she worried that everyone in the métro car could see it pulsing through the fabric. The guilt of having pilfered it from Mme Boucher's desk drawer last evening was almost too much. Several times she'd been tempted to jump off the métro early and turn up at the office like any other Tuesday morning. That way she could return the key before anyone noticed it was missing.

Yet, she didn't do that. Instead, she disembarked at the Philippe Auguste stop in the 20th arrondissement, miles from her desk at *Bonjour Paris*. It was odd that the magazine's official bank was out here, but Alice had a dim memory of hearing that Luc had grown up in this neighborhood. Presumably, Olivia had chosen the magazine's bank based on its proximity to her house, rather than to the business. Yes, much easier to think about why the safety-deposit box was located way out here than to ponder how angry the folks from the Fellowship would be if they discovered what she was about to do.

Exiting the métro station, her worries momentarily fled. To her right was an enormous stone wall adorned with massive gates. She was bewildereds until she saw a sign: Cimetière du Père Lachaise. "Oh," she said aloud, forgetting for a moment why she had come. Visiting the famous burial ground was high on her list of things to do in Paris. It was the final resting place for a bevy of famous people—Oscar Wilde, Frédéric Chopin,

Edith Piaf, and so many others, including the biggest draw—the grave of Doors front man Jim Morrison. She was jostled from her gaping by a horde of tourists hurrying toward the cemetery gates. They were a mixture of types, a large Chinese tour group, their leader holding a purple-and-white umbrella aloft like a sword before a battalion of soldiers; a bunch of Canadians with waist packs and maple leaves sewn into every visible piece of clothing; and a couple of soulful romantics perhaps planning to leave a letter at the tomb of Héloise and Abélard. The embodiment of doomed lovers, brainy Héloise and her tutor and priest, Abélard, were ripped apart after their affair was discovered. If Alice recalled correctly, Héloise was exiled to a nunnery and Abélard was castrated. Alice shivered; the twelfth century was not a good time for star-crossed lovers.

She vacillated, tempted to wander into the graveyard. If she did that, then her trip out here would be no more transgressive than a bit of skiving off. Of course, Alice had never done anything so terrible as shirk work responsibilities, but going to the bank was much worse.

The lure of the Honeybee Emeralds was a stronger draw than her own fears. She needed to see the necklace, assure herself it was there, that it was secure. Precious things—necklaces, stability, fathers—could all be taken away. If Alice could touch the necklace one more time, she could assure herself of its safety and be satisfied. She took a couple of steps toward the bank and then did a double take, thinking she saw Mme Boucher among the crowd heading to the cemetery. She looked again, but the figure had disappeared through the gates. Why in the world would Mme Boucher be here? Alice pictured the older woman throwing herself onto the lipstick-smeared grave of Jim Morrison. She laughed a touch hysterically. Her guilt was conjuring people from the office.

She inquired nervously about the safety-deposit box with a teller from the Banque Populaire. Lily had insisted that the entire Fellowship put their names down for access. Alice suspected she'd done that to create a sense of commitment to their undertaking. After signing her name in a registry, she was led down a short hallway. Alice had never seen a safety-deposit room in a bank—certainly her mother and Dale did not have anything of value to store. The one piece of jewelry her mother had not sold before leaving Iran was her own grandmother's gold necklace, and that was always around her neck. Alice had expected the experience to involve a series of high-security air-locked doors, perhaps with retinal scans at the entryway. Instead, it was a windowless room with numbered boxes recessed into three walls. The bank employee left, and Alice searched for the correct box. When she found it, she slid the drawer from the wall.

There were a bunch of papers in the box, including the lease for *Bonjour Paris*. Alice flipped through it for a minute or two. There were some other documents in the box, including what looked like M. Seguin and his siblings' birth certificates. It was funny to think of dark, hairy, large-nosed, supremely confident Luc Seguin as a tiny baby. Olivia had obviously employed the box for business and personal uses.

Straightening her shoulders, Alice couldn't postpone the moment of her transgression any longer, and she tugged out the plain white box in which the necklace was stored. She held her breath as she pulled the lid off, withdrawing the Honeybee Emeralds. She exhaled with relief when it emerged, more beautiful than she remembered. Her fingers itched to feel its weight, and she picked it up carefully, sighing with pleasure at its gratifying heaviness. The diamonds shone brightly, transforming the drab space into someplace glamorous and magical. She placed the necklace carefully on the table before her and traced the design with her fingers. Feeling the intricate gold work, she gazed in wonder at the honeybee's wings, so delicately wrought, yet bearing the burden of those deep green gemstones.

Seeing the necklace soothed an agitation she'd felt since they'd first agreed to lock it away. "You're so beautiful," she breathed.

She scrutinized it for a few moments longer and then put the necklace away. Now that she had reassured herself, she felt sick at the risk she had run. She would not do this again. She couldn't risk getting kicked out of the Fellowship.

CHAPTER 13

Louis Badinguet

THOSE FEW NIBBLES OF LILY'S PASTRY, ALONG WITH ALL THE water she was guzzling, had done a lot to ease Daphne's hangover, and she was able to enjoy their early morning walk through Place Vendôme. She loved this square: the glitzy facade of the Ritz Hotel battling the enormous Vendôme column for most photographed site, bringing in throngs of gawking tourists and Bentley-driven celebrities. This was where Cartier, Louis Vuitton, Rolex, Mikimoto, Dior, and Chanel competed for the privilege of swiping their clients' Amex Black Cards.

There was no time to linger this morning, however. Instead, she and Lily cut across the square to reach Rue Cambon, a narrow, unremarkable street that had quietly supported a thriving business for centuries. Medici dit Beauregard International Jewelers knew it didn't need flash or ostentation to survive, but rather exquisite taste, exceptional discretion, and a commitment to charging an enormous premium for both.

She and Lily walked past the display window, denuded of jewels at this still-early hour. Nothing was visible through the splendidly polished bulletproof glass except the cases where the diamond rings, glittering tiaras, and exquisite tennis bracelets would soon be placed.

"They're not open yet," Lily said anxiously as she saw the bare windows.

Daphne smiled. She was in her element, and it was nice to have Lily on her turf. Her friend might be the unofficial leader of the Fellowship of the Necklace, but years of working to recover lost art and other treasures had given Daphne an understanding of the ways of the immensely wealthy. She stopped at a discreet brown door a bit farther up the street and rang the bell. "The store won't open until noon. This is the office," she explained.

Catherine Medici dit Beauregard, a thin woman in her mid-twenties with slicked-back hair and long fingers adorned with rings, opened the door. She wore a silk dress that Daphne recognized from the Isabel Marant fall line. "Welcome," Catherine said in accentless English. "I've been awaiting you."

Catherine didn't smile. Daphne hadn't expected her to. The elegant businesswoman standing in front of them was a far cry from the frantic girl, with the red nose and smudged mascara, who three years ago had pleaded with Daphne to help cover up her boyfriend's "lapse of judgment." At that time, Daphne barely knew Catherine. They had met only the week previously, when she had gone to her father's office, this same brown door on Rue Cambon, to discuss the provenance of some recovered ruby earrings.

She had met Catherine then—a silent, surly girl with a sheet of dark hair obscuring half her face and terrible posture. When the younger woman had handed Daphne her café allongé, she had noticed her fingernails were bitten to the quick. The skin around Catherine's fingernails was raw and painful looking. Daphne had suddenly remembered coming home from university her freshman year to discover her little sister morose, angry, and withdrawn. On her second morning home she had blundered into their shared bathroom and seen Lara emerge from the shower, her forearms covered in scars from the passage of a razor blade. What had alarmed Daphne most had been the neatness of the markings—each cut spaced out an equal distance from the next, forming orderly lines down both of her sister's skinny arms. The savagery of Catherine's attack on her own body had echoed Lara's obsession with hurting herself, and Daphne's heart squeezed with compassion for the younger woman.

Perhaps Catherine had sensed Daphne's sympathy, because when her paunchy, fortysomething boyfriend had given in to impulse and swiped the Chagall and then promptly panicked, she had contacted Daphne. Twenty-four hours after the theft from the family's Villefranche-sur-Mer retreat,

Catherine turned up at Daphne's office and thrust the sketch into her hands. Daphne had examined it carefully—it was a quick, rough thing that those without training would have discarded without a second glance. She was relieved to see that it appeared authentic and undamaged.

The younger woman spent their twenty-minute meeting defending her boyfriend: "He's not a thief." Not a good one, anyway, Daphne had thought. "He has so many struggles in his life—cruel parents, difficulty finding work, challenges in keeping a job. He tortures himself, truly."

Why, Daphne had wondered back then, did good women squander themselves on bad men? At the time she had welled up with affection for kind-hearted, gentle-eyed Philip. Thank God she landed a good one.

"My parents hate him," Catherine had confessed, a resentful note entering her voice. "They'll use this as another reason why I should break up with him." Daphne made a sympathetic face at this unfairness. "Please, Mme Smythe-Baird, won't you help me?"

Daphne had hesitated. Obviously, the vile Gérard should go to prison for his greedy, impetuous, and frankly stupid act. She wasn't a police officer, however. Her job wasn't to apprehend the criminals, nor was it even to find the missing item—that was left to police and insurance adjusters. No, the International Art Registry's sole duty was to keep track of what had gone missing, when, and whether or not it was recovered. She'd be breaching no professional rules in accepting the Chagall and quietly turning it over to the officer responsible for the investigation. It would simply mean that the sketch wouldn't have to be entered into the Registry. Legally, of course, she would be in murkier waters, the words *aiding and abetting* came to mind, but she knew from experience that with art theft, as long as the piece was returned undamaged, a "don't ask, don't tell" approach was often taken.

She had, of course, agreed to help Catherine that day. Not out of compassion toward the idiot man with the poorly executed comb-over, but because of those chewed-up cuticles, a signal of so much unhappiness and a reminder of her own spiky, tender kid sister, who had blundered through that lonely, hard time and come out the other side.

The offices were still dark as they walked through a front reception area. Catherine ushered them along the plush carpet of a dim hallway. "I have your promise that we will not be mentioned in this article, yes?"

"Absolutely," Lily agreed. "Your name will not darken the pages of *Bonjour Paris*."

Catherine stopped. "Ah, is that the expatriate magazine?" she asked.

"You've heard of it?" Daphne was frankly surprised. Most born-and-bred Parisians would rather die than be caught reading an expat magazine.

Catherine shrugged. "We have many foreign clients, although they tend to read the other one—"

"*La Vie en Rose*," Lily said, her nose crinkling in distaste.

Daphne loved her friend, but Lily could not hide an emotion to save her life.

Catherine nodded enthusiastically. "Yes," she agreed. "Quite a fun read." She stopped in front of an oak-paneled conference room in the back of the office.

"I am sorry I arranged this meeting rather early," Catherine explained. "It is best if we are discreet. The others don't know of the incident that you helped me with." She nodded toward Daphne, not quite meeting her eye. "They would not approve of me sharing our old business records. We are renowned for circumspection."

Daphne was certain the Medici dit Beauregard had a lot of experience being circumspect. Emirati sheiks buying diamonds for their blond mistresses, wealthy arms dealers "investing" in jewelry to hide assets, the discreet sale of an heirloom piece to keep bankruptcy at bay—the list of people buying and selling jewelry for reasons best left undiscussed was long.

Catherine turned to Daphne. "The photo you sent me of that necklace reminded me of some of our work from the 1850s. As you said in your email, there was a mania for all things 'ancient world' at that time, and the honeybee motif was not uncommon."

Lily looked at the boxes stacked around the table. Catherine noticed her glance. "We have not digitized our records yet, but one day, perhaps." She gestured to the boxes. "These are our business files from 1800 to 1900.

I hope they prove useful. I must emphasize again, that no matter what you find, our business won't be mentioned as having assisted in your research."

Daphne and Lily nodded, agreeing to this condition. Daphne had expected Catherine to excuse herself, but instead, she moved to a far corner of the conference table and plugged in a small laptop. Obviously, the Medici dit Beauregard business records were too precious to be entrusted to two outsiders, no matter how indebted Catherine might be to Daphne.

Lily was already opening the first ledger. Daphne hesitated. She felt Catherine's story was unfinished. She had not had any communication with the girl after accepting the Chagall that day. She took a step toward her. "How is everything?" she asked.

Catherine's eyes briefly met hers, and Daphne was startled to see them filled with resentment. "All is well," she said in a clipped voice.

She shouldn't have been surprised, Daphne reflected. She had seen Catherine at her most vulnerable and knew one of her deepest secrets. Obviously, the other woman wouldn't be thrilled to be reminded of this. "I am glad," Daphne said. "I want to assure you that with this favor I consider any debt between us repaid."

Catherine nodded. "Quite," she said.

Daphne knew she should leave it alone, but she couldn't resist one more question. "How is your boyfriend? Gérard, I think was his name?"

Catherine's face registered disdain. "We broke up years ago. Now," she said, her mask of composure slipping back into place, "I urge you to begin. You only have two hours before staff will begin arriving."

The records were beautifully organized in leather-bound ledgers. Neat columns listed the date of commission, a description of the desired object, occasionally accompanied by a hasty sketch, the name of the commissioner, and the date the item was picked up.

The ink in the ledgers was faded, and although the writing was careful, it had been so long since Daphne had read a substantial amount of cursive that she struggled to make out the words. The fact that it was in French, and written in an old and elaborate script, made it all the more challenging. They'd been reading for more than an hour and had plowed through ten ledgers between them. They were now in the 1850s, and Daphne was starting to go cross-eyed with all of the jewelry she had read about—pendants, brooches, hat pins, chokers, cameos, rings, tiaras, bejeweled sword hilts, earrings, bracelets, and, of course, necklaces. So many necklaces. She read about solitaire diamond pendants, chokers brimming with rubies, filigreed snake necklaces, and delicate, carefully wrought floral chains of platinum, each petal a perfectly shaped sapphire. At last, in May 1864, a commission that fit the bill.

"This is it," Daphne squeaked.

Lily looked up, and even the poised Catherine raised her head. Lily came to stand behind Daphne to see what she was pointing to. The line in the ledger, just another business transaction, was one of the answers to their questions. "A double strand of diamonds, forty in total, pendant a gold filigree honeybee with two large emeralds in the center of each wing." To seal the deal, there was a sketch, hastily drawn, unquestionably of "their" necklace. The person who had ordered the necklace, Louis Badinguet, had picked up his commission on the 27th of May, 1864.

Lily reached for her phone to snap a photo of the entry, but Catherine spoke from the other side of the room. "I think not, mesdames. No pictures please. I can't have it known that you were allowed access."

Lily sighed but complied, jotting down the information in a notebook. "Now we need to figure out who this Louis Badinguet was."

"Badinguet?" Catherine asked, apparently interested despite herself.

"Yes, do you know the name?" Daphne asked.

Catherine shrugged. "It was a joke, a nickname."

"A nickname for who?" Daphne asked.

"Legend says it's the name of the workman who lent the emperor a disguise when he was escaping King Louis Philippe's forces."

"The emperor?" Lily inquired, but Daphne already knew.

"Louis Napoleon III," Catherine confirmed. "Thereafter the press would often refer to him by that name. Eventually he himself used it, a jab at his enemies who tried to dishonor him with it."

Sweet Jesus. Did Napoleon III commission the necklace? This doubled its value for the historical association alone. "Was the emperor a regular customer at Medici dit Beauregard?" Daphne asked, keeping her voice calm.

Catherine spoke haughtily. "We have served every French ruler from the seventeenth century onward."

"Would it have been odd for Louis Napoleon to use a pseudonym for a jewelry purchase?" Lily asked. She was in full reporter mode, notebook at the ready.

Catherine shrugged. "Not if it was for one of his lovers. He was famous for his mistresses. He had stacks of them, and each one needed to be kept happy. Half the jewelry in France was probably made for a king's cocotte."

Lily and Daphne exchanged a glance. Had their necklace been given to the emperor's mistress?

Villeneuve-sous-Dammartin

France, 1864

She had always enjoyed intimacy with men and felt no shame in that. In fact, she believed that her pleasure was the key to her success. There was no artifice to her desires, and the men, increasingly powerful as her skills and reputation grew, appreciated her authentic hunger for them. Her own fierce need to be touched, to touch in turn, to grasp and rub and lick and ride—this is what had made her so successful in the field of combatants. Indeed, was there a more challenging professional battleground in Second Empire France than that of courtesan? Certainly, dear Louis had fostered a full slate of contenders; his appetites were legendary and his wife tolerant, if not understanding.

For a brief time, she had been the champion in that particular battleground. She had held the emperor's interest for nearly two years, all while watching others of greater wealth and nobler breeding fall by the wayside. The greatest proof of her triumph was that bouncing baby at the end of the hall. Yes, this beautiful necklace was his last token for her, an end to their affair, but it wasn't his final payment. Louis was an honorable man, and young Charles's future, if not his name, was secure.

She turned back to the mirror and looked at the necklace again. This life might not be respectable, she thought as she stroked the green stones lying against her clavicle, but it would do.

CHAPTER 14

Circus Tricks

THANKS TO HER EARLY MORNING TRIP TO PÈRE LACHAISE, ALICE was late getting into work that Tuesday morning. Luckily, Lily only questioned her briefly before excitedly telling her that Emperor Louis Napoleon had commissioned the necklace. Alice thought of the Honeybee Emeralds twinkling on the table in the bank vault. She felt the urge to see the necklace growing. No, she told herself firmly, she would not sneak out again.

Instead, she concentrated on the connection to the emperor of France. It was easy to identify who Louis Napoleon's mistress was in 1864. Apparently, all of Paris talked about his passionate love affair with the scandalous, low-class, inappropriate, and ill-suited Marguerite Bellanger. Gorgeous and with a pleasingly merry disposition, Marguerite was born Justine Leboeuf in 1838, dirt poor in a backwater village near Saumur. Justine was destined for a life of obscure poverty, but a chance encounter with a dishonorable lieutenant introduced her to a bigger world. Caddish army officers seemed to abound in the nineteenth century—silly Lydia Bennet and hoodwinked Bathsheba Everdene sprang to mind. Unlike those fictional heroines, however, Justine grabbed her opportunity with both hands. She ended up performing in a circus before gaining slightly more respectability as an actress in the provinces. Somewhere along the way, she changed her name to the more posh Marguerite Bellanger and moved to the capital, where her lively personality and buxom good looks made her an audience favorite. Soon enough, she attracted many wealthy "protectors," but she chucked them over when she hit the biggest of big times by catching the eye of renowned womanizer Louis Napoleon, the self-anointed emperor of France.

Lily was practically levitating with excitement. "This is what I was hoping for," she bubbled. "We've got history, a bit of scandal, lots of bling—this is going to be an amazing June cover."

Alice heard the relief in her supervisor's voice, and it brought home to her what a risk Lily had taken, proposing this line of action.

She turned back to her research. Both she and Lily were Googling, calling out to one another whenever they found out a new fact about Marguerite. Mme Boucher wasn't paying any attention to their discussions, being deep in phone conversation with an advertiser about next month's buy. It was incredible how much you could unearth about a person once you had a few key pieces of information. Alice read aloud, "A contemporary writer said that Marguerite was 'universally loathed.'"

"Well, she may have been hated by upper-crust Paris, but she was adored by the one man who counted—the emperor himself." Lily read from her computer screen, "Napoleon III was deeply infatuated with Marguerite, and she was his favorite mistress for two years."

"Wait, *favorite* mistress? How many did he have?" Alice asked.

"He was quite the horndog . . . he'd literally line the women up," Lily said. Alice looked down, her cheeks going red. "This is a quote from one of his courtiers: 'When a woman is brought into the Tuileries, she is undressed in one room, then goes nude to another room where the Emperor, also nude, awaits her. . . . She is given this instruction: 'You may kiss His Majesty on any part of his person except his face.'" Alice glared at her lap, willing the blush to recede. Lily chuckled, oblivious to Alice's embarrassment. "God, can you imagine? You think of the past as this respectable, upright, uptight world, but it was populated by the same skeezy creeps whether it's 2019 or 1819 . . ."

Alice wasn't equipped to comment. She was twenty-three years old and had only had one boyfriend. Daniel was a skinny, nervous classmate who had seen every episode of *Dr. Who* and had strong and lengthy opinions about each one. She supposed she had loved him at the time, and it certainly was traumatic when he chucked her over for a breasty kinesiology student who wore booty shorts and false eyelashes. With the distance of a year and half, however, Alice couldn't remember what the attraction had been. Certainly, the sex had never been anything more than "nice" and was usually closer to "endurable."

Lily had to take over on the call with the advertiser but told Alice to "stay on" the mistress angle. She was happy to oblige. Alice loved research. She'd been blessed with a sharp memory, not photographic exactly but very visual. If she thought hard enough, she could often recall where on a page or a screen she had read a certain thing, and then see the text in front of her again. It was undoubtedly a trait that had helped her succeed at the University of Hull.

She'd popped out at her tea break to the local library and taken out stacks of books on Napoleon III. They were piled around her now, and having them near made her feel productive.

The nephew of the "real" Napoleon, Louis Napoleon Bonaparte, was ten when the victorious British exiled his uncle and young Louis fled to Switzerland. The rightful heir to Napoleon, Louis spent years trying to return to lead France. Finally, in 1848 he was the first elected president of France, but then, unable to resist the old family trait of autocratism, performed a coup d'état, declaring himself emperor. He was ousted after losing the Franco-Prussian War and went into exile in England. Ironically, he spent the last years of his life sheltered by the very people his uncle had waged war against.

As for his love life, he was quite the Lothario. He had many lovers, although his wife, Empress Consort Eugénie de Montijo, was conservative and called sexual relations with him "disgusting." Louis Napoleon had fallen hard for twenty-five-year-old Marguerite, who was exactly thirty years younger. Alice couldn't understand that dynamic. Older men had ear hair and paunches, although presumably the fact that he was the most powerful man in Europe would allow you to overlook a few things. Apparently, French royal mistresses were so common, there was a quasi-official position for the "chief crumpet": maîtresse-en-titre. These women even had designated apartments in the royal residences set aside for their use.

She glanced up when Alexander arrived with a toolbox. He muttered something about the small radiator to Mme Boucher and strode to the farthest corner of the room. He had stopped by yesterday to replace some light bulbs. Why was he suddenly assuming the handyman duties for *Bonjour Paris*? Didn't he have perfume to make?

She gave her eyes a break from the screen and went back to her books, looking up only when the efficient typing stopped. She saw Mme Boucher walking out the door, not bothering to say goodbye. It must be noon. Mme Boucher was off on her daily errands. She went to the market every single day, which seemed very French to Alice. The idea was to buy everything fresh and eat it immediately. Mme Boucher roamed across the entire city on her lunch hours, going to different markets depending on the day. Some specialized in vegetables, others in seafood or meat. It was an admirable system, but you'd need a pretty flexible schedule to actually implement it.

Today was Tuesday, which meant that Mme Boucher would be going to some local market. Alice had noticed that the office manager always arrived at the office later on Tuesdays, which gave her less time at lunch to seek out the specialist markets farther afield. If she had been even slightly friendlier, Alice would have asked her the location of the various markets she visited, but unfortunately, Mme Boucher was not receptive to casual chitchat. When Alice had tried to peer into her Tuesday shopping bag, she had caught sight only of some ordinary-looking celery and had received a dark glare for her troubles.

Jacob sauntered in, carrying a paper bag, undoubtedly lunch for him and Lily. "How's the research going?" he asked her. She flushed and bit her lip. "Good," she mumbled. God, she was such a berk. Here was her opportunity to network with a respected professional.

"What have you found?" he asked, pointing to her screen.

She told him about Marguerite's background and Napoleon's reputation with women. She was so enthused about the research that she forgot to be embarrassed and was able to give him a good overview without blushing once.

"Terrific work," he said. "We can use Marguerite's personal story as the hook, and then provide background on the necklace and Napoleon from there. We want to start with the most compelling, relatable elements. An underdog story is always a good opener." Jacob turned from her and wandered over to Lily's desk. Her editor was flustered by his approach. What was going on there?

Alice was hungry and opened her own lunch. She always brought something from home. Today she had leftovers. A big bowl of rice with some cooked carrots and a few small pieces of chicken. Cheap and filling. Eating at her desk, Alice resisted the urge to take out her phone and look at the image of the necklace again. She probably stared at it ten times a day. Instead, she searched for portraits of Marguerite. There were a few black-and-white images of her, probably daguerreotypes, as well as a marble bust. She had been an attractive woman with dark hair and brows and regular features. She always wore a serious expression, which was common for the time. The exposure was so long on photographs of the period that holding smiles made sitters look unnatural.

Alice zoomed in on an image, studying Marguerite's face. Even with her neutral expression, there was something mischievous about her eyes. It was hard to believe this happy-looking woman was a renowned courtesan who seduced the nation's richest and most powerful.

Alice kept researching, moving back and forth between the books on her desk and her computer. Most information on the woman dried up after her definitive break with the emperor in 1864. It appeared that the Honeybee Emeralds was a piece of "kiss off" jewelry to say goodbye at the end of their nearly two-year relationship.

Lunch finished, Alice wandered over to Alexander, bent over the small radiator at the back of the room where they'd had their first official Fellowship meeting. Filing cabinets dominated this part of the office, containing fifty years of the magazine's history. In theory this was *Bonjour Paris*'s archives, although Alice had never actually consulted them.

"I don't think we even use this radiator," she said. "We rely on the big one by the wall. The one you already fixed."

Alexander didn't look up. Hunched over at the waist, the top of his bum crack was visible over his loose trousers. She was less startled by his largeness now. She had grown accustomed to his enormous hands and wide, broad face. Even the hint of bum crack was familiar.

"It's mad about the necklace, isn't it?" she said.

No response.

"To think Napoleon III owned it. I mean, he was the emperor."

Grunt.

"And then he probably gave it to his mistress, Marguerite Bellanger. He had a ton of mistresses, but she was the only one at that time. She's even rumored to have had his illegitimate son." She stopped talking. There was a long pause.

At last a grunt and two precious words: "Go on."

She fought back a smile of satisfaction. Despite his disinterested demeanor, Alexander was as invested as the rest of them in learning more about the necklace. That's why he was inventing excuses to hang out in the office; he wanted to be on-site in case any discoveries were made. His refusal to be upfront about his motivation was rather endearing. He reminded her of Dale. Her stepfather would always tease her and her mother about their obsession with *Love Island*, but guaranteed that when it was time for Islander Elimination, you would find him at the kitchen table, with the convenient sight line to the telly, working on a sudoku or reading a footy mag.

"Well, all of Paris was scandalized by Napoleon III's relationship with Marguerite because she was working class. Usually, the emperor's mistresses were highborn ladies. Louis Napoleon didn't care though. Marguerite was beautiful, and very funny. They met in a park, and he basically bundled her into his carriage and had his way with her."

Alexander turned toward her, obviously interested.

"They were so serious at one point that his very posh wife, whose knickers were always in a twist about something, showed up at Marguerite's house—which Napoleon had bought for her—and confronted her about the relationship. The man who recorded the encounter says that the wife began by saying, 'Madame, you must end this affair. Your exertions shall kill the emperor.' Isn't that incredible? Imagine being told by your lover's wife that she was worried you'd shag him to death?"

"Then what happened?" Alexander asked. He had stopped the pretense of fixing the radiator.

"No one knows. Things were getting uncomfortable, so the witness left the room. When he came back, the two women were sitting on a divan together having a very friendly natter. Marguerite's affair with Napoleon continued for another year with no further objections from his wife. Apparently, Marguerite Bellanger had seduced the empress as well."

Alexander's eyes widened, and at first, Alice thought it was in appreciation for her story. Then she realized he was looking behind her. She turned. There was a small framed photo on the wall, one of a dozen at this end of the room. The image was a glamour shot of a slim, smiling Black woman. Her hair was in a neat bob, held back with two pins thickly encrusted with diamonds. She wore a beautiful gold lamé evening dress and a slim diamond tiara. Pendant earrings dangled with heavy gemstones. What had drawn Alexander's attention, however, and what now made Alice gasp, was that around her slim neck sat a stunning diamond necklace with a distinctive honeybee design.

"It's the Honeybee Emeralds," Alexander said, removing the photo from the wall.

"Lily," Alice called as they rushed toward her. Her heart was pounding in her ears. "Have a look at this."

Lily and Jacob glanced up from their lunch, their eyes widening when they saw the image of the glamorous woman laughing into the camera. "Holy cow," Lily said. "What is Josephine Baker doing wearing our necklace?"

CHAPTER 15

Hot Soup

LILY STARED AT THE PRINT. YOU COULDN'T LIVE IN FRANCE AND be unaware of Josephine Baker. Paris was still in love with the American singer almost one hundred years after she'd first arrived in the capital. Stylized art deco images of Josephine were everywhere—on black-and-white postcards, posters, and prints. Lily had once seen a shirt adorned with hundreds of pictures of her face—the garment polka-dotted with Josephine's wide smile and cropped, slicked-down hair. There were racier photographs, too, like the iconic one of her winking and topless in her famous banana skirt, her naked breasts barely covered by ropes of pearls.

Despite the ubiquity of her image, Lily had never actually given the singer much thought; she was one more symbol of those golden interwar years in Paris that were so mythologized, a time when Picasso, Matisse, or Pound could be found drinking at various unsavory watering holes. When Gertrude Stein held her salons and F. Scott Fitzgerald compared dick size with Hemingway. Paris had roared in the twenties, and Josephine had been in the thick of it—a sexy, exotic goddess whom the French adored, even while being almost forgotten back home in the United States.

"You're right," Jacob said. "That's the jazz singer."

"Indeed," Alexander agreed, holding the print out at arm's length. "It is she. We should remove the photograph from the frame, to see if there is anything on the back."

He placed it on the nearest desk. They held their breath as he took the backing off, but there was nothing written on the back of the photo. Handling the print at its edges, Alexander turned it over. "Look," Lily exclaimed pointing to the right-hand corner.

There was a small inscription, obscured by the frame itself: "Thank you, XOO!"

"This is pretty cool," Jacob said, taking multiple photos of the image with his phone. "This gives us a strong American angle, which is perfect for international reach."

Lily was glad to hear the excitement in his voice. He was fully invested in this story.

"We should tell the others," Alice said timidly.

Jacob scowled at the idea. He had really taken against Luc, which Lily found a bit surprising. She had thought the two men would get along.

They held an emergency Skype session to discuss it with the whole Fellowship. Luc was in London for the day, and Daphne was at work.

"What does the inscription say?" Daphne asked.

"Thank you, x's and o's," Lily said.

"Well, that's bloody useless," Luc muttered.

Lily quashed the urge to say something snippy about staying positive.

Thankfully, Jacob chimed in. "I think it's great work. We're really making progress."

She smiled. Jacob was a good writer, but more than that, he had a good sense of leadership and teamwork, something not all writers understood. She had seen him earlier offering encouragement and mentorship to Alice, and she was grateful that her friend, despite all of his successes, still took the time to help younger authors. She was relieved at this pure feeling of friendship toward him. She'd felt unsettled with him ever since that weird almost-kiss on Saturday. It was better to get things back on their usual footing.

"I'm too excited to keep working," Daphne said. "I'm going to finish early and come by to help with the research."

Mme Boucher returned from lunch then, and they ended the call. Lily slipped the photo back in its frame and put it in her desk drawer. Alexander returned to work, Jacob left to do some research for the *Hudson*, and Alice started poring over library catalogs, looking for books on Josephine Baker. If there was information about the necklace to be ferreted out, Lily was confident that Alice, with her serious nature and keen memory, would find it.

After making sure that Mme Boucher was safely ensconced at her desk, Lily pulled the photograph from her drawer and contemplated it again. It looked to have been taken sometime between the 1940s and the 1960s. Could it be a coincidence that they'd found an image of Josephine Baker wearing the necklace in the same building where they'd discovered it? Her grandmother used to say that coincidences were God's way of remaining anonymous. Granny had been a devoted churchgoer and attributed every little thing, no matter how small, to the Lord's plan. As a kid, watching her parents scrape together pennies, Lily had wondered why God didn't want her to have a Barbie Dreamhouse. It had seemed like a personal vendetta, and for a while she tried very hard to get on his good side. Despite all the mornings she scrubbed up and went to the little white church on the hill with Granny, the Dreamhouse never made it under the tree. Was that when she'd become an agnostic? When God had literally failed to deliver the goods?

Though she didn't necessarily attribute them to God, Lily didn't believe in coincidences either. Josephine had worn the necklace, and the necklace was found in their basement. They'd come to a dead end with the theater, but they should start looking at municipal records to see if they could glean more clues.

Alice stood. "I've found a number of books about Josephine Baker," she said. "I'm off to the library to do some research."

Lily nodded, still contemplating the photograph in front of her. They'd need to work on narrowing the time frame when it was taken. Given Josephine's full face of makeup, it was difficult to determine her age. Maybe Daphne could help with that.

As if thinking of her friend had conjured her, Daphne breezed through the door, saying a few words of greeting to Mme Boucher before racing back to Lily's desk. Surreptitiously Lily revealed the photo, keeping an eye on Mme Boucher, whose stolid form never turned back toward them.

"It's definitely Josephine," Daphne whispered in excitement. She snapped some photos of the image.

"We need to date this," Lily said. "It will give us a timeline for the necklace."

"It's hard to tell how old she is, though. That hair is a wig, so no clues there," Daphne said. "I'd say it's definitely later than the 1920s, but beyond that, I'd need to do a lot of image comparison."

"Alice just left for the library," Lily said. "She's found a bunch of books and research material. You could catch her if you went now."

Daphne departed. While she and Alice tracked down the Josephine connection, Lily would focus on the necklace's first known change of ownership. Why would Marguerite Bellanger part with such a valuable necklace, given to her by the emperor? Had she fallen on hard times? She looked at the notes that Alice had made on the courtesan, but they were sparse. Only one historian had anything further to say about Marguerite after the emperor had ended things: She had attended Napoleon's funeral in London. To most historians, the story of this self-made woman who had climbed out of poverty in the provinces to rub shoulders (and other bits) with Europe's elite began and ended in her relationship with Napoleon.

Presumably, at some point Marguerite had sold the Honeybee Emeralds, perhaps to the Englishwoman who wore it to the St. Ives fundraiser. Lily pulled up the enlarged image from the newspaper on her screen. The woman wearing the necklace was chubby, with carefully curled hair and a face that beamed with delight, apparently thrilled to be attending the 1881 St. Ives Church Benevolent Society gala. She was the epitome of the well-fed aristocrat—she could have been an extra from *Downton Abbey*.

Lily went back over the images from the St. Ives soiree. She might not know much (anything?) about nineteenth-century social mores, but she knew how newspapers and magazines worked. Presumably, the *St. Ives Weekly Bugle* wanted to keep its readership happy, so it wasn't going to waste precious column inches on portraits of unimportant people. The ladies and gentlemen in the sketches had to be prominent community members, people the readership would be interested in. Furthermore, they were well-known enough that the paper didn't need to mention their names; their identification by the readership was assumed.

Lily reread the short article, stopping at one sentence: "In a nod to the traditions of our esteemed benefactress, a hot soup was also served and a tremendous success it proved to be." The article stated that Sir William had sponsored the event, so the benefactress must be his wife. There was no way the paper would omit an image of so important a figure as the sponsor's wife, so undoubtedly one of the women in the sketches was the benefactress in question. Was their necklace-wearer Sir William's wife? Of the ladies pictured, she definitely had the most bling.

What "traditions" demanded hot soup be served at a fundraising event? If it warranted a mention it must be unusual for St. Ives, perhaps even for England. Could the benefactress be a foreigner? Some quick Googling and Lily learned that at that time hot soup for evening soirees was a continental custom. Was Sir William's wife continental, perhaps French? Maybe she knew Marguerite. Lily had the glimmerings of a theory: Marguerite had attended Napoleon III's funeral. This was definitive proof she had been in England in 1873. Could she have sold the necklace at that time to the woman of St. Ives?

There was a rustle at the front of the office. Mme Boucher was packing up for the day, grabbing her grocery bags and shutting down her computer. Evening was settling in. Lily loved these moments of solitude at *Bonjour Paris*. She looked around and felt the usual thrill of pride that she worked here and that this magazine, however small, however struggling, was a product of her dedication and commitment. If she could convince Luc to invest more heavily, she could do even greater things and build on the strong foundations Olivia had left her. In these moments, the dissatisfaction with her own writing, or lack thereof, faded. She couldn't lose this job.

Lily turned to the books on Alice's desk. The younger woman had said she hadn't yet had time to go through all of them. She scanned the indices at the backs, looking for Marguerite Bellanger. Most of the volumes rehashed what the Fellowship had already gleaned. Near the end of the pile, Lily came across an old, slim volume published in 1956. Alice had no notes on this one, and Lily wasn't surprised that the intern hadn't gotten around to reading it yet. The title, *Miss Howard: La femme qui fit un empereur* (*Miss Howard: The woman who made an emperor*) revealed its focus on another of Napoleon III's lovers, apparently an early mistress who was formative in his political maturity. Miss Howard was long gone by the time Napoleon commissioned the necklace in 1864. Still, the fact that the author had bothered to devote a book to one of the women in the emperor's life gave Lily hope it might contain information about Marguerite. There was no index at the back to see if the volume contained any references to her quarry. The book's faded typeface and formal French style made skimming it a hard slog.

She was rewarded for her efforts in the last chapter. The author discussed the fates of Napoleon III's other prominent mistresses after Miss Howard had been dumped to make way for the Empress Eugénie. According to the author, Marguerite Bellanger, far from pining away in her villa after being cast aside, had married. Not only that, but she managed to make quite an excellent, although surprising, match. She wed Louis William Kulback, a captain in the British army and a baronet—making him, Lily realized, "Sir William." "Lady Margaret," as she became known, spent some time in England and was famous throughout the area of St. Ives as a patron of many worthy causes.

Lily laughed aloud. The matronly lady of St. Ives and the bareback-riding courtesan who had seduced the emperor of France were one and the same.

CHAPTER 16

The Lonely Country

WALKING DOWN RUE DE BEAUNE, ALICE WAS ANGRY WITH herself. She had never heard of Josephine Baker—how could there be such a gap in her knowledge? Even Alexander, buried in that Icelandic fishing village filled with rotten sharks, had known about the banana skirt. She felt edgy to be caught out like this, exposed in ignorance.

Well, she would remedy the issue that very afternoon. The Paris library system had 194 items about Josephine Baker. There were CDs of her music, biographies, memoirs, and movies about the woman known as "the Black Pearl."

She was heading to her favorite library. Bibliothèque Saint-Simon was small, but the staff was—extraordinarily for Paris—actually friendly. They would order in any books she required from the bigger libraries within twenty-four hours. It was in a grand old building, the former 7th arrondissement mayor's office. While the building's imposing architecture reflected the French veneration of bureaucracy, its interior was bright, light-filled, and painted in fun primary colors.

"Hey, Alice," someone called. "Wait up."

She turned, and Daphne strode up in a confident way that Alice both admired and feared. The other woman smiled widely. Alice was always disconcerted by how big and white American teeth could be. It was like she held a mouthful of dominoes behind her lips.

"I'm just going to the library to do some research on Josephine Baker," Alice said.

"Yeah, Lily told me. I popped in at the magazine, and I thought I'd join you."

Alice hesitated. Daphne's gleaming hair and put-together outfits made her feel small, young, and messy. Why was Daphne offering to spend time with her? What could she possibly hope to gain? Alice forced a smile. "Brilliant," she said.

She and Daphne walked in silence. She could think of nothing to say. How was it so easy to talk to Alexander, to badger him really, about all sorts of subjects when it was so staggeringly difficult to get the words out in front of most other people? Perhaps it was because he was nonjudgmental. It meant she didn't have to worry about making a git of herself. True, he probably wasn't judging because he didn't actually care, but it did make being around him surprisingly relaxing.

"What do you say we hit the Richelieu Library," Daphne suggested.

"I was going to Saint-Simon," Alice said. She was disconcerted at the idea of changing her plans. She was comfortable at the small library. "What's better about the Richelieu?" she asked.

"Well, it's part of the national library system and specializes in performing arts. They're sure to have material on Josephine Baker. Plus, it's only a twenty-minute walk."

Alice wasn't going to admit she'd never heard of the Richelieu. "Fab," she said, injecting enthusiasm to mask her nervousness.

"Great, do you have a reader card?" Daphne asked. "You'll need one to get in."

"Yes," she said, "of course." She had her library card in her wallet. Not a worry.

They changed their route, heading back toward the river.

"So, where are you from?" Daphne asked.

Alice tensed. She hated this question. People were always trying to suss out her country of origin. What was the answer? Was she from Tehran, where she was born, but had fled after her father's death in police custody? Was she from Hull, where she didn't look like anyone in her year and where her half-sisters got teased for being chocolate milk? "England," she said tightly.

How deeply did she belong to Dale and his extended family? How to explain her mother's relationship with her stepfather? They were a strange pair. Maheen was from a cultured Persian family who, despite the harshness of the regime, ensured their only daughter could speak three languages. Her mother had been studying architecture, with a husband, a child, and a middle-class future laid out before her. Her husband's arrest at a student protest had derailed her life and forced her to flee. And Dale? His family was poor, and he was never good at school. He had taken the first opportunity to leave. He was a born tinkerer, though, and didn't fear hard work. There was always a job for him somewhere—assisting a mate in his appliance repair business, working for a bit on the North Sea Ferry, and, of course, his short but fateful stint as a security guard at the housing estate where they'd met him.

As a teen, Alice had fumed about this demotion in her mother's status. Going from studying for a respected profession to care worker taking the bus every day to Drypool to wipe drool off senile old coots' chins? Unacceptable.

The natural target for her fury would have been her mother, but that was impossible. Their exile and years of limbo in the UK had welded them too closely together for sustained anger. She tried being angry with her father, the one she barely remembered. He had died two months after being taken into custody during the 2003 student protests. Official cause of death was meningitis, though there was no way to investigate the truth of that claim. She could be angry at her father for protesting in the first place, or at least for getting arrested, but his story was too sad for genuine rage. Dale was the other obvious person to rebel against, but his personality—so genial, so accommodating, so genuinely kind—made anger against him impossible. Instead, she was left with a muddled sense of injustice and insecurity.

Daphne didn't notice her inner turmoil or seem perturbed by her introspection. Instead, she persisted with her line of questioning, "Your accent, though, I think that's Yorkshire, right?"

Alice was startled. "Yeah," she said, still processing that Daphne wanted to know where she was from in England, rather than her ethnic makeup. "Hull," she clarified.

Daphne's face lit up. "Philip Larkin lived in Hull! He called it the 'middle of the lonely country.'"

"That's right," Alice agreed, delighted to find a fellow fan. "Isn't that gorgeous?" Her enthusiasm grew, making her forget her shyness. "He was such a stunning poet. He's the reason I stayed in Hull for university. He was the librarian there for ages. I wanted to walk in his footsteps." She stopped talking, a bit surprised she had blurted out so much.

"He had some choice words for that job, though, didn't he? I think he called it the 'toad work' squatting on his life."

Alice smiled. "Yeah, they've actually got that poem up on a plaque in the library."

Daphne's eyes crinkled. "That's why I love you Brits, you're so willing to laugh at yourselves. It's a good trait."

Alice found herself blushing, not out of embarrassment, but at the sudden swell of emotion at Daphne's choice of words: "you Brits." She had been lumped into a world and a tradition she had never truly thought was hers. Did she want that? What about her Persian self?

They had turned and were walking along the Quai Voltaire. On one side were elegant buildings, on the other the black, glistening Seine.

Daphne pointed out an eighteenth-century building at the beginning of the street. "That's the Hôtel de Tessé."

"Oh," Alice said. It was an unremarkable building. Old, but nothing unique about it.

Daphne smiled. "On a particularly blustery day in March 1742, the Marquis de Bacqueville, a renowned eccentric, ascended to the roof of number 1 Quai de Voltaire, strapped himself into a pair of homemade wings, and before a crowd of onlookers, threw himself into the air."

Alice stared up at the roof, which was at least five stories high. "What happened?"

"He hovered for a moment, and then plunged into the river."

"That was lucky," she said.

Daphne's grin widened. "It would have been luckier if he hadn't hit a boat. He broke his thigh and required the use of a cane for the rest of his life."

"Oh no," Alice laughed. "That's horrible."

"Well, you've got to risk big for the big rewards," Daphne said. "If he'd pulled it off, he would have beaten the Wright brothers by 150 years."

Alice was not a risk-taker. She preferred following the rules and exercising caution. Except how did she explain her bizarre fixation on visiting the Honeybee Emeralds? The urge to see it again was getting stronger, and as much as she tried to fight it, she was sure she'd find an excuse to slip away and go out to that safety-deposit box again.

They walked along the Seine, crossing over at Pont du Carrousel, with its views of the Louvre and the Pont des Arts, before continuing on Boulevard Richelieu and stopping at the tall gates of the library. Daphne strode through the entrance without a backward glance, while Alice slowed, gaping at the gleaming wood, enormous chandelier, and the air of quiet purpose that permeated the building. This was no municipal library.

As it turned out, the national library system was not the same as the public one, and Alice's card was not accepted at the Bibliothèque Nationale Richelieu-Louvois. In fact, it seemed like Alice had personally offended the admittance clerk by presenting her public library card. The intimidating woman behind the desk reminded Alice of Mme Boucher. "You need to apply for a reader card," she said, waving at an office farther down the hall. "As a foreigner, you will need to provide your passport," the woman added.

Alice's face turned red. The woman's tone at the word *foreigner* carried a level of disdain she hadn't served up to Daphne when she had shown her card and spoken in accented French.

"Oh no," Daphne said, turning to go. "We can come back another time."

"It's all right," Alice said. "I've got my passport."

"You do?" she asked, surprised.

Alice nodded. "I always carry it with me." No need to explain that she had been issued a British passport only five years ago, after the long citizenship application. There was no way she would ever leave the precious document at home. Certainly not in her dodgy apartment, where her nasty roommate, Pauline, might pilfer it.

After a bit of bureaucratic wrangling, Alice was issued a reader pass to the National Library system of France. As with any time she succeeded in passing an administrative gauntlet, Alice was jubilant. She had triumphed over a series of forces trying to bar her from accessing a treasured privilege. She wanted to shout "Down with Imperialism" but restrained herself.

"Bummer about that registration stuff," Daphne said, "but you'll see, the reading room makes it all worth it."

They walked down a marble hallway, no different from many similar buildings Alice had seen in France, and pushed through a set of mahogany double doors. Alice gaped, trying to absorb what she was seeing.

They stood in a vast circular room that was at least six stories high. Shelves of books ringed the first four floors, with a walkway around each one. Above that, the whole thing opened up into an enormous frosted-glass dome supported by intricate wrought iron. The floor in front of them was lined with rows of desks, and about every five feet stood a tall brass lamp with a green glass shade. People were seated here and there throughout the room at leather armchairs. For the most part their heads were bent studiously over their work. A deep hush, speaking to the centuries of study and scholarship the room's walls had overseen, permeated the space. Alice's heart pounded in her ears. This was, without a doubt, the most beautiful room she had ever been in.

Alice turned to Daphne. "Thank you," she said.

Daphne nodded back, smiling.

Four hours later, Alice was happily surrounded by Josephine Baker biographies, memoirs, and reminiscences—the names of the books evoked the woman they chronicled: *The Hungry Heart*; *The Many Faces*; *An American in Paris*; *Jazz Age*; *La danse, la Résistance et les enfants*; *Naked at the Feast*; *Jazz Cleopatra*. Alice's head was swirling with Josephine facts:

dance moves that had scandalized and titillated in equal measures, a minor film career, military work during World War II, the adoption of twelve children from all over the world, civil rights activism. Josephine Baker had burned through life like a shooting star, singeing anyone who dared to get close to her. Many of the biographies held stories about Josephine's financial woes, but she always managed to triumph in the end. She wooed bankers, borrowed from former lovers (according to rumor those included dalliances with the Pasha of Marrakech, Charles de Gaulle, and even Frida Kahlo), and charmed creditors into forgiving enormous debts, while always working tremendously hard.

Josephine was showered with gifts by starstruck admirers—furs, clothes, cars, art, and, of course, jewelry. Lots and lots of jewelry. Besotted wealthy men gave her rings, necklaces, tiaras, and bracelets. Frustratingly, in all of that bling, there was no mention of a honeybee necklace.

"Pardon me, mademoiselle," a soft voice spoke at her elbow. Alice looked up at one of the Richelieu's reference librarians. "I wondered if you had finished with that book." She pointed at a thick biography of Napoleon III she had also ordered, to cross-check any potential overlapping references.

Alice had already skimmed the index, but wouldn't have time to dip deeper into it today. The Richelieu was not a lending library, which meant she could not bring any of these books home. "I'm finished with it for now," she said.

"Would you mind if I took it? We have another client who would like to review it." The librarian was pretty, with an asymmetrical haircut and dramatic black eyeglasses.

"Sure," Alice said. She looked up, curious to know who else had an interest in the emperor. Her heart jumped to her throat when she saw the well-dressed, diminutive woman waiting impatiently at the reference desk. She was surrounded by three younger people, obviously students or interns, who looked terrified to be in her presence.

Why was Yvette Dufeu, editor-in-chief at *La Vie en Rose*, interested in Napoleon III? Alice stared at her, noting that she held another big tome in her hands: *An Encyclopedia of Nineteenth Century Jewelry*. As if feeling

Alice's eyes on her, Yvette looked up and met her gaze. There was a malevolent gleam in the other woman's eyes, and Alice knew without a doubt: Yvette Dufeu was after the necklace story.

Yvette

Lily: RED ALERT!

Daphne: ?

Lily: Yvette Dufeu is nosing around.

Daphne: Oh yeah, I know—I was with Alice when she spotted her.

Lily: I am FREAKING out.

Daphne: Yeah, it's shitty. Is she trying to scoop our story?

Lily: That woman is evil.

Daphne: A bit harsh?

Lily: You don't know her. She's a black hole of nastiness disguised as a chic French woman.

Daphne: It is the perfect camouflage—you spend all your time admiring her shoes, not realizing you're being sucked into a vortex of evil.

Lily: I knew you'd understand.

Daphne: So what's the deal. How does she know about our story?

Lily: Someone must have let something slip . . .

Daphne: Wait, what are you implying with your " . . . " ?!?

Lily: Nothing—well, only, did you accidentally post something on Insta?

Daphne: I did not. I have been very careful. It wasn't me. Jesus.

Lily: Okay, okay. I'm checking in with everyone.

Daphne: Isn't it more important to find out what she's after and make sure she doesn't scoop our story?

Lily: Yes, you're right. Presumably she's got the same idea as us. Figure out the story behind the necklace and write some kind of sensational article that goes viral.

Daphne: So what do we do?

Lily: Work quicker, smarter, and get our story out ahead of hers.

Daphne: Good. Well, to start with, fantastic work on figuring out that Marguerite Bellanger was the woman from St. Ives.

Lily: I have to say, I'm feeling pretty smug about that one.

Daphne: We're an amazing team.

Lily: Team?

Daphne: Yeah—like *Guardians of the Galaxy*.

Lily: Doesn't that have a raccoon and a tree? I don't want to be that one.

Daphne: Fine, we're the cast of *Friends*. I dibs Rachel.

Lily: Yes, obviously, you're Rachel. I'm Monica, but without the fat-shaming. That makes Alice Phoebe, which kind of fits? I can't wrap my head around who the men would be.

Daphne: Yeah, those three are hard to pin down.

Lily: Right? Like, what's the deal with Alexander?

Daphne: I'm pretty sure he's very smart.

Lily: Well, he's keeping that under wraps.

Daphne: He's keeping everything under wraps. How big do you think his. . .

Lily: NOOO. We are not going down that road.

Daphne: You are no fun.

CHAPTER 17

Deux Amours

EVENING, THICK AND PEACEFUL, HAD DESCENDED ONTO THEIR little patch of Paris. Daphne sat on their postage-size patio, a thick cashmere scarf around her shoulders, a large glass of Cabernet Sauvignon in hand. Theo played quietly in the small sandbox to her left.

As April drifted toward May, the days lengthened and she was reminded again of Paris's wider place in the world. She had been stunned to realize, in that first cold, dark winter, that Paris was actually north of Montréal. In January, Parisian days ended at 4:30 p.m. and the icy drizzle made being outside intolerable. Still, all those who slogged through the early darkness were rewarded in spring when the days lengthened out with lavish generosity, like a carpet salesman unrolling his wares with a flourish.

The light now was wondrous, hovering on that cusp between day and night. *Evening* was such an elegant word. She pulled out her phone but resisted taking a selfie. It was pointless, even with all the filters; there was no way to capture the intoxication of this twilight. If you were highly skilled, you could create an echo of it with paint. Monet had managed it. His exquisite *San Giorgio Maggiore at Dusk* caught the exact moment when day has truly ended but night not yet begun. She'd made a special trip to Wales to see it on display at the National Museum Cardiff. Philip had come with her. It was years ago, before the frenzy of work and kid and life had sucked her life dry, leaving little time for pleasure. She had been newly pregnant with Theo. She frowned. That was the last trip she and Philip had taken as a couple.

She took a sip of wine, full bodied, darkly plummy, faintly peppery.

One of the trickier cases to cross her desk had involved a Monet. She'd just started at the International Art Registry, before her boss had left and she'd been appointed director. Seven paintings, including a Picasso, a Gauguin, and two Monets, stolen from the Kunsthal Rotterdam. The paintings were worth hundreds of millions of euros, but no trace of them was ever found. Instead, when they caught the thieves in Romania, one of their mothers claimed to have burned the evidence in her fireplace. Mother love used to destroy masterpieces . . . that is, if the woman could be believed. Perhaps the paintings were stashed somewhere, awaiting the end of jail sentences and the eyes of the law to turn elsewhere. For that very reason, the paintings were still listed in the Registry. If they had survived the mother's fiery protection, they would be identified, thanks to the Registry, and justice restored.

It was time to go in. She called to Theo. When Philip was away, the normal rules went out the window. Tonight they would eat dinner—thick grilled cheeses, not a vegetable in sight—in front of the TV. Inside she lit a couple of candles to increase the cozy factor. The fruity, earthy scent from the Diptyque figuier candle was a soothing base note. She and Theo snuggled on the couch under a Merci Merci cream linen throw they bought last time they were at the Boulevard Beaumarchais store. They had nipped into the home and apparel shop for new cloth napkins, and when Daphne hadn't seen any she liked, Philip insisted they buy something. He had a strange habit: If he went into a store and talked to a clerk, he felt obligated to buy something from them. It was odd, since he himself was a highly successful salesman, managing a global sales force, but he had this strange hang-up, some kind of overactive sense of politeness or duty. Like so many things, Daphne had found the trait eccentric and adorable when they first started dating. Now she found it intensely annoying, forbidding Philip from doing any shopping, except online. Still, Daphne thought as she pulled the beautiful, lightweight material around her knees, it was a gorgeous throw.

She and Theo were watching a biography of Josephine Baker. She needed to get up to speed. She'd learned a lot on her research trip with

Alice, but everything she read about Josephine told her the woman's person-ality was like a force of nature. Daphne hoped that seeing footage of the singer in action would bring her to life.

It was fantastic that Alexander had spotted the image. Daphne consid-ered the large Icelander. He was one of those silently competent men who got things done and didn't make a big deal about it. If the world were full of those types of men, rather than the smug, grandstanding Jacobs, it would be a better place.

It had been nice to show off the Richelieu Library, such a secret Parisian gem, to Alice, who was so appreciative. Seeing the girl's awestruck face as they entered the rotunda was wonderful. Daphne felt maternal to the younger woman. Alice was uncertain. She wore her insecurities so obviously, and it made Daphne want to take her by the shoulders and shake her—"Never let them see your vulnerability" was her motto, and she wished she could impart it to Alice.

The documentary was good—a straightforward narration about a woman who was, according to the movie's promo material, an international sex symbol, civil rights warrior, and forgotten American heroine. Josephine, they learned, had been born dirt poor in 1906 Saint Louis. Her mother, the daughter of a slave, had worked in a laundry, scrubbing clothes for white women. Josephine had been a showgirl in America and managed to get two marriages under her belt before the age of fifteen. At nineteen she sailed for Paris, where she shot to superstardom in a show highlighting "exotic" Black American entertainers, called La Revue Nègre. She gained immense fame and notoriety from a risqué topless dance in a banana skirt, which traded on the French love of the alluring sauvage.

The grainy black-and-white footage showed Josephine gyrating to the "Danse Sauvage"—the act that had made her famous across Europe. The woman before them had short hair plastered to her skull and a full face of thick makeup. She was lively and animated, smiling and laughing into the camera while making a series of silly faces. It was hard to understand what was scandalous, or even seductive, about the dance, which was more funny than sexy, especially when paired with the upbeat music of the Charleston.

The documentary moved on from those early successes to cover Josephine's career as a torch singer. Her French singing revealed an unmistakable American accent. Her voice was high and not particularly strong. Next was Josephine's war work and her increased interest in American civil rights—she was the only woman to officially speak at Martin Luther King Jr.'s March on Washington in 1963—but the film mainly focused on her life as a performer.

They then jumped to the 1970s. Josephine was in her sixties by then, but there she was, still singing. While she was the same trim and lively presence on the stage, Daphne got the sense they were entering the "Fat Elvis" phase of her career, or maybe it was that no entertainers made it through the decade with much dignity. Her outfit was certainly alarming. She wore a turquoise jumpsuit with a white turban around her head, and her moves were corny and false.

In the next scene a visibly shrunken Josephine tottered onto yet another stage, this time her slim neck struggling to support a hugely feathered headdress, at least three feet tall. The woman had grit.

"Is that a bird on her head, Mommy?" Theo asked in awe. He was hanging upside down off the couch; she was surprised that he was still watching the film. Usually by now he would have abandoned any semblance of interest in order to play with Lego, or he would be pestering her for yogurt or crackers. Somehow they had failed to parent Theo the so-called French way, which meant denying him snacks and instilling in him a love of Camembert, grilled asparagus, and plain water. Theo was 100 percent American in his hunger for processed cheese, salty crackers, and anything by Nabisco. He wasn't whining for the usual treats, however. Instead, he was glued to the story, granted, upside down, which now touched upon Josephine's late-career money problems and tumultuous personal life.

"Not a bird, sweetie. It's a hat."

There was concert footage from one of her last shows. Josephine wore a glittering diamond choker—Daphne leaned forward to make sure it was not the Honeybee Emeralds. The film was winding down. Josephine seemed tired and worn out in this final show, no longer exuding the vibrancy of the twenty-year-old who had taken Paris by storm. But then again, who had the liveliness of their twenty-year-old selves anymore?

Josephine carried a bejeweled mic and did less singing than talking. She exhorted the audience to "Smile—you'll feel better." Her singing was weak, her dance moves slow. Despite this, she received a ten-minute standing ovation at the end. The camera panned the audience, and Daphne spotted Sophia Loren, Mick Jagger, Diana Ross, and Liza Frickin' Minnelli on their feet, cheering. She died soon after that concert. Princess Grace, of all people, paid for her funeral, and insisted she be buried in Monaco. Not bad for the granddaughter of a slave. The film ended.

Daphne took out her phone, scrolling to the photograph of Josephine they had found at *Bonjour Paris*. How had the singer come to possess, or at least pose in, the honeybee necklace? Josephine looked ageless in the image on Daphne's phone, although certainly younger than those final years. She scrolled the documentary back to the brief portion on Josephine during wartime. There was footage of her in uniform, singing to troops. Daphne froze the screen on a particularly clear shot of Josephine and then held up her phone again. Was the Josephine on the phone younger or older than the one on her TV screen?

"What's that, Mommy?" Theo asked, grabbing at her phone.

She showed him the image. "This is the same lady we just learned about, sweetie. This is Josephine Baker," she said.

Theo startled her by singing, "J'ai deux amours/ mon pays et Paris." This was Josephine's signature song, and the documentary had played it throughout the film. Theo had an ear for music.

"That's right," she said, cuddling him close. "We're looking for this necklace," she said, pointing at the honeybee.

"It's the same one from Lily's work," he said sleepily.

"Uh-huh, honey. You saw it last Friday." She kissed the top of his head, overwhelmed for a moment by its vulnerable smallness. "Go on and brush your teeth," she said. "I'll be up in a minute."

Theo climbed upstairs, and Daphne returned to the two images. Josephine had remained in France during World War II. Daphne knew from her professional experience that the Second World War had been the biggest "redistributor" of valuable and precious items in all of human history. As soon as the conflict broke out, currency became less stable but objects, like Picassos and diamonds, carried a tangible value that became even more precious as times became more uncertain. Couple that destabilization with the Nazis' lust for treasures and rapacious interest in "reallocating" Jewish assets, and you had a perfect storm for art theft.

Miraculously, Theo had actually brushed his teeth and was struggling to put his PJs on when she went upstairs. He had the shirt on backward, and Daphne debated whether she should have him flip it around, but his eyes were heavy and she opted against. They read a chapter of his latest favorite—a book involving a retelling of fairy tales, and then she kissed him on the cheek.

He was asleep by the time she got to his door. Children were amazing for their ability to drop off like stones sinking into a pond. When did you lose that knack? When did worries about your marriage, your weight, your job start keeping you up? Theo looked so sweet, his face wide open and vulnerable. She took a quick photo, pleased with the results; the shadows in the room made him look like a sleeping angel. She was still musing about captions—a simple #blessed or something self-deprecating like "Finally got him to bed. Single parenting is hard! Missing the hubs!" What was Philip doing now? An image of him in that Singaporean infinity pool rose unbidden to her mind. Was that colleague really an older grandmother? Her mother had been blindsided by her father's affair. Why was Philip traveling so much? She frowned. Even if he wasn't cheating on her, he had ditched her and Theo, while he got to live it up.

In the end, it was too difficult to formulate a caption, and she decided that Theo actually looked slack-jawed in the photo, so she didn't post it. Back downstairs, she poured herself another glass of wine, settling on the couch with the linen throw.

Josephine had lived in occupied France but, according to the documentary, came through the war fairly unscathed. No one came out of that conflict completely unaffected, however. It was entirely possible the Nazis had confiscated some of her assets. Daphne had brought her laptop home from work, which had access to a number of databases that were off-limits to civilians. Strictly speaking, she should not be using the information for her own gain, but since she was not going to profit in any way from uncovering the provenance of the necklace, she didn't worry too much about those niceties.

Although the main duties of the International Art Registry involved tracking stolen art via a database, Daphne didn't bother logging into her own organization's catalog. She had checked its systems the very night they had discovered the necklace and hadn't been surprised when she didn't get a hit. The Registry tracked lost or stolen art, and it didn't usually cover jewelry. Tonight, she concentrated on a different series of databases.

The Art Looting Investigation Unit was formed toward the end of the Second World War with the specific aim of locating art plundered by the Nazis during their European conquest. It was a well-known story, thanks in part to a best-selling book and a Hollywood movie—*The Monuments Men*—starring George Clooney, Matt Damon, and Hugh Bonneville (or as her mother called him, "Mr. Downton").

While the movie had revealed some of the highs and lows of tracking the stolen art, it didn't capture how incredibly useful the work of the ALIU continued to be, decades after the end of the war. The ALIU documented the depth and degree of the plunder, and its reports on the networks of Nazi officials, art dealers, and individuals who were complicit in stealing artwork from Jews and any other "undesirables" was still immensely valuable. As a result, several databases of missing or looted war art had been created, and Daphne had access to all of them.

She began by describing the necklace as precisely as possible, but had no hits. Next, she entered in keywords like "honeybee" and "emerald" but came up empty. Daphne then tried another tack, broadening her search. Eventually she put in only "Necklace"—she had 698 returns and began scrolling through them all. About half way through, she hit the jackpot:

Provenance: French origin.

Type: Necklace

Material: Diamond, Emerald, insect shape

Dating: 1850s

Status: Object confiscated illegally on the Spanish-French border May 15, 1943.

Rightful Owner: Josephine Baker, Paris

Owner Information: Josephine Baker was an American singer, human rights activist, and civil rights champion. Josephine came to prominence in Paris in the 1920s and was a frequent entertainer across borders during the war. Josephine died in 1975 and her heirs claim this necklace as looted.

Daphne laughed aloud. They now had confirmation that Josephine was the necklace's owner and that the photograph from the walls of *Bonjour Paris* was taken before 1943. Two questions remained: *How did Josephine Baker come to own the necklace and what happened to it after the Nazis stole it?*

CHAPTER 18

The Rainbow Tribe

THE FELLOWSHIP OF THE NECKLACE ASSEMBLED AT BONJOUR *Paris* headquarters on Wednesday morning. Mme Boucher had a meeting with a supplier and they had a good hour before she returned. It had been a few days since they'd all been together, and everyone was discussing Alice's sighting of Yvette Dufeu. She was proud that she'd spotted their rival, but worried about what it meant for the story. Jacob and M. Seguin seemed to be fighting for who could capture the room's attention. Their voices deepened and they puffed out their chests. Alice thought there was something simian about the two of them competing to be alpha.

Interestingly, they both shut up when Lily began to talk. "Our first order of business is Yvette Dufeu. She's sniffing around our story."

"What does it matter?" Alexander asked. "Isn't our primary concern to discover the true owner of the necklace? It would be helpful to have more people looking with us."

Alice frowned. Was he being deliberately thick or did he truly not feel a sense of ownership over this story?

"We need the scoop," Jacob said. "In journalism it's the first one out with the story who matters. Everything else is echoes."

M. Seguin chimed in, as if eager not to let Jacob have the last word. "It would look very bad for the magazine if *La Vie en Rose* published their story ahead of ours. We would look like followers, second-place finishers."

Alice got the sense that M. Seguin didn't like coming in second at anything.

"What can Yvette possibly know?" Lily asked fretfully. She looked strained and tired, and Alice felt sorry for her. She knew what an impact *La Vie en Rose*'s arrival was having on *Bonjour Paris*'s bottom line. Lily continued, "At least she doesn't have the necklace itself. That's safe at the bank."

Here Alice flushed and looked down at her hands. She could vouch for that. Despite her best intentions, she had made another trip out there this morning. It was like an addiction she could appease only by holding the necklace in her hands. When she was away from it, she started to worry that it would disappear, vanish. The instant she picked it up, her concerns dissipated, along with her worries about messing things up, meeting everyone's expectations, or fitting into the Fellowship. It was as if the necklace was a security blanket, and being near it soothed her.

"I mean," Daphne spoke up, "it could be a coincidence."

Lily shook her head. "You don't know this woman. She does everything with a purpose. If she's researching nineteenth-century jewelry and Napoleon III, there is no way that it's not our story."

"A major concern," Jacob continued, and his voice held a hard edge, "is how news got out about the necklace. We must have a double agent."

"Is there any way the office manager caught wind of it?" Daphne asked.

Lily shook her head. "Mme Boucher is a straight shooter. If she knew what we were up to she wouldn't keep it secret from us." She laughed. "Believe me, she is not shy about telling me her opinions on how to run things."

Alice stared at the Fellowship members. Could Alexander have given the story to Yvette? Why would he do that? He'd be more likely to get fed up with the lot of them and grass them out to the police. What if Daphne were their mole? Was Jacob responsible for the leak? As important as this story and the Fellowship was to her, it didn't necessarily mean that the others were taking it as seriously. Alice could be sure only of herself, M. Seguin, and Lily—after all, they had a financial stake in their success.

"We're not accusing anyone," Lily said. "But be extra careful you don't accidentally let something slip to a friend, or a roommate."

Alice swallowed hard. She was the only one of this group with a roommate. Could they actually think she would betray them? Although hadn't she just been evaluating them for the very same reason? Now she recalled that the Fellowship of the Ring dissolved when one of the company betrayed the others. Did they think she was Boromir? Her illicit trips to the bank would certainly not be well received in this suspicious environment. She blushed a deep red, looked down at her hands, and prayed no one noticed.

Lily continued, "All we can do at this point is get our story out faster than whatever Yvette has planned. *La Vie en Rose*'s publication date is usually a couple of days after ours, so we still have the jump on them. This is what we know so far: The necklace was made in 1864 for Napoleon III. He gave it to his mistress, Marguerite Bellanger, who moved to St. Ives, England, and became a lady. We have a definitive sighting of the necklace there in 1881. It next pops up between roughly 1940 and 1960 when we have this photograph." Lily passed the portrait to Luc, who hadn't yet seen it in person. "We put it back in the frame to protect it," Lily explained. "There is an inscription from Josephine at the bottom, though—'Thank you,' and some *x*'s and *o*'s."

"No signature on the inscription," Jacob pointed out. "We shouldn't make assumptions."

"No," Lily said. "We assumed it was Josephine's, but you're right, she might not have written that."

"That is unlikely," M. Seguin said. "De tout façon, we can easily compare her handwriting. I think we should take it as a given it was written by her so that we don't get distracted by false trails."

"Yeah, distracted like by how the photograph of her wearing the necklace was found right under our noses in the office of your very magazine," Jacob said.

"Are you implying something?" M. Seguin asked, with amusement in his voice.

Jacob shrugged. "No, but I think we should be tracing how the necklace ended up in the basement. We've come up empty there."

Alice bit her lip; that part of the story had been her responsibility, and her pursuit of the Théâtre Rigolo angle had led to nothing.

"Why don't we confirm the handwriting is Josephine's and then try to figure out who she is thanking?" Was M. Seguin deliberately ignoring Jacob's point to irritate the other man, or did he not want them to connect the necklace and the building? Oh God, the Yvette news had really shaken her trust. Now she was questioning people's motives.

Lily chimed in. "Jacob is right. We shouldn't ignore the connection to the building." She turned to Alexander. "Did you have any luck with the landlord?"

Lily had asked Alexander to follow up that angle, but to do it subtly so as not to alert the landlord of the discovery of a valuable necklace on his premises, in case he decided he had a claim to it. Alice wasn't sure Alexander was the best person for so delicate a job, but Lily had blithely assigned him that task, and he had agreed.

"The landlord has not been able to tell me anything. That end is dead," Alexander said.

Did the landlord really have nothing to add? What if Alexander had found out more and wasn't sharing it? Perhaps he was plotting against them, in league with Yvette. Alice knew her conjecture was paranoid, the idea of Alexander—so straightforward and blunt—scheming with someone like Yvette was mad, but the thought of the Honeybee Emeralds's vulnerability jolted her.

"That doesn't mean we should stop looking," Jacob interjected. "It can't be a coincidence we found the necklace where we did."

Luc shifted impatiently in his chair. "I don't see—"

"While you boys are arguing," Daphne interjected, "I think I've got an answer to one big question."

Everyone turned toward her. Alice had noticed that Daphne enjoyed being the center of attention. "Any connection between Josephine Baker's photograph and the building is a genuine coincidence. I bet most buildings in Paris have a photograph of Josephine in them somewhere—that woman was, and is, incredibly popular. Anyway, there is definitely no link between her and the necklace being found in the building, because as of 1943, she no longer owned it."

They gaped at her. "How can you be so sure?" Jacob demanded.

"The Nazis confiscated it in '43." Daphne told them about the ALIU database and showed them the screenshot featuring the Honeybee Emeralds.

"So now we're going to have to untangle Nazi looting practices and the necklace's journey from stolen goods to forgotten pocket lint," M. Seguin said despondently.

Jacob grinned. "Are you kidding? This is going to be an incredible story. As soon as the Nazis come into anything, people get even more interested."

"What a sad commentary on the world," M. Seguin said.

"That's the way it is," Jacob replied, an edge to his voice. "The Josephine angle helps us too. Americans tend to like any story that we've got a connection to."

"I've noticed," M. Seguin said sourly.

Jacob's neck flushed red, but he shrugged. "Publishing 101: America is your biggest market and everyone is interested in the Nazis."

Alice filed these facts away. She was grateful to be learning from Jacob.

"If it is the truth about the Nazis," Alexander said, "then we know who the necklace's rightful owner is."

Alice could see where he was going with the idea, but said nothing. Jacob caught on a moment later. "Right, the necklace would belong to Josephine's heirs. That's perfect. It brings in that whole strange aspect of her personality. She adopted like twelve children from different parts of the world and raised them in some castle in the south."

Alice had read all about Josephine at the Richelieu Library. The château, Les Milandes, was seized from Josephine during bankruptcy proceedings in 1968.

Jacob laughed. "She was kind of erratic. Like a proto-Angelina and Brad. She called the children her 'Rainbow Tribe.'"

Her hope was that she could foster dialogue and peace by adopting children from distressed areas of the world. Alice didn't think the idea was that mad. The world could be a hard and dangerous place for children. She thought that Josephine's goal was noble, even if her execution was sometimes clumsy, and the Rainbow Tribe kids had had eccentric childhoods, to put it mildly.

Lily said, "Okay, so it looks like we're going to have to trace the necklace through Nazi administration somehow, which might be tough. Still, like Alexander said, Daphne's discovery gives us our end game. We'll present the necklace to the rightful owners—Josephine Baker's estate." She turned to Jacob with a huge grin. "This is going to be a gigantic story."

"You're telling me," he said, returning her grin. "We've got an emperor, a mistress, a jazz singer, and the Third Reich, not to mention that whole Rainbow Tribe dynamic. We might have to think about movie rights." He held Lily's gaze for a beat, and Alice was surprised to see her editor's cheeks start to redden. Lily wasn't usually a blusher.

Despite the flush, Lily spoke crisply. "I'd still like us to find out as much as we can about the necklace's life and journey. We need to fill in as many gaps as possible. For instance, we don't know how the necklace got from Marguerite to Josephine."

"I was researching a connection between those two," Jacob said. "They were both performers in Paris. Could there be a link?"

Lily shook her head. "I'm not sure. I mean, Marguerite left the stage by 1863, because that's when she was promoted to imperial mistress. By 1881 she was living a life of respectability. Josephine didn't even arrive in Paris until the 1920s. That's too long a gap."

Daphne said, "There is one obvious angle we haven't explored. Marguerite had a son—he was even rumored to be Napoleon III's bastard, although never officially acknowledged." She looked at her phone, reading some notes. "Presumably Charles Jules Auguste François Marie Leboeuf inherited the necklace from his mother."

That caught Alice's attention. She had seen that name, or at least a portion thereof, in her reading. Which book had it been, and what was the context? Alice closed her eyes and scrolled through the names she had plowed through yesterday. "He's mentioned in one of the Baker biographies. He knew Josephine in France—right before the war."

"Really?" Daphne asked excitedly.

Alice tried to recall the page where she'd seen it written. "Yes," she said. "He was rumored to be one of her lovers."

"One of?" Jacob asked.

"Yes, she had dozens—hundreds." Alice blushed. When would this idiotic reflex calm down? She stole a glance at Alexander. He was staring at his hands resting on the table.

"What year did they meet?" Daphne asked.

"It was 1939," Alice said. "He died a year later."

"How do you remember all that?" Daphne asked.

Alice shrugged self-consciously. "It's a thing I have—kind of a funny photographic memory."

"That's incredible," Daphne said. "You're so lucky."

Alice stared at her, startled. Had anyone called her "lucky" in those tones before? She was lucky, of course. She was fortunate to have a mother like Maheen who had built a life for them in England, to have Dale as a stepfather, and to have her sisters. She knew she was lucky to have the safety of that little house on Victoria Road. Only most people didn't see her as lucky. Not in the easy, effortless way that Daphne's tone implied. When people normally called her "lucky" like that, it meant that she should be grateful. It was a grudging statement, one intended to remind her of what had been given to her and an implication that it could be taken away.

Daphne's tone didn't imply any of that, though. It was just an acknowledgment of good fortune, of happy chance. Daphne actually sounded a bit envious, and this was new too. No one had ever envied her anything, as far as she could tell. Her large intelligence was a hindrance, her Middle Eastern features something to feel ambivalent about in Hull. Her small house filled with a loving family was wonderful, but wasn't the thing—like a thigh gap or your very own car—that sparked actual envy.

Lily spoke with excitement. "This is excellent. Charles could have given Baker the necklace then. There's our connection. It gets us from Napoleon

III to Josephine Baker in two moves."

Alice frowned. There had been nothing in the book about him giving her jewelry. She certainly would have remembered that.

"Maybe," Daphne said. "He would have been very old, wouldn't he?" she asked.

"Yeah, almost 80 in 1939," Alice said.

"Is it likely Josephine Baker would have been interested in him?" Lily asked.

They all turned to Alice. Suddenly she was the Josephine expert. "I'm not sure," she stammered. "She would have been 33 in 1939 . . . she was also at her most famous and successful. I'm not sure she would have had an affair with an old man."

"Still, that's the angle to pursue," Lily said. "Nice work on that, everyone."

These were obvious words of dismissal, and the group relaxed, people shifting in their seats, looking for bags and coats. M. Seguin was tapping on his phone; Jacob stood over him, blatantly reading his screen. Daphne was searching for her jacket.

Alexander's voice stopped them. "I have been thinking," he said in his slow fashion.

"Yes," Lily prompted him.

"I have been thinking," Alexander repeated. "About the cat."

"The cat?" Lily asked, sounding confused. Everyone else looked up from their activities, staring at Alexander.

"At the theater." Alexander turned to Alice, his big blue eyes seeking her understanding. "Alphonse Marchal's cat. Do you remember its name?"

"The cat's name?" She recalled its sleek black appearance. It was the only thing in that place that had looked well cared for.

"No," she said, bewildered.

"The cat's name was Josephine," Alexander finally said. "I think, perhaps, that there is significance there."

CHAPTER 19

A Single Red Rose

THERE WAS A LOT TO BE SAID FOR SETTLING INTO THE COMFORT of a Mercedes E-Class piloted by a uniformed driver while sipping from a chilled glass of Perrier. Daphne rested her head against the seat for a moment, breathing in the scent of the leather and the new-car smell. Alexander should make a perfume out of that combination. He could call it "Wealth" and it would probably make him a bundle.

When it was clear that the rest of the Fellowship had pressing appointments but that she and Luc had a bit of flexibility this morning, they had been assigned the task of following up on Alexander's lead and figuring out if M. Marchal, the theater owner, had a Josephine connection. Daphne was profoundly grateful they weren't schlepping over there on the métro or bus. "Do you always use a car service?" she asked Luc, who sat beside her tapping on his phone.

She'd taken the rest of her morning off for this errand. Luckily, as the director of the Registry, she called the shots.

Luc finished his message and looked up. "Not always. I have my own vehicle, of course. Still, I like the service. I can work as I travel. Efficient."

Daphne got the impression that *efficient* was one of Luc's highest words of praise. She had no idea what he actually did, other than toil in La Défense. Whatever it was, he was obviously well compensated. While she and Philip were definitely upper-middle class—affording a small house in the 16th, sending their kid to private school, making payments on the

Audi—Luc was in a different league altogether. He was bespoke tailoring, car services, and probably a five-million-euro Saint-Germain-des-Prés apartment with views of the Seine.

Whatever money Luc had, Daphne reflected, he had earned it himself. She remembered Lily mentioning that Luc was the youngest. His older siblings were all solidly middle class—maybe one was a dentist and the other an architect. His mother ran that small-potatoes magazine and his dad, she thought, had been a doctor. While a physician was a respectable profession, in a country with socialized medicine it was not necessarily the signifier for big, big bucks the way it could be in America. No, Luc had come by his car service and two-hundred-euro haircuts the honest way, by making it himself.

She looked wistfully at the crisp white edge of his shirt cuff poking out from his dark suit jacket. A hint of a gold cufflink glinted when he turned his wrist. Daphne had always loved men's wrists. They were a delicate, vulnerable point in their strong, meaty bodies—a place of movement and dexterity, yet still holding great strength. Luc's wrist was the perfect amount of both masculine hairy and ruggedly tanned. Philip had sprained his wrist last year in a squash accident. Every now and then, for no real reason, it would swell up again, and he'd spend three days icing it. The worst wasn't the swollen, taut skin that looked like a balloon about to burst and that made Daphne queasy to look at. No, the worst was that Philip would become obsessed with it, giving her minute-by-minute updates on its status in a dramatic half whisper, as if he were talking about the progress of an aggressive cancer. She sighed and looked out the window at the bustling city. She was safely insulated from it all in this smooth-riding wealth bubble. She could get used to this.

"Is there any possibility," Daphne asked, turning to the task at hand, "that going to the theater is a waste of time?"

Luc nodded. "Absolutely, but we must follow every lead. Yvette Dufeu's interest in this story troubles me."

Indeed, Luc did look concerned, his eyes pained.

"My mother built up her business over decades of hard work," he said. "She fretted over its fate in her final days. I was content to quietly close

Bonjour Paris a year after my mother's death, which would have been a gentle and appropriate end. This, however—to be bested by Yvette Dufeu? My mother would not tolerate such a fate. It is unacceptable."

"Is Yvette really such a threat?" Daphne asked.

"She is a very ambitious woman." His voice held a note of admiration.

"Well, then, the question is what does she know and when will she publish?" Daphne was surprised at how invested she felt in resolving the mystery and seeing *Bonjour Paris* succeed. She realized that it was more than keeping Lily in Paris. It was that she wanted Alice to be part of a big story. She wanted to find something that would actually impress Alexander. She wanted Luc to feel a connection with his mother, and she even wanted Jacob, yes Jacob, to write a fantastic article. She realized that over the past few days she'd come to consider these people friends. She hadn't been joking with Lily—they were a team, and true to her competitive nature, she wanted her side to win.

"I do wonder who tipped Yvette off," Luc said. "Someone in our little group has been talking."

Daphne held up her hands—"It wasn't me," she said.

Luc shook his head. "I suspect that American."

"Jacob?" Daphne asked.

"Yes, he is so arrogant."

"Oh yeah, he's a dick," she agreed.

Luc leaned toward her, obviously delighted to discover that she shared his opinion. "He has that sense of entitlement that you see only in Americans."

Having now spent five years in Paris, Daphne was inured to casual anti-Americanism. "Aren't you half 'Merican?" she asked.

Luc nodded. "Yes, but I was raised in France."

"Growing up, did you ever feel split?" she asked. "Half French, half American—belonging nowhere?" Daphne thought of Theo. Was he going to lose his roots? She had a sudden urgency to return to the States, to expose her son to Fourth of July fireworks, apple pie, vast parking lots, and openhearted American friendliness.

Her question sparked Luc's memories. "My mother was from Iowa. We used to go back every summer. Grandfather was a professor of Greek antiquities at Drake University. He was a real Indiana Jones type, at least to me." Luc's eyes lit up as he talked about his grandfather, and Daphne could feel his love for the man.

"His office was filled with dusty urns and brightly illustrated books. He'd tell me about Aphrodite and Hermes. He never softened any of the stories—tales of murder, mayhem, transformation, rage, and passion. We'd go for walks around their neighborhood; to my Parisian eye each house was a mansion—huge, with wide lawns and two cars in every driveway."

"Did you ever have the urge to live in America? To explore that part of your identity?"

Luc shook his head. "Non, my mother identified wholeheartedly as French, or at least Parisian." He laughed. "You know, she demanded to be buried in Paris? She insisted on being interred at the cemetery near my childhood home. It is not easy to be buried in Paris, however. Real estate, even in cemeteries, is at a premium. There are many rules about who is eligible. Only a "real" Parisian may be interred here. We thought Maman would be denied, but many people came forward attesting to the authorities that she truly was Parisian. Of course, it wasn't until Mme Boucher returned from a trip and took over that they really listened to us. Maman's grave is the ultimate badge of belonging."

"That's wonderful," Daphne murmured. Although she had never given it a moment's thought, now that she knew that Parisian cemeteries were exclusive, she had an urgent need to be buried in one herself.

"My father tells me there is a small mystery about her grave," Luc said. "Someone comes and lays a red rose at her headstone. Has been doing so since her death. It's been one year, now—every week, a single rose on her grave."

"That's incredible," Daphne said. "Did she have an unrequited love, do you think?"

Luc laughed. "No, you don't understand. I am sure it's my father himself who does this. He adored my mother, and that is just the type of thing he would do—continue to burnish her reputation, even in death."

"That's so beautiful," Daphne said. The problem with Philip was that he wouldn't see that gesture as romantic. He wouldn't understand what it meant for a husband to faithfully keep his love alive through a weekly pilgrimage. He thought gestures like that—futile, romantic actions that benefited no one—were a waste, and what's more, were ostentatious. Show-offy. He was a no-nonsense kind of guy, yet so much of French culture was built on exactly that kind of excess of emotion, or passion. It wasn't smart to tie a padlock symbolizing your love to the Pont des Arts, not when the city would just come along with bolt cutters. It wasn't wise to spend four hundred euros on a bottle of wine that was so good it felt like your mouth actually floated off your face, not when a fifty euro bottle would have almost the same effect. Ascend the Eiffel Tower in the moonlight? Dumb idea. Montparnasse Tower Observation Deck offered cheaper, less touristy views at a fraction of the cost. Philip had no romance.

Luc was still lost in reminiscences. "My mother and father had a very happy marriage—they were always so tender toward one another, or, at least, Papa was toward Maman. My mother was not a very demonstrative woman. She loved, I am sure she loved fiercely, but she did not express herself so well, sometimes."

Daphne could still hear a bit of hurt in his voice. Amazing how even as an adult, you carried around the wounds your parents inflicted on you. "She sounds like a complex person."

Luc smiled. "She was. She came here at age eighteen, my grandparents' only child. She arrived in Paris with rudimentary French and knowing absolutely no one. She was extremely capable, though; she got a series of jobs—nanny, dog walker, waitress."

"That's impressive," Daphne said. She couldn't imagine having a parent with that sense of adventure. Both of hers still inhabited the same Chicago suburb, having carefully mapped out who "got" which Costco, Starbucks, and Olive Garden in the divorce. They lived within five blocks of each other but dwelled in their own self-imposed isolation, never crossing paths.

Luc's tone shifted, becoming more thoughtful. "I found all of this out from my grandparents. My mother never talked about her past. She was very focused on the immediate. She'd address present realities, get her hands dirty, resolve them, and then move on." Again, Luc's voice held admiration.

"You miss her?" Daphne asked.

Luc nodded. "Of course," he said simply. "She was extraordinary. She would have loved this necklace mystery."

"Is that why you are participating in all of this—the Fellowship? I imagine you have a lot of other work you could be doing. What's the fascination for you?"

His phone pinged and he looked down to answer it, saving him from Daphne's question.

CHAPTER 20

A Javanese Princess

ALICE WAS BACK IN THE RICHELIEU READING ROOM, SURROUNDED by another pile of books. She settled herself into a comfortably worn leather chair and sighed with pleasure. As before, the room was still, interrupted only by low murmured voices at the reference desk and the sound of carefully turned pages. She loved the sense of purposefulness and dedication that permeated these walls. She also loved the fact that all of this research distracted from her peculiar mania for touching the Honeybee Emeralds. If she concentrated enough on Josephine Baker, maybe her obsession would fade away entirely.

She had already spent an hour poring over the volumes she had previously skimmed, looking for the reference she had mentioned at this morning's meeting regarding Charles Leboeuf. She found it at last in one of the thicker biographies. A quick mention of Leboeuf as one of Josephine's many prewar admirers. She flipped to the endnotes to see where the reference had come from. The source was the correspondence between Adeline Proulx, companion to Josephine Baker, and a Mr. Francis Pike. Alice smiled in delight—the letters were held at the Richelieu Library.

Alice turned to the catalog description of the Francis Pike Fonds to discover that the collection consisted of letters written to Francis, who lived mostly in Harlem, from Adeline, usually writing from Paris. The correspondence was one-way—only from Adeline to Francis. Perhaps the French woman had destroyed or lost the letters that Francis had sent back to her, or perhaps another institution held them.

According to the description, Adeline had spent about twenty years in Josephine Baker's employ, from the singer's first arrival in Paris in 1925 to shortly after the Second World War. Adeline had met Francis when he had danced with Josephine in the early Paris years. She wondered why the young Black American dancer from Harlem had kept up a long correspondence with the white Frenchwoman born and raised in Paris.

After a short wait, the librarian brought over the two boxes of letters. This was the entirety of the Francis Pike Fonds. Perhaps here were the answers to their questions.

A good couple of hours passed as she read through the letters, getting a sense of Adeline's spiky, upright personality, her deep affection for Josephine Baker, and her connection, which crossed the color and class barrier, to Francis Pike. By the 1930s Francis had given up dancing and trained as a plumber. The disparities between their lives—Adeline immersed in the glamour of the Parisian music hall world, Francis struggling with segregationist American policies, new fatherhood, and insecurities about his livelihood—didn't seem to matter, as the two evinced a deep affection for one another.

There were hundreds of letters, spanning three decades, penned in Adeline's spidery, old-fashioned script. Written in English, the letters often came with envelopes, all addressed to Francis Pike, New York, New York. The return address on the envelopes changed as Adeline traveled with Josephine; sometimes it was Paris, other times the south of France, Morocco, and even Argentina.

The first mention of Charles Leboeuf came at last in November 1938. "Dear Francis," the letter began.

You've seen the papers—the rumors about the troubles in the marriage are true. In fact, Jo's marriage to Jean Lion is over in all but name. Jo claims (dramatically, of course) that Le Beau

Chêne is not her home anymore. When she said that, I knew the marriage would not last long. It is no surprise. They are utterly incompatible: Jean is a lady's man and a spendthrift. He tries to have his cake and eat it too, but Jo won't put up with his nonsense. They are always screaming, fighting. She stays in Paris now and returns to her home away from home, the Folies Bergère, for a limited engagement. Despite the turmoil (or perhaps because of it, you know Jo), she's in good spirits.

She had a most interesting visitor last night. She'd finished her show and was changing in her dressing room before heading out to a late-night charity concert she had agreed to give at the Olympia (say what you will about Josephine Baker, she is a workhorse). A knock on the door, Paul, the stage manager, asking if Jo would see an admirer. She was displeased. Usually Paul is more adept at stopping the men—the financiers, club owners, and impoverished counts—from interrupting her toilette.

She barked her refusal. Jo is becoming ever more imperious—sometimes I hardly recognize the goofy child who first arrived in Paris, so panicked on the night of her debut, when she had burned all the hair from her scalp in her attempts to straighten it.

'Please ma'am,' Paul persisted, which was astonishing— you have never met a more servile man than Paul Guertin. (One reason he has been able to work with Jo for so long). 'Please,' continued Paul, 'He is a good man. I served with him in the war.'

Well, Paul couldn't have picked a better line—the Great War might have ended twenty years ago, but Jo has a real soft spot for the soldiers. She will always stop on the street to talk to a crippled veteran, and in Paris, they still stand on every corner— the armless, the blind, and the mad. 'Very well,' she relented, although I could tell she was impatient.

In walked a tall man, about 75, in a beautifully cut gray suit with a homburg pulled low over his eyes. He doffed his hat, just as Jo turned from her dressing table to greet him. She was naked from the waist up—oh, did I not mention that?

The man stumbled, eyes as round as saucers. Jo waited a moment, giving him a full view of the sapphire necklace nestled between those famous breasts, before shrugging into a silk wrap.

'I wanted to tell you, mademoiselle, that your performance tonight was magnificent.' He'd brought a huge bouquet of lilies and Jo tossed them on the pile with the others. There are always mountains of bouquets in Jo's dressing rooms. Jo was never terribly interested in cut flowers. (Cut diamonds are a different story!) I remember once an Italian duke had sent her a bouquet of gorgeous bougainvillea, picked that very morning in Verona and sent directly to her in Paris—they arrived in a moss basket, as fresh as if they'd been plucked from the banks of the Seine. Jo had barely glanced at them.

At any rate, the man sat down and began to gush about the performance. She was only half-listening, until he said that her 'Danse Sauvage' reminded him of another dancer he knew during the War.

This caught Jo's attention. She turned from her mirror, eyes flashing, and I could read her thoughts—How dare this man pretend to be an admirer and then bring up a rival! I knew the poor fellow was going to be screamed at and almost certainly slapped for the insult, when he casually mentioned the other dancer's name—Mata Hari. That stopped Jo cold. You couldn't be on stage in Paris and not know of Mata Hari's story of espionage and treason.

It turned out that this gentleman, Charles Leboeuf was his name, had been an officer in the Deuxième Bureau, the French Secret Service, during the Great War. He managed La Dame Blanche, a whole network of spies in neutral Holland and occupied Belgium. They monitored German movements there, especially the railroads. Their work was vital to the Entente war effort.

Margaretha—that was Mata Hari's real name—was a key figure in moving information along, and M. Leboeuf had been, what is called in the parlance, her 'handler.'

I remarked that I thought Mata Hari had been shot for spying for the Boches. Josephine looked at me in surprise for knowing my history, but I remember it was a great scandal when I was a girl in Paris.

M. Leboeuf nodded, looking sad, and sat down. 'Margaretha was a marvel.' He turned to Josephine. 'She didn't dance with your feral grace, but she had a burning passion that shone through. She was so sensual, so alive. She was a wonder to behold.'

M. Leboeuf went on, expounding on all of Mata Hari's marvelous traits. I wanted to hear more about the infamous spy, and I could tell from her shifting posture that Jo, bored with this recitation of Mata Hari's charms, was preparing to send M. Leboeuf away. I offered him a glass of champagne in an effort to change the subject. Jo wasn't happy with me, but for once I prevailed. He bowed, in a courteous, old-fashioned way that reminded me of my own dear grandfather.

M. Leboeuf continued his tale, 'Margaretha had a talent for making any man she spoke to seem fascinating. That's what made her the perfect spy.'

This, at last, recaptured Jo's attention, and she turned back to the old gentleman. I relaxed; Josephine loved a good story.

'There were always many rumors swirling around the myste-rious, exotic Mata Hari—most of them started by Margaretha herself, I should note.' M. Leboeuf's voice strengthened and deepened as he talked, almost as if he were returning to his younger years. 'The truth was she was not a Javanese princess, schooled in the art of seduction by the courtesans of the Far East, but a bourgeois Dutch girl from a stolid town in Holland. To me that contradiction increased her fascination. She had remade herself into something incredible—at one point she was the most desired woman in Paris, perhaps in all of Europe.'

Jo was enthralled. She knew what it was like to be the toast of Europe; she'd been a sensation ever since she'd first walked on stage in that banana skirt. Indeed, I think we can all agree that Josephine Baker has Paris at her feet right now. This reminds me, she is wondering if now is the time to tour America. She is ready to return home in triumph—conquer the hearts of her fellow citizens and perhaps improve the lot of her negro brothers and sisters.

The letter moved on to other topics. Alice diligently read every word, hoping for more mentions of Charles Leboeuf. No luck. Instead, Adeline wrote weekly and sometimes biweekly to her friend in New York. The letters mentioned the after-parties that lasted until six in the morning; sapphires and rubies showered on Josephine by ardent admirers; exotic pets adopted; triumphant successes on stage and equally triumphant victories in the bedroom, where Josephine was as interested in the wealthy millionaires courting her as the young chorus girls dancing for her. The approaching war did not figure in these recitations, and Alice couldn't help feel sorry for this carefree Frenchwoman, fretting about the costume fittings for Josephine's next show, when her whole world was about to go up in flames.

The next letter that mentioned Leboeuf was from December 1938, a month after his initial visit.

Jo's 'army buddy,' as we jokingly call M. Leboeuf, made another appearance last night. Jo was in the dressing room again, and one of her maids had brought her cheetah, Chiquita, along for a visit. That beast makes me so nervous. It prowls around the room, never sitting still, and it always looks so hungry to me. Jo says I'm a ninny to worry, but I think wild beasts should be left in the wild, not brought inside to threaten good Frenchwomen. M. Leboeuf's arrival was a relief. He has an air of sound competence, and I trusted that if Chiquita misbehaved he could assist. This time he carried not a bouquet of flowers, but a small box containing an exquisite cameo. Jo thanked him for it and tossed the box to the side. Ever since his previous visit, she and I had often returned to the subject of the fascinating Mata Hari. 'Tell me about Margaretha,' she commanded.

'She was an incredible girl, no, woman,' M. Leboeuf corrected himself. 'In fact, when I knew her, she was already older than you are now. She was not beautiful.'

Here Josephine smiled approvingly.

'But she was fascinating. The force of her personality shone through. Is it any wonder she was such a success?' M. Leboeuf's question was rhetorical. After more than two decades, he was obviously still smitten.

Another letter, from a month further on, January 1939.

It is funny, dear Francis, but Josephine is quite taken with this M. Leboeuf. The fascination is a bit puzzling. He has neither youth, nor looks, nor money to recommend him. In some respects, he is entirely unremarkable. He is a widower but has no designs on Josephine, and she, oddly, is uninterested in bedding him. Most strange for Jo to be devoting so much time to a man (or a woman!) she does not desire. They have, dare I say it, a friendship. He strikes me as incredibly lonely. His family is all gone— he had no brothers and sisters and his mother is dead. He never knew his father, and perhaps that strikes a chord with Jo, who herself has always been unsure of who her father was. Or perhaps the connection lies in the fact that both M. Leboeuf and Jo wanted children, and both have been unable to have any.

Of course, in truth M. Leboeuf is not as simple as he appears—no man charged with running La Dame Blanche espionage ring can be entirely ordinary. It is just that he conducts himself with a quiet dignity that is so unlike most of the people we encounter in the theatrical world. Whatever the allure, Jo always makes time for him. They talk for hours, mostly about his wartime adventures. Jo is fascinated by his stories of war and espionage, although she always comes back to Mata Hari.

Another letter, dated March 31, 1939:

Dear Francis, I must tell you about what I believe might be our final visit with M. Leboeuf for some time. He was speaking, as usual, about Mata Hari. 'I have always been fascinated by dancers and stage performers. My mother, before she settled into respectability, was an actress. She instilled in me an esteem for the hard work of the performer and a delight in their artistic ability. When Margaretha—Mata Hari—danced on stage, it was as if she was performing just for me.

'You loved her,' Jo observed.

I was surprised by this. As you know, Jo tends only to be interested in things that affect her directly. Piercing emotional insights about others are not usually her forte (to put it mildly!).

'Of course,' he said simply. 'Before the Deuxième Bureau even recruited her, I was entranced. I was one of those men who showed up at her stage door, much as I showed up at yours, to shower her with praise and adoration. We soon developed a romance, though we knew it could never be anything more. I am a devout Catholic and could not leave my wife. Margaretha needed the security and financing of wealthy protectors in her ongoing battle for custody of her daughter back in Holland. As our relationship deepened, I longed to show her that even though I could not be hers in the eyes of God and man, my heart belonged to her. On the night I asked her to assist me in my work with Dame Blanche, I gave her the one thing I had of real value, and the only piece of jewelry I still had of my mother's—a beautiful diamond and emerald necklace with a honeybee pendant.

Alice's head reared up. There was the connection to the necklace. Definitive proof of its provenance, and apparently it had once belonged to Mata Hari herself. She texted the Fellowship. This was blockbuster news.

Alice's thoughts were interrupted by a loud announcement in French: "The Reading Room is closing." She groaned aloud and bent her head to see if she could snatch a few more minutes of research.

A security guard appeared at her elbow. "Reading room is closing, mademoiselle. Your time is up."

Paris, November 1916

Charles, that adorable creature, had given her the most lovely necklace. Forty diamonds, a heavy gold honeybee pendant, and some simply delicious emeralds. He'd handed it to her after her performance of the dagger dance, telling her that her tales of Java had stirred his soul and her electric performance had reminded him of his own mother. That was not the usual reaction her clothes-shedding dance got, but the stunning necklace more than made up for his odd choice of praise.

She was wearing it now. In fact, it was the only thing she wore. Java had taught her to enjoy the freedom of nudity. *Mata hari* meant "the eye of the day," and she had named herself in honor of the burning heat of Java's tropical sun. The warmth of that thick, tropical heat had been a balm, and despite scandalizing the house servants, she had gone naked at every opportunity. She could have lived there forever—a colorful butterfly in the sun— had Rudolf not been determined to squash her.

Ah, Java. She had steamed into Tanjung Parak as a provincial Dutch newlywed, and left nearly a decade later, having lost one child, one marriage, and the full use of her right index finger, thanks to the moment when Rudolf had snapped it back like a chicken bone.

She traced her hand across the necklace's cool stones. Its weight was comforting. It signified wealth, and if not respectability, at least safety. It was a reminder that she was no longer that desperate, trapped woman. Yes, her time in Java had taught her more than how to take a punch. It had taught her how to take care of herself.

She contemplated her appearance in the full-length mirror. She was tall, her hair still a deep, almost blue-black, her eyes dark and flashing, her breasts a titch too small, but her hips amply curved. Too amply? She sucked in her belly. When she had arrived in Paris, ready to rebuild her life, the papers had described her dancing as "feline," "exotic," and even "majestically tragic." She had fascinated and scandalized in equal parts: Her apparent exoticness, aristocratic bearing, and demanding hauteur drew critical admiration, but what drew the crowds and paid the bills was her willingness to remove almost every stitch of clothing.

Her eyes were drawn again to the necklace. It truly was magnificent. Charles had presented it to her, along with a proposal, though not the kind she was accustomed to. It was neither an ardent request for her hand in marriage, nor a winking proposition to enter into a discreet friendship.

She bit her lip. She was no spy, and she didn't need more complications in her life. Not when she was still trying to win little Jeanne's custody back from Rudolf. Charles had framed his proposition as a choice, but was it really? There was a war on, and the French were desperate to defeat the Boche.

She was being foolish. She needed income, and Charles had promised her payment for this work. He loved her. He wouldn't lead her into harm's way. She could rely upon him. Her thoughts returned to the languid heat of Java. Rudolf had taught her a painful lesson about relying on a man for safety. She quashed the thought. The necklace was a gift, not a noose.

CHAPTER 21

Josephine the Cat

THE THEATER WAS DISGUSTING. ALICE AND ALEXANDER HAD neglected to mention that salient point. The chairs Daphne and Luc sat in were covered in thick, sticky dust. Dirty coffee cups littered Alphonse Marchal's desk. The entire building had an oppressive, stale smell that made Daphne itch to get home and take a shower. M. Marchal himself was creepy. He looked a bit like John Waters, but with more grease and less twinkle.

They hadn't come up with much of an excuse for the meeting, but M. Marchal hadn't appeared to need one. To his inquiry about when the article on his theater would appear in *Bonjour Paris*, she responded vaguely— "Soon, soon"—and he happily launched into a reminiscence of Luc's mother. He had fond memories of Olivia from his own brief stint at Rue de Beaune. "Your mother was so intelligent, so vivacious. I was truly sad to hear of her passing." Luc nodded, but before he could answer, a glossy black cat slunk into the room.

At last, they could get this fool's errand over with. "What's your cat's name?" Daphne asked.

M. Marchal was startled by her urgent tone, and she tried to modify her expression to one of casual interest.

"Josephine," he said.

"That's a long name for a little cat," Daphne said. She forced a laugh, but it sounded odd.

"I named her for Josephine Baker. I name all my cats after her. She had such a feline grace."

"You knew her?" Luc asked. He was more successful in keeping his tone light.

"Indeed, I did," the older man said with pride. "I was one of her dancers, you know. In the early sixties. The entertainment world in Paris, it is small. I am sure everyone over a certain age in this city who worked on the stage has a Josephine story. She was such a character. Une grande dame—a little like your mother, though much larger than life of course. And her talent, it was breathtaking. The real deal."

Daphne frowned. If M. Marchal was right, then it really was a coincidence that he'd named his cat after the singer. At any rate, the sixties was the wrong era to connect Josephine to the necklace, since the Nazis had confiscated it by then. "You didn't happen to know her before the war?" Daphne asked.

The theater owner drew his breath in with a hiss. "Madame, how old do you think I am?"

"Oh, I am sorry," she said quickly. "I wasn't thinking."

"Americans," he sniffed, and turned to Luc.

The other man smiled and rolled his eyes ever so slightly, indicating a comradeship with M. Marchal. She could see what Luc was doing—they had slipped into "good cop/bad cop" roles, although these were apparently "sympathetic Frenchman/blundering American." Daphne swallowed her irritation and went along with it. "So, to confirm, you didn't know Josephine Baker during the war?"

"Non, of course not," he snapped. He turned to Luc, willing to expand to his understanding compatriot in order to show his disdain for the foolish American. "I had the honor of performing with her in one of her later shows in the early '70s. It was a very tasteful performance. She would come out in her full military uniform, wearing all of her medals— she had the Croix de Guerre and the Légion d'honneur and Rosette de la Résistance. She would get a standing ovation every time. It was very moving."

"Josephine Baker was awarded the Croix de Guerre and the Légion d'honneur?" Luc asked, astounded.

Daphne was also shocked. This was good intel to bring to the Fellowship. Those were prestigious medals—the Croix de Guerre was for wartime heroism, and the Légion d'honneur was for faithful service to France. The Resistance Medal was even rarer. When she had first arrived in Paris, Daphne was on the bus and a wizened old man had tottered aboard, wearing a big overcoat with a bronze medal featuring a stark vertical cross pinned to his lapel. A middle-aged man had immediately given him his seat, and she had watched as several older French people nodded to him respectfully, one even shaking his hand. She had Googled the medal as she sat there, and learned that the Resistance Medal was for those who took an active part in resisting the Axis powers during the Second World War. Her eyes had filled with tears when she learned what was written on the medal's reverse—*patria non immemor*—"the nation does not forget."

"Of course, monsieur." M. Marchal sounded reproachful. "You should know your French history better. She was buried with full military honors. All of France wept."

"Josephine Baker?" Luc asked incredulously. "The G-string and the banana skirt?"

"But yes. She worked in secret with the Free French. She used her touring schedule and her celebrity to get important information out to the Allies." M. Marchal moved his hands rapidly, obviously excited to talk about his idol. "Her sheet music was covered in invisible ink. She pinned messages to her underwear when she crossed borders, because she knew no Nazi would dare strip-search the Black Pearl. She helped many, many. Josephine Baker was a great heroine of the Resistance—a world-class Allied spy."

The Loire Valley

Lily: Nice work on the Josephine war stuff. Jacob says it's great color.

Daphne: NP. I'm impressed by Alice. That's great research. A tie-in with Mata Hari?

Lily: She's fantastic. So, guess what? We're grabbing the first train tomorrow to the Loire Valley.

Daphne: ???

Lily: Jacob found a relative of Josephine Baker's who's willing to talk to us. Well, not a direct relative, but the biological brother of one of her adopted kids. He wants us to meet him at his vineyard.

Daphne: So you're taking a romantic trip to the Loire.

Lily: Cool your jets. Jacob's bringing Marie-Pierre. They're going to take Friday off, too, and have a four-day romantic long weekend.

Daphne: Gag.

Lily: Lol. Very mature. Luc's coming too.

Daphne: !!!

Lily: He was at the magazine when the plans came together and he said he wanted to tag along. I can't say no to my boss.

Daphne: He's really getting into this, it's great.

Lily: I guess. I think he mostly said he'd come to bug Jacob.

Daphne: Well, whatever. See if you can get him to spring for first-class train tickets!

CHAPTER 22

Snow Finch

USUALLY THURSDAYS WERE THE BUSIEST DAY AT THE MAGAZINE, but this morning all was quiet. Lily had left on an unexpected business trip for the day. Élise sniffed. It was most irregular. At least Alice was in her proper place. That girl did work hard. Élise appreciated that. She was glad the Viking wasn't loitering about for once. His lumbering presence had become frequent in the office and she didn't like it. She hoped he wasn't nursing any romantic feelings toward Alice. That girl had a bright future ahead of her, if she didn't get sidetracked by a man.

Indeed, none of the usual coterie of hangers-on were around, and Élise was grateful for the break from the office intrigues. No one bothered to inform her of what was at stake, but Élise heard the whispers. Lily was obviously keeping something in the safety-deposit box because the key had been moved at least twice. Did they think she wouldn't notice when it wasn't returned to its precise location? Sloppy. There was much talk of Napoleon, and, even stranger, she'd heard Josephine Baker's name a few times. References to the singer made Élise think of Olivia. They'd had a record player in those early years, when it had just been the two of them getting the magazine out. Olivia had one of the latest albums—*Olympia-Palmarès Des Chansons*, released in 1968—and they played it over and over again. All those old classics, "J'ai Deux Amours," "La Vie en Rose," and even "La Petite Tonkinoise." Undoubtedly, the young folk wouldn't approve of that song anymore, call it racist or some nonsense, but she thought the tune was charming. She'd met Josephine Baker once, but then again, every Parisian of a certain age probably had a tale to tell about the Black Pearl.

Élise looked up. Alice was gathering her things. The younger woman seemed flustered by her gaze.

"I have to go to the Richelieu Library," Alice explained.

Élise said nothing.

"Lily knows about it," Alice added defensively.

She looked so young, Élise thought, no older than she herself had been when she'd first arrived in Paris. She remembered the noise and clamor of La Gare Du Nord, and how her courage had faltered as she stood in the train station, homeless and jobless. She recalled the image of those Syrian refugees from the television, so wild-eyed and bewildered. It was a terrifying thing to launch yourself into the unknown. "How old are you?" Élise asked.

The girl's eyes widened, obviously not expecting the question. "I'm, uh, twenty-three," she said in her very good French.

Élise nodded. She had been eighteen when she had arrived in Paris and first met Olivia. She was not supposed to stay in the city and yet somehow, all these years later, here she still was, and it was Olivia who had left. Élise would be returning to the mountains soon, retired there forever. She could almost feel the peaks closing in on her. She suddenly felt immensely tired.

"Are you all right?" the girl asked, stepping toward her.

Élise meant to quell the impertinent question with a stern look and return to her work. Instead, she realized she was crying.

"Oh, Mme Boucher!" The younger woman yelped. She rushed forward and took Élise's hand, perching awkwardly on her desk. "There, there," she said, squeezing her hand.

Élise sobbed. She cried as she had not done in forty years. Her frame heaved with emotion, and the tears, great round things she wouldn't have thought her tired old body was capable of producing, washed down her face.

It was such a relief. It felt like something tight and angry was unknotting. The tears soaked into her shirt, her nose ran. She didn't even care.

The girl kept holding her hand. Far from being oppressive, Alice's presence felt like the key that had unlocked this pain. It was a balm to have someone look at her with such concern. Alice's hand was so consoling. When was the last time Henri or one of the boys had touched her in order to comfort? It was so tiring to keep people at bay all of the time. The relief of letting someone in felt so good.

Élise's sobs abated. Seeing that her crying was easing, the girl stood and went to the back of the room to get a glass of water from the sink. This gave Élise some time to compose herself. She wiped her eyes, sat up straight, and took a deep breath. She acknowledged the water with a nod.

Alice put her hand on her shoulder. It reminded Élise of the time at La Rosière when a snow finch had landed on her arm. It had sat there for a moment, tiny and magical, the barest presence, before flying off into the mountain sky.

Alice asked her no questions, but let her hand linger, conveying all it needed through touch. Élise appreciated the girl's restraint. God knows that if it had been Lily who had caught her in such a moment of weakness, Élise would be subjected to hundreds of solicitous questions and demands that she head home immediately. As if there would be any solace waiting for her there. Just blank stares and dirty underwear.

Élise straightened her spine. She nodded once more at Alice and turned back to the computer. The younger woman understood. She hesitated one moment, gave her arm a final squeeze, and then said, as if nothing untoward had happened, "If anyone is looking for me, I'll be at the Richelieu Library."

Élise blew her nose vigorously. "Good day, Aliyeh." It was the first time she had used the younger woman's real name.

CHAPTER 23

Volley of Shots

ALICE HADN'T THOUGHT ANYTHING WOULD PUSH HER IMPATIENCE to learn more about the Honeybee Emeralds from the front of her mind, but Mme Boucher weeping was an event of stupendous enough proportions to do just that. What had troubled the older woman so profoundly that caused her to break down? Her sobs had been tragic, and Alice's heart softened at the memory. She hadn't known what to do as Mme Boucher cried, and only hoped that she hadn't exacerbated the woman's obvious woes.

Alice dashed up the métro steps. She'd made a quick detour to La Banque Populaire to check on the necklace, and now she was heading to the library. Although Mme Boucher hadn't explained herself, Alice could bet on the cause. In her limited experience, that kind of crying was always the result of a broken heart. Mme Boucher was unhappy in love, and Alice's jaw clenched at the thought of her husband hurting the stalwart lady in such a profound way.

Thoughts of Mme Boucher's love life faded when she pushed through the double doors into the Richelieu. The reference librarian smiled at her. Alice was starting to establish a presence here. She took her usual seat and awaited the arrival of the boxes of correspondence. She hoped to have some good information to report to the Fellowship today. Half of them had traipsed off to the Loire without even giving her a heads up. She tried not to worry that meant she wasn't a full member of the team.

As soon as the boxes were delivered, she forgot her insecurities and dove back in to where she had left off yesterday afternoon. She read Adeline's account of events from the moment when Charles Leboeuf mentioned his gift of the Honeybee Emeralds to Mata Hari.

'Margaretha loved that necklace, just as, I believe, she loved me. Foolishly, I thought her working for the Deuxième Bureau would be a way for us to stay together. I didn't understand it would be her doom.'

The poor man, his face normally so dignified and reserved, crumbled at this. Josephine snapped her fingers at me, indicating that I should bring him a whiskey. He downed it in one gulp, and continued talking.

Explaining that his superiors were delighted with this new recruit, he spoke of how Mata Hari had access to all the wealthiest officials in Spain, Germany, the Netherlands, and France. She was a Dutch citizen and Holland was neutral, which meant that she could move more freely than most. What's more, with her dance engagements and high-placed lovers scattered across Europe, she was able to travel without arousing suspicion. The Deuxième Bureau wanted her to gather intelligence about what the Germans were planning, with the ultimate goal of seducing Wilhelm, Crown Prince of Germany. According to M. Leboeuf, somehow the Kaiser and his men realized that Mata Hari was working for the Deuxième Bureau, and they made it appear as if they had recruited her to their cause. They placed payments in her bank account and planted incriminating letters in her rooms. In short, it was a frame-up.

M. Leboeuf's tale was so extraordinary that I began jotting down shorthand notes of what he was saying so I could convey his exact phrasing to you, dear Francis.

M. Leboeuf continued: 'When the suspicions that she was a double agent came to light, I defended her to my colleagues.

I told them she would never betray France, but my superiors didn't believe me. I was driven wild with fear. But if I made a public defense of her, the whole Dame Blanche network would be exposed. That was too great a risk—hundreds of lives were at stake, as well as our greatest sources of information about German movements. I couldn't do that.'

Here M. Leboeuf looked down, his eyes filling with tears, his shoulders slumped. His voice was barely above a whisper. 'Instead, I watched the woman I loved condemned as a traitor.'

Jo rose and placed her hands around his shaking shoulders. 'You did the best you could,' she crooned, comforting him as I had seen her do with such gentleness to the animals she loved, whether teacup poodles or that infernal cheetah.

M. Leboeuf drew courage from Josephine's caress, and continued. 'I could not even attend the trial, for fear of exposing my connections to the espionage ring. I know she looked for me amongst the spectators, but I failed her. She had no friendly faces in that audience of angry, war-weary Frenchmen. Her defense was a farce. Her lawyer was not even allowed to cross-examine witnesses. The officials wanted her dead, and they made sure of the outcome.'

His voice cracked, but he blew his nose and carried on. 'I missed her trial,' he said resolutely, 'but I was there for her execution. I went to the Caserne de Vincennes, the army barracks where she was killed. I saw her—she was beautifully dressed in a thick black cloak with a rich fur ruff and a fashionable black felt hat with satin bow. I was glad she looked so beautiful. I knew that would give her comfort. She refused a blindfold. Twelve soldiers pointed rifles at her. One gun was loaded with a blank, but no one knew which. This is called the conscience round and ensures that each shooter can believe that they were not responsible for the death. The captain raised his sword and lowered it decisively. A volley of shots echoed. I forced myself to watch as she sank slowly to her knees, weaving there for a moment. Our gazes locked, and I tried to convey my love and sorrow. Then she fell backward and was no more.' He paused and closed his eyes before speaking again. 'I will forever carry the image of her beautiful form, prone on the earth, never to dance again.'

The room was silent. Then M. Leboeuf roused himself, as if remembering something. 'After her arrest, before the trial, I went to her apartments. I was part of the force that searched her rooms. No one at the Deuxième Bureau knew of our relationship. I was looking for the necklace. I couldn't bear for it to be pawed over and then disappear in some evidence room, or worse be "lost." I knew that during wartime even my colleagues weren't immune to the "sticky fingers" in your parlance. At the time, I thought I would return the necklace to her when she was exonerated. That day, alas, never came.'

M. Leboeuf withdrew something from his pocket. It was a beautiful thing—a double strand of diamonds with a central pendant in the shape of a honeybee. Two gorgeous emeralds were inlaid on the wings. Very unusual. I could see Josephine was pleased by it.

'This necklace belonged to my mother. She was once a performer, an actress. I gave it to Margaretha, but sadly, she only owned it for a short while. Now I would be honored if you, my dear Mademoiselle Baker, accepted it. Like my mother, like Margaretha, you seduce Paris with your talents. I can think of no greater spirit—a fighter, a champion of justice, a lover of France—to have it.'

Josephine sank to her knees in front of the old man (you know how she loves a dramatic gesture), but I must admit that even I teared up at the humble way she thanked him for the gift.

'Thank you, Charles,' Josephine said. 'I pledge here and now to be worthy of this necklace, and the courage of my predecessor.'

I think of all the minks, diamonds, cars, and even homes that have been lavished upon her from millionaires, sheiks, and geniuses . . . of all of those gifts, I believe this necklace might mean the most to her.

I said at the beginning of this letter that I think it might be our last visit from M. Leboeuf for a while. He has been called back from retirement. The Deuxième Bureau needs him again. He claims that the German nation is once more mobilizing for war and has urged Jo to leave Paris sooner rather than later. I only hope that his worries prove unfounded.

Alice raised her head. There was the proof that the necklace had gone to Josephine. They had their link. Emperor Napoleon III to Josephine Baker, via Mata Hari. This was going to be an amazing story. Lily was going to go absolutely mad, or as she herself might say, "batshit frigging bananas."

Madrid, December 1916

Margaretha was glad to have a break from the gray chill and dark days of Paris, though she did miss dear Charles. Madrid was brighter, warmer, and friendlier. Parisians were becoming increasingly suspicious of foreigners. The Great War ground on. The terrible trench warfare of the Somme, followed by the hard-fought battles of Verdun, had taken a toll on the population. At least in Madrid, there were no soldiers in the street, no limping war wounded.

As the conflict dragged on, it was becoming difficult to move through the neutral territories. Dear Charles's connections helped, of course. The Deuxième Bureau wanted her to have a glittering social life, traveling to all the best locales, dining out in the best restaurants, wearing the latest designer frocks, flirting with the most senior German officials. It was a difficult job, but someone had to do it.

Tonight, she was having a late supper with Arnold Kalle. One of those frightfully enthusiastic Prussians, Herr Arnie, as she playfully called him, had a direct line to Crown Prince William. Her ultimate mission was to seduce the prince. When she was feeling tired or defeated, she worried that she wouldn't be able to manage it. She was nearing forty, after all. Perhaps her days as Mata Hari, exotic dancer, effortless seductress, were over. What if she managed to secure a meeting with the prince and that jaded playboy found her too dull or, worse indeed, too fat?

No. That was not the way to think. Vile Rudolph had promised that she'd be allowed to visit with Jeanne the next time she was in Amsterdam. It had been over a year since she had seen her daughter. She was squirreling the Deuxième Bureau payments away; those, as well as the gorgeous necklace that Charles had given her, would be enough to cover another round of legal fees. On her next trip to Amsterdam, she would spirit Jeanne away and then fight to keep her legally.

She adjusted the strap of her satin evening dress and reached for her fox stole. From her jewelry bag, she withdrew the honeybee necklace. It had become her talisman. With Charles's necklace around her neck, she felt she would be able to do whatever was necessary. When the time came, it would bring her back her daughter. For now, it would simply bring her good luck.

CHAPTER 24

Color TV

DAPHNE PRODUCED HER READER CARD AND WAS ABOUT TO breeze past the sleepy security guard at the Bibliothèque Nationale's Mitterrand building when the elderly man stood up from behind his desk. "Non, non mademoiselle," he called.

Daphne paused and assumed a haughty look; she was going to have to bluff this one out. "A problem, monsieur?" she asked in French. "My pass is up to date." She flashed the card again. She didn't want him—or anyone—dwelling on the photograph. The image was taken in darkest January and she looked washed out.

The guard wasn't interested in her photo, however. "The child, you can't bring the boy in."

They both looked down at Theo. His shirt was untucked, his shoelace was undone, and there must have been an old juice box kicking around the back of the car, because he was dribbling it onto the gleaming floor. A thin line of snot, the reason he wasn't at school today, leaked from his nose. She grabbed the juice box and briskly wiped his nose with a Kleenex.

Most areas of this huge complex, which was part of the Bibliothèque Nationale suite of facilities, were open to everyone, but children under sixteen were forbidden on the Haut-de-Jardin level. A rule wasn't necessarily an impediment, however. Daphne had lived in France long enough to know that this could play out in one of two ways. The guard could rigidly enforce the rules—there was nothing the French loved more than a bureaucratic decree they were in charge of administering. Yet that sense of officious entitlement could also work in her favor.

She'd once been on a crowded city bus when the driver mistakenly deviated from the route, taking the wrong street. When the people around her complained, instead of apologizing and correcting his error, the bus driver doubled down. He turned on the passengers, shouting furiously, "My bus, my route!" It was that sense of small fiefdom that she was now relying on. French bureaucrats loved bending the rules when it suited them. Plus, Parisians, for all of their self-importance, genuinely loved small children, and Theo, despite his current condition (Good lord, was he now blowing his nose in his sleeve?), was a cute kid.

"Can't my son come up with me?" she asked. "I have nowhere else to send him." Daphne had used Theo's slight cold as an excuse to absent herself from work, but she didn't think he'd be harmed by a few hours of research. She wondered what Lily, Jacob, and Luc were uncovering in Chinon. She was determined to come up with some good information today. The threat of Yvette's scoop was all too real.

The guard initially remained adamant in his refusal, but after Daphne wheedled a little longer, he relented with the magnanimity of an emperor granting a stay of execution.

"Come on," she said, hustling Theo along before the guard changed his mind. "This is going to be fun."

They squirreled themselves away in the dark, overly warm microfilm center. The hum of the dozen microfilm readers created a muted buzz, making it feel as if a creature were actually alive in the room. Over the course of her education and career, Daphne had spent a lot of time in rooms like this, carefully threading the film through machines in order to see photographed images of text pop up on the screen in front of her. More and more microfilm was being digitized, and while she appreciated the convenience of having everything online, she did mourn the experience of coming to this kind of room. It was quiet, people were deeply concentrated on their subjects, but there was a thrill when you found something relevant to your research. She was glad to share this with Theo.

They scrolled through hundreds of pages of newspapers from the 1920s to the 1960s, looking for mentions of Josephine Baker and, more specifically, of her jewelry. The more Daphne learned about Josephine, the more fascinated she became. This woman had left America to remake herself and spent her entire life striving for greater success, greater love, greater adulation. Josephine wasn't the best dancer or strongest singer, but she triumphed on the stage. She was terrible at managing money, burning through it at a ridiculous rate; no matter, she just made more. Unable to have children, she didn't just adopt one baby, but a whole tribe. She was selfish and egotistical, but she had friends and lovers falling over themselves for her because she was also generous, interesting, and wild. Many biographies described her as a seeker—always looking for the next thing. Driven by a restlessness, it made Josephine Baker difficult, but it also made her a star.

Unfortunately, while Daphne uncovered many stories of Josephine's excesses, she didn't spot any mentions or images of the necklace. Theo started out like a champ—learning to thread the machine and delighting in the whirl of images as they scrolled through the old newspapers. This had lasted about half an hour, after which he became squirmy. Luckily, Daphne was not an amateur at this parenting business and produced a coloring book of dinosaurs and some Lego men. At the hour and a half mark, she brought out the big guns and handed over her smartphone, with the promise of pizza from the café as soon as they finished.

By hour two, even the allure of PixelArt on her iPhone had faded. Theo splayed out on the floor, drawing on the back sheet of his coloring book. He was humming Josephine Baker's signature song, "J'ai Deux Amours."

Daphne stretched, ready to call it a day. They hadn't found anything. Hopefully the others were having better luck. "What are you making, sweetie?" she asked Theo.

He looked up. He'd sketched a picture of a woman standing next to a box, her black hair piled up on top of her head. He'd colored her skin brown. Her neck was long and elongated, and hanging from it was the Honeybee Emeralds.

"That's very good," Daphne cooed. The child was a genius. He'd only seen the necklace twice. Once back at the *Bonjour Paris* offices when they'd started out on this adventure, and then when they'd watched the documentary and she'd shown him the photo on her phone, yet he'd captured it perfectly. She was going to have forceful words with Miss Lucy at the school. She refused to take Daphne's assertion that Theo should be in the gifted class seriously, but this drawing was proof. Obviously, he had superior visual memory. "You remembered that necklace from our visit with Lily, right, sweetie?" she asked.

Theo looked at her blankly.

"Or was it when we watched the documentary? I showed you the photograph." She pulled out her phone with the image of Josephine wearing the necklace that had been hanging on *Bonjour Paris*'s wall.

"No, it was in the big picture we looked at today. The one from the singing lady's house." He continued drawing the box beside the woman, and Daphne realized it was a television.

Her excited pride dimmed. "That's not possible, sweetie." They hadn't seen an image of the necklace today. Furthermore, Josephine would never be wearing the necklace, standing next to a television—those weren't popularized until after the war, by which time the Honeybee Emeralds had been confiscated by the Nazis.

Theo shrugged. "I saw the necklace in the picture, Mommy. I saw it today."

He sounded so sure, and he did have quite a good visual memory. Should be in the gifted class, etc. Had she somehow missed the necklace? Theo was only looking at images with her for the initial half hour of research. She looked through the pile of reels and threaded in one of the first they had viewed.

She found the image in an article on Josephine from 1966. It was in the color supplement, and everything was rendered in bright hues despite the fact that both age and the microfilming process had faded the cheap newspaper ink. The article was a puff piece about the work Josephine was doing at her château, Les Milandes, to make it a tourist destination.

It included many photographs of Josephine around the estate. Shots of her with her herd of sheep and of the chapel she had had moved to the grounds stone by stone. There was a group photograph of her staff, more than fifty people lined up in neat rows—gardeners, maids, shepherds, cooks, nannies. The singer had hired an army to bring her vision to life in the French countryside. No wonder she'd gone bankrupt. Then, there it was, a big double-page spread from the center of the supplement. Josephine Baker standing proudly in her living room, next to her color television. This was still a major technological advancement in rural France, and a full paragraph extolled its wonders.

Daphne leaned in closer. Josephine was not wearing any jewelry. "Is this the picture you drew?" she asked Theo, more sharply than she would have liked.

He stood up and peered at the image. "Yes," he said happily. "I told you, Mommy."

"There's no necklace in this picture, sweetie." She was annoyed with herself that she had gotten excited. "She's not wearing any jewelry."

"There it is," Theo said. He pointed to a low table next to the television that held a number of jewelry boxes. Daphne enlarged that portion of the image, zooming in. A large diamond ring twinkled from the table next to a huge panther brooch with glittering red ruby eyes and there, at the very edge, was their necklace. The honeybee motif was unmistakable. The emeralds shone bright green.

How was this possible? She checked the date of the newspaper article again. 1966. Had the Nazis not confiscated the necklace? No, the Art Looting Investigation Unit database clearly listed it as stolen. The necklace had been taken, but perhaps it had also been recovered. These things happened. In fact, that was Daphne's entire job—recording the losses and recoveries. When artwork was found again, however, the relevant databases were updated. Unless no one had reported its return. Josephine was in serious financial trouble after the war. She was on the verge of bankruptcy countless times. Eventually Les Milandes was repossessed for a fraction of its value. She died in massive debt.

Could Josephine have recovered the necklace but failed to declare its return? It would make sense if the necklace had been insured against theft. Insurance fraud was an unseemly fact of Daphne's job.

Well, however it happened, one thing was clear: Josephine Baker still owned that necklace in 1966. This shifted all of their thinking. If Josephine owned it after the war, then she could have sold it. Perhaps their assumption that her estate was now the owner was wrong. Head spinning, she texted this update to the Fellowship, half of whom were living it up in the Loire Valley today.

As much as she wanted to celebrate this break in their investigation, she'd promised pizza to a five-year-old, and she knew that she had to deliver, or face an outraged meltdown.

The Café du Temps was the Bibliothèque Nationale's bright on-site restaurant. She and Theo sat in comfortable chairs while he demolished his plain pizza. "No pepper-pony, Mommy, it's too spicy!"

The place was humming with activity. A group of attractive young mothers dominated one area, their strollers, bottles, diaper bags, and offspring taking up the central tables. Daphne noticed they all drank soda water or small espressos without milk. Despite what any book might claim, French women were nothing if not calorie conscious. Seeing these young mothers, Daphne recalled her own time with an infant. She received sixteen weeks of maternity leave from the United Nations. Her American friends had drooled with envy, but she couldn't have imagined going back to work any earlier. She'd been a hormone-crazed zombie for the first three months. It was only in the last few weeks of leave that the fog lifted—Theo started sleeping longer, and she remembered deodorant again. At that point, she cleaned herself up, found all the other mommies pushing UPPAbabys and Bugaboos in Jardins Luxembourg, and joined a new gang. That's when her Instagramming really took off; there was something very satisfying about putting out a photograph of a sleeping Theo under a plane tree, the sun dappling perfectly on his cheek. It was a reassuring announcement to the world, and more importantly to herself, that she had figured things out, that she was succeeding, that she had managed to have it all.

In a far corner of the café, five students were arguing passionately. Their scarves were long, their vape pens peeked from their pockets, and every now and then, a word or two of their argument carried over: "Deleuze!" "Barthes!" "Posthumanism!" Listening to them, Daphne felt profound gratitude that she was no longer required to pretend to care about critical theory.

At another table, two professorial types sat hunched over laptops, not speaking. One woman had long gray hair and the kind of shapeless, baggy dress that not even a Parisian could make stylish. The other had an adorable pixie haircut and wore bright-red lipstick. Daphne stared at her, wishing she had the bone structure to pull off that kind of hairdo. She knew, from a regrettable period in her mid-twenties, when she looked like a mulleted hockey player, that she did not. The two were both so intent on their work that Daphne was surprised when the shorter-haired woman leaned over and carefully tucked a strand of her partner's hair behind her ear.

Daphne found herself blinking back tears. This private moment of tenderness was devastatingly touching. It wasn't the love it implied, or the intimacy. What spoke to her was the kindness. She and Philip had lost that over the last year. She couldn't point to one thing—a specific moment where they stopped being loving toward one another. They were both over-worked and their lives were overscheduled. The safest place to lash out about all of their job and parenting stress was at each other. Their marriage was like a complicated machine with many moving parts—Theo, sex, career, commute, work travel, groceries, in-laws, bills, house repairs, and a dozen other stressors. Somewhere along the way the lubricant that kept all of those pieces moving well together—the small thoughtful gestures, the words of encouragement or love, the little gift that signaled you were thinking of the other person—all those moments dried up. Now the machinery of their marriage ground on, but with nothing to grease the gears, the parts were wearing out. The rate of deterioration was increasing, and soon the thing might fall apart. At least then the noise would stop. Did Philip feel that too? Was he preparing to flee? Daphne dabbed at her eyes with a Kleenex.

She gave a shaky sigh. "Theo, sweetie," she said. He looked up, and she swung her head close to his, snapping a selfie. She assessed the image.

The lighting was good, not great; she'd have to erase the crow's feet. Her hair was fine. Theo had a smear of pizza sauce on his cheek. She'd leave it, because it was cute and made the photo seem more natural. Her fingers hovered over the phone—what to caption? "Sick day at the Bibliothèque Nationale"? No, that might generate questions about what she was doing. What about "Mommy and Theo time"? That wasn't very interesting. Something about pizza? "Eating the za"? No, that was stupid. She put her phone down without posting anything.

Instead, she bit into her croissant and tried to take pleasure in the white, clean modernity of the café. This is what all the major cultural heritage institutions had realized: in order to pull researchers away from their computers and make them discover all that had not yet been digitized, you had to lure them on-site. You did that not with the richness of your holdings, but with the flakiness of your pastry crust and the Scandinavian inspiration of your design aesthetic. Daphne was pleased with this new approach. She had spent grad school working in institutions that had not yet received that all-important memo. At one archive with no café, there had not even been a restaurant within ten blocks. She was forced to subsist on hot dogs dispensed from a vending machine. You'd drop ninety-five cents into the slot and then wait for the "plop" as the wiener and bun fell onto the dispenser. That sound, the defeated smush of a hot dog landing, could be the soundtrack to grad school drudgery. The horrors didn't end there. Once you had secured your dog, you were meant to microwave your meal in a machine that had not been cleaned since the first George Bush was president. Things were better now. Researchers had more amenities, and Daphne, as a woman who liked amenities, was pleased.

"Did you know Josephine Baker had twelve children?" she asked Theo. "She was a very famous dancer in Paris, but she was from America."

"Like you," Theo said.

"Yes, and like you," Daphne agreed.

"I'm from America?" he asked.

"Yes, honey. Daddy and I are both American. You are too."

She thought again of that last month of maternity leave, when Theo was sleeping through the night. She wasn't working, commuting, or stressing. Instead, she spent her days with her baby, going to parks, puttering around, planning elaborate meals. She had space and time and kindness for Philip when he got home.

Another baby. Maybe that's what their marriage needed. Philip used to say that he wanted a "brood"—an expression that conjured an image of a sow with piglets. Still, one more child, a tiny baby carrying all the hope and possibility that her marriage was missing. Maybe that was the answer.

Her mind churning with the possibility, Daphne stared absentmindedly at a well-dressed woman crossing the café. She wore the most adorable pair of By Far Este crocodile ankle boots. They went beautifully with her tan Givenchy trench. Daphne was impressed; the woman was tiny, but able to carry off the large coat without it overwhelming her. She had seen this woman recently at another library. Yvette Dufeu had looked put together and confident at the Richelieu. She moved with even more assurance now, striding through the café, a large biography of Napoleon III tucked under her arm and two young interns trailing behind.

CHAPTER 25

The Grape Flower

EVEN AFTER THE LONG TRAIN JOURNEY, LILY STILL COULDN'T quite believe she was in the Loire Valley with this random assemblage of people. She, Luc, Jacob, and Marie-Pierre sat at a cute café by the river Vienne, contemplating their lunch order. Thursdays in early May were apparently quiet in Chinon, because they were the only ones at the restaurant.

Their train trip had been uneventful. Luc had indeed sprung for first-class tickets, which Jacob had pointedly refused, paying for his and Marie-Pierre's seats himself. Luc had immediately disappeared into his work laptop, while Lily tried to work on the rest of the June issue. *Tried* was the operative word, because there were many muffled giggles and a few unpleasant kissing sounds coming from Jacob and Marie-Pierre, who sat in the seats behind her.

Surprisingly, Jacob's girlfriend was a rather plain woman, with brown hair and eyes, a large-ish nose, and of middling height. She was dressed in some kind of boho French style, involving lots of linen and big gold bangles. She certainly looked put together and interesting, but the way Jacob had talked about her, Lily expected her to be a flipping Aphrodite. The depth of Jacob's passion for Marie-Pierre had actually blinded him to the fact that she was a regular-looking woman. This was somehow even more depressing than if Marie-Pierre had been drop-dead gorgeous.

Lily was glad to have left the train, and pleased with the spot they had picked for lunch. The ancient fortress loomed above them, a reminder of the town's strategic place in medieval France, but the swans swimming placidly in the river weren't troubled by old battles. Sparrows tweeted a springtime song from a nearby lilac bush.

They placed their orders with the café's waiter, and Lily turned to Marie-Pierre: "Jacob tells me you're a lawyer?" Jacob's hand was resting lightly on Marie-Pierre's thigh. Their intimacy was obvious, the way their bodies curved toward each other as if pulled by magnetic force. They had that new-lovers vibe. Outwardly, they were smiling and talking to her, but she could see that inwardly they wanted to find a bed and rip each other's clothes off. "That must be interesting for you." The faintest note of sarcasm edged into her voice, and Lily hated herself for it.

"Oh, it's terribly boring. I opened my own real estate law firm so that I could maintain a good work-life balance. I do love to travel."

Her English was adorable, with that wonderful French accent making even the most banal statement seem exotic and somehow sexy.

"And that's how you met Jacob, in New York?" Lily confirmed. Jacob had, of course, already regaled her with the story of their meeting in a Manhattan bookstore. Who even dated without the internet anymore? Jacob was literally the only person she knew who had met a partner IRL.

"Yes, it was serendipity," Marie-Pierre said.

Jacob smiled, listening to the conversation, while Luc looked on. Disconcertingly her boss was wearing a T-shirt and jeans paired with a leather jacket, rather than his usual suit. Without his business uniform, he seemed younger and more approachable.

"Wonderful," Lily said. "Have you lived in Paris your whole life?"

"No," the other woman said, shaking her head. "Like so many, I am a transplant. I am actually from"—her voice dropped to a whisper as she glanced at Luc—"Brussels."

"A Belgian!" Lily exclaimed in surprise.

"Shh," Marie-Pierre said in mock horror. "We don't want to attract attention. Luc may turn on me if he realizes I am a Belge!"

Her boss smiled. "I knew the instant you spoke, mademoiselle. Your accent is charming."

While Jacob frowned at this little flirtation, Lily mused that she still hadn't cracked the various rivalries and snobberies that were sewn through European life as tightly as threads in the Bayeux Tapestry. She did know that the French considered the Belgians to be coarser, less sophisticated, and maybe even a little bit stupid.

"How do you sink a Belgian submarine?" Marie-Pierre asked.

"How," asked Lily, disconcerted.

"Just knock," Marie-Pierre replied with a smile. Luc and Jacob laughed. "Trust me," Marie-Pierre said, "I've heard them all."

Lily smiled. "That's terrible," she said. She could see why Jacob was attracted to Marie-Pierre. She was effortlessly confident and quite entertaining.

Marie-Pierre shrugged. "Eh, it could be worse; we could be at war with one another."

Lily poured herself a glass of champagne. Her heightened awareness of an attraction to Jacob had come at a very awkward time. She was literally sitting in front of him as he and Marie-Pierre intertwined their arms to sip bubbly from their own glasses.

"You'll spill it all," she said sharply, but the couple ignored her and took their drink amid much giggling.

Lily downed her own glass and refilled her flute. She just needed to get through today. She glanced at Luc and put her glass down. They may be outside the office, but she needed to remain professional.

Marie-Pierre and Jacob's friskiness subsided when their meals arrived. Lily focused on her food, and indeed, it was sublime—the steak cooked to tender perfection and the french fries the perfect mixture of salty crunch. A small green salad, enough to feel virtuous, but not so much that she felt like a rabbit, completed the meal. If she concentrated on her food, she was almost able to push unwanted thoughts away and enjoy herself.

Lily's phone chimed. Alice was at the Richelieu Library for more Mata Hari research. She had no updates as of yet, but was going to keep a sharp eye out for Yvette. There had been no sighting of her since Tuesday, but Yvette was obviously—probably?—after their story. The juiciness of the article was now a double-edged . . . melon? If Yvette scooped them with this—Napoleon III's blingy necklace, worn by Mata Hari and Josephine Baker and then stolen by Nazis—they'd be blown out of the water.

They needed a win today. Their interviewee was a winemaker on the outskirts of Chinon. The plan was for the Fellowship members to rent bikes and cycle out the half hour to meet with him, while Marie-Pierre stayed behind and explored the historic center. Luc had raised an eyebrow at the idea of renting bikes, but had come around when Jacob had boasted of his mountain biking skills.

"Should we get a move on?" Lily asked the men as they sat back after eating.

"Sure thing," Jacob said, and reached over to give Marie-Pierre a kiss. Lily's stomach knotted with jealousy. She wanted someone, anyone, to care for her as solicitously as Jacob did for Marie-Pierre. Maybe it was time she dove back into the dating pool, although her latest swims in those waters had not been productive.

The Fellowship members had been scrupulous not to discuss the Honeybee Emeralds in front of Marie-Pierre. Lily wasn't sure what Jacob had told her about the article, or what they were up to, but the other woman seemed uninterested. Lily could only assume he hadn't spilled the beans.

The trio left Marie-Pierre and picked up their bikes, immediately embarking on the trail to Montsoreau. Like most Parisians, Lily had occasionally used the bike-sharing system, Vélib', to get around town, but dodging buses and scooters while whizzing through roundabouts was a different experience than cycling down a dedicated pathway along the river. Jacob and Luc immediately entered into a silent but ferocious race, and they sped away from her down the path.

She stared after them for a moment, and then her mind returned to her worries. How had Yvette found out about the Honeybee Emeralds? Was it Daphne and her manic social media posting? Jacob blurting something out to Marie-Pierre? Alexander was unlikely since he barely spoke two words at a time. Alice was equally quiet, although she was a bit jumpy lately. The other day, the intern had been quite cagey about getting to work late. She'd stammered out some excuse about a métro delay and blushed. Then again, Alice blushed at everything.

Lily pedaled on. The light glinted off the water, the banks were bursting with springtime flowers, the songbirds flitted from tree to tree, tweeting merrily above her head. The only thing missing from this perfect, romantic scene was a Disney bunny hopping past with hearts for eyes. Lily inhaled the sweet air and began to enjoy herself. Why shouldn't she relax?

She rounded a corner and saw both Luc and Jacob standing with their bikes, sweaty and glowering at one another, waiting for her. She didn't ask who won. They left the path and spent a hair-raising five minutes zipping down the side of a busy highway, which at least forced the two men to go slowly. At last, they turned off onto a long driveway indicated by a sign reading Domaine du Taureau. They cycled up the drive, surrounded by hills covered in well-ordered grapevines.

They parked their bikes in front of an old stone farmhouse. Clematis vines climbed up along the side of the building and a burst of lush pink roses festooned a big bush by the front door. A line of white linens flapped in the breeze. The air smelled fresh. A beagle came bounding out of a nearby barn to greet them, its bark announcing their arrival. Daphne would love this. It was Instagram heaven.

The door opened and a smiling sixty-something woman in jeans and a work shirt came out. "You must be from the magazine," she said to them in French. "I am Denise Latendresse." She extended her hand. Lily translated for Jacob and made her own introductions, apologizing for her shaky accent.

"Not at all," Denise said in French. "I'm delighted you speak my language. Come, my husband, Pascal, is working on the north field. We can walk up and see him."

Lily translated, and the four of them made their way through the vineyard. The individual grapevines looked like trees, carefully trained to have two major "arms" sticking out about chest height. Denise explained that this was the optimal shape for a high-yield harvest and had been developed over centuries of trial and error. The vines themselves had only started to bud with new green leaves.

"They are waking from their winter sleep," Denise said. She had a pleasantly low voice. "In a few weeks they will be in flower; it is very hard to see the blossoms, and most people don't care so much for them. It is the grapes that matter, after all."

Lily translated as the Frenchwoman spoke.

"I love the flowering, though," Denise said. "The aroma—it is very special."

"Ask her what it smells like," urged Jacob. He was always curious about the world around him; it was what made him such a good writer.

Denise stopped at the question, her brow furrowed as she considered her answer. She spoke slowly. "The scent is delicate, but sweet. It is like a pear warmed in the sun or a clutch of violets."

Lily concentrated on finding the right words to convey Denise's meaning. Jacob asked several follow-up questions, and they had a detailed conversation about the process of winemaking. Lily knew that most of this probably wouldn't make it into the article, but Jacob wanted the background to convey a sense of place. She admired his thoroughness.

Farther up the vineyard hill they encountered Pascal, a burly man, older than Denise, and dressed in overalls and a plaid shirt. His English was quite good, and for a few moments they discussed the farm as they surveyed the view. Luc surprised her by being quite knowledgeable about French agricultural practices. When she looked at him curiously, he shrugged. "A couple of years ago my bank invested heavily in a company specializing in organic root crops."

She smiled, having a hard time imagining the urbane Luc as a farmer.

He met her smile and grinned back, Lily noticing the small dimple in his left cheek for the first time. "I am now quite an expert in beetroot," he murmured, and she laughed aloud.

Jacob glanced over at them, frowning. Lily turned her attention to the view. They were at the highest point of the property. The soft hills of the Loire Valley dipped before them, the carefully regimented grapevines lined up like small soldiers, their leaves unfurling in the sunshine. Far off, on a hill rising in the west, was a château, its peaked roof looking like something out of a fairy tale.

Turning from the view, Jacob broached the topic of Josephine Baker.

Pascal squared his shoulders, as if recalling the past required fortification. His eyes stayed trained on the view. "She adopted my younger brother in the early 1960s," he said.

"Were you in foster care?" Jacob asked.

Pascal shook his head. "No, we were poor village children in a forgotten part of France. He was three years old, with a head of white-blond hair and piercing green eyes. She noticed him playing in the village square and that was it. She was like the queen, selecting one of her peasant subjects. She had to have him for herself."

"But that's insane—it's feudal," Lily exclaimed.

Pascal smiled wryly. "I wouldn't say postwar rural France was feudal, but we were struggling. My parents saw it as a boon. A chance for him to have a better life."

"As I explained in my email, we're trying to trace a particular necklace that Josephine might have worn." Jacob handed his phone to Pascal, letting him see the photographs they'd taken of the Honeybee Emeralds.

The winemaker frowned. "She had this huge estate, Les Milandes, in the Dordogne. It was very chaotic there. So many children, all of her exotic animals. She was trying to make a business out of it, but it was always on the verge of bankruptcy. Staff came and went, a revolving door. We visited a couple of times. I missed my little brother. The mansion was like nothing I had ever seen. Filled with beautiful treasures." Pascal shook his head. "I don't remember that necklace, however."

The image Pascal conjured, of a glamorous woman, a touch divorced from reality, trying to remake the world in a way that suited her, seemed quixotic and tragic.

"Do you recognize this photograph?" Lily asked. She showed him her phone with the image of Josephine wearing the necklace, taken from the wall at *Bonjour Paris*.

Pascal shook his head. "No, I've never seen this."

"Are you sure?" Jacob asked.

Pascal smiled wryly. "Trust me. I've had a fascination with Mme Baker my whole life. It took me a long time to stop wondering why she didn't choose me that day she swept into our village."

Lily heard a wistfulness in Pascal's voice. What was it like to define your life by one moment, the instant when you were not chosen? There was a whole novel packed into his one sad sentence. Unfortunately, Pascal didn't have any useful intel about the necklace. Lily tried not to think about Yvette and what information she might have about the Honeybee Emeralds. Was she preparing her article right now as they lolled around the Loire on a fool's errand?

They walked down the hill as a group. At the house, Pascal and Denise insisted on giving them a bottle of the new red they had just vinted. The sun was starting to fade in the west as the three returned to their bikes.

Jacob checked in with Marie-Pierre, who said she was touring a château and not to hurry back. Since their train wasn't leaving until that night, Luc suggested they nip into the nearby town center to pick up some food for the ride. As luck would have it, the weekly market was winding down. They filled their bike baskets with bread, meats, local cheese, olives, and some apples. They continued on the path toward Chinon until they found a spot under a large weeping willow. The afternoon was ending and golden light now glistened off the river. The state of mellowness cheered Lily. Despite the absence of hard information on the necklace, the interview with Pascal Latendresse had gone well. Lily knew that Jacob would weave a compelling story with the details they had gleaned.

They sat beneath the willow, with their backs against the tree, and spread out their food on the scarf that Lily had been wearing. The bread was fresh and chewy, and combined with the strong cheese, salty olives, and crisp apples, it felt like a decadent feast.

Luc opened the wine, and they realized with a laugh that they didn't have glasses.

Lily reached for the bottle and took a sip directly from it. She gave a sigh of appreciation.

Jacob grinned. "Reminds me of our college years," he said.

She passed him the bottle and he took a swig. "Wow, that's good," he said.

It was Luc's turn, and he carefully wiped the bottle with a handkerchief before taking a sip and nodding.

She and Jacob talked about the possibilities the story afforded. "It's going to be fantastic," he promised. Jacob paused, and it seemed as if he was picking his words carefully. "You know, you could be writing this one," he said to Lily. "You've got so much talent. I never understood why you stopped."

Luc, who had been making himself a little sandwich of baguette and prosciutto, looked up with interest.

"I didn't stop," she said defensively. She didn't want to talk about this, definitely not in front of Luc.

"Didn't you?" Jacob asked.

She drew her knees up to her chest, hugging them. "I have to earn a living, so that kind of intense writing takes a back seat."

"Come on," Jacob chided, using a gentle tone that set her teeth on edge. "Aren't those just excuses? Are you afraid of trying?"

God, she much preferred the self-involved pre-girlfriend Jacob to this patronizing armchair psychologist.

Thankfully, Luc spoke before Lily had to reply. "Marie-Pierre seems like a very nice woman," he said.

If Jacob was startled by the abrupt change of topic, he couldn't resist talking about his favorite subject. "She's great," he agreed, nodding grudgingly to Luc. "One of the things I love about her is her competence. Nothing fazes her. She just handles it."

Jacob lay on the grass and stretched out his legs, taking a sip from the bottle. "You know, it's funny, but when I first started seeing Marie-Pierre, she reminded me of you, Lily."

"Really?" she asked, uncertain how to feel about this revelation.

"Yeah, she's confident and has her shit together. Like you used to be—so sure of yourself and who you were going to be. I loved it."

Lily closed her eyes for a moment. The past tense was a kick to the gut. New, new topic.

Jacob looked at his watch. "Oh boy, we'd better be getting back." He stood and began gathering up the picnic mess.

Lily stood.

"There is no hurry for us," Luc spoke.

She looked at him, surprised.

"Our train is not for another two hours. If we go back to Chinon we will just have to hang about the town. This," he gestured to their riverbank, "is much more pleasant."

Lily considered. Returning to Chinon meant watching Jacob and Marie-Pierre make goo-goo eyes at each other. The thought was not appealing. The light was dancing on the water and the air smelled faintly of wisteria. She drank again from the bottle. Velvety and rich. She passed it to Luc. "Fair enough," she said. "Let's stay."

"What?" Jacob asked, looking startled. He'd already wheeled his bike to the path. "You're not coming?"

Lily shook her head. Luc grinned at her, that little dimple making its appearance again. He really was quite charming.

Jacob frowned. "Lily, can I have a word."

Luc raised his eyebrow, but then lay back on the ground, closing his eyes. Lily went to Jacob.

He urged them farther up the path, out of earshot. "I don't think you should stay with him," he whispered.

"What, why not?" Lily laughed.

Jacob glared at Luc's prone body. "I don't trust him."

"Oh, come on, Jacob. Isn't this macho rivalry kind of ridiculous? We're all on the same side."

"Are we?" Jacob asked.

"What do you mean by that?" she demanded.

"Listen, Lily Pad," he said. "I didn't want to have to bring this up, but I need to tell you."

Lily tensed.

Jacob stared into her eyes. "I don't think Luc has been honest with us."

"He's my boss, and he's always treated me fairly," she said impatiently, tired of Jacob's immature dislike.

"I did some nosing around. A bit of investigating," Jacob said.

"Of Luc?" Lily whispered, lowering her voice to make sure he didn't overhear. "You investigated my boss? He could fire me for this." Lily's heart pounded in her ears. How dare Jacob jeopardize her job.

"Don't worry, I was discreet."

This was so typical of Jacob. Arrogant, dismissive of her feelings, sure he was in the right. "I'm not going to listen to any more of this," she said, turning to go.

Jacob grabbed her arm, lowering his voice to hiss at her. "If Seguin is such a great guy, why didn't he tell us that he and Yvette Dufeu used to be in a relationship?"

"What?" Lily demanded. Luc and Yvette dated? It was weirdly hard for her brain to process that piece of information. It was literally not computing.

Jacob met her gaze, his face telegraphing his concerns. Her friend was many things—self-involved, complacent—but he was not a liar. "A couple of people confirmed it to me yesterday. There's more," he said.

Lily stared at him, waiting for the other shoe to drop.

"I saw him texting her yesterday after the Fellowship meeting."

Lily felt a headache begin. Had Luc betrayed them? It made no sense, but why had Luc kept his relationship with Yvette a secret? She glanced over at her boss, dozing under a tree. If he wanted to shut down the magazine, he could. Yet, he had had a relationship with Yvette. Perhaps that was the piece that was so hard to comprehend. Yvette was a conniving manipulator. What did it say about Luc that he had willingly spent time with her? Lily realized that more than her shock or her suspicions, her overriding emotion was disappointment. She had expected more from Luc Seguin, and now she didn't know how to feel about him.

Lily's phone chimed and she realized with a start that she hadn't checked it since lunch at the café. She tapped her text messages. Her smile at Alice's excited message about Mata Hari turned to a scowl when she read Daphne's latest update. If Luc had betrayed the Fellowship to Yvette, she would never forgive him.

CHAPTER 26

Himalayan Salt Butter Tea

A SHARP PAIN PULSED THROUGH LILY'S LEFT TEMPLE, BLOOD pounded in her head, and even the hairs on her arms were standing to attention. Is this what it meant to bristle with anger? She needed to scream at someone to vent all of this emotion, and she was viciously pleased that that someone was going to be Yvette Dufeu.

Ever since last evening, Lily hadn't been able to think about Yvette without wanting to either kick someone or burst into tears. Thanks to Daphne, they knew she was unquestionably moving in on their story. Compound that knowledge with Jacob's revelation about Luc, and it was almost too much.

Last night's train ride back from Chinon had been horrible. Luc was blissfully unaware that anything was amiss, while Lily tormented herself with questions. Why would Luc have told Yvette, when it undermined his own magazine? Why had he lied to them about the nature of his relationship with her? What had he told Yvette? Then the circle of questions began again, Lily unable to escape the loop. Her angst meant she hadn't slept last night. She'd risen this Friday morning with a plan to take action. She might not be able to confront her boss, but she could talk to Yvette.

She and Daphne sat together on the off-white sofa as the morning sun filled *La Vie en Rose*'s sumptuous waiting room. Irritatingly, her friend had cooed with delight when they sank into the couch, murmuring that it was a Pierre Frey, but Lily kept her back ramrod straight. She would not allow herself to relax into the perfectly crafted splendor, or recline into the delightful fluffiness of the wool-cashmere Bella Coola cushions. Daphne, on the other hand, was literally lolling on them. "I think they're goose down," she whispered joyfully.

If she were thinking rationally, Lily could admit that a rivalry with *La Vie en Rose* was to be expected. The expat market was too small to support both magazines. It was natural that they would compete, but there was something about Yvette's personality that made this rivalry so much worse. Yvette was the kind of person who would complain about how hard it was to make women friends, because they were so often "catty."

Anyway, if Luc was capable of dating such a woman, could she really believe that he hadn't sold them all out? She had a lot of respect for her boss's intelligence, but men could be demonstrably stupid when it came to spotting subtle feminine maneuvers. Yvette might profess sweetness and light, but she had the stone-cold heart of an assassin. Every day in the expat magazine business was *The Day of the Jackal*, thanks to Yvette's presence at the top of the heap.

"Would you ladies care for some Perrier or perhaps a Himalayan salt butter tea?" the slim, impossibly tall receptionist with short dreadlocks asked.

"No," Lily snapped before Daphne could get in her order.

They were in the 8th arrondissement, just off Avenue Montaigne in a wealthy neighborhood of beautiful nineteenth-century buildings. Huge bouquets of freesias and lilies filled large urns in discreet alcoves, and the sounds of classical music wafted out of what must be a state-of-the-art sound system. Lily sniffed. This was not what a legitimate house of journalism should look like. It should be frantic and noisy and staffed with ambitious people, hungry to make a difference in the world. People with bad social skills and worse personal hygiene. Certainly the receptionist, her flawless black skin set off to perfection by her tight-fitting gold dress, did not fit the bill for scruffy, impoverished scribe.

"That's a Samy Chalon dress," Daphne whispered as the receptionist returned to her sleek standing desk.

Lily had no idea what that meant, but by Daphne's appreciative look, she assumed it was some trendy designer, probably located in the Marais, who only made dresses in size 0 to size 2.

Lily was seriously regretting bringing her friend. Daphne now had a thick *Italian Vogue* in her lap and was contentedly flicking through the pages. Lily got the impression that Daphne could happily check in for a four-night stay in *La Vie en Rose*'s waiting room. "Hey," Daphne asked idly. "What do you think about Philip and I having another baby? Good idea?"

"What?" Lily asked, startled. She was not in the headspace to think about her friend's marriage.

"A baby," Daphne said, her eyes dreamy. "Maybe that's what we need. I feel an emptiness, like I need more, like life's not enough—"

Before Lily could respond to this alarming train of thought, Yvette Dufeu emerged through a frosted glass door at the far end of the room. She sauntered over to them, totally comfortable in spiky ankle boots that made Lily's feet ache to look at. She wore a simple sheath dress—"Chanel," Daphne whispered at her unhelpfully—accessorized with a heavy gold choker.

Yvette went in for the double kiss, but Lily thrust out her hand for a good old-fashioned handshake. She was starting this meeting on her terms. Yvette hesitated for a moment, and they shook. The other woman's hand was so delicate it reminded Lily of the time she had found a baby bird in the grass behind the old barn. It had fallen from the nest and been so tiny and brittle, she had sensed she could crush it with one squeeze. There had been something intoxicating and terrifying about that feeling of power. Yvette's hand was as fragile as that bird, but she would not be as easy to quash.

"Leelee, such a surprise you should come here this morning," the other woman trilled sweetly. She bared her teeth, but Lily wasn't fooled into thinking it was a smile. "I would invite you back to my office, but I am so terribly busy. Fridays are always a madhouse, and I'm afraid that without an appointment—"

"This won't take long," Lily said curtly. She knew how to handle the Yvettes of the world. They were expert manipulators, but they didn't react well to direct confrontation. Excelling at the passive-aggressive, the actual aggressive overwhelmed them.

"Whatever is the matter?" Yvette asked.

"What's your endgame here?" Lily demanded.

"Why, Leelee, I don't know what you're talking about."

Lily was short, but she felt enormous next to the tiny woman. She drew herself up as tall as she could and leaned toward Yvette, channeling her inner Tony Soprano. "Come on, Yvette. I know you're sniffing around my story."

"What story would that be?" she asked.

She wasn't going to fall into Yvette's trap. "What do you think it is?" she asked.

"I don't know, Leelee, are you writing about how to avoid bedbugs in youth hostels or where Americans can purchase extra-large bottles of Diet Coke?" Her "smile" widened.

Lily didn't rise to her bait. "You know what I'm talking about. Why were you at the Richelieu Library and then at the Bibliothèque Nationale?"

Yvette didn't blink. "Perhaps I will be writing a story about conducting research in Paris."

"Is that what you're doing?" Lily asked sarcastically. Damn, sarcasm was not a weapon of intimidation—it was weaselly and weak. Yvette's wheelhouse.

"No," Yvette said simply.

"We're getting this story, Yvette. Us. *Bonjour Paris*."

"Ah yes, of course. Darling Luc's magazine." Yvette's eyes glittered. "So surprising when he simply didn't sell after Olivia's death . . . sometimes I wonder if he hung on to it because of our past relationship. A way of staying in contact with me." Here was confirmation of Jacob's intel. Why did it still feel like a slap?

Daphne reacted quickly. "So, you and Luc dated." Her friend shrugged. "That's hardly news." The small part of Lily's brain that was working admired Daphne's poker face. She'd always suspected that Daphne herself had once been a Mean Girl. She knew how to play the game.

"Dated? Yvette smiled. "What a quaint American custom. No, no, my dears, we were engaged, or didn't Luc mention that?"

The blood rushed to Lily's head, and she closed her eyes for a moment. Luc must love those fragile, ultrafeminine women, the ones who deprecate their own competence in order to pump up male egos; the ones who tell you they think Robbie Fowler is a loser, only to turn around and go to the Spring Fling with him. The idea that Luc could be attracted to someone like Yvette was maddening. The sex was probably fantastic, she thought sourly.

She would not let Luc's lies distract her now. She had to bring the conversation back to her purpose. "Cut the bullshit. What story are you going after?" Her voice sounded desperate to her ears. She was losing the advantage.

Yvette must have sensed it, because her smile was smug. "An item of jewelry."

Lily's heart jumped in her throat. She felt Daphne tense beside her, and she put her hand warningly on her friend's arm. Yvette noticed the gesture, and Lily was mad at herself. Had she revealed more than she intended?

Now was the time to display a tough stance. "I won't let you steal my story, Yvette. It's not going to happen."

"I can't steal something that does not belong to you," Yvette replied.

"So you admit that we're chasing the same story?" Lily asked.

"I admit nothing," Yvette declared.

Lily stepped forward, towering in a satisfying way over the smaller woman. "I am warning you, Yvette. This is ours." Now was the time to put Yvette on blast. "I want to know how you heard about this story, understand?"

Yvette did not collapse. Instead, her eyes narrowed. "I understand that you are threatening me, and I will not tolerate it. Do you honestly think I would allow you to dictate how I run my magazine? Don't be absurd." She stepped away from Lily and said to the receptionist, "Madeleine, see Mademoiselle Wilkins and her guest out." She then turned on her heel and stalked toward the frosted glass door. Before disappearing behind it, she spoke over her shoulder. "If you're so concerned about where I heard about this story, ask my darling ex-fiancé," she said.

Damn it, all Lily had succeeded in doing was letting Yvette know how important the Honeybee Emeralds was to them. She felt tears pressing against her eyes. She wasn't sure if she wanted to cry out of rage or despair.

Madeleine stepped gracefully from behind her desk and murmured in French, "This way, ladies."

Lily and Daphne followed her to a glassed-in elevator area that let in the blue Parisian sky and had piped-in birdsong. A large urn filled with ferns made the space feel like they were in the countryside, and suddenly all Lily wanted to do was throw herself on the nearby off-white couch ("Maison Margiela," Daphne murmured unhelpfully) and stay in this lavender-scented haven forever. Instead, she remained beside her friend, awaiting the slow arrival of the elevator. Madeleine stood next to them, obviously intending to make sure they left the premises.

"Well, that was totally pointless and stupid," Lily muttered to Daphne.

"Yes," her friend agreed. "You kind of lost it, plus we learned nothing about the necklace."

Lily was about to snap at Daphne, when they were interrupted by the receptionist.

"The necklace?" Madeleine asked, stepping in front of the elevator doors.

Lily looked at her in alarm but recovered quickly. "No, no, you must have misunderstood," she said to the girl in French. She and Daphne had been speaking English.

"I don't think I misheard," the girl replied. She smiled malevolently, and Lily's heart sank. She was going to take this intel straight back to Yvette.

The girl's next question confused her, however. "Have you ever seen *The Devil Wears Prada*?"

"Sure, the Meryl Streep movie," Daphne said.

They could hear the well-engineered mechanism of the elevator approaching their floor. The girl leaned in, speaking quickly. "Working for Yvette Dufeu is a million times worse than working for that devil." Her voice dropped. "Yvette is researching a story—she's obsessed with it. She wants it to be our June cover, but she's going to be publishing to our website first . . . it's all about this one necklace—diamonds, emeralds."

"How did she hear about it?" Lily asked urgently.

With a loud ding, the elevator arrived, and the girl leaned in conspiratorially. "She got a call from an old friend. Someone who made us promise not to reveal their identity."

Lily's heart sank. She lunged blindly toward the open elevator doors, almost missing the end of Madeleine's sentence.

"Her goddaughter, Catherine Medici dit Beauregard."

CHAPTER 27

Madame Bovary's Wedding Feast

ALICE PUSHED OPEN THE DOOR TO BONJOUR PARIS. SHE'D BEEN out all morning, doing a bit of fact-checking for the Honeybee story, as well as taking a quick trip to the safety-deposit box at the Banque Populaire. That was definitely her last time sneaking out to touch the necklace. She felt ill every time she thought of the risks she was running.

She was thankful that Mme Boucher had already left for lunch. She thought it best to avoid the other woman since yesterday's emotional outburst. Alice wasn't embarrassed by what had happened, but she suspected Mme Boucher would appreciate some space after revealing her vulnerability.

Lily and M. Seguin were in conversation by the editor's desk. He had really been hanging around a lot lately. It was a bit unnerving. M. Seguin was a posh businessman with presumably quite a lot to do.

The two weren't paying attention to her, so she took the opportunity to drop off the note and gift she had purchased for Mme Boucher at the Japanese dollar store. It was a little blue whale cartoon figurine with an upright tail, big googly eyes, and a goofy grin. She hoped the memento would cheer Mme Boucher up, or at least let her know that Alice was thinking about her. She was pleased with this nicely muted recognition of a shared moment. Acknowledging without acknowledging seemed very British.

She walked over to her desk to discover that M. Seguin and Lily were arguing. They both glanced at her as she sat down but didn't lower their voices.

"I still don't understand why you would go to *La Vie en Rose*," M. Seguin said.

Lily must have gone to Yvette's office this morning and confronted the other woman. No one had told her about that plan. Coupled with yesterday's trip to the Loire, that was two things she hadn't known about.

"I told you," Lily replied. "Daphne and I wanted to find the source of the leak."

M. Seguin waved his hand dismissively. "Catherine Medici dit Beauregard."

Blimey. The lady from the jewelry shop.

"The knowledge doesn't do much good, does it?" Luc continued. "Why did the leaker's identity matter so much, anyway?"

Lily bit her lip and looked down. "I thought it was you," she said in a small voice.

Alice blinked. Why would M. Seguin have betrayed them?

"What?" he demanded.

Lily's voice suddenly had an angry edge Alice had never heard before. "Why were you texting Yvette Dufeu?"

M. Seguin froze. "How do you know about that?" he asked, his tone neutral.

"It doesn't matter."

His eyes darkened. "It's Jacob. Did he tell his 'Lily Pad'?"

She shook her head. "Why were you texting her, Luc?"

M. Seguin's eyes flashed. Lily had provoked a reaction. "You really think I would betray you like that? Have you such a low opinion of me?"

He sounded hurt.

Lily didn't notice, because her tone was still hard. "Come on. What's going on?"

Luc's voice was exasperated. "I could shut this whole magazine down right now if I wanted to. Why would I deceive you?"

Lily's face remained hard, and Luc seemed to realize she was expecting an answer to her question. "I was asking Yvette directly what she was up to, trying to clarify things so no one panicked."

"And why would Yvette Dufeu tell you anything?" From Lily's tone, she already knew the answer.

Luc sighed. "I didn't want to get into this, because I know what you will all think, but once, many years ago, Yvette and I had a relationship."

"Really?" Alice blurted out, unable to hide her astonishment.

The two turned toward her, seemingly only remembering she was there. Lily took a step back, inviting Alice to join them in their conversation.

M. Seguin shook his head ruefully. "Yes, when Maman was still alive. Yvette worked for a brief time at *Bonjour Paris*. We kept our relationship secret. Maman would not have been thrilled that I was bothering the staff. Frankly, I think the illicitness was what made the relationship so exciting."

"Oh, so this was an exciting relationship?" Lily said. She wasn't nearly as surprised by this revelation as Alice. Instead, she was sarcastic, something Alice had never heard from her editor before. Lily, who was usually perfectly professional, seemed to have forgotten that M. Seguin owned the magazine.

"It was a very fiery relationship," he said with a crooked grin, as if remembering something particularly outrageous.

This statement seemed to enrage Lily, who leaned forward and said, "She was more than your girlfriend though, wasn't she? She was your fiancée." Her voice was shrill.

Luc shrugged. "For about ten minutes, before I came to my senses. It was nothing. I didn't even get her a ring." His tone was sincere, but now it took on a note of impatience. "Take my word, I didn't reveal anything to Yvette."

Alice frowned. Lily had once described Yvette as a "least weasel" and Alice had dutifully Googled it. The tiny animal would sneak up behind its much larger prey, like a rabbit, and when its victim was at its most relaxed and calm, the weasel pounced, its razor-sharp teeth effortlessly finding the jugular. The little she knew about Yvette Dufeu made her believe the comparison was apt. Perhaps M. Seguin wasn't even aware of what he'd let slip—bleeding information unaware of the weasel's teeth in his artery.

M. Seguin continued, "Besides, why would I hurt *Bonjour Paris*? I want us to succeed. I'm taking time out of my day to attend meetings and visit vineyards. I want to discover the truth as much as anyone, not just for my mother's legacy, but because I believe in what you're doing. I believe in you."

Lily opened and closed her mouth, obviously surprised by this revelation. She took a deep breath, and Alice could almost see her slipping back into her professional persona. "I'm sorry for my tone. I was startled to learn you'd been texting her."

"I promise you, I hadn't been in contact with Yvette for years. I only sent her that text on Wednesday when her involvement was clear."

"Wait, let me understand this," Lily said. "You broke off the engagement and ghosted Yvette for years . . . then, just as she's trying to screw over your magazine, you send her a text demanding to know what she's doing, and you expected to get a response?"

He blinked. "That's correct." Seeing her incredulous expression, he asked, "What did I do that was so wrong?"

Lily met Alice's eyes, and the two women shared a look of understanding. It was always shocking to discover how emotionally clueless men, even sophisticated ones like Luc Seguin, could be about women. No wonder the Least Weasel wanted to destroy *Bonjour Paris*. Alice honestly felt a bit of sympathy rage on her behalf.

Seeing that Lily wasn't going to answer, M. Seguin let out a loud, very French, sigh. "Well, ladies," he said. "Can we move on from this?"

Lily nodded. "Absolutely." She seemed quite cheerful now. "I'm sorry I reacted like that. I was out of line."

"It's fine," Luc said, and his voice softened. "I'm glad we could clear it up."

There was something oddly heartfelt in his tone. Wait. Was M. Seguin crushing on Lily? Was that why he was hanging around so much? But he was her boss. Was this a #MeToo moment? Alice had never worked in an office setting before—her main part-time jobs had been at the chippy and then, blissfully free of grease and fish, at the university library. If M. Seguin were interested in Lily, was that okay? It probably depended on what Lily thought of the situation. She couldn't imagine discussing the issue with Lily, but maybe she could talk to Daphne about it on her boss's behalf. Who was she kidding? Daphne was more intimidating than Lily. Her self-confidence was breathtaking, and while Lily at least could get mustard on her shirt or admit to yanking chin hairs, it seemed inconceivable that the polished Daphne ever did anything less than perfectly. No, Alice wouldn't take her concerns to Daphne. She'd talk the whole thing over with Alexander. He'd say little, but she knew he'd listen closely.

"So where are we with the Honeybee Emeralds?" Luc asked.

Lily responded equally energetically. "Thanks to Daphne, with an assist from Theo, we've established that Josephine recovered the necklace after the war, which gives us a new twist. Our print deadline is in three days, so I think it's time to consolidate everything we've gleaned and get ready to go to press. We might even want to consider publishing the story early on our website to get the jump on *La Vie en Rose*. We have the advantage, since we actually have the necklace in our possession, something Yvette doesn't know."

"Excellent," M. Seguin said. "What's the status on all our fact-checking? The last thing we need is a lawsuit."

They both turned to her. Alice had to ensure that every single item in Jacob's article could be corroborated. With their eyes on her, Alice panicked and could think of nothing to say. The silence continued for another beat, M. Seguin's question still hanging there. This was incredibly awkward. There was a loud gurgling noise. Lily looked startled and then flushed; it was her stomach growling.

The interruption helped Alice find her voice. "I've gone over everything we've discovered so far—Marguerite Bellanger, Mata Hari, Josephine Baker—our timeline on ownership fits, but we'll have to couch the story in some speculative language, because I haven't been able to confirm all the details."

"Good work, keep at it," Lily said.

Luc slapped his hands together, "Now," he said, grinning at Lily, "I think we should order some lunch."

"Perhaps that would be best," Lily said demurely. "Alice, are you hungry?" she asked.

She shook her head. She'd brought her lunch from home. There was no way she could afford whatever fancy place M. Seguin and Lily chose.

"You will eat," he declared. "My treat."

She couldn't argue with him, and she appreciated the way he had discerned the reason for her hesitation. People with money didn't always remember that not everyone had it. Without consulting anyone, Luc dialed a number and spoke in rapid French. He hung up, pleased with himself. "I'm having the daily lunch special from Chez Lucien sent over for all of us. Their veal stew is sublime."

Alice had never had veal. The thought of the animals, big-eyed, soft-fleshed, horribly treated was a bit daunting. Then again, there was that wedding banquet scene in *Madame Bovary*. Flaubert, in his careful, perfect way, listed a series of mouthwatering items. She had reread the passage many times . . . She closed her eyes and conjured up the description—"chicken fricassee, a veal stew, three legs of mutton, and, in the middle, a nice roast suckling pig, flanked by four chitterlings," whatever those were. She had loved that scene the way she had loved the moment in the Mister Men book when Mr. Strong got all the eggs. It was a joyous celebration of abundance, filling her soul to read it. Now she was going to taste the same dish that Emma Bovary ate on her wedding day. She grinned.

The three chatted about the necklace as they waited for the food to arrive. M. Seguin turned to her. "You did a fine job uncovering the Mata Hari connection."

She blushed and looked down. "Thanks," she mumbled. God, she couldn't even take a compliment properly. She should smile graciously, or be like Daphne and revel in her own powers, embracing his words with confidence and poise. Instead, it sounded like she resented them.

Neither Lily nor Luc seemed to notice her inadequate response, and Alice was saved from further self-loathing when the conversation shifted back to what Daphne had uncovered.

M. Seguin spoke excitedly. "Perhaps this changes our end game. The Baker estate might not own the necklace. If Josephine sold it or gave it away before her death, then it could belong to anyone."

"Maybe," Lily said, with doubt in her voice.

"You don't think that's a possibility?" he asked.

Lily put her hands up, "I didn't say that. I'm only wondering at the coincidence of finding a photograph of Josephine wearing the necklace in the same building where the necklace was discovered. There might be a connection."

This was the same argument that Jacob had made the other day, but this time M. Seguin didn't seem so resistant. He nodded. "The key will be to learn who left it in the wardrobe room."

Lily chimed in. "Alexander hasn't been able to get any info out of the landlord, at least not without arousing suspicion."

M. Seguin turned to Alice. "I think we should go down there again. Perhaps we missed something when we last looked."

Alice nodded. She thought of the feathers, buttons, sequins, and ribbons. Headdresses, gowns, and sailor suits. It was a giant, glorious, vibrant mishmash of clothes. It had given her that same surging sense of abundance and satiety as the *Madame Bovary* feast scene, or Mr. Strong's eggs.

M. Seguin nodded. "Good. We go down after lunch, then."

"We'll need Alexander," Alice said. Her voice cracked slightly at his name. Lily looked at her inquiringly, and Alice rushed to explain. "He's the only one who really knows his way around."

M. Seguin continued, "We've established that it wasn't Théâtre Rigolo's wardrobe room, but that doesn't mean that those clothes don't belong to another theatrical company. I do remember there was a theater in the neighborhood that went out of business. Maybe there is a mention of it in the local paper."

"That seems like quite a long shot," Lily said doubtfully.

"What other options do we have?" M. Seguin asked.

Lily's lips pressed into a thin line. Alice could tell she wanted to make some kind of smart remark but was biting her tongue. After their argument, Lily seemed intent on reestablishing her professionalism.

"We should check the neighborhood paper," M. Seguin said. "It went out of business about five years ago, but it documented everything that happened in this area. Google 'Le Petit Quartier.'"

As great as Lily was, it was rather nice to see her editor being bossed around, especially because she was obviously unused to it. Lily turned to her computer and typed in a few words. "Got it," she said, reading her screen. "They digitized their archive, but it isn't open. You need a membership."

M. Seguin frowned. "I know Mother had one. She said its back issues were a godsend."

Just then, the lunch delivery person arrived. M. Seguin rose to pay.

"I've popped in your mother's email address," Lily said. "Now I need her password. Any guesses?"

"Xanthia," he called back. "With an X. It was her password for everything."

M. Seguin paid the bill and came back holding two big bags of food. He passed a heavy cardboard box to Alice. It smelled heavenly. He gave the other to Lily. "This is quite a meal. Hopefully you and your large American don't have dinner plans tonight."

Lily flushed and replied with heat. "He's not 'my' American." She typed in the password. "We're in," she said happily.

Alice opened the box, pulling out a heavy plastic bowl. The restaurant must be very fancy indeed, if they used such good-quality plastic for their takeaway orders. This bowl was much nicer than any of the six that she and Pauline shared back at their hovel. She pulled off the lid and a wonderful smell, rich and with a tinge of rosemary, filled her nostrils. The stew was a deep gold color, the meat and mushrooms visible in the creamy sauce. She dug her spoon in and withdrew a piece of veal. It literally melted in her mouth, its soft, meaty flavors combining perfectly with the wine and herbs in the sauce. She closed her eyes to better savor the experience.

When she opened them, Lily was busily typing in keywords to the database. She and M. Seguin had foolishly not even opened their lunches. "'Xanthia,' that's a random password," Lily remarked.

"It was my mother's real name—her father was a bit of a Greek nut. She hated it and went by her middle name, Olivia."

Alice looked up from her third bite of buttery veal. Had M. Seguin said his mother's name was Xanthia Olivia?

He and Lily hunched over her computer, arguing about what terms to enter into the database.

"Excuse me," Alice said softly. She wiped her mouth on a tissue. They didn't hear. "Sorry to interrupt," she said more loudly.

Lily looked up and said a trifle impatiently, "What is it, Alice?"

"Um, I just wondered," she addressed M. Seguin. "What's your mother's maiden name?"

"Her maiden name?" he repeated. "Owens, why?"

Alice couldn't keep the excitement from her voice. "So, your mother's full name was Xanthia Olivia Owens?"

"Yes," he said, staring at her in puzzlement.

Lily grasped the significance. "Oh my God, of course," she exclaimed. "Luc, your mother's initials are X.O.O."

He still looked confused, but Lily bent to the bottom drawer of her desk, pulling out the framed photograph of Josephine Baker that Alexander had found on the wall. Carefully, she removed the image from the frame and pointed to the inscription at the bottom left-hand corner: "Thank you, XOO!"

Lily spoke quickly. "We thought it was a standard 'hugs and kisses' sign-off, but that photo is actually addressed to your mother. This inscription directly connects Josephine Baker to Olivia."

M. Seguin gazed at the photograph, his brain taking a moment to catch up with what he was seeing and hearing.

Lily turned to Alice. "Fantastic work, kid!" she said. It looked like her editor was enthused enough to attempt a hug, so Alice quickly forked up a mouthful of veal to fend her off.

"How on earth would she have known Josephine Baker?" M. Seguin's voice almost held a note of resentment, as if he disliked uncovering new information about his own mother.

"This makes sense," Lily said, following her own line of thought. "We assumed the image was from before the war, but now that we know that Josephine still had her necklace, this photo could be more recent. It might have been taken specifically to be given to your mother."

M. Seguin shook his head decisively. "No, no. This is a coincidence with my mother's initials. The inscription is a standard fan autograph."

"Maybe," Lily said, but the look she shot Alice said she didn't agree with his assessment. Even if M. Seguin didn't want to admit it, it seemed his mother was connected to the Honeybee Emeralds.

Dallas

Daphne: What's our weekend game plan?

Lily: ??

Daphne: How do we connect Luc to the necklace?

Lily: We're Skyping with his father on Monday to see what he might know.

Daphne: Monday! We need to get moving on this. Can't you talk to him over the weekend?

Lily: Nope. His dad is at some model train conference and is unreachable.

Daphne: WTH? That is a super lame excuse.

Lily: I don't want to push Luc. He was kind of weird after learning about the connection to his mother. Also, he's my boss, so he gets to decide.

Daphne: Ugh, this is so frustrating. Yvette is breathing down our necks.

Lily: I know, but I can't be pushy.

Daphne: Fine, fine. I guess the rest of us can keep researching our angles. Hey, what about Yvette being Catherine Medici dit Beauregard's godmother?

Lily: Well, upper-class Paris is a small world.

Daphne: I guess I'm not surprised Catherine sold us out. She resents me knowing that secret about her ex-boyfriend.

Lily: Makes sense. I'd be really pissed if someone blackmailed me over my love life choices.

Daphne: Ha ha. Like the guy you dated with the soul patch and the hand-rolled cigarettes?

Lily: Oh man, trust you to remember Dallas.

Daphne: Oh God, I forgot his name was Dallas. A Frenchman named Dallas. DALLAS!!!!!!!!!!!!!!!!

Lily: Yup, here comes the resentment . . .

Daphne: Ha ha, consider him forgotten.

CHAPTER 28

A Hole in the Heart

DAPHNE PUT THE PHONE DOWN, SMILING AT HER EXCHANGE with Lily. Theo was watching some special Friday evening TV and she was prepping dinner while sipping a glass of Chardonnay. She thought about her day—the *La Vie en Rose* offices had been something else. She was definitely going to buy one of those Bella Coola cushions. Divine.

Skype sang its song. Time to talk to Philip. She took a glug of wine and stepped into the backyard.

"Hi, babe," he said. He looked tired.

"Hi," she replied. She suddenly longed to have him standing in front of her, but of course, that was impossible. He launched into a work story. She listened, but felt that sense of frustration and loss that they weren't connecting. She wanted her old marriage back, the one where they actually talked face-to-face.

"Listen, things have been happening here too. I've been working with Lily on a special project." Surely, their secrecy vow was over now. Yvette, their greatest threat, would be publishing something soon. Daphne told Philip the story of the Honeybee Emeralds, finishing up with the extraordinary development—the connection between Olivia and Josephine Baker. She held her breath. She had betrayed the Fellowship in order to connect with her husband; she hoped it was worth it.

Philip was silent after she finished and then spoke. "So that's what you've been up to?" His voice held a note of querulousness that set her teeth on edge. "Seems a bit silly."

Breathe in, breathe out. Do not lash out but respond with empathy. You are Pema Chödrön. You are Mother Teresa. You are the Buddha. Daphne's voice was shrill. "This is so typical of you, Philip—only considering your own point of view. This story matters. It's important."

"Of course it is," he said tiredly. "It's just that if we don't end up landing the Beijing account—"

He was about to start talking about work again. Daphne thought she'd scream if she had to listen to more. "Hey, what if we had another baby?"

There was a startled pause. "What did you say?" Philip asked.

"Another baby. Maybe we'd have a little girl this time. We'd all be together. We'd be a family."

"But we are a family," Philip said. His bewilderment was grating.

"No, we're a couple who happen to have a kid. Two children would make us more serious, we'd be an undertaking." You would have to be home, she wanted to shout. You would have to be here. You couldn't leave so easily.

"I don't think a second child is a good idea right now," Philip said. His tone, so supercilious, was maddening. It implied that she was being ridiculous.

"Why not?" she demanded.

"We have a very comfortable life right now. More children would mean a bigger house, a bigger mortgage, more bills, more stress, more worries."

"That's what I want," Daphne said. "More. I want more life."

"We haven't been very good about contraception, Daphne. Maybe we're not meant to have another child. The universe—"

"Fuck the universe," Daphne said quietly. "It's not the universe preventing us from having another kid; it's your travel schedule."

"Daphne, I told you, once we get through next quarter, things should settle down."

Daphne spoke without even formulating her thoughts. "I have a hole in my heart, in my soul. I am standing around waiting for life to give me something and it's not happening."

"A hole in your heart?" Philip asked. "Aren't you being a bit dramatic? Be reasonable. We have a nice life. It's quiet and contained. We can afford the best of everything. Another child simply isn't in the cards."

Daphne's throat filled with acidic mockery. "'Another child simply isn't in the cards.' Would you listen to yourself? You sound like a robot." She heard the anger in her voice but could do nothing to modify her tone.

"What?" Philip demanded. His voice contained hurt outrage, but she knew at some level he was pleased she was being so unreasonable; it made him look all the better. This would be excellent ammunition at their next therapy session. Poor Philip, stuck with Daphne, that ball-breaker. His tone softened. "I miss you and Theo. I feel terrible about being away so much."

This is what he told himself. This is what he told the therapist. Philip had everyone convinced, even her, that he was a good guy and she was the needy, unreasonable woman.

"Bullshit. You love getting away from us, from me. Who knows, maybe you even asked for all this extra travel." It felt wonderful to tell him her deepest suspicion.

"That's insane," Philip said.

"Insane." Her voice was angrier still, but underneath was a thread of satisfaction. He shouldn't have insulted her, his first mistake. Name-calling meant he could no longer claim the moral high ground. "You are gone half the time. You swoop back in and confuse Theo, disrupt everything, and then you get on a plane. What's insane about that?"

"Listen to me, sweetheart." His voice was soothing, and it made Daphne even angrier. "This isn't the time for a big discussion. I'm home in a week. Let's talk then."

She thought of Josephine Baker, and how she had fought her whole life to live the way she wanted. Shouldn't she, Daphne, be doing the same? Things she didn't even know she was feeling came tumbling out of her mouth. "We've grown apart. Half the time it feels like we don't even like each other anymore. You've checked out of our marriage. I'm lonely, I'm sad, and I'm mad at you."

She had never expressed her feelings so bluntly, but as she uttered them, she knew them to be real. "Every time I need you, you're gone. I'm sick of explaining to Theo why Daddy is away so much. I'm sick of telling myself that Skype conversations are enough. I'm sick of worrying that you've lost interest in me."

"Daphne," Philip started, his tone telling her he was about to argue. "I'm not the one who has checked out—that would be you. As soon as I started traveling more, you stopped trying. It's like you're waiting for me to screw up, waiting for me to leave."

How had Philip made this her fault? "That's ridiculous," she spat.

"It's true, and I think it goes back to your father and how he left—"

"Are you fucking kidding me?" she yelled. "You're trying to blame your failures on my Daddy issues? No way."

Now Philip was angry. "This is exactly what you always do, Daphne—you amass a litany of complaints and use them as weapons instead of honestly trying to resolve something. I'm not going to let you do it this time."

"Not going to let me? You don't control me."

Philip took a deep breath and once again spoke in a calm voice. "Daphne, I hear what you're saying and I feel—"

She couldn't do this therapy-speak dance with him—couldn't listen to his "I feel" statements and respond with her own. "We want different things," she said flatly.

"What are you saying?" From his tone she could tell he had heard her. Suddenly they left the usual steps of their usual dance. The old grievances, the old slights, and the old insecurities were laid aside. Daphne sensed they were at a fork in their relationship.

He repeated his question. His voice took on a tentative note, and Daphne felt a twinge of tenderness toward him. He was just like her, blundering along in the dark, trying to find a way through.

She felt sad. "Maybe we should think about a separation," she heard herself say.

CHAPTER 29

Speak Not of Fate

THAT MONDAY MORNING ÉLISE ARRIVED EXTRA EARLY TO THE office. She hadn't been sleeping well and was glad to have a few hours to herself before the others arrived. Logging into the computer, she looked up. Her eyes sought the little whale figurine that Alice had left on her desk on Friday. It was a cheap, stupid thing. Probably made in China. It wasn't even clear what species it was—just a generic whale. Yet, she couldn't resist running her finger over the slope of its back and down the flip of its tail. The girl had included a poem with the statuette. Élise had never understood poetry. She felt itchy looking at the shape of a poem on the page. Ridiculous format, waste of paper.

This poem was called "A Persian Song," and at the bottom of the page, beneath the many stanzas, the girl had written, "By Hafez, 1315–1390. Sufi poet."

Élise had read the poem many times on Friday, trying to understand what the girl meant by it. Searching for the coded message. She had looked at it so often she memorized parts—now, snatches of the poem came to her at odd times. Saturday night as she brushed her teeth she thought "'Tis all a cloud, 'tis all a dream; / To love and joy thy thoughts confine, / Nor hope to pierce the sacred gloom."

She recharged her métro card this morning and some lines danced before her eyes, "Speak not of fate:—ah! change the theme, / And talk of odors, talk of wine, / Talk of the flowers that round us bloom." There was something about that exhortation—"ah! change the theme"—that gripped her imagination. How had the girl known?

Over the weekend she had Googled "Sufi" and was surprised to discover it was a branch of Islam. She hadn't known there were different forms of the religion, or that one branch could be so complex.

On Sunday afternoon, breaking with her normal schedule, she'd gone out to the cemetery. She'd cried at the gravesite, something she had not done in all the months she'd been visiting it. Oddly, it wasn't just Olivia's death or the thought of leaving Paris to return "home" as Henri called it. No, she had also cried for the girl, Aliyeh. Élise remembered the loneliness and uncertainty of trying to make her way in a big, unknown, and unforgiving city. She and Aliyeh were so alike; Élise could see that now. The girl was shy, tentative, unsure, and Élise wanted to tell her that she had nothing to fear. She wanted to take Aliyeh by the shoulders and tell her, "This is it, the only life you have—live it! 'Talk of the odors! Talk of the wine! Talk of the flowers that round us bloom!'" Instead, she whispered it as she laid the usual red rose on Olivia's grave.

Élise touched the whale again. She had always longed for a daughter. If she had had one, surely the girl would have been like Aliyeh. A tear streaked down her face, and she brushed it away. Crying again. She was going soft in the head. She could not continue like this. Mooning around the cemetery, crying at her desk, weeping over a cheap statuette. Henri was right. It was time to move on. To return to the mountains. To go home.

She would hand in her letter of resignation at the end of the day. She stood and lumbered to the back of the office. Somehow, it seemed important to write out her resignation on the old electric typewriter she used to use. She found it at the back of the room and lugged it to her desk, pulling off the dust cover. She turned it on and rolled in a sheet of paper. She typed a few words. It still worked.

She would give the letter to Olivia's son. Luc had been around a lot lately—always whispering about necklaces, Josephine Baker, and their big, secret project. She was glad she had not involved herself in this latest excitement, easier to leave if she didn't know what they were up to. She concentrated on the letter. Her throat tightened as she typed out the words, each tap of the key sealing her fate. A return to the beginning. What else could she do? She had made her choice and she would abide by it, as she always had. Her days of wine and flowers were over.

She finished the letter. It was straightforward. No emotion. Élise rolled it out of the machine and folded it into an envelope. She would spend the day putting the office affairs in order. Technically, she should give two weeks' notice, but she knew that once she handed in her letter, she wouldn't be able to bring herself to return. When she left *Bonjour Paris* tonight, it would be for the last time. They would do fine without her. Henri was right, she wasn't needed anymore.

She turned to her computer, its keys much more yielding than the old typewriter's, but less satisfying to use. An email in the administrative *Bonjour Paris* inbox caught her eye. It was from Yvette Dufeu. Élise's nostrils flared. That woman was like Coco Chanel—a fascist in great lipstick. The subject line, "Emerald Bee Necklace," attracted her attention, ringing a long-forgotten bell.

"Dear *Bonjour Paris*, I hope this email finds you all well. After Lily's impromptu visit to our offices last Friday, I thought I would send this along as a professional courtesy. *La Vie en Rose* has moved our publication date forward; by the time you get this, our story will be up on our website. The more fulsome Emerald Bee Necklace article will be at newsstands shortly. Thanks so much for all your help and interest. We certainly couldn't have done this without you. Bisous to all of you, especially Luc."

Élise stared at the email. Could it be? Was it even possible?

She clicked on the attachment. It was a long article, the headline reading "An Emperor's Lost Treasure." But it was the image, a sketch of a beautiful necklace rendered in exquisite, vivid color that astounded Élise. The diamonds sparkled off the screen, the honeybee pendant glittered, and the emeralds, a deep magical green, shone with a heat she could almost feel. Élise remembered when she had first held that necklace, and her eyes once more filled with tears. Suddenly, everything that had gone on over the past couple of weeks, the safety-deposit key, the whispered conclaves, the snatches of conversation she had overheard, and even that broken furnace, the pieces all fit together.

Élise stood from her desk. She knew what she had to do, but she'd have to move quickly.

Scooped

Lily: You saw the article I forwarded? From the *La Vie en Rose* site?

Daphne: Yup.

Lily: Yvette has already published it online.

Daphne: She is diabolical.

Lily: She's shafted us.

Daphne: So what's the next step?

Lily: We have no choice but to give the necklace to the police now. We'll use its discovery as the hook for our article.

Daphne: We should still try to fill in the gaps in our timeline. Are you and Luc going to talk to his father?

Lily: I guess. I'm pretty bummed though.

Daphne: Why?

Lily: Dude, we've been scooped. Even if we publish something now, *La Vie en Rose* will always have broken the story.

Daphne: Yvette's article is missing key elements. We've got the better story.

Lily: Yeah, but Yvette got there first.

Daphne: It's not a slam dunk for her—she's right that there was a necklace created by Napoleon for his mistress, and that Josephine Baker owned it. She doesn't know about Mata Hari, and she has nothing about a possible connection to Olivia. She doesn't even know that we have it in our possession. They had to use an old sketch as an illustration.

Lily: I guess.

Daphne: No guessing. Positive vibes only. I really need something good to focus on.

Lily: ?

Daphne: Philip and I had a huge fight Friday night. We haven't spoken since and I've been obsessing all weekend.

Lily: Oh no—want to talk?

Daphne: Not now—I'm still processing. Anyway, La Vie en Rose did us a favor. Their article builds up buzz about the necklace without answering everything. Then we come in with how it has been discovered, recovered, and returned to its heirs. Bam! That's a story.

Lily: Bam?

Daphne: Bam!

Lily: Maybe you're right.

Daphne: Of course I am!

Lily: BAM!

CHAPTER 30

The La Cornue Stove

THE EXCHANGE WITH DAPHNE BUOYED LILY'S SPIRITS, AND SHE texted Luc to confirm she'd meet him at his place to Skype with his dad. Alice remained behind at the office, while Jacob went to fetch the necklace to hand over to the police. Their article would be published tonight and would include everything they had learned about the necklace, plus the police reaction to its recovery. That way they'd build on Yvette's momentum, taking the wind from her sails. By the time the June issue hit the newsstands, with the Honeybee on the cover, *Bonjour Paris* would own the story.

Mme Boucher had texted to say she wasn't feeling well and wouldn't come in. This wasn't unusual; the older woman took the occasional sick day, which Lily certainly didn't begrudge her. Still, Lily was disappointed. Now that the story of the Honeybee Emeralds was out in the open and there might be a direct connection between Josephine and Olivia, it would be good to pick their office manager's brain to see if she knew anything. Such discussions would have to wait for tomorrow.

Had Lily given much thought to Luc's home, she would have assumed it was a sterile penthouse overlooking the Seine or an overstuffed maison de maître, brimming with antiquities and views of the Eiffel Tower. She was surprised to find his apartment was actually a little down at heel, and not the kind of shabby that was secretly cool. Located in an unflashy apartment building in a nondescript part of the 13th, it was as far from chic as you could get in Paris.

Inside was no different. The furniture wasn't cheap, but it wasn't a two-thousand-euro sofa from Miliboo, either. The parquet floors were battered and scratched; there was no extraordinary art on the walls or expensive champagnes ostentatiously displayed in a wall-mounted wine fridge. Instead, the place had a comfortable, lived-in feel—lots of framed photographs of Luc's friends and family, a couple of cool vintage lamps, an obviously homemade blanket thrown over an overstuffed chair, large windows. The home, oddly enough, felt *cozy*—not a word she would have associated with Luc Seguin.

"Nice place," she said, but he must have heard the question in her voice.

He shrugged. "I'm comfortable here. I bought it when I first started making money, and it never seemed worth it to move."

"They make flat screens now, you know," she said, pointing to the television. It had been years since she had seen such an old relic—a big cumbersome thing that jutted out like a triangle.

He shrugged again. "I hardly watch it. I keep it for my father, when he comes around. He's happy. Why would I get a new one?"

Lily couldn't argue with the logic. For all of Luc's fancy haircuts and pricey suits, he obviously spent money only on things he valued, rather than flaunting wealth for wealth's sake. Was that a product of having been raised in a comfortably middle-class family, where coupon cutting was unnecessary and worries about the electricity being cut off nonexistent? Irrationally, Lily still held her breath when paying with a credit card—those couple of seconds between punching in the code and awaiting approval were tense, even though she always paid her balance off. Her childhood and young adult life were dominated by a sense of scarcity, and she didn't think she'd ever fully shake that anxiety. Luc didn't have any of that angst; money was simply a tool to get the things he wanted. What a liberating outlook.

He led them into the kitchen, a smallish, poky room with cheap cupboards and thin linoleum. There was one jarringly luxurious addition, however—an enormous Provence blue La Cornue stove, with its distinctive copper accents. More than a Maserati in his parking spot or a Picasso on the wall, this custom-built French stove was a giant, flashing signal of wealth. She had a friend who had bought a house in Paris solely because the owners included their La Cornue in the sale.

Luc didn't give her a chance to absorb the incongruity. "Would you like some brioche?" he asked.

"Sure," she said, still processing the presence of the stove. Each one was handcrafted to the owner's specifications. Her friend said the one in her house was worth more than $40,000. Lily's stomach rumbled, distracting her from the appliance. She realized that the sweet, yeasty smell of brioche filled the kitchen. She looked around for the brown paper bag with the pastries, but Luc surprised her by pointing to a braided wreath of bread resting on a wire rack.

"You didn't make that," she said in disbelief.

"Of course," he said. "Baking is my hobby. My father taught me."

She was literally stunned into silence. The whole thing—Luc's run-down, comfy home in an unfashionable part of the city, his deft hand with a rolling pin, the way he seemed approachable and handsome in his casual jeans and V-neck T-shirt, the stove that cost more than a car—combined to throw Lily completely off balance.

He didn't appear to notice. He was breaking apart the warm, dense bread, staring at it intently. "Not sure it has risen as much as it should have," he murmured to himself.

The golden loaf looked perfect to her, and the smell was amazing. Her stomach rumbled again.

"I'm sure it's delicious," she said.

He frowned. "I am constantly tweaking the recipe. My father is much more consistent with bread and pastries."

"I never would have guessed this was your hobby," she said as he placed a thick piece on a plate for her and took one himself. They moved to the small table beside the window in the corner of the room.

"Baking is very precise, very exact. So many things affect the outcome—quality of flour, purity of water, activity of the yeast, how the ingredients are put together, how the dough is kneaded, the temperature of the oven. All are important factors that must be considered."

Lily took a bite—it was perfect, slightly sweet, light, with a pillowy interior. She closed her eyes in pleasure. "It's amazing," she said.

"I'm pleased you like it."

For the first time she noticed his hands—strong and capable with slender fingers. "I'm so glad you were free this morning," she said.

Luc shrugged. "I moved some meetings. A perk of being the boss."

"I know you doubt your mom knew Josephine Baker, but I am sure there is a connection."

He nodded. "Upon reflection, I believe you might be correct. Friday's news startled me—I have an image of Maman: focused, hardworking, driven. It is hard to reconcile with what I know of Josephine Baker."

Lily nodded. His mother had died only a year ago. She kept forgetting he was still grieving. Lily had been lost for years after her father's sudden death. She could empathize with his need to understand his mother.

Luc glanced at his watch, heavy-looking and undoubtedly expensive. "I told Papa we'd call him about now."

"Great," she said. "Let's give him a jingle." She instantly regretted the dorky expression. She was feeling keyed up and awkward around Luc.

"Papa," Luc said as M. Seguin's face—high forehead, haughty expression, so similar to Luc's—filled the screen. "J'ai une question pour toi."

"Who's there?" the older man responded in French. "I saw a lady behind you."

Lily popped her head in front of the screen, waving at the camera and speaking French. "Bon matin, M. Seguin. I'm Lily Wilkins from *Bonjour Paris*. I'm the editor there now."

"The new Olivia," M. Seguin said, looking at her keenly.

"Oh, I couldn't replace your wife," she rushed to say. The older man's eyes were sharp, and she was suddenly frightened he would judge her. "She was such a force. I am hoping to keep her legacy alive."

M. Seguin nodded.

"Would you mind if I recorded our conversation? It's for a story."

"Oui, that is fine." He focused on his son. "Luc, I am surprised you haven't sold the magazine yet. I thought that was your plan."

"It was Maman's life's work, Papa," Luc responded defensively.

"Sentimental, just like Ollie," the older man said, but his voice was fond. "What can I help you with? Something to do with *Bonjour Paris?*"

"A little, Papa. We've found something in the basement at Rue de Beaune."

"The basement? Ah, I remember it was horrible down there. Dark and like a labyrinth. I told Ollie that she should complain to the landlord and get it modernized, but she brushed me aside. It didn't matter, no one had been lost yet. She called it Murk Woods—some English reference," he said. "At one point they had explored every inch of it, I think."

"They?" Lily asked.

"She and Élise, the office manager now, but she was called the receptionist back then."

Lily frowned. In retrospect, it had been shortsighted to keep Mme Boucher in the dark. She sent her a quick text, asking if she felt well enough to talk.

M. Seguin continued, "Ollie told me they had found all sorts of things down there—a whole storage room devoted to a nineteenth-century family home. The remains of a watchmaker's business. Many cast-offs. It seems like things end up in that basement and they are never recovered."

Lily glanced at her phone to make sure it was recording. M. Seguin had a nice turn of phrase, and she was sure Jacob would be able to use this interview effectively in the story.

"Well, Papa, we found something down there, and we think Maman had a connection to it."

"What is it?" the man asked.

"I've emailed you some photographs. Can you take a look and tell us if you remember ever seeing it before?"

"Ah yes, I will look."

"Just click into your email inbox, Papa, you don't need to hang up . . ."

It was too late, their screen had gone blank. Luc looked at her and shrugged. "He's seventy-two—I am amazed he manages to Skype."

Lily laughed. "My mother is completely wired. My brother bought her an iPhone and she has a tablet . . . she can't stop texting or updating Facebook—she's a fiend with Giphy."

"We should introduce them; perhaps your mother could be a good influence on my father."

She couldn't imagine her mother, who had never traveled abroad, coming to Paris. Lord knows Lily had offered to fly her over enough times. She had hoped after she retired her mom might spread her wings, but she wouldn't visit Lily's younger brother in Boston, let alone travel to Paris.

Before she could reply, Skype flashed back onto their screen. M. Seguin was beaming at them, and Lily's heart lifted. He must have recognized the Honeybee Emeralds.

Luc obviously thought the same thing. "You know the necklace, Papa?"

"Necklace? No, I've never seen it before. A bit garish for my taste."

Lily's heart plummeted and Luc's shoulders slumped.

M. Seguin was oblivious to their disappointment. "I didn't recognize the necklace, but I remember that jacket. It was Ollie's."

Lily's head snapped up. "What?" she demanded.

"The photo of the jacket—I recognized it at once."

Lily looked at the photos that Luc had sent. One had included a partial view of the jacket, its green sleeve and the pocket that had held the necklace visible in the image. This was the coat that Alice had found.

"It's easy to identify," M. Seguin continued. "Handmade—I don't know by who, but Olivia told me that Élise had embroidered those olives on especially for her. Élise was a real seamstress—knitting, sewing, all the womanly arts. I teased Ollie once, told her I should have married Élise so I could have a real wife. Your mother smacked me." He laughed fondly at the memory.

Lily and Luc stared at one another in surprise.

M. Seguin carried on. "Anyway, the jacket. It was a wonderful garment. Very sumptuous. She wore it the first time I met her—Christmas Day, walking down the Canal Saint-Martin with the sun in her face and Élise by her side. It was a coup de foudre on my part—a thunderclap. Love at first sight. She was elusive, like a rabbit, and I was the fox. She had no interest in me, even though many considered me quite the catch, or at least so my mother kept telling me." M. Seguin chuckled.

Luc nodded. "Yes, Papa. You've told this story often. The first time you met Maman she was rude to you. The second time you met, she had forgotten who you were. It was only on the third attempt that you managed to capture her attention."

M. Seguin nodded happily at the memory. "You know I always suspected she only agreed to go out with me because someone else had jilted her, though she never said a word to me about it. Your mother was extraordinarily discreet. One of her many sterling qualities."

"What happened to the jacket?" Lily asked.

"Eh? Well, I don't know. She wore it on the day I met her, but I'm not sure I ever saw it again, actually. It obviously made quite an impression on me."

"Yes, it's beautifully made," Lily said. How had it ended up in the wardrobe room and, more important, with a priceless necklace in its pocket?

"No, no, the history of it," he said.

"History?"

"Yes, my goodness, I haven't thought about this in fifty years, but it's coming back to me now. When we chatted that first day, she told me that Joan Baez had once owned that jacket."

Mistaking their surprised expressions for lack of comprehension, he explained. "She is an American folk singer."

"We've heard of Joan Baez, but how on earth did Maman know her?" Luc asked.

"Well, well. Your mother had quite a life before settling down. She met all sorts of extraordinary people."

"How? I thought she was a waitress in Paris before starting the magazine."

"Oh, she may have waitressed at some point, but she spent a few years working in the Dordogne. She didn't speak of it much, you know, the ending was painful, and she felt such responsibility for the children."

"What children, what are you talking about, Papa?" Luc was clearly frustrated.

"Why, she was the nanny. The nanny for the Rainbow Tribe. She looked after Josephine Baker's children."

"Maman worked for Josephine Baker, the singer." Luc's voice was flat, almost disinterested, but there was something about his body language—tightly coiled and intense—that made Lily glance at him in concern.

"Yes, yes," his father said.

Lily wanted to pump her fists in the air. Here was a clear connection between *Bonjour Paris* and the necklace itself. This was going to blow Yvette's damn story out of the water.

"How come I never knew this?" Luc asked.

M. Seguin shrugged. "I'm surprised you didn't. It wasn't a secret, but then again, you know your mother—no dwelling in the past. Parts of her life were closed to me. I had to accept that when I married her."

"The fact that Maman worked as a nanny for Josephine Baker seems like something she should have shared," Luc said.

Lily now heard the frustration in his voice, and she grimaced in sympathy. As much as she had come to admire Olivia over her year working at *Bonjour Paris*, having such a forceful, and apparently secretive, mother couldn't have been easy.

"I don't know what to tell you, son. Your mother was who she was."

That explanation struck Lily as cavalier. This latest revelation obviously hurt Luc, but M. Seguin was still too busy defending his wife's actions to try to help his son. Had it been like that for Luc's whole life? His mother active, incandescent, and energetic and his father too besotted to pay their youngest child much attention? Suddenly Lily's own childhood, plagued with money shame and anxieties but also populated with two loving parents, a doting grandmother, and three rough and tumble siblings, looked good in comparison.

M. Seguin seemed determined to finish the story of the jacket, still thinking it was the source of their questioning. "Anyway, Joan Baez met Josephine Baker at the March on Washington—that was a big civil rights event in the 1960s. Apparently, Josephine said she liked the jacket, and the singer gave it to her on the spot. At some point, Josephine then gave the coat to your mother."

Could the necklace have somehow slipped into its pocket while Josephine was wearing it, and the singer handed it over to Olivia without realizing that a valuable piece of jewelry was nestled inside? That didn't seem likely. The necklace was heavy. Josephine or Olivia would have noticed the weight.

"Ollie said that Josephine was always generous with gifts, although absolutely terrible at paying wages on time or managing money."

Could Olivia have stolen the necklace and hidden it? That didn't square with what she knew about Olivia. Besides, why steal a valuable piece of jewelry and then leave it languishing in an unlocked basement storage room for years?

M. Seguin was on a roll, addressing Luc. "If you're so interested in that period, you could try to find that journal of hers—a little red one. Ollie didn't keep a regular diary, but I remember her saying that she'd had one when she arrived in France. It is probably amongst the things you took of hers last time you visited."

They hung up, and Lily and Luc looked at each other with excitement. "I think I know where that journal is," Luc said, turning to his bedroom.

Before they could take another step, both of their phones chimed—a text message.

It was an SOS from Jacob. "Emergency—meet at Café Neptune now."

Berlin, 1965

The venue was tiny, and the sharp, unpleasant tang of old sauerkraut was a thin under-smell whenever she breathed in too deeply. The last time she had performed in Berlin was, oh, 1937, right before that terrible little man had banned her. He hadn't approved of her erotic dancing, and he had positively hated the color of her skin. Back then, the club was packed with people, the manager wringing his hands and muttering worriedly about fire department violations. The air, filled with the warm smell of tobacco and the rich odor of schnapps, had crackled with anticipation. She had blazed out on stage, performed her famous "Danse Sauvage," waggled her banana skirt, and held them firmly in the palm of her hand.

This time it was different. Her bones ached and the crowd before her, a sea of old, wrinkled faces, beaten down by the war, that terrible wall, and age, were as tired and as uninspired as her show. Perhaps it was time to stop. Give up performing. How could she, though? Bills to pay, mouths to feed. So many mouths.

Her dressing room was shabby, and there was no one to help her from her costume at the end of the show.

"Mademoiselle Baker?"

He was in his mid-forties, balding and a bit pudgy in a cheap suit. So this was her fan base now? One lone man, who hadn't even thought to bring flowers? Once her dressing room would have overflowed with roses.

She smiled graciously at him. "Yes," she said.

He took a step inside the room, breaking into a wide grin, and for a moment she could glimpse the young man he had once been. "That was wonderful," he said with a thick German accent. "What a show. Magical to see you on stage again."

The "again" was the kicker. No one who had seen her perform before could truthfully have found that arthritic shuffle inspiring. She had once been described as "electrifying," but now the only thing she inspired was nostalgia. Her performance hadn't been about what she could still do, but about reminding the audience, this man, about what their lives had been like back when they had hair, and waistlines. Back before the war.

His next words confirmed it. "I saw you perform in Berlin, 1937. I was sixteen—I snuck in. I had never seen anyone like you before. A negro lady dancing as you did. I didn't know people could be so free, so open with who they were. You inspired me."

She was tired of being told how important she *had been*. So very close to *has been*. "Well, it was the wrong time to be inspired, wasn't it?"

"Yes," he agreed, a shadow crossing his face.

She was ashamed of her causticness. It wasn't this man's fault that his youth was engulfed, swallowed by the monstrous events of the war. "Thank you for coming tonight," she said.

"I wouldn't have missed it. To see you up there, on stage again. It reminded me of what I had once felt all those years ago."

There was the "again" again. Her performance, her art, the urgent feeling she still harbored in her chest to wow, to seduce, to connect, was trapped— she couldn't get that message across. She felt deeply, heavily depressed. "Well, thank you for stopping in," she said, turning back to her vanity mirror and picking up a sponge to begin removing her makeup. "It was lovely to meet you," she lied, dismissing him.

She swiped at her cheek, the thick pancake makeup coming off brown on the sponge. She looked up; he was still standing in the doorway, and she sighed with impatience. In the old days, she would have had a bodyguard there, waiting to eject overeager fans. Now she would have to do it herself, and it would make this depressing encounter perhaps unpleasant as well. "I have to get changed now," she spoke in a firm voice.

Rather than leave, however, he took another step into her small dressing room.

Josephine gathered her dressing gown around her neck, for the first time conscious that she was alone with him. Her chest tightened in fear.

CHAPTER 31

Café Neptune

USUALLY ALICE LOVED THE FELLOWSHIP MEETINGS, THAT SENSE of excitement and camaraderie was intoxicating. But this time she felt only worry. Something about Jacob's text, so curt and urgent, caused her concern. Alice left the office and headed over to the nearby café.

The first to arrive, she selected a long table at the back of the room and ordered a mint tea. Despite Lily's chipper texts, assuring the Fellowship that they would carry on, regardless of *La Vie en Rose*'s scoop, Alice wondered if they were actually going to disband the Fellowship. That would be calamitous. All of their hard work, all of her research, for nothing. What's more, did that mean M. Seguin would shut down the magazine? She'd be out of a job. How would a truncated internship look on her résumé?

Lily and M. Seguin arrived together, almost immediately followed by Daphne. The three began talking excitedly. Apparently, Olivia Seguin nannied for Josephine Baker. The news distracted Alice from her worry. Alexander slid into a chair beside her. He smelled nice—something lemony—and his hair was less wild than usual. Had he taken a comb to it? He sensed her stare and frowned at her, but she smiled back at him.

Jacob arrived, and one look at his grim face made their chatter die away. He stalked to the table. "I won't beat around the bush," he said. "The Honeybee Emeralds is gone."

The blood drained from Alice's face, and she thought for a moment she might faint. She closed her eyes and felt a steady hand on her wrist.

Alexander had noticed her wooziness.

"What are you talking about," Daphne gasped.

Jacob spoke quickly. "Lily asked me to go to the bank this morning to pick up the necklace. We were going to hand it over to the police as part of our story."

A feeling of dread, like a thick weight, compressed Alice's lungs, making it difficult to get a full breath.

"When I opened up the box, the necklace was gone."

"How is this possible?" Lily demanded, her face green. "It was in a safety-deposit box, locked up tight in a bank. It couldn't have been stolen."

"You're right," Jacob said. "Someone with a key got there first thing this morning and strolled out with it. I questioned the tellers. They keep a register of who goes in and out."

Alice nodded. She knew all about that register. She had signed it on every visit to the bank. How many times was that? She closed her eyes for a moment, willing this news to be different.

"Well, who was it?" Luc demanded impatiently.

Jacob shrugged. "No one had a useful description, but it was a woman. She signed the register 'E. Nadeau' and had a key. It could be a false name. The teller didn't check her identification, even though they are supposed to."

It was true, Alice thought queasily, she had never had to show ID when she went to the bank. In retrospect, their security was lax.

"Yvette Dufeu," Lily said, her face flushing with anger. "It must have been her. Somehow, she learned we had the necklace. She could have snuck into the office, got the safety-deposit box key, and stole it."

"It might be Yvette," Daphne said, "but maybe you're letting your dislike cloud your judgment. Should we consider your office manager? The key was in her desk drawer. Maybe she read the article this morning and somehow realized we had the necklace and grabbed it."

M. Seguin spoke forcefully. "Nonsense. Élise Boucher has served *Bonjour Paris* for almost fifty years. Her loyalty is unimpeachable."

"But . . ." Daphne said.

M. Seguin simply shook his head, and Daphne stowed her argument.

Alice considered Daphne's point. If Mme Boucher had been to the bank this morning, she must have gone quite early and returned the key to the drawer before Jacob showed up. It didn't make sense to steal a necklace and then bother to return the key.

Jacob put up his hand. "I actually think there's an explanation that's closer to home," he said. "I asked to see the bank register, and someone has been to the safety-deposit box five times in the last ten days."

"What?" Daphne yelped. "Who?"

Jacob's eyes met hers.

Alice's whole body was on fire, sweat sprang to her hairline, and she stood reflexively. Everyone turned to her. It was like she was seeing them through a wall of water, or a thick pane of glass. Lily looked confused, Daphne was speculative, M. Seguin's eyes were hard, and Alexander—well, she couldn't even look at him.

"I didn't take it," Alice said quickly. "I just went to see it a few times."

"A few times?" Jacob interrupted. The disappointment in his eyes was like a slap. "You went there five times, and you never told any of us."

"Did you steal the necklace?" Daphne asked, her tone serious.

Alice's eyes filled with tears, but she blinked them back. This was too important to cry. "No!" she said vehemently. "I didn't take it."

Lily's voice was soft. "What were you doing there, then?" she asked.

"I don't know." Alice bit her lip. She stepped back, as if she could escape the questions, but she was against the wall, literally. "I wanted to touch it. I felt such an incredible connection with it," she said pleadingly. "It was like it was calling to me."

"So you snuck out to visit with a necklace?" Daphne's voice held incredulity and perhaps contempt.

Alice flushed with shame. She felt so stupid. She was so stupid. "I don't know," she sputtered. "I would just look at it, touch the stones, then I'd put it right back. I didn't take it," she repeated.

"And we're expected to believe that?" Jacob asked.

"Wait a second," Lily said, standing up. "If Alice says she didn't take it, I believe her."

Alice's knees wobbled in gratitude.

"Lily, you can be really naive," Jacob said. "I hate to say this, but we all might have been played."

M. Seguin now stood. "I think we're getting a little overexcited," he said calmly. "Alice has admitted to going to the bank, she's here right now, so she obviously hasn't absconded. She could have stolen the necklace at any point, had she wanted to."

"I didn't," Alice said fervently. "I didn't steal it. I just visited it." It sounded so pathetic when she said it aloud. She wanted to die from humiliation.

"What were you thinking, Alice?" Lily's voice was confused rather than accusatory. "Why were you sneaking around? What if your visits alerted Yvette to the necklace's existence?"

Lily's words pierced her heart. "I'm sorry," she blurted. She hadn't thought that her actions would jeopardize the Honeybee Emeralds.

"I told you all we should have gone to the police right away," Daphne cried. Her voice held a note of panic that was all the more disconcerting coming from such a normally calm woman. "How do you think this is going to look to them now? *La Vie en Rose* publishes an article on a necklace that we claim we found and then lost?" Daphne's hands twisted together. "If they even believe our story, they'll think we're responsible. Oh, God," she said. "What will this do to my career?"

A fresh wave of embarrassment and remorse overwhelmed Alice, and for a moment she couldn't speak. "I'm so stupid," she mumbled. "I didn't mean for this to happen." She had ruined it all.

She looked at their faces—unfriendly, questioning, angry. These people didn't want her. She was the idiot who had broken their trust. She had wrecked the Fellowship.

Alice had to get out, away from the accusation and disappointment in their eyes. She pushed the table away. The tears she'd been trying to hold back came rushing out. Alexander put out a hand to stop her. "Leave me alone," she cried, stumbling to the door and racing out onto the street.

CHAPTER 32

Hair Dye

THERE WAS A MOMENT'S SILENCE AFTER ALICE LEFT, AND THEN
Alexander stood. He towered over Lily, and she took a startled step back.
His face was as impassive as always, which somehow made his words worse.
"You people are terrible," he said, and strode out of the café.

"Alice didn't take the necklace," Lily said, sitting back down and
feeling exhausted. She had seen the intern's face. There was no way she was
involved in any kind of theft.

"I want to believe you're right." Daphne's voice held a righteous note,
and annoyance flared in Lily's chest. Her friend could be very judgmental.
"But how do we explain her sneaking around?"

Luc frowned. "I don't believe she took the necklace. Why would she
sign the register? Let's end that line of speculation."

"Well, we shouldn't be hasty," Jacob said. "Someone stole it. We need
to call the police."

"And tell them what?" Luc asked contemptuously. "That we found a
valuable necklace and didn't report it? We're not even the owners."

Jacob's fingers balled into fists. Lily felt the beginnings of a headache,
a sharp, piercing pain that squeezed her temples. She moaned softly and
rubbed her head.

"Well, if we're sure it wasn't Alice, who took it?"

Luc turned with decision. "I'm not saying Yvette is the thief, but it
must be related to the *La Vie en Rose*'s story. It is too much of a coincidence

that the necklace disappeared the morning she published the article. I'll go to Yvette now, demand answers."

Lily's headache was slowing her thinking process, and he was already at the door by the time his words computed. He was going to confront Yvette? His former fiancée? Was there an eagerness to his step? The tension in her head increased. The Least Weasel would have him wrapped around her finger in a minute. Her skin felt hot and itchy. There was a moment's silence after Luc's departure.

"Well, you really served up a shit sandwich," Daphne said to Jacob.

"What?" he asked aggressively.

"You were so accusatory," she said. "You should have eased off on Alice."

"Are you kidding?" Jacob asked. He was pacing now, still agitated. Lily wished he would sit down and take a beat. Daphne downed her coffee and waved the waiter over for another. Why was Luc so sure he knew where to find Yvette?

"You were just as aggressive," Jacob flung at Daphne.

"Me? I hardly said anything."

"Exactly, you weren't much help. We need to keep thinking. Now that Seguin is gone, we should seriously consider Mme Boucher," Jacob said. "She is the logical suspect."

"She called in sick, and she's not answering my texts," Lily said. She tried calling her, but there was no response.

"I can't handle this," Daphne said. "I can't be involved in a missing necklace, especially one with the Honeybee Emeralds's pedigree. It was one thing when we were looking for the owner, but now that it's gone . . ." Daphne's voice trailed away.

Lily stifled her impatience with both Jacob's aggressiveness and Daphne's self-absorption. "We're all upset, let's try to get along and be logical. We have a story to finish."

"Oh, come on, Lily," Daphne said. "It's over."

"What?" she asked, confused.

Now Jacob and Daphne seemed to be in agreement. He stopped pacing and dropped back into his seat at the table. "The Fellowship, or whatever this was—is over," he said. "We got scooped by Yvette, we lost the necklace, traumatized Alice, pissed off Alexander, and now Luc has stormed off God only knows where. Were we ever sure of his loyalties?"

"I told you," Lily said. "They were engaged, but it's long over."

"Come on, Jacob," Daphne interjected. "Do you honestly think he stole the necklace? Get over this infantile rivalry."

"Rivalry?" Jacob laughed. "What are you talking about?"

"Really?" Daphne asked. "You're going to make me spell it out?"

Lily looked at her friend's angry red face. She remembered their chat at the Coutume Café where Daphne had insinuated that she had a crush on Jacob. Oh God, what was she about to blurt? "Daphne—" Lily said warningly.

It was too late. "Come on Jacob," Daphne said, "you've been acting like a pissy jerk to Luc because you think he might take Lily's attention away from you."

"What?" Jacob asked, genuinely flabbergasted.

"Daphne!" Lily said more firmly. "Shut up, you don't know what you're talking about."

Daphne ignored her, intent on saying her piece. "You can't stand having Lily pay attention to another man. Just because you've led her around on a string for years doesn't mean she's just going to keep waiting for you."

There was a roar in Lily's ears, and she thought her head might split wide open. "Daphne!" she shouted. Other patrons turned to look at them, and Lily lowered her voice. "Shut the hell up. You don't know what you're talking about."

Daphne turned to her, surprising Lily with the anger she saw in her friend's eyes. "It's true," she said fiercely. "I'm sick of watching you get hurt by this guy, and I'm also sick of you dismissing my opinions."

Lily closed her eyes, having trouble following her logic.

"I've contributed to this project—I'm the one who connected us with Medici dit Beauregard. I'm the one who realized the necklace had been confiscated in the war. I'm the one who did the research and found the necklace postwar."

"I know," Lily snapped, wondering how the conversation had swung from her righteous anger at Daphne to a discussion of her friend's contributions. "I'm grateful, but—"

"Are you?" Daphne interrupted. "You haven't said 'thank you' once."

Lily lost what remained of her patience. This was so typical of Daphne—never satisfied, always unhappy with people, always hard done by. "Well, I'm sorry I haven't been catering to your almighty ego, Daphne, but we've all been a bit busy."

"Let's be honest about your true motivation," Daphne said. "This whole necklace thing has been a pretext for you to spend more time with Jacob."

Lily gaped at her, unable to formulate a reply.

Her silence seemed to aggravate Daphne. "You've been in love with him for years."

Jacob's eyes widened.

Lily's pulse pounded in her ears. "Where the hell do you get off saying something like that?"

"Come on, Lily, I'm your best friend. I know you."

"My best friend? Oh really? And yet the only time we hang out is when Philip is out of town or you need a sitter for Theo."

"What?" Daphne asked.

"Look at our friendship, Daphne. We were super tight when you moved to Paris, but you ditched me the instant you met Philip."

"That again? It was years ago. You've been carrying a grudge around this whole time?"

Lily shrugged, feeling foolish but refusing to concede. "You really hurt me."

"Well, I won't apologize for falling in love and having a child."

"Of course not," Lily said impatiently. "Obviously I understand that, but you made it hard to accept because you seem so pissed off about your own choices."

"What does that mean?"

"Daphne, you've got everything—a husband, a house, Theo." The words were spilling out of her without thought. "You have everything you want, yet you never trust it. You carry around a list of reasons not to be happy, adding up your grudges like Scrooge McDuck with his gold coins."

Daphne's eyes reflected startled pain, and Lily belatedly remembered her friend saying she and Philip had had a huge fight. She didn't mean to be piling onto Daphne, but Lily couldn't stop the flow of words. "Whatever you are looking for, and I know this sounds woo-woo, but it's the goddamn truth—whatever you're looking for is inside. You've got to get right with yourself. Your marriage, your life, would be better if you could just be happy with what you had instead of looking for reasons to be pissed off."

There was a long, painful silence, and though she wished she could have softened the words, Lily was glad she had said them. Daphne needed to hear it.

Her friend stood, smoothing out her cream-colored pants. "Well, thanks for the observations, Lily, but I'm not interested in being psychoanalyzed." She walked out of the café with her chin held high.

It was quiet for a moment, and then Lily turned to Jacob. "I'm sorry; I don't know what that was." She dug in her purse for some pills for her head. She gave a shaky sigh. "I don't know what we're going to do about the necklace."

Jacob came to sit beside her on the bench. "I don't care about the Honeybee Emeralds."

"You don't?" she asked, startled.

He was sitting so close she could count his eyelashes. The angle of the café light was such that she noticed something—Jacob's hair was gray at the roots, yet the rest was the same shade of deep blond he'd had as a nineteen-year-old. He was dying his hair. Her heart squeezed at this realization. Jacob was all confidence and bravado, acting like the man who had life figured out, but here he was, dyeing his hair because he didn't want to get old. There was something heartbreakingly vulnerable about it.

"What Daphne said—about you and me, was that true?"

Lily couldn't look at him, and she gave a weak shake of her head.

Jacob sighed, a ragged sound. "Lily, I remember the first time I saw you—stomping across the Commons Lawn with a load of books in your hands. It's like a scene from a movie that I can replay over and over. That night we were together—grad night—was another moment like that. A touchstone."

"What are you talking about?" she asked.

"We both freaked out so badly after we slept together, and then you didn't talk to me for six months because it was so awkward. Going that long without you was the loneliest time in my life. I told myself that I wouldn't risk our friendship by making another play for you, so I threw myself into writing and tried to stop thinking about you like that."

He couldn't have had actual feelings for her. He was always too handsome, too confident, too much. Lily leaned away from him and crossed her arms. She shouldn't be hearing all of this. Not when her head hurt so badly. "You're with Marie-Pierre."

"Exactly. I am with Marie-Pierre, doing the same thing I have done in every single relationship I've ever had. Tricking myself into believing I'm happy with someone because I didn't want to admit the truth."

"Oh yeah?" she said. "And what's that?"

"The truth is that I love you."

Lily barked out a laugh. "You don't know what you're talking about."

"I know you," he said, and the fierceness of his voice more than his words made her listen. "You're smart and fierce and funny and sexy as hell."

Lily couldn't meet his eyes.

"I also know love, Lily. Real love is being challenged. Real love is this attraction we share. Real love is going cross-eyed with jealousy when Luc Seguin swoops in on your damn girl."

Jacob grabbed her by the arms and pulled her to him. His mouth found hers and she closed her eyes, allowing herself to melt against his chest. The kiss was tender at first, questioning, but Lily responded and it deepened. Lily was lost, floating and drowning all at the same time. Her headache vanished and her desire for more overwhelmed all other thoughts. Jacob was so strong, so handsome—this is what she had been fantasizing about for days, months, years. It was so good to give in to her attraction. She felt like she was soaring, and she deepened the kiss further.

They were interrupted by a loud chime.

A text from Luc, all caps: "LILY: I'VE FOUND MOTHER'S DIARY. COME AT ONCE."

CHAPTER 33

Pistachios

THANK GOD, PAULINE WASN'T HOME. ALICE WAS IN NO MOOD FOR her roommate's sharp, malicious inquisitiveness. She pulled out the old suitcase Dale and her mother had loaned her when she left for Paris. The thought of returning home, back to the safe confines of Victoria Road, consumed her. She had believed she could make a place for herself in the city, in this country, but she didn't belong here. The Fellowship—what a joke that was—had turned on her. She recalled Jacob's face as he leveled his accusations. Disgust had radiated from their bodies like angry stink waves.

If only she hadn't been so foolishly weak. Why had she felt that compulsion to see the necklace? Good God, she gave a shaky laugh. She wasn't Legolas or Frodo or even Samwise Fucking Gamgee—she was Gollum, obsessed with her "Precious." That stupid necklace had made her feel safe and a part of something, but it had been her downfall.

Her phone chimed again. Probably a text from Lily. Alice ignored it. Undoubtedly she was fired, but she couldn't face the final confirmation. Better to tell herself she was quitting.

She looked around. The tiny, shabby flat didn't hold much of hers. It had come "furnished," the landlord throwing in the mold in the bathroom and the chronically leaking kitchen sink for free.

She threw her clothes from the hall closet into the suitcase, but paused when her hand touched the velvet jacket. It had been too warm to wear it this past week, but it would serve her well in windy Hull. She placed it carefully in her suitcase. Next she dropped to her knees and dug under the futon for her pistachios. Every evening after work she treated herself to five roasted Iranian pistachios, spiced with lemon and saffron. Her mother had given her a big jar as a leaving present when she had departed for Paris. She allotted herself only five because they were very expensive and she wanted them to last. She had almost cried the day she had come home to find Pauline nonchalantly popping her costly pistachios into her mouth as if they were salt and vinegar crisps. Since then, she had stored them under her futon, mad maybe, but no quarter could be given in the flatmate wars. Now she threw the precious nuts into her suitcase. No way was she leaving them for Pauline.

She looked at her phone, trying to figure out the coach schedule. Damn it, she only had twenty percent battery. Would she have time to charge it before leaving? There was a knock, or more like a pounding, on her door.

She opened it to Alexander.

"What are you doing here?" she squeaked. "How do you know where I live?"

"I went to *Bonjour Paris*. I found your address."

"You shouldn't have done that," Alice said sharply.

Alexander shrugged. "I did."

There was his breathtaking confidence again. He just *did* things when it suited him. He felt entitled to take up space in the world. What would her life be like if she could have just a pinch of that attitude? She wouldn't be tied up in knots about a few innocent visits to a bank vault, said an unexpected inner voice that sounded an awful lot like Daphne.

Alexander looked around, taking in the cramped space, the cracked walls, and the half-packed suitcase on her bed. He gave a deep sniff and nodded. "Patchouli," he said.

"My roommate burns incense all the time."

"Yes, you always carry the faintest scent," Alexander said. "I had wondered."

For some reason, Alice blushed. "I didn't steal that necklace," she said, jutting out her chin. "You can search the flat if you must."

"You're leaving?" he asked, ignoring her statement.

She shrugged. "I can't stay."

"We are not done. We haven't found the whole story. We don't know the ending."

"What do you care?" she asked. She turned back to the cheap dresser and threw more clothes into the suitcase. "Were you ever really interested in solving the mystery? You wanted us to go to the police from the get-go."

Alexander said nothing.

"How can I be expected to stay here and go in to work tomorrow when everyone has accused me of theft?"

He didn't answer.

In the face of Alexander's silence, Alice was forced to be fair. "Well, Lily defended me." She recalled that awful moment when they had all stared at her. "I mean, I was sneaking out to the bank, so I could see how they might leap to an accusation." Her haphazard packing slowed. "I guess if I were in their shoes, I might come to the same conclusion." She bit her lip, holding a pair of socks meditatively in her hands. "I probably should have waited for them to decide on a course of action." She put the socks down and picked up a pair of jeans from the suitcase. She carefully refolded them, smoothing out the creases. She shot a glance at Alexander. He was leaning against the wall by the kitchen sink. His face was still, but she knew he was listening. "My whole life I've never felt like I belonged anywhere. The Fellowship was different." Her voice cracked. "It was just so hurtful to have everyone turn on me like that."

"Not everyone," Alexander said.

Alice's eyes filled with tears. "No, you're right. Not everyone. You're here, aren't you?"

Silently he handed her a handkerchief. She nearly laughed at the sight of its delicate white lace. Trust enormous, slovenly Alexander to have such a tiny, pristine cloth at the ready. She wiped her eyes and squared her shoulders. She didn't have to scuttle away. She didn't have to quit the Fellowship. "You're right," she said again. "I can't go home like this, my tail between my legs. I did nothing wrong. At least, nothing too terrible. I'm not a quitter."

She could stay and help find the necklace. She could undo the mistakes that she had made.

She started to unpack her belongings. "I don't know why I was so obsessed with touching that necklace. It was almost like a compulsion. I worried so much it would be gone, and I found it soothing to confirm it was still there. Now my worst fear has come to pass . . . and yet I'm not falling to pieces." Her tone was wondering. "Maybe it wasn't about the necklace at all. Maybe I was going to the bank as a test, to see what would happen if I was discovered." Even as she said those words, she realized their truth. She recalled her Intro to Psychology class. Did she so fear rejection from the Fellowship that she self-sabotaged in order to prove her fears correct? "Oh God," she said. "Who knew I was such a nutter?"

"Not a nutter," Alexander said. "Complex."

She shot him a grateful look. Her phone chimed again. Another text from Lily. This time she didn't ignore it, but read the whole string.

Lily: Are you okay? I'm sorry about that. No one thinks you stole the necklace.

Lily: I'm in a cab heading over to Luc's. He's found another clue.

Lily: I'm sorry we were all such schmucks. Tell me you're okay.

Alice texted back. "I'm all right. I'm so sorry I was such an idiot. Let me know how I can help." Her phone was at fifteen percent. She put it on battery-saving mode and stared at the image of the Honeybee Emeralds on the wallpaper. "How are we going to find this?" she asked.

"May I see?" Alexander asked.

She handed him the phone, and he stared at the image. Then, with his thick fingers he zoomed in. "Why are those diamonds missing?" he asked musingly. He pointed to where he had enlarged one of the four unfilled settings near the clasp.

Alice wasn't sure where he was going with this, but answered. "We know from Adeline's letter to Francis that there were forty diamonds on the necklace when Charles Leboeuf gave it to Josephine," Alice said. "Now there are only thirty-six." She examined the missing spaces more closely. "Look at the settings," she said. They were bent, as if pried open by pliers. "Someone pried the diamonds out."

"Why?" Alexander asked thoughtfully.

"Well, probably to sell them, don't you think?"

"Removing those diamonds has damaged this necklace. Reduced its worth because it is not complete. That reduction in overall value is probably much higher than what someone would get for each separate diamond," he said.

Alexander was volunteering more of his thoughts than he normally did.

"Yes, but they were removed from near the clasp where they would be least noticed when the necklace was worn." Alice pursued the thought. "The person who took the diamonds didn't necessarily want to sell the whole piece, but may have needed money. Maybe they were skint."

Alice began to pace. "We know from her biographies that Josephine had terrible money problems, especially after the war. She sold much of her jewelry to keep her château afloat and her family together." It was difficult to pace in the cramped space. She kept running up against bits of furniture or walls. She felt they were close to figuring something out. "Now that we know the necklace was still in Josephine's possession after the war, would it make sense that she pried out some diamonds to pay the bills?"

She paused in front of Alexander. He was listening intently. "According to Adeline, this necklace had great sentimental value for Josephine, but then again her bills were mad. She had twelve children, multiple divorces, all of the relatives she was supporting, plus that château—it was an absolute white elephant. One biography talked about how she had cars, art, furs, and jewels repossessed on a regular basis. She took to stashing valuables around the city, often under other friends' names so her creditors couldn't find them. She even did it with the costumes she wore for her performances . . ."

Alice's voice trailed away. She was remembering her many visits to the safety-deposit box. There were a lot of legal papers related to *Bonjour Paris* and to Olivia Owens's life in there. One of them had been the magazine's lease. She had glanced through it very quickly on her first visit. She closed her eyes, concentrating on the pages she saw. Yes, she thought. She was remembering correctly.

Her eyes snapped open. "We need to get to *Bonjour Paris*," she said. "We have to go back to the basement. Back to the wardrobe room where it all began."

CHAPTER 34

Pandora's Box

"THE JOURNAL IS IN HERE," LUC SAID, LEADING LILY THROUGH his apartment. She had left Jacob at the café, not needing him and the confusion of that kiss following her to Luc's. Locating the necklace was their priority, and if Luc found a clue that meant dropping everything (and everyone).

Luc's bedroom was monochromatic beige with good-size windows and a huge bed. He was more agitated than she had ever seen him. "When Yvette wouldn't return my calls, I came back here. I thought if I couldn't find Yvette, I could at least locate Maman's journal."

A battered green metal box, like something you could buy at an army surplus store, sat on the floor by a walk-in closet. "I found the journal in here," he said.

He and Lily knelt down on the carpet.

"This chest fascinated me as a child. I was never allowed to open it. Mother called it her Pandora's box." He smiled at the memory. "Papa gave it to me last time I visited. I hadn't looked at it yet. Still too soon after her death."

Was Luc ready for this? Lily forced herself to say, "If you don't feel up to it, we can wait."

"Are you mad?" he demanded. "I opened it as soon as I got home. The journal was at the top. I texted you when I spotted it. I didn't want to read it without you."

"Really?" Lily asked.

Luc shrugged. "It seems I never knew my mother that well. I need some moral support."

Lily wanted to take a moment to absorb the intimacy of this confession, but the journal and the answers it might contain were too alluring.

It was a small red diary, easily fitting in the palm of Luc's hand. He met her eyes, and she nodded.

The writing was large and sprawling, a few sentences taking up a whole page. The entries were usually short—three or four lines only, and they began June 4, 1965. "Landed and smelled my first breath of Paris. I am intoxicated! Vive la France!" The next was a month later, mentioning a concert Olivia had attended: "John Coltrane—Salle Pleyel—amazing music. Smoked my first reefer."

Luc looked up. "We had this album. *John Coltrane Live in Paris 1965.* Maman never said she'd attended. She used to play it on summer evenings. The whole house would fill with the sound of that saxophone." He shook his head.

They scanned the entries quickly, until Lily clutched Luc's arm. "There," she said, pointing to a name on the page.

November 3, 1965: Met Josephine Baker tonight. Talked about America and Saint Louis. Told me she liked my 'Yankee confidence.' Tried oysters. Did not care for them.

A month later, another entry, this one marked "Les Milandes."

"That's Baker's estate in the Dordogne," Luc said. "Josephine must have offered Maman a job."

Met the 'Rainbow Tribe.' So many kids. I don't know what I will do with them. Played hide-and-seek and lost one for three hours. This place is huge. Josephine is traveling.

Another dated April 1966:

JB back from a trip with a new infant in her arms. Demanded the children be roused at eleven p.m. to greet her. I have not been paid in three months. The baby is gorgeous.

October 1966:

Beautiful day today. Picnic. Children wonderful. JB arrived and in a good mood. Presents for all and a small payment for me. Back pay coming, she promises. Meanwhile, I see that the Oriental rugs in the main house have all been rolled up—presumably for sale?

There were similar notes until at last, on January 3, 1968, there was a much longer entry. It seemed that Olivia had needed to express her feelings.

JB home from a long trip—Lisbon, Barcelona, and points beyond. Exhausted and dictatorial. Displeased with the children. Says that Akio is growing too quickly. How can that be a complaint?! I had enough. I waited until the children were in bed and she was alone in the salon. "I quit," I told her. She begged me to stay. I told her I hadn't been paid in over a year. I told her I had to go. It was too hard. My heart breaks for those children. And for her. Just yesterday workers removed all of the chandeliers from the ballroom—paying a debt, undoubtedly. JB didn't argue with me. "You lasted longer than most, Olivia." She is so seldom home, I was surprised she remembered my name. We reminisced about my time with them. I was amazed at how much she recalled of the children. She was paying more attention than I realized. She loves them in her complicated fashion. At last I said, straightforwardly—American to American—"You owe me two years of back pay."

"I am a bit cash poor at the moment, darling," Josephine said. She closed her eyes, and I thought she'd fallen asleep—she was working so hard, traveling so much, and in such poor health. At last, she opened her big brown eyes. "I will give you something," she said with decision. "It was given to me by a man who had suffered a terrible heartbreak during the Great War. It was my inspiration during my Resistance work. I thought I lost it forever, but a few years ago it found me again. Now I want you to have it. Lord knows, it will only be sold eventually to cover some debt."

She walked over to a small safe and withdrew a necklace—a double strand of diamonds, a bee-shaped pendant, two thick emeralds like expensive Brussels sprouts. She laid it on a small side table. "You'll see it is missing a couple of stones. I've had to use them to pay certain debts. I want you to start your life out properly, though," she said. "To do that, money helps. Use this necklace to get what you really desire."

I took it, doubting it was real. Now, here I am in Paris, and to my surprise, I discover it is genuine. JB paid me my wages and then some. I am truly in her debt, and have enough money to start a new life. Like JB, I've pried out a couple of diamonds, selling them. I open my magazine, and a new chapter of my life, tomorrow.

The diary ended there, the sprawling writing having eaten up all the pages of the small book.

"Your mother was the owner of the necklace," Lily said, stunned by this revelation and its implications. "That means that your family owns it now. It's yours, Luc, the Honeybee Emeralds belongs to you." They had the perfect ending to the article. This would destroy Yvette's small scoop. Lily texted the members of the Fellowship, letting them know there had been a big development and instructing them to reconvene at *Bonjour Paris* as soon as possible.

Before leaving, she and Luc looked for another notebook, emptying the trunk. It contained a number of treasures—a jar filled with beautiful shells and richly colored sea glass; a stack of black-and-white photographs held together by an old elastic. Luc looked at these quickly. "They are from Iowa—Maman's childhood." They pulled out a beautiful scarlet wool scarf, and a sprig of dried lavender fell out as it unraveled, the faint scent tickling their nostrils. Toward the bottom of the box were some drawings. Bright children's works—straight-limbed trees with green clouds of leaves, smiling people in triangle dresses, yellow suns with pointed rays and happy faces, the colors unfaded despite the brittleness of the paper and their obvious age. "These are not by me and my siblings—I think they are by Josephine's children, the Rainbow Tribe," Luc said.

Unfortunately, there was no other journal in the trunk. They did find, however, a tissue-thin sheet of paper with an old-fashioned scrawl: "I, Josephine Baker, do hereby and unreservedly give my diamond and emerald honeybee necklace to Xanthia Olivia Owens." It was signed by the singer.

"It's official," Luc said, looking stunned.

Lily felt a fierce tide of gladness. This twist was great for their article, but more than that, she was pleased that Luc would have such a tangible reminder of his mother. "The necklace is yours," she repeated.

"Now we just have to find it," he said grimly.

CHAPTER 35

The American Women's League Excursion to Chartres

DAPHNE SLAMMED HER FRONT DOOR SHUT AND MARCHED directly upstairs. Not bothering to remove her Jimmy Choo espadrilles, she climbed into bed fully clothed, pulling the duvet over her head. Only safe in her bed-nest did she allow herself to think: The necklace was gone and she was implicated in its disappearance. Why, why, why had she allowed herself to get embroiled in this stupid Fellowship? She groaned in anger. If Philip had been home this never would have happened.

She remembered how shattered Alice had looked as she left Café Neptune. She groaned louder, recalling her fight with Lily. She shouldn't have said all of that stuff about Jacob, but what the hell had Lily said about her? That she'd taken their friendship for granted? What other "truth" bombs had she dropped? That she was never satisfied and didn't know how to be grateful? That was patently false.

Daphne rolled over. She wrote in a special gratitude journal every night, as dutiful as a schoolgirl. She grabbed the leather-bound Smythson Soho notebook in moss green, opening it to a random page: "Today I am grateful for: Clean drinking water; Theo missing the lice outbreak; the scent of my Byredo Rose hand soap." She flipped through the pages, which went back two years. Her gratitudes carefully listed out, proof that she didn't take her privilege for granted.

As she was scanning the notebook, she noticed something. The further back she went, the more entries there were about Philip. "Grateful for my husband's amazing back rubs; grateful for Philip's firmness with his mother; grateful that Philip gave Theo his bath; grateful for a husband like Philip." She flipped forward, looking for the moment when her Philip gratitudes petered out, trying to find the place where her marriage changed. What were the words that Lily had flung at her? "Your marriage, your life, would be better if you could just be happy with what you had instead of looking for reasons to be pissed off." She didn't do that.

Daphne groaned again, remembering the things she had said to Jacob about Lily's crush. Why had she lashed out like that? She was upset about the necklace's loss, annoyed with Lily, and, underneath it all, panicked about the state of her marriage. She had blurted out words from a place of vulnerability. Hurt people hurt people. When would she learn?

She pushed the covers back and got out of bed. She had taken a vacation day and dropped everything to get to Café Neptune. She grabbed her gratitude notebook. She'd go downstairs, have a coffee, and write down everything she was thankful for. That would show Lily. She was stopped by the biography on her bedside table: *Josephine Baker: The Hungry Heart*. It was an apt title: Despite how talented and successful the singer was, it seemed that she always needed more—more children, more animals, more staff, more jewels. She was never content. Oh God, what had she told Philip during that awful fight? That she had a hole in her heart? Was she just quoting some biography? She'd told Philip she wanted another baby, but that wasn't really true. He was right; she loved the life they had now. Having a baby to save a marriage was a terrible idea. That's what her parents had done, and it had not worked in truly spectacular fashion. Had she just been overidentifying with Josephine Baker?

Her phone chimed, distracting her from unpleasant introspection. A text from Lily, instructing them to meet at *Bonjour Paris*.

Her spirits lifted. Her other worries faded from top of mind. Maybe they could recover the necklace. She grinned; if she was honest, she was also delighted that the Fellowship hadn't disbanded. She loved being in the thick of this adventure. She checked the text distribution list; yes, everyone was being summoned.

She looked at her Hermès H watch and cursed. It was Monday, and normally Theo went to music lessons right after school, but the instructor was sick. She was due to pick him up. She called Sasha to see if she could do it, but she had a Pilates class; Corinne was at the American Women's League excursion to Chartres; Vanessa had a big work deadline.

Five minutes later, Daphne found someone, or someone's nanny, to pick up Theo for an impromptu playdate. Babbling her thanks into the phone, she grabbed the car keys. She felt like a kid on Christmas Eve, excited but also queasy with worry that something calamitous might happen, making her miss the great reveal. She needed to get to *Bonjour Paris*. She yanked open her front door and jumped back, startled by the figure on her doorstep.

"You," she blurted. "What the hell are you doing here?"

CHAPTER 36

The Motorcycle Ride

"WHAT HAVE YOU REALIZED?" ALEXANDER ASKED AS ALICE grabbed a sweater and headed to the door.

"I looked at the lease in the safety-deposit box," Alice said, closing her eyes and seeing the paragraphs she had skimmed ten days earlier. "There was an addendum on the last page. Rental of a basement storage room, paid for by *Bonjour Paris*. It had been rented for over forty years."

"You had that in your head the whole time? Why didn't you tell us sooner?" Alexander asked.

Alice bit her lip. "That's not how my memory thing works," she stammered. "It's like my brain takes pictures, but I don't compute what's on the images unless I'm looking for it. I wasn't paying a lot of attention to the lease. I was focused on the necklace." She blushed, remembering her all-consuming desire to touch the Honeybee Emeralds. She was amazed she even remembered there had been a lease in that safety-deposit box.

"Well, I am glad you remembered now," Alexander said.

She smiled at him, grateful he accepted her strange brain makeup.

Her phone chimed, a text from Lily summoning them to *Bonjour Paris*. Perfect, they were going there anyway.

They hurried down her stairs. "The clothing has to be Josephine Baker's, don't you think?" Alice asked Alexander. "She knew Olivia, and she got her to store them for her. Josephine's costumes always belonged to her show producers. Josephine never liked that. She considered the clothing hers—this is in loads of the biographies. On closing night, she'd often steal the outfits—expensive things, designer stuff—and get friends to stash it for her until the producers stopped looking for it." They burst onto her street, and Alexander steered her eastward, toward the métro.

Alice felt newly alive to the sights and sounds of a Parisian springtime. There were birds in the trees, a soft blue sky overhead, and the feeling of infinite possibility in her heart. She practically had to stop herself from skipping. "After Josephine died," Alice continued, "tons of people came forward with all sorts of her possessions that they had tucked away and hidden from creditors. I'd wager that's what the wardrobe room is—a stash of Josephine's treasures."

Alexander stepped toward a group of parked scooters and then bent over and fiddled with one before handing her a helmet. She stared at it. "You drive a scooter?" she asked.

"Motorcycle," he replied.

He pointed to a large black machine, which he straddled with surprising nimbleness. She hesitated. "I didn't know you had a bike," she said.

He shrugged. "It was in the shop."

Alice had never ridden on a motorcycle before. The thought had honestly never even occurred to her. Her mother would definitely go spare if she ever found out.

Alexander waited, not saying anything.

She plopped the helmet on her head and did up the chinstrap, then slid on behind him. "Let's do this," she said, pleased at how rock 'n' roll she sounded.

Within twenty seconds of revving the engine to life and zipping into traffic, any shyness Alice may have felt about sitting behind Alexander whipped away. She wrapped both her arms around his waist and gripped as if the tighter she held on, the safer she would be. They weaved in and out of traffic, Alexander maneuvering around slow-moving vehicles and nipping through roundabouts. The wind beat Alice's face, making her eyes stream, the roar of the engine drowned out all rational thought and her heart pounded in her ears. She thought she was terrified, or at least furious with him, until she realized she was laughing.

Alice was still laughing when she got off the bike in front of *Bonjour Paris* and handed Alexander her helmet. What surprised her was that he was laughing too; his whole face opened up, his eyes crinkling in the corners, and for a moment she could glimpse the little boy he had been. "You liked that, then?" he asked her.

"It was brilliant," she said.

"I thought you would enjoy it," he said with satisfaction, and Alice's stomach did a funny flip-flop to think that he had been considering her like that.

Alexander headed to his workspace to get the key to the basement, and Alice popped into the office to grab a notepad. There was an envelope on her desk addressed to "Aliyeh Ahmadi." It was in Mme Boucher's handwriting. The office manager must have come back into the office while they were all gone, but she was supposed to be sick.

Alexander entered as Alice opened the envelope. She read the short note aloud. "Aliyeh my dear. I know how your story ends. You will find the answers you seek in the basement wardrobe room, where I believe this adventure of yours first began. Sincerely, Élise Boucher."

Her heart banging in her chest, Alice met Alexander's eyes. "Mme Boucher knew about the wardrobe room. I think she knows about the necklace, maybe even where it is. We have to get to the basement."

She texted the others, telling people to meet in the wardrobe room, reminding them to follow the red thread. She hit send and blinked at her phone. Down to five percent. Her old battery wasn't going to last.

She urged Alexander back onto the street and then through the building's main doors to the entrance to the basement. She didn't want to wait around for the Fellowship. Mme Boucher might still be in the wardrobe room. Alexander left the basement door propped open for the others, and the two of them raced down the stairs.

They navigated the confusing jumble of hallways, walking purposefully and in silence. Alice's heart beat rapidly. It was only when Alexander paused for a moment, looking for the red thread, which could be hard to see in the gloom, that Alice realized they'd been holding hands. It was only as his fingers squeezed hers that she realized that this, more than the discoveries they'd made about the necklace, more than being readmitted into the Fellowship, this—her hand in his hand—was what was making her so happy.

Alice smiled to herself and concentrated on the twists and turns. They were nearing the end of the story; she could feel it. It felt right, somehow, that Mme Boucher, who had been so peripheral, was at the center of things. She and Alexander had been walking for some time, carefully following the red thread, when there was a loud electric hum and then darkness.

"Fjandi! The fuse has blown again," Alexander said. He dropped her hand, and Alice felt momentarily vulnerable and alone. "I will go and repair it," he said. He turned to her, and she felt his heavy hands on her thin shoulders. He spoke fiercely. "You stay right here, understood? You could trip and fall in the dark. It is dangerous. Do not move. I will come back for you. I will find you."

Alexander left so abruptly that Alice didn't have the chance to tell him her phone was dead. She moved tentatively, but wasn't panicking. The darkness, the basement, even that faint sound of dripping water somewhere far away, this was all old hat now. Alexander was down here, and as absurd as that was, the idea made her feel safe.

CHAPTER 37

Porcelain Doll Heads

PHILIP STOOD IN THEIR DOORWAY. "WELL, THAT'S A CHARMING greeting, sweetheart." His smile was tight. He looked exhausted, the way you do after a twenty-hour flight from Singapore.

"Why are you home early?" she asked, stepping to the side so he could enter. She forced a wide smile, stifling her impatience as best she could. She knew she should be pleased at his arrival home, but she was desperate to get to *Bonjour Paris*. "Come in, come in. You must be wiped out. Have a shower. Theo's at his friend's. I have an errand. I'll be back in an hour."

Philip's tired expression changed to anger. "I came home early, to surprise you," he said.

"That's wonderful. I really appreciate it," she said. He's tired. He tried to do something nice. He was responding to their last fight. She should be grateful that her husband was home; grateful that he'd cut his trip short; grateful that he was here in front of her.

His voice was querulous. That exact tone that set her teeth on edge. "What do you have to do that's so important, anyway?"

Gratitude slipped away, and her voice hardened. "This is so typical of you, Philip—only considering your own needs. I have plans that I can't change," she said.

His lips tightened. "Well, I'll come with you," he said.

She was suddenly frantic to get away from him. To immerse herself in the mystery. To join the others—people with whom she carried little emotional baggage. She tried to inject a note of affection into her voice, but it came out as false jollity. "Don't be silly. You're exhausted. Have a sandwich. Take a nap. I'll be home in an hour."

"I'm coming," he said. His bottom lip stuck out, just as Theo's did when he was being obstinate.

Her phone chimed, Alice telling them they'd made another discovery and now everyone was to meet in the wardrobe room. They must be close to finding the necklace! She didn't have time to argue with Philip. "Fine," she said. "Come with me."

She drove across town in silence. Daphne was not going to speak. Why should she give him the satisfaction? Did he really think she would fall to her knees in thankfulness when he cut his trip short by a day or two? He couldn't expect to constantly swan off and then have her stop her whole life when he deigned to show up again.

For his part, Philip pointedly did not ask where they were going. He gave a grunt of surprise when she pulled up to the magazine but said nothing when they bypassed the door to the office and headed straight for the basement. Daphne thumped down the narrow stairs, hoping to get away from the man behind her, but he followed close on her heels.

Once down in the basement, the air felt moist and chilly. The hallway was dimly lit. If the lights were on, did that mean that Alice and Lily were already down here? Damn it, she didn't want to miss anything. Philip was so irritating. Why had he come back now, of all times?

Like the first time she visited, the place was creepy. Daphne tried not think about the spiders that must be scuttling around. Which way should she go? She strode down the hall, but shortly came to a fork. Now what? Wait, wasn't there a thread she was supposed to follow? Flustered by Philip's arrival, she'd forgotten to look for it. Damn it all. She couldn't retrace her steps now; Philip would know she was lost, and it would give him another opportunity to roll his eyes at her. She forged ahead. She'd find it.

"What in God's name are we doing down here?" he asked.

His tone, so supercilious, was maddening. It implied that she was being silly and frivolous. She ignored him and plunged down the hallway to the right. She was almost running in her haste.

Philip followed, panting behind her. "Seriously, Daphne. What are we doing?"

"Why are you even here?" she shouted at him, increasing her speed.

"Stop," he said. "This is crazy." He tried to grab her arm, but she shook him off and ran farther down the hall, ducking into a narrow corridor lined with tiny storage spaces. She looked in one and saw a whole room filled with porcelain dolls' heads. She stopped, transfixed by the horror movie-ness of it. Just the thing to haunt her nightmares for the next decade.

Philip caught up to her again and put a hand on her shoulder. She turned to tell him to get his hands off her, but there was a loud electrical hum, and suddenly the lights went out. "What the hell?" Philip shouted, his voice sounding more startled than frightened.

Daphne remembered Alice saying that the wiring was tricky down here. Had they somehow tripped a fuse? "Don't freak out," Daphne said. She couldn't see anything, and her words were as much for herself as Philip. They were in absolute darkness. Despite her anger at Philip, it was comforting to feel his hand on her shoulder. She resisted the urge to grab hold of it and squeeze, taking reassurance from the strength she would feel there. "The others are down here—Lily, Luc, Alexander, Jacob, and Alice. One of them will fix the fuse. The lights will come back on soon. We have to wait."

Despite her brave words, Daphne really wished they hadn't stopped right in front of nightmarish doll central.

"So, this is about that necklace thing?" Philip said.

"Yes," she said defensively. "The 'necklace thing' has become very important to me."

"I can see that, but I ended my meetings early, rebooked my flights, and flew across continents to be here. The last time we talked you said you wanted to end our marriage."

"Don't be dramatic. I said we needed a break," she responded. "I didn't expect you to show up on my doorstep."

"Our doorstep," Philip reminded her, his tone still carefully reasonable. "I came home for you, for us, for our marriage."

"You always did love to be a self-sacrificing martyr," she said.

"Better than being a cold bitch."

Daphne gasped—he'd never said anything so harsh.

"I'm sorry, Daphne, I didn't mean it," Philip said. "I'm so tired, and now we're in this damp basement—"

"What's the point?" Daphne interrupted. "We don't even like each other. I'm starting to wonder what we ever saw in each other."

His grip on her shoulder tightened, and his words came through the darkness. "I saw you—a beautiful, pushy, funny, self-absorbed woman who had every reason to expect the best out of life. I loved that person. I still do."

What had she seen? A kind man who was devoted to his job and the people he loved. A man who was loyal and would never leave.

"You've always worried you won't get enough, Daphne." Philip's voice was tender now. "It's what's pushed you to be an amazing mother, a fantastic employee. But you've got everything, Daphne. You don't have to strive. You can rest now."

"I can't relax," Daphne found herself saying. "What if you leave me? Leave us?" Out came the fear, the big one. The real one. She thought about what Lily had said, how she nursed grudges. She did—she cast out blame and carried hurts with her. Why did she do that? Better to expect the worst so she was prepared for it.

"Daphne, I literally came running back to you. I'm right here. Why can't you see that? Accept that I am here."

She felt the darkness closing in on her and she blinked. Why couldn't she be happy that Philip was back and that he wanted to fight for their marriage? Instead, his presence made her feel tense, anxious, uncomfortable. She always blamed Philip for those feelings of irritability and unhappiness, but what if he was right—what if they came from her? From her refusal to believe that Philip wouldn't leave one day? He wanted her to trust him, but how could she? Philip was a good man. What would a good man like him want with her?

Her stomach churned.

Did she hear footfall ahead of her? Where were the others? She didn't want to feel this confusion and pain anymore. "I have to go," she said. She broke away from him, blundering down the hallway, deeper into the darkness.

CHAPTER 38

Hung Up

LUC DROPPED LILY OFF AT THE BONJOUR PARIS ENTRANCE AND said he'd find parking and meet up with her in the wardrobe room. Down in the basement she remembered which direction Alexander had led them the last time, and she found the red thread. She set off, but within thirty seconds there was a weird humming noise and then the lights flickered and went out. She was in absolute darkness. Panic choking her, she turned and stumbled back to the stairs.

Unfortunately, she got turned around at the meeting of two corridors. Now she was wandering around alone in the dark. She scrambled in her pocket for her phone before realizing she'd left it in Luc's car. She stopped walking. She'd wait here and someone from the Fellowship would be along soon.

What was that scuttling sound? Don't think about it. Concentrate on the necklace. Now that they had discovered that Luc's family were the true owners, it was even more urgent to find it. She heard a noise ahead of her. "Hello?" she called. "Luc?"

A figure using a cell phone as a flashlight approached. "Jacob," she said, startled. She hadn't thought of him since the café. Oh God, that kiss. What was she going to do about that?

"Lily," he said, and rushed toward her, pulling her into a tight embrace. She allowed herself to relax against his hard chest. It was a relief to be down here with a friend.

"How are you doing?" he asked tenderly. He brought his head down for a kiss, but she pulled back.

"Are the others down here?" she asked.

"I don't know. I got Alice's text and came right over. I was looking for the wardrobe room when the lights went out."

She stepped away from him. Was that a soft footfall behind them? She whirled around.

"What is it?" he asked.

"I thought I heard something," she said.

"There's no one," Jacob said confidently. His voice deepened. "I'm glad I found you."

He reached for her hand, but she evaded his grasp.

"What's wrong?" he asked.

She wasn't sure herself. She had always been attracted to Jacob. Grad night had been amazing, but he was right—the aftermath, when they were awkward and strange and didn't talk for months, hadn't been worth it. "About what you said in the café . . ." she began.

"I meant every word."

She took a deep breath and sought out his eyes in the dimness. "I call bullshit."

He reared back. "What?"

She shook her head. "I've known you for almost twenty years, Jacob. You don't love me, not like that. I'm your buddy."

"That's not true. We've got chemistry. We've always had chemistry."

"You're with Marie-Pierre," she told him. As the words left her mouth, she gained more confidence. She was tapping into the truth. "You guys are good together. You're freaked out that it might get serious, and you've grabbed hold of your old pal Lily as a convenient way to put some distance between you and Marie-Pierre."

"That's garbage. You can't tell me what I feel. I've loved you for decades—it's epic."

Lily laughed gently. "No, it isn't. What we have is friendship, plus mutual physical attraction that we've been bottling up since our twenties.

You don't love me like that. I saw you with Marie-Pierre. She's perfect for you, and that scares the pants off of you. You really like her, man. Don't screw this up."

Jacob's face looked bewildered in the murky lighting. "What about you—don't pretend you don't have feelings for me."

"I don't," she said simply, and an immense wave of relief washed over her. She had spoken the truth.

"But Daphne said—"

"Daphne got it wrong," Lily said. "I've always been attracted to you, but I don't love you. Not like that. It was honestly a little crush. Nothing more."

Jacob's face turned red, and he persisted. "I'm going to break up with Marie-Pierre. You're the one I'm interested in."

"But Jacob," she said as gently as she could, "I'm not interested in you."

Jacob's face darkened. "It's Seguin, isn't it?"

Lily laughed. "Absolutely not."

"Come on, he's been sniffing around you since this whole thing started. The problem is he thinks you're some great businesswoman with smart ideas about running a magazine. He doesn't know the real you—the one who has more writing talent than anyone I know, but who's too scared to try."

Lily stiffened. "That's not true, I don't have the time—"

"Well, I call bullshit on that," he snapped.

Before she could stop him, he turned and stomped off, leaving her once again in the darkness.

CHAPTER 39

The Medicine Ball

ALICE MOVED SLOWLY THROUGH THE DARK. SHE AND ALEXANDER had been walking for a long time when the lights went out. She must be close to the wardrobe room. She heard a noise ahead. "Alexander!" she called.

"Hello?" a voice yelled back.

"Hello," she said. It wasn't Alexander. Who else was down here?

"Alice." The voice held a note of panic, making it difficult to identify the speaker. They were closer now. "What the hell is happening, do you know?"

"Daphne!" Alice exclaimed.

They had reached each other, or at least she thought they had. The darkness was absolute. She put her arms out tentatively. Her hand brushed against Daphne's shirtsleeve and touched her shoulder. The other woman was doing the same. There was a need, in this complete shroud, to reassure oneself that the person opposite you was real. She would have skimmed her fingers across Daphne's face, traced the planes of her nose with her fingers to confirm who it was, but that was far too intimate. She settled for rubbing the soft silk of her shirt.

"Do you have a mobile on you?" she asked Daphne.

"Of course."

"Use your torch app—it will help us see."

"Ah yes. Good thinking," she said. Daphne's voice sounded stunned, befuddled. Was the other woman okay? Earlier at Café Neptune, Daphne had been angry at her for jeopardizing the necklace.

The pocket of illumination was a bright yellow and Daphne sighed in relief. "That's more like it."

"Alexander has gone to the fuse box to fix the lights," Alice said. "We won't have long to wait until they come back on."

"Oh good." Daphne stopped dead in her tracks. "Did you hear that?"

"Hear what?" Alice asked.

"I thought it was footsteps behind us."

Alice listened, but could hear nothing.

"Hello!" Daphne called. Her voice echoed. There was no response.

Alice shivered, but Daphne seemed preoccupied rather than scared. "Philip is down here somewhere," she said.

"Philip?" Alice responded.

"My husband," Daphne explained. "He changed his flight, came back early from his work trip. We fought, and I left him down here when the lights went out." Daphne's voice cracked. "Now he's alone in the dark."

"I'm sure he's fine," Alice said consolingly.

"Thank you," Daphne sniffed. "He came all the way home to surprise me, and all we did was fight. I really am ungrateful."

"Let's find the wardrobe room. Alexander will meet us there, and he'll help us find Philip."

They walked for a moment in silence.

"Alice, listen. I'm sorry I was such a bitch at Café Neptune," Daphne said.

"No, I'm sorry I lied to you all. I don't even know why I did it."

"It's okay," Daphne said. "We're all running around sabotaging ourselves. I'm ashamed at how I treated you. I tend to overreact to things—lash out. My therapist always says, 'Hurt people hurt people.'"

"It's all right," Alice said, embarrassed. How profoundly American to casually bring up your therapist in conversation.

"No, it's not okay," Daphne said. "I'm beginning to realize that I don't always approach things with the best attitude. I need to do some soul searching about my marriage, about myself."

Alice murmured soothing noises, uncertain what else to do.

And just like that, Daphne was unburdening herself. As they walked through the darkness, the older woman poured out a story of resentment, guilt, and confusion. Daphne knew she had been deliberately distancing herself from Philip; was that because she was scared he'd leave, or was it because he was really a terrible person? After all, according to Daphne, he spent too much money on their car, was too hard on Theo, didn't clip his toenails short enough, needed babying when he was sick, and had politics that were too right-wing.

As Daphne went on about her own insecurities and her husband's failings, Alice became increasingly confident. She might be awkward and unsophisticated, but she knew something that Daphne Smythe-Baird hadn't figured out yet: Alice knew what a good relationship looked like. She thought of the way her mother's eyes crinkled when she saw Dale. She recalled Dale's hand lightly touching Maheen's shoulder as he passed her in the kitchen while she stirred the spaghetti. She remembered looking out at the audience when she graduated from university—seeing Maheen and Dale watching her, their hands tightly clasped. She also knew what it took to keep a relationship like that going. She had seen it with every argument she'd heard between Dale and Maheen—where they would raise their voices, yes, but that always ended on common ground. No one gave too much, no one asked too much. They truly respected each other, and it shone through all their interactions.

"My parents were miserable, and even though I know he's a good guy, I can't seem to be happy with Philip," Daphne finished. "I don't think I know how to be married." Her voice held real pain.

Alice spoke, surprised at the words coming from her mouth. "About six months before I finished university, my boyfriend dumped me," she said. "I was devastated. I was balled up with my betrayal and a sense of injustice. I couldn't move beyond it. My grades were slipping. I wasn't leaving my room. I was hanging on to so much anger it was choking me.

"Finally, my stepfather called me out to the garden shed. He had set up a little gym back there—he had a weight bench and some skipping ropes, that sort of thing." Alice was lost in her story, hardly conscious of Daphne as she remembered that time. "He made me do a workout with him— pumping iron to sweat out my rage, he said. I did it grudgingly, but you know, Dale was right. It did feel good to be accomplishing something— moving my arms, building muscles."

"I don't think I need to work out," Daphne interrupted. "I already do a Yoga-Barre class twice a week."

"That's not what I'm saying," Alice said. The darkness had emboldened her to speak firmly. "By the end of the session, I felt better for the first time in weeks. Dale handed me a medicine ball—you know, one of those twenty-pound weighted balls? He told me to hold it in front of me with my arms straight out. I started shaking almost immediately. It's very difficult to hang on to something that heavy in that position. Sweat poured down my fore-head, my arms were quivering, my stomach muscles were tense, my shoul-ders ached. Dale kept saying to me, 'Hold on to it, hold on to it.'

"Finally, when I was near the breaking point, he said, 'Now put it down.' I dropped it and turned on him. I was furious that he had made me do that. He held up his hand and asked, 'Didn't it feel good to let that weight go? Just put the medicine ball down. Let it go. You don't have to hold it.'" Alice finished speaking, and they walked in silence.

Finally, Daphne spoke. "So, you're saying—"

Alice couldn't believe she was daring to give advice to Daphne. "Stop counting the ways you've been hurt or disappointed. Put it down. Let it go. You're only hurting yourself by carrying it around."

Alice held her breath, waiting for Daphne to yell at her for being a nosy parker or an immature idiot.

Instead, the other woman murmured to herself, "Just put the medicine ball down."

CHAPTER 40

Ausina's Golden Mane

A BRIGHT LIGHT AND A HEAVY FOOTFALL COMING TOWARD HER.
Lily's heart leapt into her throat. A psychopath? A ghost? A monster? A
psychopathic ghost monster? Suddenly she relaxed. It took her a moment
to register what had calmed her. She caught a whiff of a scent—fresh, light,
and lemony, but somehow also masculine. It was familiar.

"Alexander?" Lily said, her eyes struggling to adapt to the powerful
beam of the flashlight.

"Yes," came a curt reply.

His very gruffness was reassuring. They weren't about to be murdered
by a demigorgon if Alexander sounded so irritated. "What happened?"

"The fuse has burned out again."

Alexander held an enormous flashlight. It was eerie to see the basement
laid out in such high relief. The dark areas even blacker against the brightness. Every hanging light looked like a potential bat waiting to nest in her
hair. She shuddered. They'd had bats in Vermont. Every summer, the juve-
niles nesting in the attic would "sleepwalk" down the farmhouse walls
during the day, subconsciously searching for the cooler temperatures in
the lower part of the house. When they awoke to feed at night, they'd find
themselves in the basement. Disoriented and unable to locate their entry
hole, they'd burst out of cracks in the basement walls and flap around the
house in the middle of the night.

"Where are you going?" she said as he turned and began walking purposefully away from her.

"To the furnace room, the fuse box is there. I will repair it."

"Wait for me. I'll come with you," she said. She didn't want to be by herself, a target for the bats.

"Very well. After I must return to Alice."

"I was sorry for how things went down at the café. You were right, we were unfair to her."

"You should tell Alice this, not me."

Fair enough, Lily thought. He strode down the hall, and she jogged after him. "So," she said. "What's the deal with you and Alice?"

He stopped dead in his tracks. "Deal?" he said. "There is nothing going on between us."

"No, no," Lily said. "I meant what did you discover about the necklace? We have to find it."

"We have determined that *Bonjour Paris* rented the wardrobe room. We suspect it was to store Josephine Baker's stage costumes. Mme Boucher has a connection to all of this. She directed Alice to return to the wardrobe room. Perhaps she is there. Perhaps she has the necklace."

Mme Boucher again. Lily could kick herself for excluding the older woman from the Fellowship. As the office manager, she would have known about the lease. If Mme Boucher wasn't waiting for them in the wardrobe room with a big smile and the Honeybee Emeralds, Lily was going to drive over to her house tonight to get to the bottom of things.

"*Bonjour Paris* leasing the wardrobe room jibes with what we found out. Josephine Baker owed Olivia for her nannying work, and get this—she paid her with the Honeybee Emeralds. Luc owns the necklace. We have the whole thing in black and white."

Alexander grunted in response.

"What did you mean when you said there was nothing going on between you and Alice?" she asked, coming back to his earlier statement.

"Nothing."

Now Lily was thinking about the interactions she had observed between Alice and Alexander. "You've been spending a lot of time together." There was a long silence. She got the sense that his brain was working, like the massive water mill she had once seen at the Shaker Village in Massachusetts. It had thundered and churned with a great creaking noise, pushed by the water from a small stream under the floorboards. "It seems to me there might be a bit of a romance brewing."

More mental churning. "Why do you say that?" he asked eventually.

"I don't know. Alice's face lights up when you walk into the room. She literally blushed when you guys touched hands the other day. That kind of thing."

"She's only twenty-three," he said.

"Twenty-three is not eighteen," Lily replied. "Alice seems young because she's so sweet, but she's got steel in her spine. How old are you, anyway?"

"Twenty-eight."

"Twenty-eight," Lily repeated, astonished. She definitely would have put him in his thirties—it must be his silence. You associated maturity with the good sense to be quiet. "Well, there's nothing stopping you, then. You should ask her out. Go on a date." Even as she said the words, Lily recognized their absurdity. There was something tragic about Alexander, precluding the possibility of anything as prosaic as dinner and bowling.

"I am not sure she would like that," he said after a long pause.

"Only way to find out is to ask," Lily chirped back. Sometimes these damn Europeans, with their heavy histories and lugubrious self-doubt, could be so draining.

Alexander seemed disinclined to discuss her solution. They walked for what seemed like a long time in the twisty darkness. Alexander moved with purpose, and Lily kept close to him, occasionally running a hand through her hair to check for bats. As they walked, she considered how the news of the necklace would affect Luc. If they recovered the Honeybee Emeralds, would he then have to prove ownership to the Baker estate? Presumably the note from Josephine transferring ownership could be authenticated. What would Luc's family do with the jewelry? She doubted that he would advocate keeping it. She could see him donating it to a museum, or perhaps auctioning it off and using the money for a charitable cause. She realized she had a lot of faith in his good intentions. A couple of weeks ago she had barely known the guy. Now she was sure he'd give hundreds of thousands to charity.

As they continued walking in the dim light, seemingly never getting to their destination, the faint sound of their footfalls and Alexander's deep, even breathing began to lull Lily into a meditative calm. Her thoughts drifted until she found herself blurting out something unexpected. "I'm not writing anymore."

Alexander kept walking, and she wondered if he had heard her. "I'm not writing anymore," she repeated more loudly. Her words echoed.

He turned, keeping the flashlight trained at her feet so as not to blind her. It created a strange, almost churchlike space. His face was only dimly visible above the pool of light below them. "Oh yes," he said.

His voice was polite. Lily knew that this didn't matter to him, that they had more pressing things to do, but suddenly it was urgent that she confess to someone. She recalled Jacob's words. He'd said she had more talent than anyone he knew. Rather than inspire her, it made her sad. She would never get the chance to prove him right. "I've always been a writer. As a kid I would write these stories—I even had an old typewriter that my dad fixed up. I loved that thing; using it made me think I was a 'real' writer, like Hemingway or Woolf."

Alexander nodded and turned back down the hall, but Lily wasn't done. She trotted beside him, talking.

"For a while I was really into fantasy—I wrote about a girl who rode a white winged stallion. Her name was Ausina." Lily laughed, self-conscious. She had never told another living person about those stories.

Alexander gave no indication he had even heard her, which gave her the courage to plow on. "Ausina had a golden mane of hair. I was fixated on my characters having 'manes.' She also wore a kirtle. I didn't know what a 'kirtle' was, but I knew Ausina had to have one . . ."

Alexander made a small "hmm" sound and continued walking. Lily followed him, finding it strangely soothing to talk to his broad back. "College was great. I finally met my people. Everyone was like me. Well, not with the typewriter or the manes, but they were all dreamy nerds who wanted to create stories. I had the most amazing professors, too. So inspiring.

"My writer's block started after college. I moved to New York and was supposed to make it big. Become the next Sontag or Didion. I used to get up every day and write in my journal. I knew, *I knew* that I needed to keep writing. Stick my butt in the chair, churn it out. 'I'll take care of the quantity, universe, you take care of the quality.' That sort of thing." Lily laughed and glanced at Alexander's form, moving slowly and steadily through the dark.

"I landed a job in publishing—working for a small magazine. It was my big break, but the work was exhausting. I got home at nine every night. I stopped getting up early to write in my journal. I stopped writing on weekends. I just stopped writing. Now it's been a decade. Ten years! I don't know where the time went. I guess that's what happens when you grow up. You realize that the dreams you had as a kid, the vision you had for who you would be, was uninformed. You have to give it up and face reality."

She spoke more slowly now, coming to a realization. "I need to stop thinking of myself as a writer and make my peace with what I am—a magazine editor, and a damn good one." She was never going to write that novel. She paused, expecting tears as she finally admitted it to herself. Instead, she found herself speaking. "I didn't live my dream. Maybe that's okay."

They walked on. Lily had no idea if Alexander had even been listening to her meanderings, but she was grateful for his presence. She felt lightheaded and somehow free. An enormous burden had lifted off her. She had verbalized her greatest failure and nothing bad had happened.

At last, they arrived at their destination. They were in a decent-sized room. She could see the large furnace to her left. To her right was a wall of fuse boxes. Alexander walked over to one, playing the flashlight along the wall.

He was facing away from her, so it took her a moment to realize he was speaking. "You should get a typewriter," he rumbled in his deep voice.

She stumbled forward, perhaps mishearing him. "What?"

"Buy a typewriter. Write about that girl with the hair."

Lily wasn't sure what to say. "Ausina?" she asked to be clear.

"Yes." He was looking through a box of fuses.

"That's what you got from all of that?" Lily couldn't keep the frustration from her voice. It had been one thing to confess her deepest secret to Alexander when she thought he was a silent cipher, it was quite another to have him offering unsolicited life advice. "You think I should write some ridiculous fantasy story?"

"Yes," Alexander said, now studying the complex number of fuse boxes on the wall.

"That's crazy. If I were going to return to writing, I'd work on something serious, something edgy that would shake things up. Let people know I had arrived. Write a fantasy story about a woman on a winged horse? That's nuts. Fantasy isn't a respected genre. Why would I do that?"

"In the whole time you were talking," Alexander said, unscrewing a fuse, "it was the only moment you had a smile in your voice. You should write that story."

His words were like a divine edict, issuing from the dimness. As if to underline his higher power, he screwed in the new fuse and the lights burst back on. The darkness was banished and now she could see.

CHAPTER 41

A Fox-Fur Stole

WHEN THE LIGHT RETURNED, DAPHNE SOON SPOTTED THE RED thread, and with Alice's help they navigated to the wardrobe room. It was just as Daphne remembered: gowns in rich jewel tones, mannequins sporting feathered cloaks, wig stands holding up elaborate coifs.

Lily and Alexander arrived soon after she and Alice.

"You are okay?" Alexander asked Alice.

The younger girl nodded, smiling sweetly at him. "Yes, I'm fine."

Jacob and Luc showed up next; both looked grumpy.

Jacob took a couple of steps toward Lily. "We need to talk," he said.

She put up her hand. "Please Jacob, not here." Instead, Lily turned to Daphne. "I'm sorry for what I said at the café."

Daphne recalled Alice's words. Was that medicine ball of resentment the thing that prevented her from being happy? Lily, Philip, and Alice had essentially told her the same thing. She was so tired of carrying that weight. She smiled. "I'm sorry too, Lily. I shouldn't have said all that stuff." She glanced at Jacob. "I didn't know what I was talking about."

Lily grinned. "You're telling me." She stepped closer to Daphne and put her hand on her arm, lowering her voice. "We are going to need a major debrief when this is over," and she jerked her head toward Jacob.

Daphne laughed, relieved their friendship was still intact.

She looked toward the door, hoping to see Philip. If he didn't show up in the next three minutes, she would have to get Alexander to lead a search party to retrieve him.

Lily turned to Alice and gave her a hug. The intern looked uncomfortable. "I'm sorry things got intense at the café, kiddo. I was freaked out that the necklace was gone."

"No worries," Alice said, extricating herself from the embrace. "I think I overreacted."

Jacob came up to her. "Yeah, sorry. I was kind of an asshole."

"Don't worry about it," Alice said. "I'm simply glad the Fellowship is back together." She grinned. "We texted you to meet us here because Alexander and I discovered that *Bonjour Paris* rents this room. Our theory is that Olivia was storing some of Josephine Baker's costumes for her."

Daphne looked at the treasures spread out in front of her, a fox-fur stole hung next to a stunning red silk gown, which sat next to a bejeweled bolero jacket. There was so much here, and yet Josephine hungered for more. Why wasn't this enough?

Lily spoke. "That makes sense. We know that Olivia was Josephine Baker's nanny, but Luc and I found Olivia's diary from that time. Josephine gave Olivia the Honeybee Emeralds in lieu of back pay. We have a signed note from Josephine. Luc's family are the rightful owners."

Daphne could see her own shock reflected in Alice and Jacob's eyes. "That's incredible," she said. Luc's ownership of the necklace actually made her involvement with the Honeybee Emeralds less problematic—at least she had been working with the owner (however inadvertently) when it was stolen.

"Well, it's a good twist for the article," Jacob said grudgingly. Daphne was sure he resented that Luc was playing such a prime role in the story. "But the fact is that the necklace is missing, and none of this helps us find it."

"There's more," Lily said. "Mme Boucher is involved. Alice, can you read the note?"

The young woman stepped forward, blushing. "Yes," she said. "This was sitting on my desk when Alexander and I stopped by the office before coming down here." Alice read them the message.

"So did Mme Boucher take the necklace?" Lily asked. "I was hoping she'd be waiting here with an explanation."

"What does she mean by writing that the end of the story is here?" Daphne wondered.

"We should search the room," Luc said.

There was a noise in the doorway, and Daphne's heart squeezed at the sight of Philip standing there, looking rueful. Then she gasped at the person who stepped out behind him.

"Yvette," Lily said. "What are you doing here?"

Daphne automatically cataloged her outfit—her dress was black Lagerfeld, and the stiletto ankle boots had to be this season's Amélie Pichard. Yvette strode forward, but the surprising amount of color in the room shook even her self-assurance. "So, this is one of La Josephine's hiding spots," she said. She was almost speaking to herself. "I'd heard rumors about these for years . . . storage lockers, attic trunks, forgotten closets filled with her treasures—jewelry, costumes, even cash, all hidden from Josephine's creditors. I had never seen one with my own eyes." She turned to Lily and bowed with a flourish. "Thank you, Leelee."

Lily's face darkened, and she stepped toward Yvette. "What the hell are you doing here?" she snarled.

The other woman batted her eyes. "The same as you, Leelee. Fighting for my magazine. Already our website has received quadruple the usual hits, but we've promised a series on the necklace, so I must provide more content. We're going to print shortly, and I'm looking for fresh information to really move it at the newsstand."

"How did you get the story?" Lily asked.

Yvette shrugged, walking into the center of the room, naturally assuming her role as expository villain. "When my darling goddaughter Catherine told me about your interest in a diamond and emerald necklace, I had my research team do their own digging. Naturally, we discovered the connection with Napoleon III and of course the subsequent link to his illegitimate son. We only discovered the Josephine Baker association yesterday. One of my interns found an image of her wearing the necklace."

"But why are you here, in the basement?" Luc asked.

"I came to chat with Lily, and then I saw you, darling." She smiled sweetly at him. "You were disappearing down the basement stairs. I thought there might be something intriguing afoot, so I followed. Hélas, the lights went out and I was in darkness. I might still be wandering about down here, were it not for my knight in shining armor." She turned and placed a hand on Philip's arm. "He rescued me. I could never have found this place without his help."

Daphne stared at Philip. "What did you do?" she gasped.

He shrugged. "I didn't know it was a secret," he said. "Miss Dufeu and I bumped into each other as we wandered around, and it made sense to help her out."

Yvette smiled at him. "Yes, Philip was most forthcoming." She turned to Luc. "He's given me much useful background on the story that will help tremendously."

Oh no. The entire time she was talking to Philip, despairing that he didn't really understand or care about the project, he was absorbing everything. Now, in his sweet, honest way, he had ruined it all. She couldn't be angry with him. He was being true to his nature.

Yvette smiled again. "If you don't mind, I must be getting back to the office. I have a lot to do."

"Wait," Lily called.

Yvette turned back.

"Where is it?" Lily asked urgently, putting a hand on Yvette's arm. "Where is the necklace?"

"The necklace?" Yvette asked, startled. "Do you mean to say, you actually located it?"

Daphne was pretty good at reading people, and there was no way that Yvette was feigning her surprise.

Lily opened her mouth, but seemed to recognize Yvette's shock and its implications. She said nothing.

Yvette shook off Lily's hand, and her voice was gloating. "You found the necklace? You actually found it. That's what inspired you to write the article. This is incroyable," she said. "What a story. And am I to understand you've now somehow lost it?" The other woman's laugh was delighted. "It is too much! *Bonjour Paris* really is amateur hour." Yvette cast them all a contemptuous look before walking up to Luc. She patted him gently on the cheek. "What would your poor mother think of your failure, Luc, chérie?" She swept from the room before he could answer, leaving glum silence in her wake.

"Well," Lily said, her voice cracking. This was the most upset Daphne had ever seen her. "That's it for the story. Yvette is going to publish her article, making us look like morons. The necklace is lost, and there's nothing we can do about it."

"Not necessarily," Philip muttered.

"I think you've done enough," Jacob snapped.

Daphne bristled. She could be mad at Philip, but no one else could. "Why don't you shut it, Jacob," she snapped.

Lily turned to Philip. "What do you mean?" she asked.

He stepped forward. "Hi," he said. "For those who don't know me, I'm Daphne's husband." He gave an awkward half wave. Alice was the only one to return it. "I, um, bumped into Yvette in the dark. I knew who she was, because Daphne told me what you guys were up to. Anyway, the way she was talking, it really sounded like she was going to get the jump on you, so I took action."

"Action?" Daphne asked wonderingly. Philip thought this whole thing was a waste of time. "What did you do?"

Philip didn't meet her eyes. "I hope I did the right thing, but I, uh . . ." He coughed. "I lied. I told her that Daphne had said that the necklace belonged to a Hindi princess. I said that Brigitte Bardot had owned it. I also told her that Elizabeth Taylor's dog once wore the necklace as a collar . . . I was pretty sure she wouldn't buy that one, but she was recording everything I said on her phone and was pretty excited."

Daphne was having trouble computing this. Philip was a rigid, upstanding, by-the-book kind of guy. He'd once called up the IRS when they had mistakenly given him too big a refund.

"You fed her false stories?" Lily asked.

"Well, yeah," Philip admitted.

"Why?" Daphne asked.

At last, he met her eyes. "I knew it was important to you," he said.

"Oh," was all she could manage. They'd had a massive fight where she told him that she thought their marriage was over. Philip had left work, changed his ticket, flown home early. He was completely fried from jet lag, and he'd been wandering around in a dark, damp basement for the past half hour. And yet Philip, good, loyal Philip, had deliberately misled Yvette for her. That was the whole point of marriage, wasn't it? It was to have an ally beside you so when apocalypse happened and the zombie armies rose, your partner would be by your side. They would be there despite seeing how small your eyes looked without mascara or knowing that you thought reindeer were mythical animals until your midtwenties.

The secret to getting that sawed-off-shotgun, zombie-killing ally, Daphne now truly understood, was just letting some things go. Let go of the need to control, let go of the slights and grudges. Alice was right; you needed to put the medicine ball down. She took a step toward Philip, and he filled the space between them, pulling her into a hug. She pushed him away, grasped his face, and planted a giant, swooping kiss.

When she came up for air, Daphne noticed that Alice was blinking back tears. "Sorry about that," she said to everyone else. She took up Philip's hand. "He's been away for almost two weeks, and I really missed him." They were in this for the long haul.

CHAPTER 42

Le Sentier des Chasseurs

ALICE WANTED TO APPLAUD AT THE SIGHT OF DAPHNE AND Philip's kiss. Instead, she leaned slightly closer to Alexander, whose warm, reassuring bulk stood next to her in the chilly basement. If she shifted her body ever so slightly, her waist would tuck in to his side, nestling nicely into his hip. Her skin tingled at the thought. Then, as if she had willed it, his hand reached out tentatively and engulfed hers. Now it was easy to lean toward him, and he toward her.

A sense of peace flooded through her. This was good. She'd never experienced such a feeling with a man before. Her one real relationship had been uncertain, tentative, and wracked by her own worries. It wasn't like that with Alexander. Instead, she felt steady and secure. It wasn't as much about trusting him, although she did of course, as it was about trusting *in* him. She knew he was there and present, as immovable as a glacier . . . although the whole point of glaciers was that they moved. Also, weren't they melting?

"Okay everyone," Lily said, calling for their attention. She stood by the door where Alice had found the sewing kit all those weeks ago. "We've got to figure out our next move. We should comb this room, see if we can find another note from Mme Boucher. If we don't, Luc and I will go to her house and have a conversation with her. Jacob, I'll need a final draft from you. Alice, I'll get you to do a copyedit, and then we publish online with everything we've got. If Yvette doesn't fact-check Philip's wild stories, she'll have a bunch of fake news. She'll be discredited and we'll become the trusted source for this story."

Alice stepped forward and noticed a large manila envelope on the sewing table behind Lily. It hadn't been there ten days ago.

Her name was scrawled across it. She picked up the envelope, and as soon as she felt its weight, she knew. Alice's heart pounded and her mouth went dry. Sure enough, when she ripped it open, among a thick sheaf of pages, was the necklace. She gasped.

Lily and the others gathered around. "Is it real?" Jacob demanded.

Alice nodded. She pointed to the missing diamonds, but then stopped. Before there had been four missing. Now two more were gone.

"What the hell?" Jacob muttered.

Daphne took the necklace from her numb fingers. "This is legit," she said. "It's the same necklace."

"What does it mean?" Lily breathed.

Alice's knees shook with relief, and she could see the same emotion reflected in everyone's eyes. She blinked back tears and yanked out the papers from the envelope. It was a typed letter. "Dear Aliyeh" was scrawled in blue pen across the top. She flipped to the end to see "Élise Nadeau Boucher" signed at the bottom.

"It's from Mme Boucher," she said.

Alice began reading. It was written in English.

Dear Aliyeh, I presume you have found my note on your desk and have quietly made your way to the basement to retrieve what you first discovered so many days ago. No need to alert the others, this is for you, and you alone. That is why I've left it down here, away from prying eyes.

Alice glanced up at the rest of the Fellowship, all staring at her. "I honestly don't know what she's talking about," she said.

"It's okay, Alice. Keep reading," Lily said.

Alice resumed:

I know the true story of the necklace, or at least, the final piece of the puzzle. The part that is undoubtedly elusive. Read my tale and perhaps you will understand how I knew of the necklace, though never of its true value. I want to set down all my memories, so they are recorded for posterity.

Daphne put the Honeybee Emeralds back down on the table, motioning for her to keep reading. Alexander came to stand beside her, and she was grateful for his presence.

When I came to Paris from La Rosière in 1970, I had never been to the city. It is hard for young people, so cosmopolitan now, to realize how isolated one could be, even in the center of Europe. At La Rosière my life was not about iPhones or Xbox. I had grown up in the shadow of war. Though I was born well after the conflict had ended, my parents, both older when they had me, had been shaped by it. All around my village was the sadness of *la* guerre. Remnants of old army equipment, my father's wound, my mother's grief. Our religion reinforced this sense of oppression. The god we worshipped was judgmental and harsh. I grew up hating my home. There was no path for women beyond housewife. I learned cooking, sewing, cleaning—all the "necessary" arts. It felt like the very heaviness of the mountains seeped into my house and into my soul. All I could dream of was escape.

Nowadays, of course, I would give almost anything to smell my father's tobacco, or to brush my mother's thick dark hair again.

Luc shifted impatiently. "Where is this going?" he asked.
"Shh," Lily admonished. "I want to hear."
Alice resumed her reading.

My family disapproved of my move to Paris. My father, a pious Catholic, a strict parent, forbade me to go. I was meant to marry the boy next door, the grocer's son. We had been sweethearts for years. He was from a prosperous family. My father said that to renege on my promise would bring dishonor. It was not that I didn't feel my obligations, but I knew something with greater certainty—if I stayed in La Rosière and married Henri Boucher, my soul would die.

My mother spoke to my father, and at last, he relented. He gave me one year to explore the world, and then I was meant to come home. If I failed in this, he would renounce me as his daughter. It seems so harsh as I type this now, but La Rosière was a place out of time, perhaps almost like a fairy tale. Henri, for his part, was confident that I wouldn't last more than a week in Paris. He let me go easily because he knew I would return to him with my tail between my legs, abashed and ready to be a good wife.

Paris was a marvel. The noise, the crowds, the expense! I almost turned around at La Gare Du Nord and caught the first train home. Only the thought of Henri's "I told you so" kept me in the city. I answered Olivia's advertisement. The magazine had been open for nearly two years, but it was a one-woman operation and she needed help. I had no skills, but the pay was so low that I thought she couldn't be expecting someone with great abilities. I had my interview in this very room, where I now compose my letter to you. Olivia had a small inheritance and wanted to run a magazine that would show off the real Paris and help people like her—outsiders, foreigners—uncover the city's truths. I didn't tell her that I, too, felt like a foreigner in Paris. Instead, I embraced her mission. It became mine.

She talked little of her past, but I knew she was American and had traveled internationally before coming to France. Her life was much larger and more glamorous than mine. I felt intimidated and resorted to malice and haughtiness. She didn't care how barbed I got, however; she was always so kind, so easygoing, that eventually it wore me down. I realized that her friendship was genuine. She saw things in me that I had never even seen in myself.

One night we went to the Eiffel Tower and climbed to the very top to see the city lights. We stopped in a café on the way home. We drank too much wine, and she began telling me about her life. She didn't usually talk of her past, and I listened closely. Her father had dragged the family to Greece every summer on archaeology excavations, and she told me about pulling two-thousand-year-old pottery shards from the earth. She said she always felt different from the girls she went to school with in Iowa, and she became fascinated with France. When she turned eighteen, she demanded to go. This was 1965, and her parents were very nervous to let her travel on her own. She was their precious only child, but she was so strong-willed, she got her way. I remember marveling when she told me that part of the story—I couldn't imagine bending my father to my will the way she had. I told her this, and she pointed out that whatever I had said or done had worked because here I was, in Paris on my own, like her. Perhaps, she said, my father was more sympathetic than I realized. I shook my head. I was here on sufferance, and the thought of my oppressive La Rosière life lingered like a shadow over all present joy. That shadow lifted, for a moment, when Olivia slid her hand over mine and said, "Perhaps we are more alike than you realize, Élise."

I was happy in those months. I didn't know the first thing about journalism or how to run a magazine. I didn't even speak English at that point. Olivia and I worked well together. We shared a determination and a passion. We spent long hours in the office, she chasing down stories, me securing advertisers and promoting our work. As a break we would roam around in the basement. I forget why we went down there in the first place—perhaps that temperamental furnace. At any event, we loved what we discovered. Our own little wilderness beneath the city—a place, unbound by rules or maps—a secret hideaway.

We were inseparable. When work ended, we spent our evenings in the city, conquering it together. Olivia had entrée into parts of Parisian society I would never have known existed. My friend was striking, rather than beautiful, but her attraction was more compelling than mere looks. She was tall, confident, likable, and friendly. She had a way of making people feel seen that was simply intoxicating.

I was not the only one entranced by her. Her forthright manner and curiosity won her many admirers. Don't fear, Aliyeh, I was not left to the sidelines in our sorties. In those days I was young and slim, and I think my haughty attitude attracted a certain type of man—the ones who like to "conquer" uninterested women. Still, despite the beaux who lined up to pay us tribute, I was chaste, and I think Olivia was as well. We flirted and we danced, but we did nothing more. We were far more in love with Paris than with any man who crossed our path. We saw every show and concert the city had to offer, danced all night at after-hours clubs, and drank too much sauvignon blanc at art openings and galas. We consorted with brilliant poets and middling philosophers, filthy musicians and passionate artists. We weren't tasting Paris, we were devouring it.

Olivia wasn't done surprising me in that year. I remember it was six months into my time in Paris, a perfect September day. I sat at my desk, trying not to feel melancholy about the passage of time. The magazine was starting to find its footing, and I was happy in my work. Bonjour Paris's door opened, and I was dumbfounded when Josephine Baker sauntered in. Although by 1970 she was an old woman, I recognized her immediately. My father loved her music and had all of her albums. I used to stare at them as a girl, entranced by the beautiful Black woman, so exotic and glamorous. Despite the brightness of the day, she wore a white mink hat and carried a matching muff. I had learned in my time in Paris to recognize a few distinctive designers, and her dress looked like Pucci. She sported enormous sunglasses, which she kept on for her entire visit. She seemed to suck up all the energy and life in the room, pulling it into her very presence and then reflecting it back on Olivia and me, two small planets orbiting her sun.

She knew Olivia, and they spoke rapid American English together, which made it difficult for me to follow. It seemed like Josephine was asking for something back. Olivia refused, telling Josephine it had been given to her in lieu of wages and it was now rightfully hers.

"My God," Jacob interjected. "This is amazing."
Alice looked up from her reading. The others were rapt.

Where I had thought Josephine might argue or cause an unpleasant scene, the singer accepted Olivia's stance. I remember she spoke with a laugh. "Fine, Olivia. I see that like me, you know how to drive a hard bargain. I won't welch on our deal. Keep it, and may it bring you happiness." The singer then stood, smoothing her dress, and spoke again. I sensed that she was coming to the real reason for her visit. "As someone who has shown you a great deal of generosity, may I ask a small favor?"

"Of course," Olivia said. "I'd be happy to help you."

It transpired that Josephine had "liberated" her costumes from the producers of her latest show, men who erroneously (at least in Josephine's view) thought they owned the couture clothing that had been custom-made for her. There had already been some unpleasantness with lawsuit threats, and the police had come around to a friend's place, looking for the outfits.

Could Olivia find a spot to store the costumes until Josephine was able to sell them? "A couple of weeks tops, darling."

Now it was Daphne's turn to interject, crying out, "This is wonderful. It confirms everything we suspected."
Alice resumed.

The costumes were delivered in a removals van, and we found a spot for them, well you know, in the basement. Olivia arranged it all with the landlord, rolling the cost up into the rent we paid. Of course, Josephine was never able to retrieve the gowns; some creditor or other was always suing her, and she had liens against every single valuable she owned. Over the next few years, I know Olivia accepted a few more clandestine deliveries from the singer. Olivia herself always paid the costs and continued to fill that little room in the basement. Eventually those late-night deliveries wound down, and by the time the singer died in 1975, I think Olivia must have forgotten about the existence of the storage room. I certainly had.

After our brief Josephine excitement, things settled down again. As 1970 came to a close, and the days became shorter and darker, work was busier. We spent more and more time here, in the office. I learned how to cajole advertisers into taking a chance on us. Olivia built up a stable of good writers and wheedled them into writing for a pittance. She and I worked hand in glove. I'd never been valued like that before, for my common sense, for my intelligence. No one in La Rosière considered me smart. Brains in a woman were not something particularly desired or praised. Now things were different. I knew then that I could never go back to La Rosière. That idea, and the idea of Henri Boucher's dull brown eyes, held no appeal.

It was a dark, rain-swept evening in late November, the waning days of the year. The city was quiet, deserted of students, of tourists, of everyone, it seemed, but us. We worked late, toiling in the warm yellow glow of the desk lamps. Olivia reached across me to get something, and I turned my face toward her. Our kiss felt right and natural. I knew love between two women was evil, the priest had certainly made that clear, but it didn't feel wrong. It, she, felt perfect.

Luc made a strangled noise, and Alice stopped reading. She glanced up and noticed Lily touch his arm, and that he shifted, grasping her hand. Luc's eyes met Alice's. "Please keep reading," he said.

For a girl like me, marriage to a man was the natural order of things. As inescapable as gravity. Yet here was Olivia, offering me the chance to fly. She was beautiful and young and strong and so was I. We were together for six weeks. We spent our days working and our nights making love. We laughed and talked and touched. It was the best time of my life.

I told my family I was too busy and wouldn't be home for the holidays. On Christmas morning I presented her with my secret project—I had stealthily been embroidering her favorite green velvet jacket—stitching in olives and leaves on the pockets to make it entirely hers, Olives for Olivia. She loved the embroidery and told me that she loved me as well.

She gave me a small box, and inside was the most beautiful necklace I'd ever seen—two strands of diamonds with a honeybee motif. I gasped when I saw it and told her I could not accept such a gift. She insisted, saying it was fake—the diamonds made of glass. She convinced me to take it by telling me that it was a thrift store find. She even showed me the four missing diamonds as proof—assuring me that it was a cheap trinket. I believed her and accepted it. We had a magical day together.

"Holy fucking shit balls," Lily breathed. Her words encapsulated exactly how Alice was feeling. Olivia had given Mme Boucher—Mme Boucher!—the necklace . . . She looked over at M. Seguin. His face was completely stunned.

"Should I keep reading?" she asked tentatively.

"Yes!" everyone shouted. She picked up the tale.

It must have been a few days later, the city still quiet over the Christmas holidays. We dragged ourselves from Olivia's flat and went to the office. It was cold. Olivia insisted I wear her green velvet jacket. I slipped my necklace in the pocket, intending to return it to my flat later that day when I picked up a change of clothes.

Work was quiet, everyone still in lazy holiday mode. We wandered down to the basement, to the room where Olivia was storing Josephine's costumes. We played like two girls amongst those beautiful dresses, trying them on, twirling around, giggling like fools as we slipped into turbans and flung boas around one another's necks. We were hot and exhausted when we were done, and I forgot the jacket, with the necklace in the pocket, down there.

That afternoon, while Olivia was out on a story, my father arrived at the office. Who knows, if she had been present, perhaps I would have found the courage to defy him. He knew nothing about what had gone on between us, but staying away at Christmas had been a mistake. He had been stewing over the holidays, convincing himself that I had been corrupted by the city. He was cutting my promised year short and taking me back to La Rosière immediately. It was time I return to the life that awaited me.

I refused, I stormed, I cried, I begged. It was all in vain, however. I was not an indulged child like Olivia, and I did not get my way. The dutiful daughter must return home. Everything I thought I had discovered about the world and about myself was quelled with one look from my father's eyes. I left without saying a proper goodbye to Olivia, but I knew my lack of courage had devastated her. When I think of how weak-willed I was, I am utterly disgusted with myself, but you must remember, Aliyeh, that is how I was raised. To defy a parent, a father—especially over an illicit love—it was not done.

I packed up for my return to La Rosière. I could not locate the necklace anywhere—I had forgotten that I had slipped it into the jacket pocket. I ransacked my flat looking for it. I had no notion of how much it was worth, but I wanted it for the sentiment that it held. At last, I concluded that I had left it at Olivia's, and I thought it was fitting that she keep the beautiful piece, since I was so ashamed of my own weak actions.

I returned to La Rosière and dutifully married Henri.

"Nadeau," Lily said, interrupting Alice. "Élise Boucher's maiden name was Nadeau. She's the one who signed the bank registry." Lily's voice rose with excitement. "I bet she had to use her maiden name because she and Olivia set the safety-deposit box up back before she had married Henri Boucher."

The others nodded in agreement, and Alice resumed reading.

Thinking of Paris was too painful for me, and I returned all of Olivia's letters unopened. I struggled to accept my home, struggled to find a place for myself in the village, tried to conjure some passion for Henri. Nothing worked, and I felt doomed to a half-life of sorrow, just as I had witnessed my parents endure. It's funny to say that Henri's injury saved me, but it did. One morning, while unloading the truck, he wrenched his back terribly. He never recovered and could no longer stand for long periods. His life as the village grocer was over.

La Rosière, and the whole region, was in a terrible recession. There was no employment. My family could not help. Henri's parents were dead. The shop had to be sold. We did not get a good price. I'd had David by then and was pregnant again with Yanick.

Henri was always an edgy man with a quick temper, but he had also been funny and fun-loving. The injury and pain changed him. The witty man was replaced by an angry and embittered person. He was in constant pain and felt like a failure. We had moved back in with my parents, and we fought constantly. I didn't know what to do. I had thought I was unhappy after leaving Olivia, but this was a new low, as if sorrow and pain were layers in a cake and I had sliced into a new one. I, too, grew embittered and angry, impatient with David, exhausted by the stress.

One night, I went for a walk. It was a wild, windy evening, and I climbed partway up the mountain on one of the old trails— Le Sentier des Chasseurs. I needed to clear my head. The terrain was jagged and slippery with rain. I was heavy with pregnancy, and awkward. A few times I nearly fell on the steep and winding path. Such a fall might have resulted in a broken leg, or perhaps worse. I didn't care, instead welcoming the possibility of escape. I didn't fall, however, and eventually, soaked through and exhausted, I returned home.

My father was sitting up, waiting for me. He looked furious, but I wasn't scared of his anger. I didn't feel anything anymore.

He must have read my state of mind in my expression. Perhaps he understood why I had gone for a walk on such a dangerous night, what I was half-seeking. I am sure that he himself had contemplated suicide over the years of pain he had endured. His words surprised me. "You need to leave La Rosière," he said. "You must take your family and find happiness elsewhere."

In my mind I was still trying to comprehend his words, but my heart had already grasped their meaning, and hope was blossoming. "Where can we go, Papa?" I asked him.

"Paris," he said. "Go back to Paris. There is work there. Help your family."

I protested. "Papa, I can't do anything in Paris. I have no skills. I am good only for a wife."

"Go back to that magazine," he said. "You can do that work." He bent his head so I could not see his eyes for his next words. "That friend of yours, the editor. She will take you back."

"Olivia?" I laughed sadly. "It's been more than two years. She's probably forgotten me. If she does remember, she won't be happy to see me. I left her." My voice cracked as I said this last, and I worried that I had revealed too much, but still my father didn't look at me.

"She came here." He said the words so softly that at first I wasn't sure he had spoken, or if it was a flame sputtering in the fire. He cleared his throat and spoke louder. "She came here, to La Rosière, only a few weeks after I brought you home. She wanted to see you. I told her you were already married. That you didn't want to go back. That you had chosen Henri." His eyes met mine at last, and I could see then that he somehow guessed the nature of my relationship with Olivia.

I am proud to say I didn't blush or flinch as he looked at me. I felt no shame about the love that Olivia and I had shared. "You should have told me she had come," I said calmly.

He surprised me by saying, "Yes, I should have."

His next words surprised me even more. "I was wrong to interfere at all. I should have left you in Paris. You were happy there. You deserve that, Élise."

With my father's blessing, Henri, David, infant Yanick, and I returned to Paris. I swallowed my pride, went to Rue de Beaune, and threw myself on Olivia's mercy. She was married by then and happy. I could see at once that her love for me had been a youthful emotion, raw and quick burning. True to her nature, she forgave me immediately. She welcomed me back, gave me my old job, and we carried on. The love we had shared was over. This was for the best; we were two mothers, with responsibilities and marriages we took seriously.

Henri found work that did not hurt his back. Eventually he got a good job as a bus driver, but he never recovered his youthful disposition. After the revelation of his anger and malice during those hard years, it was impossible for me to trust him again. When he started work as a driver, he tried to insist that I quit *Bonjour Paris*, but in this one thing, I refused. I was not to be separated from her again. And so Henri and I have muddled along, two people who might not like each other so very much, but we have built a life and raised three boys together, so that is not nothing.

Olivia and I worked side by side, never acknowledging or discussing our shared past. I think Olivia had consigned it to a youthful experiment. For me, however, it was something deeper. Those few weeks we shared as lovers were the truest and best days of my life.

It was only in the last year of Olivia's life, after she had the diagnosis, that we began talking of the past, remembering our romance. Illness had softened Olivia's usual dislike for rehashing history. Enough time had elapsed—nearly fifty years!—that our relationship was no longer painful to revisit. Indeed, I think those memories of our shared youth, our shared passion, were very comforting to her in her final days. It was then that she told me how Josephine Baker had given her the necklace, and of its true value. She had never had an inheritance, she confessed, instead using two of the diamonds to finance the magazine. One gem had covered the first few months of rent on the office. Another bought our equipment and furnishings, and helped pay my wages.

I was flabbergasted and so glad that I hadn't kept such an expensive gift. I explained that I had accidentally left it at her flat. She told me she had never seen the necklace. That's when I realized the depths of my foolishness. She was surprised that I had lost it. She had assumed I had eventually discovered its value and sold it. She forgave my carelessness, I forgave her extravagance. After that, we speculated about the necklace but could not figure out where it had been lost. Eventually we settled on my roommate, an angry Ch'ti from Lille, who had moved home soon after I left Paris.

Those last few months with Olivia are so precious to me. I remember them with gratitude. It was Olivia who encouraged me to take my dream trip to Québec City, to see my eldest boy, David. I didn't realize how close she was to the end, or I would never have left. She died while I was away, on another continent. I wasn't there for her in her final days. I abandoned her once again.

So at last, I come to the end of my long tale. I do apologize for my rambling, but I wanted to give you all the details, since I know how important "color" is to a good story. Tell Lily I give her permission to use it in the magazine. Write the article (as long as Luc agrees) and tell the world the story of the necklace . . . It's not my necklace anymore, however. I don't need it. I hereby happily and without reservation give over full and legal possession to someone who reminds me of the girl I once was—Aliyeh Ahmadi, may this necklace help you on your next great adventure.

Élise Nadeau Boucher

P.S. I hope you do not object, but like Josephine and Olivia before me, I will pry off two more diamonds to fund my own adventure . . .

Alice stopped reading and the room was silent for a long moment.

M. Seguin moved first, carefully picking up the Honeybee Emeralds; he weighed it in his hands for a moment, his thumb passing over the hard diamonds, and then cleared his throat.

"This is yours," he said, passing it into Alice's cold hands. "The necklace is yours."

Alice looked down at the beautiful piece of jewelry, and for a fleeting moment she thought she could feel heat coming off the sparkling emeralds, then she closed her hand over the gems.

Tone Loc

Daphne: Yo yo yo.

Lily: What's up?

Daphne: We're heading home early!

Lily: Oh no, what's wrong?

Daphne: Nothing—just rain in the forecast for the next two days, and we miss Theo—I hope he was good for you.

Lily: Angelic—only two meltdowns, but one was totally understandable—I didn't cut his bread the right way. The other one was also my bad. I forgot SpongeBob's best friend's name.

Daphne: Patrick, obvs.

Lily: How was the trip?

Daphne: Amazing—gorgeous weather (until today), sparkling blue sea, scent of wild thyme in the air . . . How can I have lived in France for so long and never made it to the Riviera?

Lily: And Philip?

Daphne: Delicious. Yesterday I looked over at him sitting on our seafront patio . . . He had the coolest Armani sunglasses on, a bit of stubble on his chin, his white Etro linen shirt with the sleeves rolled up . . . mmm mmm MMM.

Lily: That's right; you have that weird wrist fixation.

Daphne: Philip's wrists are amazing. So's the rest of him. Rrrow.

Lily: LOL. Settle down. Was your phone broken? I didn't see a single Instagram post.

Daphne: Pffft. I'm over social media. Nowadays the cool cats go for authenticity. Plus our therapist told me I need to stay in the "now." We can be at your place in an hour to get Theo.

Lily: Perfect, then I could get some writing in.

Daphne: Writing? What's this?

Lily: Nothing. Never mind.

Daphne: LILY!

Lily: I will tell you, but you can't comment in any way. Understood?!?!

Daphne: Yes.

Lily: I've started writing a novel. I'm even doing it old-school on a typewriter.

Daphne: What? That's amazing. What's it about?

Lily: Do not judge me, promise?

Daphne: I promise.

Lily: It's a fantasy about a golden-maned princess who has to retrieve her father's lost sword from a band of roving trolls.

Daphne: . . . golden-maned?

Lily: I AM NEVER TELLING YOU ANYTHING EVER AGAIN.

Daphne: No, it sounds amazing. I can't wait to read it. You're brilliant.

Lily: Tks. I think it's actually pretty good. Jacob said he'd show it to his agent once I get far enough along.

Daphne: How's he doing, anyway?

Lily: Oh God, I can hear your studied casualness even through text. He's fine. Returned to New York yesterday. He and Marie-Pierre got back together.

Daphne: And Luc?

Lily: The magazine is doing really well. I can hardly keep up.

Daphne: I didn't ask how the magazine was. I asked how Luc was.

Lily: Dude. Nothing is going on with him. He's my boss.

Daphne: Uh-huh.

Lily: There's that tone again.

Daphne: You're going to get the Tone Loc and the Funky Cold Medina until you stop stonewalling me.

Lily: You're such a dork. Fine, the night he bought everyone the champagne? We stayed in the office after you all left and we might have shared ONE kiss.

Daphne: !!!!!!!!!!!!!!!!!!!!!!!!!!!!!!!!!!!!!! And?!?

Lily: It was nice. Very . . . French.

Daphne: Ha. I bet it was. What's the next step?

Lily: No next step. Back to strictly professional. I'm a busy lady. I've got a novel to write and a successful magazine to run.

Daphne: Uh-huh.

Lily: TONE!

CHAPTER 43

Wonderland

ALICE LOOKED UP FROM HER COMPUTER. SHE WAS THE LAST TO leave the office. These past two weeks she, Lily, and Jacob had been pulling extra-long hours. The first of their Honeybee Emerald stories had gone online the night they recovered the necklace. Their story, about the lost necklace and its sensational ownership details, had gone viral; especially because it debunked several falsehoods printed in *La Vie en Rose*'s coverage. Indeed, the two magazines had had a little war of words over this, which had driven traffic to both. The story had trended on Twitter for three days, Stephen Colbert had made a wisecrack about it on the *Late Show*, and every single "Must Read" newsletter had cited *Bonjour Paris*'s crazy story about the Honeybee Emeralds. Their June newsstand issue had held even further coverage and beautiful images. They were in talks with Netflix about a TV show. When the article hit ten million views, Luc brought champagne and all the Fellowship (except for Alexander, who was too busy) had toasted their success.

Jacob had written the original story, of course, but Alice had written every follow-up. Suddenly she had half a dozen stories with a million-plus views and an international profile. Chelsea Clinton followed her on Twitter. Even better than that was the coaching Jacob had given her over the past couple of weeks—great advice not only about writing, but how to network, how to build a career, and how to make it last. According to Jacob, she needed to move to New York yesterday, but Alice wasn't going to rush into anything. She was committed to *Bonjour Paris* for the summer. Not only did she need to catch her breath and figure out her next move, but she couldn't leave Lily in the lurch. They were run off their feet with new advertisers and authors clamoring to work with them, and they were brutally understaffed. No one had seen Mme Boucher since that day. After typing out her "confession," she had gone to the bank, accessed the safety-deposit box, pried out two more diamonds from the Honeybee Emeralds, and disappeared. They'd called Henri Boucher. She'd gone to Canada, he said, sounding bewildered.

Alice lingered at her desk, delaying her departure. She'd been practically living at the office these past two weeks, and yet she had barely seen Alexander. She tried not to feel hurt by his absence. She had been daft to read anything into their hand-holding—after all, they were swept up in the excitement of the Honeybee Emeralds.

Alice still couldn't believe she actually owned that beautiful necklace. Daphne had been a true friend—still so odd to think of her that way—helping her navigate the ins and outs of ownership. First, she'd had the Honeybee appraised by a reputable jeweler who authenticated everything they had uncovered. Then Daphne had helped establish her legal claim. Once she had indisputable ownership, Alice had been faced with the question of what to do.

She was surprised to realize that she didn't have any qualms about selling it. The lure the necklace held over her had faded away. Perhaps it was the fact that she was its genuine legal owner. Maybe that's what poor Gollum had needed to shake the hold of the One Ring. If he had been secure in his title, he could have chilled out about it. At any rate, the necklace had served its purpose: she counted Jacob, Lily, Daphne, and even M. Seguin—Luc—as friends now. The Fellowship was the Honeybee Emeralds' most lasting legacy. Well, that and the sizeable bank deposit she'd get when it sold.

Daphne had organized insurance and security, telling Alice she could pay her back with the proceeds from the sale. At last, they had started the process of finding a buyer.

She, Daphne, and the lawyer had met in his book-lined office on the Right Bank. "I strongly advise you to bring the necklace to auction," he had said in a dry voice. "There you will get the best price."

"What about that interested buyer, the one from Los Angeles?" Alice had asked.

The older man sighed. "Ah yes, the singer and actress?" He coughed. "She's got a reputation as demanding and erratic—she's been married four times." The older man radiated disapproval.

"She also has a penchant for jewelry—the size of her latest engagement ring made international headlines," Daphne put in.

"I know it's a bit silly," Alice said timidly. "But I think we should sell it to her."

Daphne frowned. "Alice, you'll make more money at auction."

"Young lady," the lawyer said sternly, "you shouldn't be swayed by celebrity. The fact of the matter is that an auction is the most sensible course of action."

Alice shook her head. "I don't care about celebrity." She thought of Marguerite Bellanger, Mata Hari, Josephine Baker, Olivia Seguin, and Élise Boucher. "Given its history, the Honeybee Emeralds should belong to someone larger than life, a big personality—a diva."

Daphne's face cleared, and they shared a smile of understanding. "Of course," Daphne said. She spoke crisply to the lawyer. "Make sure we get a good price from that singer—we want to squeeze her for all she's worth."

No matter who Alice sold it to, the necklace meant an end to money worries for her mother and Dale, and a chance for Alice herself to take some risks, such as moving to New York.

It was time to go home. She might be almost-rich, but she still had to return to that squalid flat and her angry roommate. She stood from her desk.

"Oh good," said a voice from the doorway. It was Alexander. "You're still here."

Her heart leapt in her throat. "You just caught me," Alice said, nervously running a hand through her hair. "I'm calling it a night."

"It's late and dark," Alexander observed, scowling.

"I know," Alice said. "We're so busy right now. I mean it's all good, of course, but it is a lot, especially for Lily."

Alexander frowned.

"At least she hired a replacement for Mme Boucher today," Alice continued, babbling because she wasn't sure what to say. "You'll never believe who—Madeleine, the receptionist from *La Vie en Rose*. Apparently, she really disliked working for Yvette."

Silence again.

Alice was suddenly impatient with Alexander. Why couldn't the big oaf talk? Why was he lingering there, blocking the door? "Anyway, I have to get going," she said. She didn't bother hiding the annoyance in her voice.

"I made this," he said roughly. "I've been working on it for the last two weeks."

He thrust a small glass bottle at her.

She took it. "A new perfume?"

He gestured for her to open it.

She pulled out the stopper and took a sniff, closing her eyes to fully capture the scent. It held the aroma of roses and a faint trace of that honeysuckle she had sniffed the first day she had met him. There was another odor. "Is that saffron?" she asked.

"Yes," he said. "It's traditional in Persian perfumes."

There was another scent, too, one that undercut and played with the sweeter florals. It was the faintest whiff of lemon—a smell that always reminded her of Alexander. "It's lovely," she said, opening her eyes and smiling at him.

"I call it Wonderland," he said.

She looked at him questioningly, and he continued.

"After you, Alice." His blue eyes met hers, and something unclenched within her. His head bent down, and she stood on tippy toes. Her hand slipped up to his broad shoulder as she leaned into his steady, solid bulk, and his lips, surprisingly soft, found hers.

When they came up for air, Alexander looked at her with his usual steady gaze. Only the crinkles in the corner of his eyes revealed his happiness.

Suddenly her summer in Paris was looking better than ever.

CHAPTER 44

September

INITIALLY ÉLISE HAD THOUGHT THE YELLOW SOU'WESTER WAS ridiculous, a cartoon prop they made her wear for tourists. It offended her dignity, made her feel like a fool. The first day on the boat, however, she understood its importance. Even though it was a bright, sunshiny September day in Trois-Pistoles, the weather could be different, more blustery out on Québec's Saint Lawrence River.

The flat she had rented was small, but it had a garden. She planted wildflowers from a seed packet, and they emerged as promised by the end of summer. Lupines, brown-eyed Susans, asters, milkweed, it all came up. None of these North American flowers were as delicate or impressive as the masses of edelweiss she remembered so well, but they were good in their own way.

Henri still called her most nights, and she listened as his anger turned to bewilderment and then resignation. The boys were doing fine. Yanick was dating a promising girl, a nurse, who sounded sensible. Thierry had moved out. She refused to think about what it said of her own parenting that they couldn't flourish until she left. What mattered was that the birds had finally flown. Perhaps her own transatlantic flight had inspired them.

When winter came, she would leave Trois-Pistoles and move upriver, to Québec City. David was keeping an eye out for an apartment. She didn't intend to interfere too much in his life, but perhaps he and the family would come for Sunday dinners. She could, occasionally, pick her granddaughters up from school. She would stay for one winter and see. David said the cold was like nothing she had ever felt. She thought of the taste of a tiny mountain strawberry, sweetened by the sun. She thought of the soft feel of Olivia's skin as she traced the line of her jawbone. She was ready to feel something new.

She looked out over the water, and her heart raced. There was a form below the surface; this close to shore and this large, she knew what it must be. Élise Boucher turned to the crowd of awestruck tourists behind her and began to tell them about the blue whale. It was the largest animal on the entire planet. A smile stretched across her face.

Epilogue

Berlin, 1965

Josephine kept calm, not showing any fear. The man, surely just an over-eager admirer, took another step into her shabby dressing room.

"We have met before, you know." His voice held an unexpected note of urgency.

"Oh yes," she said, keeping her tone even.

"In the war," he confirmed. "I believe it was the best performance of your life."

"My best performance?" she asked. Had he been at the Théâtre des Champs-Élysées in '45? Impossible. That had been a victory performance, and this blond German would certainly not have been welcome there.

"Yes," he replied, and he took another step toward her. He filled the small room now, towering over her. She noticed his bearing for the first time—upright, rigid—he held himself like a well-trained soldier. She stood, feeling small and fragile in her thin wisps of silk, the dressing gown a laughably flimsy protection.

"We were in a border hut on the Spanish-French frontier. You arrived suddenly, and I knew precisely who you were. Even that night, in the dark, in the middle of nowhere, I recognized you. Your aura of power, of enticement. It was just as I had seen you on stage."

She stared at his face, willing herself to remember him. Imagining him in a Nazi uniform.

"You spoke to my superior officer. He was questioning you, demanding to see papers. Insisting he go through all of your belongings with a fine-tooth comb. You were haughty, you were cold. He was not swayed. He was suspicious. He thought perhaps you were spying for the Allies. He wished to detain the man who traveled with you. The one you claimed was your bandleader. Of course, in later years, I have learned the truth. You were indeed a spy. You smuggled much information across the border, aiding the Allied cause. I have seen the photographs—you were decorated by de Gaulle himself for your work in the Resistance. Your so-called bandleader was a Jew you were helping to flee."

Josephine's stomach clenched. Was this former soldier bent upon revenge for her perceived treachery?

He was still lost in reminiscences of an evening that was like so many others, Josephine had trouble recalling it.

"At last, you drew yourself up to your full height. You spoke with an imperious authority. 'There is nothing to see here,' you said. I almost laughed. It was such an absurd statement. When Josephine Baker was in a room, she shone as fiercely as the sun. She was the *only* thing to see.

"It was only as you and your bandleader were given safe passage and departed that I realized what you had done. My captain was tucking the package you had thrust into his hands inside his coat pocket. I waited until he retired for the night, and then I snuck over to his coat and opened the thin linen bag hidden there."

Now Josephine recalled the night. Albert Weiss needed to get out of France. She had been terrified but determined. Her heart had pounded so hard it had almost choked her. She willed the fat-faced Nazi officer in front of her to let her pass. None of her charm worked, and she was scared he'd demand to see Weiss's papers.

She had been carrying the necklace with her like a good-luck charm, a reminder of dear Charles Leboeuf's story. A reminder of Mata Hari's tragic life. She had known that one day she might have to use the necklace for this purpose, and she parted with it without a qualm. Cold stones for a human life. There was no question about such a trade.

The man continued reminiscing. "We were deployed the next day. In the confusion of packing up, I slipped the bag into my pocket. I was sent to Italy. I never saw my superior again. I learned later he died in the Battle of Nuremberg."

The man thrust a small bag into Josephine's hands, turned smartly on his heels, and left before she had a chance to say anything.

She held it in her hand. Its weight a comfort. She could see the necklace in her mind's eye. A reminder of who she was and what she had done. She might not attract the audiences she once did, she might feel old and tired, but she had done some good.

She imagined that the emeralds, even muffled and covered in their shroud, emitted a faint, warm glow.

Author's Note

The *Honeybee Emeralds* is a work of fiction, but it is based on the real lives of three extraordinary women.

Marguerite Bellanger was a dirt-poor washerwoman who used her talent and charm to escape Saumur by performing as a trick rider and acrobat. She leveraged those skills to rise to the highest ranks of imperial courtesan. For several years she managed to supplant the well-born mistresses Emperor Napoleon III favored and in so doing captured the ear and attention of the most powerful man in France. She did indeed bear the emperor an illegitimate son and was well-rewarded for her efforts. She died a rich and respected woman, renowned for her charitable endeavors.

While the romance between Marguerite Bellanger's son, Charles Leboeuf, and Mata Hari is a figment of my imagination, she was another extraordinary woman who used her charm to carve an unconventional life for herself. Born into a bourgeois Dutch family, Margaretha MacLeod (née Zelle) reinvented herself after escaping an abusive marriage. She fled to Paris where she mined the years she had spent with her colonial officer husband in the Dutch East Indies to create a seductive persona as an exotic dancer. Claiming to be a Javanese princess, Mata Hari garnered widespread acclaim for her performances, partly because she ended her dances by shedding most of her clothes. Titillating and scandalizing Paris in equal measures, Mata Hari was recruited by the French government to spy on the Germans during the First World War. In 1916, she was accused of counterespionage by the British and French governments. Although there was no concrete evidence against her, Mata Hari was nevertheless executed by a French firing squad in 1917.

Only a few years later in 1925, the last of my novel's divas, Josephine Baker, burst onto the same Parisian entertainment scene that both Marguerite Bellanger and Mata Hari had once dominated. The granddaughter of slaves, Josephine was born into poverty in Saint Louis, Missouri. Like Marguerite Bellanger, Josephine's mother was a washerwoman, and like Marguerite, Josephine used her talent and force of personality to escape her fate. A dancer and singer, she won renown for exotic and scandalous performances. More comfortable in France than segregationist America, Josephine married several times and adopted twelve children, her "Rainbow Tribe." She did indeed work for the French Resistance during the Second World War and received the Croix de Guerre and the Rosette de la Résistance, among other awards, for her wartime service. She became active in the American civil rights movement and was the only woman invited to speak at the March on Washington. Josephine's lavish lifestyle caused many money troubles in her later years. She continued performing right up to her death, and she is the only American to receive full French military honors at her funeral.

Acknowledgments

Thank you firstly to Stephanie Beard at Turner Publishing, who took a chance on an unknown writer and plucked me from the slush pile. Thanks to Todd Bottorff for backing that decision. Thanks to Ezra Fitz and Claire Ong for their editorial direction and support. I owe a debt of gratitude to Jessica Easto and Shayna Sobol for their keen editorial advice and sharp eye for a missing accent aigu. Big thanks to Lauren Ash for her marketing enthusiasm and know-how. Thanks to Emily Mahon for creating such a beautiful cover. Thanks to Melory Mirashrafi, who improved my story with her sensitive insights and thoughtful comments.

I am lucky enough to be part of an amazing twenty-year-old critique group filled with smart, insightful, and brilliant writers. To Chris Crowder, Wayne Ng, and Alette Willis, this book wouldn't exist without you. A separate shout-out to my bonus critiquer and unstinting cheerleader, Trish Lucy.

Thanks to my fabulous friends who read my book and spurred me on: Kathryn Moore, Sara Trew, Amy Turner, Paddy Harrington, Johanna Smith, Dara Price, Meghan Hall, and Ash Seha.

Profound thanks to my earliest readers, my sisters: Susie, Emily, and Tina Tector. Your encouragement and suggestions were so helpful, it almost makes up for the childhood teasing and torment. Thanks to my brother, Mark Tector, who provided excellent legal advice despite contributing to that childhood torment. Thanks to my mother, Sarah Tector, for her love and support.

To Violet, who I am so proud of, and who I hope is proud of me. You're my number one best.

Lastly to Andrew, whose overseas posting introduced me to the expat life, and who has listened to and encouraged me for years as I worked on this story. Thank you for helping me with plot problems, reading my earliest drafts and for doing all of the quarantine grocery shopping. I love you very much.

Book Club
Discussion Questions

1. How does the Parisian setting impact the story? Could the story have taken place in another setting? What does Paris mean to the four protagonists?

2. *The Honeybee Emeralds* connects the lives of four contemporary women with three historical divas: Marguerite Bélanger, Mata Hari and Josephine Baker. How do you think the historical women changed, inspired or influenced the four modern-day protagonists?

3. The three historical divas all shared some commonalities; what traits do the three divas share? Would these women have gotten along, had they had the chance to meet in real life?

4. The Honeybee Emeralds is a fictional necklace, but the main characters are all fascinated by it. What is it about expensive jewelry and rare gemstones that captured their imagination? What is it about such treasures that interests people more generally?

5. What did Alice's fascination with the necklace tell us about her character?

6. The characters spend some time connecting with the past, either through research, Google searches, archival digging or interviewing people with a connection to history. What is it about the quest to uncover secrets from the past that is compelling?

7. Daphne objected to her husband referring to their marriage as "the long haul." What did the events of the story help Daphne see about her marriage? Do you think they really are in it "for the long haul"?

8. Alice and Alexander form a tentative relationship. What is the attraction for each of them?

9. How has Madame Boucher's attitude shifted by the end of the novel? What truths and changes has she embraced?

10. By the end of the novel Lily is faced with a romantic choice, did she make the right one?

11. Displacement and belonging are themes in the book. Where do we see those themes enacted?

12. In the final scene, why do you think the author doesn't allow The Fellowship to know how Josephine Baker recovered The Honeybee Emeralds? What impact does that have on our understanding of the story?

About the Author

Amy Tector was born and raised in the rolling hills of Quebec's Eastern Townships. She has worked in archives for the past twenty years and has found some pretty amazing things, including lost letters, mysterious notes and once, a whale's ear. Amy spent many years as an expat, living in Brussels and in The Hague, where she worked for the International Criminal Tribunal for War Crimes in Yugoslavia. She lives in Ottawa, Canada with her daughter, dog and husband.